carrington cove: book three

SOMETIMES YOU *fall*

HARLOW JAMES

Copyright © 2025 by Harlow James

All rights reserved.

No part of this publication may be reproduced, distributed, or transmitted in any form or by any means, including photocopying, recording, or other electronic or mechanical methods, without the prior written permission of the publisher, except as permitted by U.S. copyright law. For permission requests, contact [include publisher/author contact info].

The story, all names, characters, and incidents portrayed in this production are fictitious. No identification with actual persons (living or deceased), places, buildings, and products is intended or should be inferred.

Book Cover by Abigail Davies

Edited by Jenny Ayers (Swift Red Pen)

Proof Read: Emma Cook

ISBN: 9798300218058

Contents

Dedication	V
Epigraph	VI
Prologue	1
1. Chapter 1	12
2. Chapter 2	28
3. Chapter 3	38
4. Chapter 4	51
5. Chapter 5	64
6. Chapter 6	73
7. Chapter 7	88
8. Chapter 8	99
9. Chapter 9	122
10. Chapter 10	147
11. Chapter 11	154
12. Chapter 12	168
13. Chapter 13	196
14. Chapter 14	210

15.	Chapter 15	236
16.	Chapter 16	263
17.	Chapter 17	268
18.	Chapter 18	276
19.	Chapter 19	288
20.	Chapter 20	295
21.	Chapter 21	316
22.	Chapter 22	328
23.	Chapter 23	332
	Also By Harlow James	337
	Acknowledgements	340
	Connect with Harlow James	343

To the women who fight for what they want day in and day out.
Trust your intuition.
Manifest your future happiness.

And don't be afraid to fall...
because you might fall into exactly where you're supposed to be.

Sometimes we lose people just to find them again. Sometimes the second time just makes more sense. Honestly, that timing in life has a lot to do with everything. Sometimes, you just aren't ready for each other yet, and that's okay. Now you are. Make it magical, make it amazing, and enjoy every moment.

Erin Rose

Prologue

Grady

Senior Year of High School

"Good luck today, Grady!" one of the JV players shouts at me as he shuffles down the hallway past the lockers.

"Thanks." I turn back to my open locker, shoot a text off to my mom about what time my game starts, then grab my math book and secure the lock on my locker before heading to class. Nerves run through me, the kind that usually fuel my focus to win our games, but today's game is different. Today's game could determine my future.

A few more kids offer their good luck wishes as I amble down the hall, and even the teachers standing by their doors chime in as I pass by. Over the past three years, Carrington Cove High School has had a winning baseball program, and much of that has to do with my performance on the pitching mound. So today's game is just as much about me as it is about the school.

Settling into my desk in my math class, I flip open my textbook to the section we've been working on, cleaning some of the grease left under my fingernails from working at Carrington Cove Auto

Repair. While I wait for class to start, a familiar voice pulls me from my thoughts. "Have you thrown up yet?"

Green eyes meet mine, the same green eyes that have become a source of comfort for me over the past year, as Scottland Daniels takes her seat right next to me, her bright smile making my own lips curl up in response.

Chuckling, I reply, "No, not yet, Scottie. I haven't eaten much today, so hopefully that will help."

She shakes her head at me as she digs her notebook out of her backpack. "You need to eat something, Grady. If you don't, you could end up passing out on the mound in front of the scouts, and that would be even worse than you playing a shitty game."

I swallow hard, envisioning what she just said and the embarrassment that would follow. "Crap. You're right." I dig out the protein bar from my backpack I keep for emergencies, tear open the wrapper, and shove the entire thing in my mouth as Mrs. Williams, our Algebra II teacher, signals that class is about to start.

Scottie laughs at me. "That was a little dramatic, but at least you know how to listen."

"My mother taught me well."

Smirking, she directs her attention to our teacher, and for the next twenty minutes, we take notes on the lesson until it's time for us to work on today's assignment. I twist in my desk to face hers and try my best to focus on the problems I need to complete, but Scottie is the only person who understands what today means for me, so our conversation drifts back to the topic neither one of us can ignore.

"So how many will there be?" she asks as she jots down the steps to the problem, rushing toward her answer. The NSYNC stickers plastered all over her folder catch my eye, and for the millionth time I find myself wondering how the hell she listens to that god awful music, but I keep that thought to myself.

"I think five." My stomach twists in knots at the reminder.

"That's amazing. Five scouts coming to see you, Grady!" She grins across her desk at me. "That's everything you've been working toward."

"I know, but now that it's happening..."

"It's becoming more real," she finishes for me.

"Yeah. What if none of them make me an offer?"

"Or what if they all do?" she counters. "Have you thought of that?"

It's a possibility. I know that. And then the problem becomes making a decision. "I doubt that will happen..."

She glares at me, snapping her fingers in front of my face. "Haven't you heard of positive thinking? You have to manifest what you want, Reynolds. Negativity isn't going to get you anywhere."

Huffing out a laugh, I lean back in my desk chair. "Yeah, I guess. But what about you? Have you heard from any scouts?"

The pride that shows through her smile reminds me of why Scottie is the one friend I can talk to about this stuff. She's the pitcher for our varsity girls' softball team and has just as much promise and drive to play professionally as I do. It's what solidified our friendship. She's the only one who loves the sport and wants the same things out of it as I do. Plus, she's smart, sassy, and gorgeous. I couldn't help but want to get to know her.

"Of course. I was just letting you have your moment today, Grady. I didn't want you to feel bad about how many scouts were coming to watch *me* play next week. I didn't want to tear up your heart."

"Was that an NSYNC reference?"

"Maybe."

"Stop while you're ahead, Daniels." Laughing, I write down the next problem, then drop my pencil to my desk. My concentration is shot, so there's no point in pretending I'm going to get any work done right now. I'll finish these problems later tonight after the game is over and I can breathe. "Your cockiness is showing."

"What can I say? I know what I have to offer these schools. They're the ones that need to prove to *me* which one I should choose, not the other way around."

"I wish I had your confidence."

She tucks one of her soft, brown curls behind her ear, tilting her head at me. "You need to find it, Grady. That's the only way to get where you want to go. Don't doubt yourself. You're a really freaking talented pitcher and you deserve this."

"Likewise," I tell her, and it's the honest-to-God truth. Scottie is a beast on the mound. Other schools are scared of her because she's ruthless. I freaking love watching her play, but part of that may just be because staring at her has become one of my new favorite pastimes besides baseball.

Pointing at her desk, she continues, "Go out there today, own that mound, and believe that this is the start of your professional baseball career." Then she glances down at my hands stained with grease. "And if it doesn't work out, at least you know how to turn a wrench."

Laughing, I pick up my pencil again, not wanting to draw Mrs. Williams' attention. "I like working on cars, Scottie. You should try it sometime. It's far less stressful than pitching."

She arches a brow at me. "Really? *Less* stressful?" Leaning closer to me, she continues, "You do realize that if you mess something up on someone's car, it could mean life or death, right? Have you ever had that thought about pitching, Reynolds?" She blinks at me slowly.

"Shit. Okay, you're right."

Swinging her hair around, she goes back to work. "Again. I know." Smirking, she glances up at me, and just that small purse of her lips has me fighting to stay firmly planted on my side of the line that defines our friendship.

My chest grows tight with that familiar twinge that seems to grow every time I talk to Scottie. I'm pretty sure I know what my heart and head are trying to tell me, but I can't listen. I don't have time for a girlfriend, and hell, high school is almost over. We're both headed in different directions, possibly to opposite sides of the country.

Scottie is my friend, and that's just the way it has to remain, even though the thought of tasting her lips has occupied my mind more nights than I care to admit.

"I'm going to give it my best today," I say, breaking through our silence.

"I know you will," she says, brushing her hair over her shoulder with a confident lift of her lips. "And I can't wait to hear from you later when all five scouts start begging you to play for them."

***

"I hope you get drafted to the Atlanta Braves so we can drive down and see you play," Blane, one of my friends on the team, says as he takes a sip from his red Solo cup.

"Nah. He needs to play for the Red Sox. Since I'm gonna be in Boston, I can cheer him on," declares Derek, our shortstop, to the group of my now former teammates gathered at the house party his parents are letting us throw.

It's only a few days after graduation, but my life at the University of California, Santa Barbara, officially starts in a week. Just as Scottie predicted, all five scouts at my game made me offers. I gelled best with the coach from Santa Barbara, though, and their D1 baseball program is famous for sending players to the draft. Plus, their offer of a full ride made the decision a no-brainer. I fly out on Monday to start training and begin my journey to the MLB.

"Look, I gotta make it through the next three years with no injuries and hope to get drafted at twenty-one. There's still a long road ahead of me, guys."

Blane slaps me on the shoulder. "Yeah, but you're living the dream, man. It's not like any of us got an offer like you did. We're gonna live vicariously through you, all right? You get to leave this town and hopefully never return."

I chuckle, nod my head, then take a sip from my beer. I usually don't drink at these parties because it makes me sluggish on the mound, but this is the last time I'm gonna see my friends for a while, so I gave into the peer pressure and filled my cup from the keg.

"I'm not the only one that's leaving, though. Dallas is shipping out just two days after me." I jerk my chin toward one of my close friends, Dallas Sheppard, who's been standing there stoically, listening to the conversation.

"That's right. You joined the Marines, huh?" Blane slurs and then salutes him.

Dallas scowls. "I did. And…" But he doesn't get a chance to finish his thought.

"Scottie! Scottie! Scottie!" Cheers ring out from the crowd gathered around the keg, pulling all of our attention to the sight. And when the crowd parts, I see an upside-down Scottie doing a keg stand better than most guys I've seen.

Once she's had enough, the boys holding her up bring her feet back to the ground where she wobbles a bit before shooting her arms up in the air in celebration.

Jesus, she's something else.

"Scottie!" The group around her cheers again, and she high-fives several of them before our eyes lock and she heads in my direction, her eyes glazed over but her smile wide.

"Reynolds!" She throws her arms around me, pulling me down to her for a hug before shoving me back and brushing her curls from her face.

"A keg stand?" I ask, shocked to see her drunk. Scottie is normally as disciplined as I am when it comes to her health, prioritizing her performance on the ball field.

"It's a party, Grady." She shoves at my shoulder. "You don't have to be such an old man all the time."

My friends laugh at her dig. They know she's right. I get shit from them on the regular because I don't partake in the typical teenage activities. I've worked too fucking hard to risk my future, though, so they can laugh all they want.

I hold up my cup. "Hey, I'm having a beer, okay?"

She plants her hands on her hips. "Well, until you do a keg stand for longer than I just did, I'm not going to pretend that I'm impressed."

My friends move toward the other side of the yard where more commotion has started, leaving the two of us alone. "I'm happy to let you keep the keg stand champion title."

She smiles, a hint of challenge in her voice. "Wuss."

I wrap my arm around her shoulders, pulling her close to me, and begin walking to a more secluded area across the yard. There's a tire swing attached to a huge oak tree, and Scottie slides her legs through the tire while I set my beer on the ground so I can push her.

"You ready for what comes next?" she asks, tilting her head all the way back and gazing at the sky through the leaves as she swings back and forth.

"California?"

"Yeah."

"As ready as I can be."

"Have you thrown up yet?"

Laughing, I say, "Nope. And I think if anyone is going to throw up tonight, it's going to be you."

She giggles. "You're probably right."

"You don't usually drink, Scottie. Everything okay?"

She twists her head to the side so our eyes can meet as her entire body continues to lie flat while she swings. "Just trying to have a little fun, Reynolds. You should try it sometime. Life doesn't always have to be serious."

"I know how to have fun."

She scoffs. "Okay..."

"You don't think I can have fun?"

"I think you're afraid to have fun." She grows quiet for a moment, and then speaks again. "Promise me we'll keep in touch."

My chest aches instantly. "Of course, Scottie."

"I'm serious. I'll be cheering you on, Grady. I know you're going to make it to the major leagues."

"You're going to make it too, Scottie."

"Duh," she says, making us both laugh.

"It's going to be tough getting there."

"Nothing we can't handle though, right?" She smirks back at me. "I mean, we're both kinda the shit in our respective sports."

"Yeah, I think we're definitely top-tier talent."

"I can't wait to watch you on TV," she says, dragging her feet on the ground as if she wants to slow down. When she swings back toward me, I grab the tire and pull her to a stop. Our eyes meet and everything around us grows quiet. Offering her my hand, I help her out of the tire, and she falls into my chest, her body off-balance from the alcohol and the swing. I wrap my arm around her back, holding her against me.

"You promise you'll be watching?"

Her lips spread in a huge smile as her eyes bounce back and forth between mine. "Hell yeah."

I smile back at that beautiful face and drag a finger down her cheek, making her breath hitch. For a moment, I wonder if I should kiss her, taste her since I know I'll probably never get the chance again. She's headed to the University of Georgia to play softball, and I'm headed to the opposite side of the country.

It's only one kiss, one that I might regret not taking while I have this chance.

"Scottie..." I say, my voice nearly cracking from my nerves. Our eyes bounce back and forth between each other, and in that moment, I swear she's leaning toward me. I can feel the heat of her breath on my lips, the scent of beer on her breath, or maybe that's mine.

But then her eyes widen, she takes a step back, and turns away from me just in time to throw up her beer all over the grass.

"Shit." I grab her hair as her body empties all of the alcohol from her system. "It's okay, Scottie. Get it out."

She heaves a few more times, and then stands up slowly. I release her hair but continue to rub her back. "Ugh. That was..."

"Disgusting," I finish for her, turning away from the mess she left on the ground before I add to it with my own.

Laughing, she wipes at her mouth and then glances up at me. "Sorry about that."

"It's all right. But I'd just like to point out that clearly it's not *me* you need to be worried about throwing up all the time." I shrug, but she rolls her eyes at me.

"Gloating isn't a good look on you, Grady," she says as she heads for the base of the tree, sitting down on the ground and lying back against the trunk.

I join her, motioning for her to lay her head down in my lap, and she does. Even though I know I should be hanging out with my friends and probably getting ready to head home soon, a part of me doesn't want to leave.

That part of me just wants a few more moments with Scottie.

"I think I need to close my eyes for a few minutes," she murmurs.

"Go ahead. I'm not going anywhere."

"I wish you didn't have to leave, Grady," she mumbles as her eyelids flutter closed.

And in that moment, that same part of me from moments ago wishes the same.

***

Three Years Later

Scottie: *Oh my god! You did it! You're going to the minors, Grady!*
Me: *It's fucking happening, Scottie! I fucking did it!*
Scottie: *I'm so proud of you!*
Me: *Thanks! What about you? I've been trying to keep up with your career, but life has just been crazy...*
Scottie: *Same here, but I'm still working. My coach says I have potential to make it to the USA Women's National Team, I've just got to get through this season.*

Me: *That's fucking awesome! You can do it, I know you can.*

One Year Later

Me: *Scottie! I'm getting called up! One year in the minors and the San Francisco Giants are calling me up!*

One Month Later

Me: *Scottie? I'm worried about you. I've been watching this season and haven't seen you play. Is everything okay? Text me back.*

Life has been insanely busy this past year, but Scottie and I still check in with each other occasionally. Not hearing from her as soon as I texted her has me worried to the point that I decide to call her. We never talk on the phone, just a text here and there, but I can tell something's not right.

The line rings only once before a voice that's not Scottie's comes through.

My stomach plummets when I hear it.

"The number you are trying to reach is no longer in service."

And instantly I know that I just lost the only person who ever truly understood me and my dreams.

Chapter One

Grady

Present Day

"There you go, Mrs. Hansen." I rip the invoice from the printer tray and hand it to her across the counter. A smudge of grease transfers from my fingers to the paper, but that's pretty par for the course when you work on cars for a living.

"Thank you, Grady."

"My pleasure."

"I'll see you in another five-thousand miles." She winks and heads for the door.

"I'll be here." Watching her leave the office, I sigh as I file away the invoice for processing later, wondering if all my days will feel this way from now on—monotonous and dull.

At least Mrs. Hansen doesn't flirt with me when she comes in. That's a welcome reprieve from my normal customer—single, female, and plenty of cleavage on display.

I swear, it's like these women don't realize I don't play professional baseball anymore. They still act like I'm some big star and practically throw themselves at me. Any normal red-blooded male would tell me to stop complaining and take the bait that's being offered, but those days are behind me.

Now that I'm back in Carrington Cove and far from no-strings hookups, it's been just me and my hand. My days are filled with running my business: oil changes, tire rotations, radiator leaks—the list goes on and on. I guess I shouldn't complain about my life now... Working on cars was my second passion, one I left behind willingly for the chance to play professional baseball.

I should be grateful that Carrington Cove Auto Repair was available to purchase when I moved back home. Mr. Rogers practically begged me to buy the place, knowing that I was familiar with the ins and outs of the business. He was my boss during the summers once upon a time. From the age of fourteen, I followed him around the property and absorbed everything he could teach me about cars. I sure as hell wasn't going to learn it from my own father, who took off shortly after my younger sister, Astrid, was born. And my mom was so busy working two jobs to keep us fed and housed that the last thing on her mind was worrying about me learning skills any self-respecting man should know.

Besides, she pushed me to play baseball since she knew my aspirations of playing professionally were something I actually had a shot at. She saw my talent and so did my coaches, and she didn't want me to miss out on an opportunity so few actually get.

But working here, learning a skill besides how to pitch, brought me extra money and pride. So, when I lost the main part of my identity almost five years ago, I gravitated toward the only other thing I knew, hoping it would help mend the hole in my chest left by the end of my baseball career.

"Hey, I need your expertise on this car." Chet, my right-hand man, pokes his head in the main office from the garage, pulling me back to the present.

"Be right there." I click around on the computer, take note of the open customer files we still have, and glance at the clock, counting down the minutes until lunch time so I can fuel the never-ending pit of my stomach and catch up with my friends. Taking hour-long lunch breaks on Thursdays is one of the perks of being the owner, and today I have another place to go as well, giving me a break from the monotony of the day.

Grady's Garage smells of oil, rubber, and hard work as I walk over to where Chet is leaning over the engine compartment of an '81 Z28 Camaro a customer has asked us to rebuild. To keep the business afloat, I knew I had to expand our services beyond routine maintenance. Between Chet and me, our knowledge of classic cars is extensive, so to bring in extra revenue, we rebuild and repair older cars in between our regular customers from Carrington Cove. This Camaro actually belongs to a guy who lives in Georgia.

I glance toward the '73 Nova sitting in the corner, wondering if I should bite the bullet and finally start working on my own project like I said I would when I moved back home. But this new life of mine kind of got in the way.

"Are you seeing what I'm seeing?" Chet asks as I bump my shoulder against his and peer down inside the engine compartment.

"Fuck. Yup, that's the water pump. Should have known to look there first. It's a notorious problem with these cars."

He nods. "Just wanted to make sure I wasn't seeing things."

I clasp him on the shoulder. "Nope, your eyes are fine. I'll contact my parts guy and see how long it'll take to track one down. Let me call him before I go to lunch. Hopefully, we'll have an answer before I get back. I also planned to stop by the bakery to see my sister since she was gone this past weekend and has her big event in two days. I just want to make sure she's not going insane."

Astrid recently bought the old Sunshine Bakery in town, renaming and renovating the place to make it her own, and this weekend she's catering a Morgan Hotel party in Raleigh that Dallas's new girlfriend, Willow, orchestrated with her connection from her advertising business.

I'm so fucking proud of her. She spent years not chasing her dreams because her husband didn't support her and made her feel less than. But after he died, she started living her life differently and finally took a risk a few months ago to pursue the career she's always wanted. This past weekend she ventured out of town for a break, and I'm proud of her for that too. She's been working so hard since she bought the bakery, and she deserved the reprieve.

Maybe I should take a page out of her book and take a break too. Maybe I'm getting burned out.

Or maybe I'm going a little nuts since I haven't gotten laid in eight months.

A dry spell can do weird things to a man.

Chet laughs. "No problem. I can hold down the fort."

"I know you can. Thanks, man." He tips his chin in acknowledgment and then turns back to the car just as my cell phone vibrates in my pocket. But when I take it out and see the name on the screen, I silence the call immediately and let it go to voicemail. Irritation fills my veins as reminders of my former life flood my mind, pushing me even harder to take care of my responsibilities and head to lunch, grateful for the distraction since I really need it today.

***

"You're here early." Dallas Sheppard, my childhood friend, greets me with an arch of his brow as I head for the bar he's standing behind. As planned, Dallas left for the Marines right after high school and returned to Carrington Cove around the same time I did to build a life outside of the service. He now owns Catch & Release, a coastal bar and restaurant, and turned it into the hot spot in town for tourists and locals alike.

"I'm starving," I reply, feeling my stomach growl as the smell of grease and food fills my nostrils.

"Well, Jimmy just started the burgers, so it's going to be a minute."

"No problem." I push a hand through my hair that's in bad need of a cut and intercept the glass of Coke Dallas pushes my way. "Thanks."

"Of course. How's everything going?"

"Fuck. That's a loaded question, man," I say, unsure if I want to get into this with Dallas right now. It's not that I don't trust him. Hell, he was one of my closest friends before we both left our hometown, and we picked up right where we left off when we returned.

In fact, we actually have a lot more in common now than we did back then. After twelve years in the service, he retired and bought this restaurant from the owner who was looking to sell at the time, much like I did with the garage. And for a while there, he was single too.

But then he met Willow Marshall, the owner of a multimillion-dollar advertising company who inherited a house in town and stole Dallas's heart in the process. Now he's happy, in love, and living a life that I never allowed myself to even think about because baseball was the only thing I cared about for the longest time.

And now I don't even know what I want out of my life anymore.

Dallas smirks, crossing his arms over his chest. "You know, owning a bar has made me great at listening to other people's problems. Comes with the territory."

Huffing out a laugh, I lean back in my seat. "I just feel stuck."

"With...?"

"Life."

He nods thoughtfully. "Sounds like you need to shake things up a bit."

"What needs to be shaken up?" Parker, Dallas's youngest brother, interrupts our conversation as he slides onto the stool next to me.

"Grady's in a funk." Dallas fills a glass of Coke for his brother and sets it in front of him.

"Yeah, I get that. I'm so fucking busy at the clinic right now, by the time I get home, I just zone out on the couch watching TV or scrolling on my phone before passing out."

"And then get up and do it all over again," Dallas says. Parker and I nod in agreement.

"Maybe we need to take a page out of Penn's book and just take a fucking vacation," I grumble as the bell on the kitchen counter rings, signaling that our burgers are done. Dallas grabs our plates from under the heat lamps and delivers them to us. The plate barely hits the bar top in front of me before I pick it up and take the biggest bite I can fit in my mouth.

"I still can't believe he did that," Parker mumbles around the fry he's chewing. And honestly, I was shocked too. Penn is a fucking workaholic, and now that he's starting his own contracting business, I don't see that changing anytime soon. "Although the week I'm taking off between Christmas and New Year's is all I can fucking think about, so I know I need the break. Dr. O'Neil was adamant about it too, so I really didn't have a choice but to take it off," Parker explains, referring to his boss. I'm pretty sure Dr. O'Neil has been the owner and main doctor of the veterinarian's office since I was kid.

Dallas nods. "You should consider it, Grady. Maybe it will help turn that frown of yours upside down." There's a teasing lilt to his voice, but I know he's trying to give me real advice that I should probably take.

I scowl at him as the door opens and closes behind us. Parker and I both turn our heads to find Penn striding toward us, happier than I've seen him in a long time.

"Oh, look. It's Mr. Well-Rested," Parker teases his brother as Penn finds his stool and Dallas slides him his burger. Penn is the second oldest of the three Sheppard siblings and the one I'm closest with, probably because he's close with my sister, Astrid. They have a younger sister, Hazel, who is also friends with Astrid, so our families have no shortage of ties to one another.

I moved back to Carrington Cove just before Brandon, my sister's Marine husband, died in combat. Being there for her when her life was turned upside down made me beyond grateful to be back home. But it was Penn, Brandon's best friend, who stepped up and helped her the most. He has an uncle-like bond with my niece and nephew, and I'm glad she has more than one man she can count on, especially since our dad was never around and her marriage was less than stable.

"Yeah, those bags under your eyes are a lot smaller. It must have been your mini-vacation." I grin as I pop a fry in my mouth. Giving each other shit is what we do, but honestly, I'm grateful for these guys. Lord knows life would be a lot less interesting without them.

Penn cups his hand around his ear. "Do I detect an ounce of jealousy from both of you?" He nods his head. "Yup, I think I do."

Dallas scoffs from behind the bar as he crosses his arms and his legs, leaning against the counter behind him. "I think I hear it too."

Parker rolls his eyes and I go back to eating, mumbling around my food. "So, you had a good trip, then?" I ask.

"I did. The mountains are gorgeous in the winter—but fucking cold."

"I can imagine. I'm just ready for the warmer weather in general, which reminds me…I got a rather interesting phone call yesterday," I continue, thinking back to the call from earlier that's still irritating me.

"From who?" Penn asks before taking a bite of his burger.

"The new baseball coach at Carrington Cove High School." I wipe my mouth with a napkin. "Coach Larson retired, and this new guy thought that by reaching out to me directly, he'd get a different answer than the one I gave Larson."

Parker shakes his head. "I don't get it. Why don't you want to help coach the team? You could help shape the next prodigy."

Grumbling, I say, "I'm busy. I don't have time for that." That's what I keep telling myself, but honestly, I don't know if that's what I want. Coaching seems like the logical way to keep baseball a part of my life, but dealing with teenage boys? Teaching the game instead of playing it? I just don't know if I'm cut out for that shit. I was a hell of a player, but that doesn't mean that I'd be a worthwhile coach. And the only kids I have experience with are my niece and nephew. Not sure teenage boys and I would jive, and I sure as fuck didn't have an example of a father to pull experience from.

"Yes, you fucking do," Dallas counters. "I mean, hello? You're sitting in my restaurant on a Thursday taking an hour-long lunch. You'll go back to your garage, finish out a few jobs, and then what?"

"Running a business takes a ton of time," I fire back, wondering why he's pushing this so hard. "You of all people should know that, Dallas."

"I do, but I also know that we make time for things that are important to us, like having a life outside of work. You already have a guy that can run the place for you for a couple of hours, so why not take advantage of it?"

"Because I don't want to fucking coach, all right?" I snap, my voice booming through the empty restaurant. Fury races through me because I thought of all people, he would understand. He saw me at my worst those first few months. He knows what losing the game did to me. If it weren't for Astrid and the kids needing me, who knows how many bottles of whiskey I would have taken down since then?

Parker and Penn share a look, but Dallas continues to push. "Because it reminds you of what you lost, doesn't it?"

I stand from my stool and toss my napkin on my plate, my meal only half-eaten. But I'm no longer hungry. "You know what? I don't fucking need this. I'm going to go see my sister since she has her big event this weekend and she was gone this past weekend too." I turn to walk away, but only move three steps before I freeze. Slowly, I turn back around and drill my line of sight into Penn.

Holy shit. It can't be…

"Uh, Dallas? Didn't you want to show me that…thing about the…stuff?" Parker stutters as Penn and I remain eye-locked, tension building.

"Sure. Yeah, we can do that." Dallas heads to the back of the restaurant, Parker scurrying after him. And then it's just me and Penn, the man that I'm fairly certain has some explaining to do.

"Is there something you need to tell me?" I ask, walking back over to the bar where Penn is still seated.

He doesn't flinch before he replies, "Is there something you want to ask?"

"I don't know." I rub my jaw, dragging my nails through the thick scruff I've been growing lately because I've found myself too lazy to shave. "I just find it odd that you and my sister went away on the exact same weekend…"

"That's because we were together, Grady," he says, immediately laying the truth out there.

I glare at him harder. "*Together*?"

Penn stands now so we can see eye to eye, even though he has a few inches on me. Penn has a few inches on everybody at six-foot-five. "Yes. Together. I'm in love with her and I took her away to tell her that."

My face softens almost instantly. "Holy shit."

I've always wondered if there was something more between them, but I also figured that if Penn felt that way, he would have done something about it by now.

"I'm not going to lie to you. She and I have been torn up about it, but I'm not going to stop living my life because of what other people might think. I've been in love with her for a while."

"So when did things change?"

"About a month ago."

I run my hand through my hair and sigh. *Fuck*. If Penn is finally making moves in his life, I should be happy for him. Maybe he's learned something I haven't.

"Well, I know what I think about it doesn't really matter because you're grown-ass adults, but if there's anyone I would pick for her, it would be you." I reach out my hand to him, and just like that, everything is good again. That's how men handle our issues—cut and dry. "But don't fucking take her for granted, Penn," I say, our hands still clasped. "She doesn't need to go through that again."

"Again?" His brow furrows.

"Yeah. I mean how Brandon never appreciated her. Their marriage was long over, but I'm sure you already know that." The second the words leave my lips, his face shifts from elated to confused. "Wait…you *didn't* know that?" My pulse starts hammering in my ears, my mind starts to race, and within seconds I realize I just revealed something that wasn't mine to reveal.

"Uh, no. What do you mean?"

"Fuck." I release Penn's hand and blow out a breath. "Dude, they were going to get a divorce when he returned from his last deployment, but then..."

"Shit," Penn mutters, turning away from me as he takes in this information.

"Look, I thought you would have known. Don't be mad at her."

"I'm not mad at her. I just..." He tilts his head at me. "I just...I need to fucking talk to her."

My heart rate is borderline alarming, but my brain continues to function normally, which leads me to a very important conclusion. "Yeah, and I know that when you do, it's going to be my neck on the chopping block, so why don't you let me talk to her first?"

Astrid may be younger than me, but she can scare the shit out of me too. I need to make this right. I need to let her know that it's my fault Penn knows about Brandon now.

Penn nods. "Yeah, probably a good idea."

"And Brandon never said anything to you either?" I ask, hoping I didn't really just create a clusterfuck of epic proportions.

"Never, Grady. In fact, he told me the opposite." Penn grabs his Coke and drains the rest of the glass, shaking his head as he places it back on the bar.

I scoff. "Sounds about right. He always was about keeping up appearances."

Penn shakes his head for an unsettling amount of time before finally speaking. "I...I need to get back to work."

Jesus, I do too, but who knows how long it's going to take for me to talk my sister down off a ledge now. "Yeah, okay. I'll text you when I've talked to her."

My half-eaten burger now churning in my gut, I head for the door and hop in my truck to race across town to the bakery, hoping my sister doesn't have any sharp objects around her when I tell her what I did.

At least your day isn't boring now, is it, Grady?

Yeah, not sure this was the excitement I was looking for.

***

"Pour me another," I say, gesturing toward the bartender at Ricky's Bar. Located just on the edge of town, it draws some unfamiliar faces from surrounding towns. I needed a place to sulk that wasn't Catch & Release, where I'm sure I'd suffer the inquisition from Dallas and anyone else there that knows me.

In small towns like Carrington Cove, there's no privacy. Almost like it was being a famous baseball player. There was no privacy in my life then either, but fuck, do I still miss it. Being able to play made up for the other bullshit I had to deal with.

The whiskey goes down smooth, easing the tension in my neck and shoulders after a long fucking week. It's just a few days before Christmas, and everyone I know is spending time doing things with their families. But I don't have one of those and probably never will at this rate.

Astrid forgave me rather quickly for spilling her secret to Penn, and now that I see the two of them together, I'm glad he pulled his head out of his ass so he could be the type of man that my sister deserves. Now, if only I could get her to stop pushing *me* to date. I swear, people in love just want everyone else to have it too, but sometimes, being alone is just easier. It's how I've operated for most of my adult life. I didn't have time for relationships when I was playing, and the only women interested in me now are the ones who think I have something to offer them from my former life.

Don't get me wrong. I'm doing very well for myself. I didn't piss away the money I made in the major leagues—I invested and saved so I'd be set for life. The garage does well too, but that's beside the point. Those women want Grady Reynolds, the star pitcher. Not Grady Reynolds, the grumpy, injured man who channels his inner Clint Eastwood most days.

Earlier, Astrid and Penn insisted I go with them to my niece Lilly's dance recital, so of course I did. But after, they all wanted to go out for dinner and dessert, and the only thing I wanted was to be alone—again.

It's been a long few days, finishing up projects around the garage and dodging phone calls from the high school coach. With the holidays approaching, I'm looking forward to a much-needed break. I'm headed down to Florida where the weather is warmer and I can go fishing, catch up with a buddy of mine from college, and escape small-town life for a while.

I need it. The boys were right, and I'm starting to feel suffocated by this life that I didn't choose.

But part of you did, didn't it, Grady?

The twinge of pain that shoots through my arm at any given moment decides then to remind me of my own selfish foolishness. I reach up and rub the spot, circling my arm around while trying not to hit the person sitting next to me at the bar, then take another drink of whiskey to help numb the pain.

It only does so much, but still better than being sober at the moment.

Tennessee Whiskey by Chris Stapleton plays from the jukebox in the corner as the sound of pool balls scattering across felt echoes in the bar. A group of men are gathered around the pool tables dressed in Carhartt jeans and work boots, sharing pitchers of beer and a few good laughs. Harold, Baron, and Thompson are playing darts in the corner. They usually play at Catch & Release, but Dallas has been closing the restaurant and bar early this week because of the holiday.

Several bikers are seated in another corner, black leather vests encasing their chests and red bandanas covering their heads. A group of women giggle at a table near the center of the room, one of them wearing an "I'm Divorced!" sash across her chest.

But as I survey the group of women more closely, a head of curly brown hair catches my attention. The woman those curls belong to stands from the table and heads toward the back corner where the bathrooms are located. I can't see her face through her hair, but her curves give me more than enough to admire.

She's wearing dark denim that is practically painted onto her wide hips and thick thighs. Her waist dips in just enough to hint at an hourglass figure under her red top, and she's wearing wedges that make her appear taller than she is.

There's something eerily familiar about her, and for a moment, I convince myself I've just had too much whiskey. I stare down into my glass, listen to the music playing throughout the bar, then swirl the amber liquid around, and toss back the rest of my drink before catching her walk back out from the hall.

And that's when my stomach drops.

"Scottie?"

Her eyes swivel around the room before landing on mine. And then her lips spread so wide as mine mimic the same movement. "Oh. My. God."

"Holy shit."

Biting her lip, she strides over to me as I take in the entirety of her. Damn, Scottie Daniels is all grown up, a fucking woman now—a woman I haven't seen in almost seventeen years.

"What are the freaking chances?" she asks as she stands right before me, the shock on her face just as pronounced as my own.

I rise from my stool to pull her into a hug, inhaling her still familiar scent while wondering if this is all just a fucking dream. "Scottie Daniels," I murmur in her ear as I inhale a little too deeply.

She clears her throat and then breaks our embrace. "Ha. I haven't been Scottie Daniels in a long time, Grady Reynolds. But you?" She places her hands on the sides of my face. "Holy shit, it's really you."

My eyes can't stop taking her in, from those familiar green eyes to the freckles on her nose that are barely concealed by her makeup, to those full lips painted a deep rose shade that brings out the color in her cheeks. Her hair is just as wild as I remember, yet somehow also tamer, and her smile just as addicting. Standing here in front of her now is like taking a ride in the DeLorean—it feels like I'm back in high school staring at the girl who always made me wonder, *what if?*

"So what do I call you then?"

"That might take a while to explain," she says, rolling her eyes and peering over at the group of women she left earlier.

I follow her line of sight. "Do you need to get back to your friends?"

"Not really. Those are my mom's friends. She dragged me along tonight and told me I needed to have some fun, so here I am."

"The girl I knew used to say the same thing to me."

The corner of her mouth lifts, but it's a sad smile. "I haven't been that girl in a long time, Grady."

Studying her face, I say, "What happened, Scottie? One day we were texting, and the next, your number was disconnected."

She sighs. "It's ancient history."

"Well, I've got all night to travel back in time with you."

She shakes her head at me, clearly debating whether she should stay or just treat this as a coincidental passing. But then a familiar spark of determination lights up her eyes, and she says, "I'm gonna need a drink to get through that story, if that's the case."

I signal to the bartender. "Then let's make that happen."

Chapter Two

Grady

Scottie takes a large drink of her vodka cranberry, keeping her eyes locked on the bar in front of her.

"Easy there, tiger."

"Trust me. This conversation will go a lot faster with a little liquid courage."

I huff out a laugh and take a sip of my drink, still reeling from how quickly the evening turned around. Being back in Scottie's presence is like taking a breath after being underwater for hours. I know it's impossible to hold your breath that long, but now that she's sitting in front of me, I feel alive again, like a weight was just lifted from my chest.

And fuck. She's even more gorgeous than I remember.

"Start talking, Scottie," I say, trying to remain patient, but my mind is spinning. I need something from her so the pieces of the puzzle that comprised our friendship can start to make fucking sense. Losing contact with her fucking stung, but I don't think I realized just how much it affected me until now. I'm simultaneously elated and angry seeing her tonight, and the last thing I want is for our reunion to go sour. But damn it, I have questions and she's the one with all the answers.

She pats my thigh. "Let's talk about you first."

"If you start this, we're just going to keep going back and forth all night."

She reaches over and covers my hand with her palm, the heat of her touch sending a bolt of electricity straight down my spine to my groin.

Jesus. She practically just electrocuted me.

"I'm sorry about your arm," she continues with a sad tilt of her lips.

A grunt escapes me, the same reaction I give anyone who offers me their condolences about my career. "It is what it is."

"Still. You were at the top of your game. It sucks to go out like that."

"Believe me. I lived it. I know." I drain the rest of my glass and motion to the bartender for another.

"Torn rotator cuff?"

Blowing out a breath, I wipe my palms on my jeans and nod. "I knew something was wrong the game before."

"Grady…" Her brows draw together, but I continue before she can say anything else. "But I didn't want to believe it. I kept telling myself I was just sore. We were on a three-day game series, and my age was catching up to me. Years of beating up my body was finally taking its toll, so I didn't tell anyone and kept playing through the pain."

"And then it was beyond repair when you tore the tendons."

I nod, intercepting my fresh whiskey, taking down a large gulp. "Yeah."

"Shit, I'm sorry."

I cast my gaze in her direction before taking another sip. "No one to blame but myself."

Scottie reaches for my hand again, squeezing it, but then a twinkle in her eye appears. "Can I ask you one more thing about baseball and then we can leave the topic alone for tonight?"

I arch a brow at her. "Okay…"

Leaning closer, she flashes me that smile I didn't realize I missed so fucking much and says, "Did you throw up before your first MLB game?"

My head falls back as laughter pours out of me, a deep-rooted laugh that I feel all the way down to my toes. *Fuck, I needed that*. When I gain my composure, watching her sip her drink around the straw tucked between her teeth, her mouth spread with pleasure, I reply, "I did."

She shakes her head at me. "It was only a matter of time."

"What about you? Any more keg stands gone bad while you were in college?"

She chuckles. "A few, but like you, my focus was on the game. I didn't party nearly as much as my teammates, but I did enough damage the few times I went out." Her smile falls and just like that, the light in her eyes starts to fade as well.

My heart hammers as I repeat my question from earlier. "What happened, Scottie?"

"You made it to the big leagues, Reynolds," she says quietly. "And I didn't."

I swallow down the lump in my throat. "I know. Right after I got drafted you were telling me about the national women's team, and then you weren't on the roster the next season at Georgia. What went wrong?" I remember trying to find as much information as I could about her, but there was nothing to find. It was as if her entire softball career vanished overnight.

She blows out a breath, tilts her head at me, and says something I wasn't expecting. "I got pregnant, Grady."

My eyebrows climb up my forehead. "Holy shit."

"Yeah." She takes another sip from her drink as she stares off to the side of the bar. "He just turned fourteen. His name is Chase and..." A soft smile spreads across her lips. "He changed my life in the best way." Our eyes meet again. "I thought I had my future planned out, but God showed me that I was meant for more. I was meant to be Chase's mom, and I don't regret having him for a second."

My heart hammers again as I think about how that must have felt for her. "Why didn't you tell me? Why didn't you text me back?"

"It's complicated," she mutters, draining her glass and then motioning for another from the bartender.

"So uncomplicate it."

She stirs the ice cubes around in her empty glass, avoiding my eyes. "Chase's dad..." My hackles instantly rise. "I thought I knew him, but if I've learned anything, it's that people can surprise you. He was controlling and I didn't realize it until it was too late."

"Did he hurt you?" Murder wasn't something I thought I was ever capable of until this moment, but if I find out her ex put his hands on her, I might just accept my fate to make sure he never does it again.

"No, he didn't hurt me, not physically," she interjects quickly. She blows out a breath and forces a smile. "But thankfully, that's not something I have to deal with anymore. I'm proudly divorced and have no regrets about leaving him."

"I'm sorry." Reaching between us, I grab her hand, our fingers threading together. It feels so natural touching her like this, hearing her voice again, waiting anxiously for what's going to come out of her mouth next. I swear, I'm seventeen all over again, sitting in math class, wishing our time together wouldn't end.

"No need to apologize. Things worked out the way they should have." Her words sound rehearsed, like she's said them so many times now they come out with ease.

Guess I'm not the only one who's gotten good at giving people the response they want rather than the freaking truth.

"So please tell me your girlfriend knows you're out drinking alone tonight," she says next, her assumption catching me off guard.

"Is that your way of asking if I'm single?"

She smirks around the rim of her glass. "Maybe."

"No girlfriend, Scottie. No wife either."

"You never married?"

"Didn't really have time to focus on that aspect of my life."

"I always wondered. There wasn't much about your personal life in the news articles and stuff."

"You were keeping tabs on me?" I pinch her knee, making her squeal.

"Hey! I told you I would be rooting for you. I just did it…quietly."

"What are you up to now?" Our hands remain linked between us as I wait for her reply.

"I work in education now. My degree was in early childhood development, so I decided to become a teacher. Now I'm in administration."

"Good for you. I bet the kids love you."

"Not as much as I love them." She clears her throat and directs the conversation back to me. "I heard you turned into a grease monkey."

I lift my glass to my lips. "You heard right. I bought the Carrington Cove Garage from Mr. Rogers shortly after I moved home."

She studies me for a moment. "I don't see it."

"See what?"

"You. Working on cars." She pauses, a pinch in her brow. "Wait. No shirt on." She draws a check mark in the air. "Overalls with one strap undone." She shakes her head. "No. Just a pair of jeans with grease stains and a rag sticking out of your back pocket." She nods, drawing another check mark in the air. "Sweat trailing down your temple." Another check mark. "Grease covering your forearms, and the band of your briefs sticking out of the top of your jeans." She licks her lips. "Yeah, okay. I can definitely see it now."

The temperature in this bar just rose twenty degrees—because while Scottie was describing her little fantasy right there, I was imagining spreading her out over the hood of my Nova and eating her pussy until she screamed.

Yeah, I can definitely see it too.

Clearing my throat, I swirl my glass in my hand. "I can't believe you're here, Scottie." And then I ask the question that instantly pops into my mind. "Are you staying?"

She shakes her head twice. "Just here for the holidays."

"When will you be back?"

She shrugs. "I have no idea. I don't come home very often. In fact, it's been years, but something told me it was time to face the past."

Her words hit me square in the chest. The past—*our past*—is sitting like a ghost right between us, haunting me with everything I never said, everything I never did—and the girl I never chased because I was too busy chasing something else.

"It felt hard coming back home after everything...and Chase." She swallows hard. "His life is down in Winterville."

"Where is that?"

"It's a suburb of Athens. I stayed close to UGA so I could finish school, and then I got hired at the elementary school down the street just after Chase turned four. It's home now, and I..."

"Don't leave tonight," I interrupt, almost commanding her to stay.

She licks her lips, bites her bottom one, and then says in a sultry voice that travels straight to my dick, "I'm not going anywhere just yet."

***

Scottie slaps the bar beside her. "God, that last game was a nail-biter!"

"You don't have to tell me. I've never felt pressure like that in my entire life, but damn, what a rush."

We've each had two more drinks since Scottie sat down on the stool across from me over three hours ago, and both of us are beginning to slur our words. It's nearing one in the morning, and I have no desire to leave. But the glares from the bartenders tell me that our time is coming to an end sooner rather than later.

Ricky's has nearly cleared out. Scottie's mom and her friends left hours ago, but I assured her mother I'd make sure she got home safe. Scottie is the spitting image of her mom and it felt nice to meet the woman responsible for raising her to be the spitfire I knew and the strong woman she is now.

"But you won, Grady." She reaches over and squeezes my arm, touching me for the hundredth time tonight.

I may be reading this all wrong, and it could just be the alcohol talking, but Scottie's made it a point to touch me any chance she gets, scooting closer and closer as the night goes on. And I'd be a fucking liar if I said I wasn't thinking about how this night could end if I give in to the same draw I feel toward her.

So much time has passed, and yet it feels like none has at all. The girl who offered me her friendship all those years ago is still in there, but she's different too. I can tell her life trajectory has changed her, made her strong in ways she never knew she'd have to be for her and her son.

But as I sit here and stare at her, I can't help but wonder what would have happened if I had chosen a different path myself. Would the ache of losing baseball even be there if I had never tasted a World Series title? Would the extra time with my friends and family have made it worth it, not missing all those milestones and birthdays?

And what if I had gone after the woman in front of me? If I hadn't held back and had let her know how I felt all those years ago?

These feelings are flooding my chest, my body humming with energy and making me feel alive for the first time in years—almost five years to be exact.

"I did. The team won, and it was a night I won't ever forget." *Much like this one.*

"Do you have your ring with you?" she asks, peering down at my hands even though she's been touching them all night and already knows the answer to that question.

"No," I scoff. "I don't wear that thing around, Scottie."

"Why not?" She throws her hands up in the air, nearly falling from her stool but I catch her before she hits the ground.

"Easy there."

She shrugs me off. "I'm fine. But seriously, Reynolds? If it were me, I'd be flashing that thing in anyone's face I could. You won a freaking World Series! Do you know how freaking amazing—"

"We close in ten minutes!" the bartender from earlier interjects, cutting Scottie off. The irritation on his face tells me he doesn't give a shit if I won the World Series or not.

"Here." I toss my credit card to him over the counter, then turn back to Scottie. "We'd better be going."

"Yeah." She stands from her stool, gaining her balance before brushing her curls from her face. "I'm just gonna use the bathroom."

"You gonna be okay walking over there?"

She rolls her eyes at me. "Yeah, I'll be fine."

My eyes trail her ass as her hips sway from side to side until she disappears down the hallway to the restrooms. While she's gone, I order an Uber and settle our bar tab. I'm grabbing my coat from the back of my stool just as she reappears.

"Thanks for the drinks." She reaches for her own coat, and I help her slip it on before putting on my own.

"Thanks for coming out tonight."

"Yeah, who knew the night would turn in a completely random direction." With my hand on the small of her back, I lead her outside, the frigid air hitting us the second we walk through the door. "Jesus, it's cold," she murmurs, pulling her coat tighter around her body.

I wrap my arms around her, pulling her into my chest to help keep her warm while we wait for our ride. "It's almost Christmas, Scottie. Don't you remember how brutal the winter air can be?"

She laughs, her breath forming a visible cloud. "I guess I forgot. Back in Georgia, I'm more inland, so the air isn't as frigid..."

Her voice trails off as we stand there in the silence, nothing but the sound of the wind whipping around us and her eyes twinkling in the dim lighting outside. But I don't want to let her go. I don't want this night to end yet. Hanging out with her tonight has woken up a part of me that feels like it's been dormant for far too long, and the most irrational part of me that woke up is my fucking dick.

He's been ready to go since the first time Scottie touched my leg earlier.

I know I can't be the only one that wants to cross that line. I've felt it from her all night. And hell, we're adults now, right? I have no idea when I might see her again, and I think we owe it to each other to see where the rest of this night could lead.

"Don't go home tonight, Scottie," I say, breaking the silence, waiting on pins and needles for her response. If she turns me down, then at least I know where we stand. But if she's feeling what I'm feeling, then trying to pace myself will be my next obstacle.

Please tell me you want this, Scottie.

"Give me a reason not to, Reynolds."

A breath of relief leaves my lips as I press my cock into her stomach, backing her up against the building we were just in, showing her what the night can hold if she gives me permission. "How's that?"

She hums and reaches down between us, rubbing her hand over my erection straining against my jeans. "That feels like a pretty strong reason, but I might have to take a closer look to be sure."

"Oh, it'll deliver. I fucking promise that."

She licks her lips and says, "I hope you're ready to prove it."

Chapter Three

Grady

I help Scottie out of the car, thank our driver, then walk her up to the garage.

"God, this place hasn't changed," Scottie murmurs as I unlock the office door and pull her inside, locking it behind us. The only light in the space comes from the moon and street lamps outside the windows. Scottie wanted to see everything about my new life, so I carefully guide us through the office and into the garage.

"Oh, come on. The outside has a new coat of paint and the name is different. You've got to give me credit for that." I flip the lights on just as the smell of rubber and oil hits our noses, followed by the sound of the lights buzzing to life.

Scottie's eyes scour the space. There are several cars in the bays still, customers who needed more than just routine maintenance. The Camaro that was giving us trouble last week is ready to be picked up on Monday, and in the far corner, under the sheet that keeps her safe, is my '73 Nova—my own project that I'll get to someday.

"This is a big change from swinging a bat and wearing a glove." She meets my eyes.

"Yeah, it is. But working on cars is the only other thing I really liked besides baseball."

She reaches out her hand to me and I take it. "Show me around."

I give her the tour, showing her the tire balancing machine, the welding station, and how to use the vehicle lift before we end at the tool shelf.

"It's a lot cleaner than I expected." She wrinkles her nose at me. "But this stands out like a sore thumb." She strides over to the Nova. "What's under here?"

I lift the sheet and rip it off the car. "My project."

She tilts her head at the car. "Doesn't look like you've done much."

Laughing, I reply, "Haven't had much time." That's a lie. I could make time, I just haven't. I haven't had the motivation—for this or much of anything lately.

She runs her hand over the hood, dust collecting on her hand before she wipes it on her jeans. "She sure is sexy though."

I wait for her gaze to meet mine again before replying. "Yeah, she sure fucking is."

My pulse hammers as our breaths grow shallow, but neither of us moves.

"Are you ready to prove that coming here wasn't a mistake?" she asks breathlessly, her chest rising and falling rapidly. My self-control snaps, and I quickly close the distance between us, burying my hand in her hair.

I pull her head back slightly, grip her hip possessively, and say, "Nothing between us could ever be a mistake, Scottie," before crashing my mouth to hers.

With one taste I know that this woman just might ruin me.

Scottie's lips mirror my own, licking, seeking, and when our tongues meet, a groan travels up my throat and vibrates against her mouth.

"Fuck," I mumble against her lips.

"Don't stop, Grady."

Lifting her up by her hips, I place her on the hood of the Nova and press her against the cool metal surface. God, I want to devour her right here, but she deserves better than this. Better than a rush to get each other naked, better than fumbling sex on the hood of my car. Our mouths move over each other, my hands trace her body, memorizing her curves, how soft her skin feels as I run my palms up her arm, how fucking incredible she tastes and sounds, dragging me even further under her spell.

But before I can suggest we go to my house, she pushes me backward, hops down from the hood, and strips off her jacket, tossing it to the ground. Then she unbuttons her jeans, kicking off her wedges before peeling them down her legs, leaving her standing there in her red top and black G-string.

I drag a hand down my face, trying to pick my jaw up off the floor. "Jesus Christ, Scottie."

"Touch me, Grady," she whispers, and I fight every ounce of my control not to pounce on her immediately.

I lift her back on the hood of my car, spread her legs open, and lower my face to her pussy, dragging my nose through her slit and inhaling her scent through the thin strip of silk before biting the inside of her thigh, trying to pace myself. She moans, lifting her head up to watch me as I apply pressure to her clit through the fabric with my fingers.

"You're sure you want this, Scottie?"

She nods hurriedly. "Hell yes."

Without any more hesitation, I grab the strings at her hips, rip the thong from her body and drag my tongue through her slit, watching her eyes roll into the back of her head. "Oh God, yes..."

I lick her slowly, drawing a moan from her as her fingers dig into my hair.

Jesus Christ. Even her pussy tastes like heaven—pure, unfiltered heaven.

My cock weeps behind my jeans, begging for his turn, but not yet. This woman is going to come on my mouth and then I'll sink into her tight heat, bring us both to the edge, and fuck her over and over until we both can't keep our eyes open any longer.

I need it. I need to feel *her*. And by the way she's riding my face right now, I have a feeling she needs this too.

I circle her clit with my tongue and suck, feeling her grow wetter against my mouth. Lapping up her arousal, I make sure to explore every inch of her before coating two of my fingers in her wetness and sinking them inside her.

"God damn," I grate out, watching my fingers disappear in and out of her before bringing my tongue back to her clit, teasing her with soft strokes and circles. "I could eat your pussy all night."

Her body slides down the hood of the car, but I fall to my knees so I can still reach her, not wanting to stop for anything. Her thighs shake, her hands tighten in my hair, and just when I feel her constrict around my fingers, she screams through her orgasm, her pleasure echoing in the empty garage. I peer up just in time to watch the ecstasy paint her features, her eyes squeezing shut as moans escape her lips.

And right then and there, I commit the sight to memory because nothing is more perfect than Scottland Daniels climaxing on the hood of my car.

"Holy shit," she breathes as I pull my fingers out of her and lick them clean, locking eyes with her as I do.

"We're not even close to being done, Scottie," I say, rising from my knees.

"Good. Because now it's my turn to taste you." She slides off the car and drops to her knees, reaching for my belt buckle.

"Fuck, woman." I push her curls from her face so I can see her eyes. "This is really fucking happening, isn't it?"

"Don't ruin the moment, Reynolds," she teases as she pulls my zipper down, pushes my pants down, and pulls my cock dripping with pre-cum from my briefs. "God, yes," she says as she admires my dick, licking the slit before circling the head with her tongue.

"That's it, baby. Suck me."

She pulls me in halfway, flicking her tongue on the underside of my shaft before pulling me all the way out. And then she takes me deep, so deep that I hit the back of her throat, making her gag, but she handles it flawlessly, easing me out just enough to find a rhythm that brings me to the breaking point quicker than I wanted.

"Fuck, Scottie. Keep doing that and I'm going to come down your throat."

She releases me long enough to say, "Please," and takes me back in her mouth, using her hands in combination with her lips, cupping my balls as she works me over, pulling my orgasm from me.

Facing the ceiling, I brace for the white-hot pleasure that's about to shoot out of me, but I drop my head back down just in time to watch Scottie's eyes flutter shut as the first spurt of cum hits her tongue.

"Fuck…yes…" Groaning, I keep fucking her mouth, watching her take every last drop until she releases me and smiles up at me, proudly. I lift her up and pull her to my chest, cupping the side of her face before planting my lips on her. "I think it's safe to say our friendship is effectively ruined."

She shakes her head. "I think we just unlocked a new level of friendship."

I reach down to pull my pants up, then toss her jeans at her. "Come on. Let's go to my house. It's warmer and there's a bed."

She pulls her pants up, fluffs her hair, and says, "Lead the way."

When I worked here as a teenager, Mr. Rogers lived in the apartment above the garage, which was fine for a single man without a family. But I wanted an actual home, so I built a house on the back half of the property—and I spared no expense.

We trek across the field that separates the garage from my house, treading lightly through the grass so she doesn't fall. But before we reach the front porch, Scottie deviates toward the huge oak tree in front of my house, staring up at it as I put a few feet of distance between us so I can watch her.

"Wow. Now that's a tree."

"Is that the alcohol talking, or are you seriously mesmerized by it?"

She smirks at me over her shoulder. "Am I not allowed to appreciate a good tree, Grady?"

I walk over to her, wrapping my arm around her waist and slowly backing her up until her back hits the trunk. "I think you should appreciate anything that makes you happy, Scottie."

Her eyes crinkle at the corners. "Do you remember the last time we were under a tree?"

"You mean the night you did a keg stand at Derek's party?"

She laughs. "Yeah. Swinging in that tire wasn't a good idea."

"I tried to tell you that, but you were always more concerned with me throwing up than yourself."

Her smile falls and then she reaches up and pushes my hair back. "If I hadn't thrown up, would you have kissed me that night, Grady?" Her voice is a whisper, but those words travel right down my spine.

That night lived rent free in my head for years. I would think back to my missed opportunity, but then remembered that kissing her wouldn't have mattered. I still would have left, and so would she.

"I wanted to, Scottie. Fuck, I did." I lean my forehead on hers. "But we were both leaving and…"

"Would you kiss me now? Under this tree?"

Our eyes are locked on each other's. All I can hear is the sound of crickets chirping in the distance and the beat of my heart in my ears. I just had my mouth between this woman's legs, but for some reason, this feels more intimate.

"I'd love nothing more than to kiss you, Scottie. And I plan on doing it all night long until we pass out."

Wasting no time, I dip my mouth to hers and savor the taste of her once more, but without feeling rushed, without feeling like she might evaporate from my arms. Our tongues meet in a slow swirl, blood rushes right down between my legs again, and I reach down to grab Scottie's leg, curling it around my hip while I press her against the tree.

I bury one hand in her hair and pull her closer to me with the other as I angle her head to the side and deepen our kiss.

Scottie pulls away, breathing heavily, and says, "Fuck me, Grady."

And my body jolts back to life with desperation, pulling her toward the house.

The second we're inside, I spin her around, push her against the door, and dive my tongue into her mouth again. Both of us just came but I know my dick is eager for more.

"Take everything off, Scottie. Now."

"So bossy." She giggles as clothes go flying. And when her bra falls to the floor, my mouth waters at the sight of her breasts.

"I want these in my mouth," I say as I cup both of her breasts, pinching and rolling her nipples.

"Yes," she mewls, pulling my face down to her chest, making me bend over to reach her pebbled peaks. So instead, I hoist her up, wrap her legs around my waist, and push her back against the door, sucking on her nipples as she rubs her pussy against my stomach. I can feel how wet she is still, more than ready for me. But I want her in my bed. I want my sheets to smell like her. I already know that one night with her isn't going to be enough, but I can't think about that right now.

Right now, the only thing I need to focus on is making her come on my cock this time.

Her arms tighten around my neck as I lift her from the door and start walking down the hallway, locating my room in the dark with ease. We fall to the bed with her beneath me, her legs still wrapped around my waist.

Our lips continue to move, exploring and drawing pleasure from each other as she rubs her pussy against me again. I settle in the cradle of her hips and all it would take is one thrust to bury myself inside her. But I have to be level-headed in some respect. The whiskey is already clouding my judgment.

"I need to get a condom," I say between kisses, forcing myself to pull away as I head for my nightstand and take out a rubber. I've had these condoms for so long that I almost forgot they were there, but thank God I have something. I tear the wrapper, cover myself, and walk back over to the sight of Scottie splayed out on my bed. "Jesus, you look perfect like this."

She opens her legs to me, giving me the perfect view of her glistening, pink pussy. "Like how?"

"Ready for my cock. Willing to let me own you." I crawl over her and bracket her head with my forearms as I stare right into her eyes. "Like this was how you were always supposed to be—mine."

Her lips part on a gasp. "Grady…"

Dragging my nose up the side of her throat, I line my lips up to her ear and whisper, "Tell me this isn't a dream."

I can feel her shake her head against me. "It's not."

"Tell me you want this just as badly as I do."

"God, yes. Please…please fuck me, Grady."

I don't say another word before lining up my cock to her entrance and sliding home. Ecstasy races through my veins as her tight heat surrounds me, pulling me in deeper. Her heel slides up the back of my thigh, pulling me closer until my pelvis hits her clit, and we grind together, moaning at how good it feels.

How fucking *right* it feels.

"So good. You're so fucking tight, Scottie. Squeezing me so hard."

"More, Grady. God, don't stop."

I search for her nipple with my mouth, sucking and nibbling on her as our bodies writhe, our hips collide, and my dick grows impossibly harder. Her moans and trembles are cues I listen to as I find a pace that feels so fucking natural. I can feel Scottie dig her nails into my back, marking me, claiming me the same way I'm claiming her. With each thrust, I let my hands explore her body—brushing my knuckles along her soft skin, kissing and licking her neck, squeezing her thigh tighter around my hips as I work us higher and higher, chasing that release that I know is going to be fucking mind-blowing.

Her pussy spasms around me, signaling that she's close. "Come on my cock, Scottie. Fucking milk me, baby."

She moans loudly as I reach between us and apply pressure to her clit while circling my hips, thrusting in long strokes that make her moan with each pass of my dick inside her.

"I'm coming," she moans against my lips before I cover her mouth with mine and swallow her cries. She tightens even more around my dick, and then I let myself join her as numbness crawls down my legs and it feels like my soul leaves my body.

Collapsing against Scottie's chest, I fight to catch my breath as she pants beneath me. That was over much quicker than I wanted, but I'll be damned if she leaves my bed without me having her again.

When I finally feel stable enough to stand, I pull out of her, press a quick kiss to her lips, and head for my bathroom to deal with the condom.

Scottie lets out a yawn as I walk back into my room.

"None of that," I say as I crawl back into the bed, positioning her across my chest.

"Sorry. It's just way past my bedtime." Her hair tickles my nose, and I brush it out of the way so I can stare down at her. The heat of her body warms me all over, and holding her in my arms makes me realize how long it's been since I've had someone else in my bed.

But nothing compares to having her here.

"Then close your eyes. Rest for a while. You don't have to leave yet."

"I don't want to leave at all," she whispers, before we both drift off to sleep.

***

"Ride me, Scottie." I smack her ass again, urging her to move faster and fuck me until she comes. "Make yourself come. Make me break with you."

"Grady!" she cries, rubbing her pelvis over me, working herself closer to her climax. "I'm there!" And then I feel her tighten before she screams and takes me over the edge with her.

When we come down from the high, she turns to her side to face me. "So good."

I huff out a laugh. "Fucking amazing."

"I definitely didn't anticipate my night ending like this when my mom told me to go out with her."

It's three in the morning. Scottie and I drifted off for about an hour before I woke her up with my head between her legs again. And then she climbed on top of me and rode me until we both saw stars.

"It's not over yet."

"No, but at least it was memorable. I mean, you ate me out on the hood of a car for crying out loud."

My lips tip up like they have a mind of their own. And the memory of Scottie splayed out on my Nova like that will live on in my brain for all eternity. "I can do it again if you want."

She shakes her head at me. "Are you ever going to rebuild that car? Does it even run?"

I blow out a breath and turn to face the ceiling as she rests her head on my chest again. "I want to. I just…"

"I get it. But maybe it would help to have something to focus on, Grady." She draws circles through my chest hair. "I know I said I wouldn't bring up baseball again, but…"

"You're going to anyway."

She nods against my chest. "Have you ever thought about coaching?"

Just the mention of the word has my entire upper body tightening. "Why do you ask?"

She's silent for a moment before she speaks again. "Well, after I found out I was pregnant, I wasn't ready to give up the game entirely. I asked my coach if I could still practice with the girls, but as an observer. It sucked not being able to play, I'm not going to lie. But watching and being able to help the girls improve, especially the girl that replaced me, made it a little bit easier to let go." I trail my fingers up and down her spine. "I still loved the game, I just got to appreciate it on a different level."

My jaw is tight, but I manage to say, "I'll think about it." And that's not a lie. I have been thinking about it, especially after Dallas called me out at lunch last week and the new coach at the high school is still pursuing me. He even showed up at the garage a few days ago. I just don't know if it will make things better or worse for me.

But it might help you feel unstuck.

Scottie glances at the clock on my nightstand. "I need to get home soon. It's late, or early, however you want to look at it."

Reaching for her hand between us, I intertwine our fingers. "It's still dark. Get some more sleep first."

She lets out another yawn, and then snuggles in deeper to my body. "Just a little bit of sleep and then I'll go."

I don't argue with her. I just savor the feeling of her in my arms. But I do know one thing for certain—before she leaves, I'm going to get her number. This isn't going to be the last time I see Scottie or feel her wrapped around me. It can't be, not when my soul feels like a piece of my past and present just snapped into place.

Unfortunately, Scottie didn't feel the same way, as evidenced by her stealth departure after I fell asleep.

She didn't leave a note. Hell, not even a scrap of paper with her number scribbled on it.

And when I drive to her mom's house the next afternoon, eager to confront her on the matter, her mother can't look me in the eye when she says, "She's gone, Grady."

"What?"

"She went back home. Something about an emergency." Crossing her arms over her chest, she eyes me up and down, but there's a hint of something behind her eyes I can't read.

"What kind of emergency?"

She arches a brow at me. "The kind that doesn't exist."

"Lisa," I start, but she cuts me off.

"I know my daughter, honey. And if she left, there was a reason, one she didn't want you or me to know." She shrugs, but I can tell she's not happy with her daughter either.

I push a hand through my hair and blow out a breath. "Well, can I get her number then? Please?"

Shaking her head, she looks down at the ground. "If she didn't give it to you herself, then I can't help you."

"Seriously?"

"I'm sorry, Grady." She moves to shut the door. "This is what Scottie wanted, and I have to honor that. As her friend, I hope you understand."

The sound of the door clicking shut is like a nail being driven into a coffin, and with it I bury my feelings back where they belong—six feet under, where all my dreams have gone to die anyway.

Chapter Four

Scottie

Eight Weeks Later

I let out another yawn as we pass the state line into North Carolina, the hum of the tires beneath us lulling me to sleep yet again. This is one of those moments when I wish Chase were just a little bit older and could drive, but then again, he's not happy about the journey we're on right now, so that would probably be just another thing for us to fight about.

"Are we there yet?"

I glance back at my son in the rearview mirror, wondering how the hell he grew up so fast. It wasn't too long ago that he was five and sitting in his car seat, swinging his feet while eating Goldfish crackers, asking me the same question.

"A few more hours, baby."

He rolls his eyes and returns his attention to the game on his phone. "I'm hungry."

"What else is new?" Reaching for my purse, I locate the bag of sour peach rings I grabbed at the gas station at our last pit stop. "Wanna share some of these with me?"

He wrinkles his nose. "Those are gross."

"What? Since when?" I rip open the bag with my teeth and hand it to him, but he shakes his head. "Really?"

"I want a burger. And a milkshake." He licks his lips. "Can we stop for some food soon?"

Sighing, I glance at the clock on the dash. The length of this drive can be taxing, but at least I won't have to make it again for a while—or ever, if I have it my way.

Two months ago, when we visited Carrington Cove for Christmas, the last thing I anticipated was moving back to my hometown just eight short weeks later. But life had other plans for us, and my gut told me this move was what my son and I needed—a fresh start, and distance—distance from the suffering we'd both endured for long enough.

"There's a rest stop with a few fast-food chains in about twenty-five miles. We'll stop then," I reply, tossing a sour peach ring into my mouth, loving how the combination of sweet and sour bursts on my tongue. But as I chew, a sudden wave of nausea washes over me.

Whoa. That came out of nowhere.

Traveling at seventy miles per hour, I debate whether I need to pull over or wait for the churning in my stomach to subside.

Am I...am I really about to be sick right now?

I signal to my right, heading for the shoulder as I jerk the wheel to maneuver the car across two lanes of traffic.

"What the heck, Mom? What's going on?" Chase asks, concern lacing his words.

Not wanting to risk opening my mouth to reply, afraid vomit might escape, I slam on the brakes, jump out of the car, round the hood, and barely reach the dirt on the side of the highway before emptying the contents of my stomach.

Every snack I've eaten for the past five hours reappears as the sound of a car door opening and closing rings out behind me.

"Mom? Are you okay?" Chase comes up on my side, rubbing my back.

Once the heaving subsides and I'm fairly certain there's nothing left in my stomach, I brace my hands on my thighs, take a few deep breaths, and slowly stand upright. "Holy crap."

"You just threw up on the side of the road," he says, as if I didn't just experience it myself.

"I'm aware."

"Was your stomach bugging you earlier?"

"Not really. It just came on out of nowhere."

He snaps his fingers and gives me one of those looks that I usually give him, like he's the adult and I'm the child that never listens. "You probably ate too many snacks, and they didn't agree with your stomach." He waves a finger in front of my face. "You always tell me not to eat too much junk, and look what happened to you."

Swatting his hand away, I head back to the car, opening the passenger door to reach in and grab my water. I take a few small sips, rinsing the inside of my mouth before spitting the water in the dirt. I gulp down a few drinks to see how it feels in my stomach. "I didn't eat that much junk."

Chase starts ticking off items on his fingers. "Chips, candy bars, sour candy..."

"All right," I cut him off. "I may have gone a bit overboard with the road trip snacks."

"Honestly, I was a little worried. You normally would pack us crackers, cheese, meat, and some sort of fruit. You know, healthy crap."

"Well, I wanted to get on the road and live a little. Road trip snacks are a treat, and I know you weren't excited about this drive..."

"I didn't want to leave Winterville, Mom." His expression turns angry in an instant, the playfulness of his voice gone.

"I know you didn't, honey, but I promise..."

"You can't promise anything." He walks away from me, over to his side of the car where he throws himself in the back seat again, leaving me alone as cars whiz past.

Closing my eyes, I take a deep breath and blow it out. Being a mother is hard, especially to a teenager. I'm convinced that the inventor of alcohol had a teenager at home.

Shielding my eyes from the sun, I glance back at the car. Chase may think his whole world is ending, but I know in my bones that it's really just beginning.

He needs this. I need this. I can't stand seeing my son hurt anymore. The broken promises, ignored texts, and lack of support—he doesn't deserve any of it. If putting some distance between us and a place that holds more pain than joy is the only way for him to see his worth, I will gladly make that happen. Even if it means enduring his attitude, leaving my job in the middle of the school year, and moving back to my hometown that holds painful memories from my own childhood.

It also holds Grady, but that's a problem I can worry about later.

I settle into the driver's seat, start the car, and ease back into traffic, feeling a million times better than I did before I got sick. Maybe Chase was right. I just ate too much junk. Lord knows that's not how I normally fuel my body, and now I know to take it easy on any future road trips.

***

"They're here! Brenda, they're here!" Gigi—my grandma—comes traipsing down the front porch steps of my mother's house just as Chase and I exit the car. She pulls Chase into her arms for a hug, ruffling his curly hair that falls over his eyes as he stands nearly a foot above her. "What is with the mop on your head, boy?"

"Uh, that's my hair." He pushes it out of his eyes, but it falls right back into place.

"It looks like you haven't cut it since we saw you for Christmas." She glances over at me. "Why haven't you taken this boy to get a haircut?"

"He doesn't want to cut it. This is how the kids are wearing it these days."

The corner of her lip curls up in disgust. "I don't understand today's youth, but if looking like a cross between a poodle and boy is the trend, there's no use fighting it." She shrugs. "Just don't get upset when you run into shit because you can't see where you're going." She pats him on the shoulder and then moves around him to greet me. "Speaking of, you *look* like shit."

"Good to see you too, Gigi." I pull her into an embrace, knowing not to take her criticism to heart. My grandmother has always had a way with words, in the sense that she doesn't care about which ones she uses. She's honest, opinionated, and doesn't take shit from anyone. She's honestly my idol and part of the reason I had the courage to move me and my son away from our home of the past fifteen years. I channeled my inner Gigi.

"Seriously. You're kind of pale."

"She got sick on the side of the highway," Chase says as my mother comes down the porch from the house.

"You threw up?"

"I think I just ate too much junk." I rub my stomach. "But I feel fine now."

My mother pulls me in for a hug. "Yup. You probably just ate something that didn't agree with you." When she releases me, she cups the side of my face. "My baby is home."

I laugh. "I'm hardly a baby, Mom."

Shaking her head, "You'll always be my baby, Scottie. And I'm proud of you."

My eyes start to sting. "I still don't know if I made the right decision," I whisper, not wanting Chase to overhear.

She strokes my cheek. "All you can do is listen to your gut."

"I know. And I did."

"Then everything else will work itself out."

I stifle a yawn as we break apart. "God, I'm exhausted."

My mother jingles a set of keys in my face. "Well, let's show you the house and then you can get some rest. I'm sure the drive took it out of you."

"You have no idea."

The four of us cross the lawn of my mom's house into the yard of the house next door. That's right. I'm going to be living next door to my mom and grandma. But honestly, I'm really grateful. Having them close makes me feel safer, and not just because I know Gigi sleeps with a rifle next to her bed. For the first time in fifteen years, I'll have my family close by, help when I need it instead of having to rely solely on myself, and a place that doesn't have reminders of the life I tried to make work but couldn't.

Lord knows I couldn't rely on Andrew for anything anyway.

My mother unlocks the front door and then we all shuffle inside.

"This is perfect," I say as I take in the space. The living room is to our left, which already has furniture, thank God. The kitchen is straight ahead with the dining room to the left of that, and the hallway which leads to the bedrooms is to our right. My mom said there are three rooms, which means Chase can pick which one he wants, a detail he was less than enthusiastic about. I'm learning that teenagers are very difficult to impress.

"I told you. Just enough space for the two of you. When Colleen told me she was looking for new tenants, I had to swipe it up for you two." My mother turns to Chase. "What do you think, Chase?"

He shrugs. "Looks like a house."

My mother and I share a look, but Gigi speaks first. "Very good, Chase. It is a house. Good to know they're teaching you *something* in those good-for-nothing schools."

"Gigi..." I warn. She flicks my son in the back of the head.

"Hey! What was that for?"

"Don't disrespect your mother, your grandma, or me."

Rubbing the spot where she flicked him, he grimaces. "Sorry. It's just not home."

"But it will be." I step up to him. "You'll see, Chase. Carrington Cove is a great place to live." I keep telling myself that too, hoping it will click because for the past four weeks, all I've felt is nausea about the move. But now that we're here, I'm excited to show my son that living in a small town has its perks.

I've barely been home since leaving for college. Most of the time my mom and Gigi would venture down to Georgia to see Chase and me, partly because I couldn't get Andrew to stop working long enough to make the trek ourselves.

Well, at least I don't have to worry about that anymore.

Turning and walking toward the hall, Chase says over his shoulder, "I'm going to check out the rooms."

The three of us watch him walk away before I turn back to my mom and grandma. "It's going to get better, right?"

They nod in unison. "It will," my mother says. "Once he starts school and baseball, he'll adjust."

"I hope so."

"Speaking of school, when do you report?"

"Monday. I gave myself the weekend to get settled in, and then Alaina said she needed me as soon as possible."

"I knew we'd get her back home somehow," my mother says to my grandma, bumping shoulders with her.

"Yeah, more money and a handsome man." Gigi bounces her eyebrows. "Speaking of the cover model that came by here looking for you a few months ago, what do you plan on doing about him?"

"Cover model?" I ask, even though I'm fairly certain I know who she's referring to.

"Oh yeah." Gigi smirks. "That man belongs on the cover of those smutty books your mother and I read."

"Mom!" my mother admonishes.

"What? You act like he wouldn't sell thousands of books with that face and those muscles." Gigi glances back at me. "And I'm going to guess he's packing too." She bounces her eyebrows and then holds her hands nearly a foot apart from one another. "Just tell me. Am I close? Bigger or smaller?"

Groaning, I stare up at the ceiling. "What the hell have I gotten myself into?"

***

"And this will be your office." Alaina Bell, the principal of Carrington Cove Elementary, gestures for me to enter the office, where sunlight pours in through the open blinds. The box of décor I brought with me makes my arms ache, so I move toward the desk to set it down before gazing out the window, admiring the view of the campus.

The office is spacious, with a large mahogany desk sitting under the window. There are a few matching shelves on the wall to my left, along with two chairs with navy cushions for visiting parents and students. The walls are bare, but that's an easy fix. Most importantly, it's the fresh start I needed, and I'm grateful for it.

Turning to her, I say, "It's perfect."

"I'm glad you think so." She lets out a deep breath. "I can't tell you how grateful I am that you took this job, Scottie."

"Part of me still can't believe that I did, but it was the push I needed to leave Georgia."

"I'm glad it worked out then. Finding a new administrator in the middle of the school year is tough, but our last assistant principal just wasn't a good fit. I got a lot of complaints from staff and parents."

"It happens, but I promise I'll do whatever I can to keep fostering the culture and atmosphere that you've built here."

"Our teachers need someone they can count on to support them. Discipline is harder than ever these days. These kids are dealing with issues at home and have access to information that is beyond anything you and I dealt with as kids."

As a former teacher, I know what it is like to be in the classroom and the decision fatigue you battle every day. Teachers are the backbone of the schools, and my job now as an administrator is to help them make their lives easier any way I can. Getting my administration credential was a decision I didn't make lightly, but once my divorce was final, I needed a way to financially support Chase and me on my own. I didn't want to rely on Andrew for anything, especially since he's already shown that he's a lost cause in that respect.

"Believe me, I know. I saw some cases down in Georgia that would shock you."

"Your experience is exactly what we need, and I'm really excited to work with you."

"Same here," I reply, feeling genuinely excited for the first time in a long time.

Alaina is a few years older than me, but I remember her from our high school days. She was always friendly and one of those girls who could hang out with any group. She wasn't popular, but she was well-known. For the past five years, she's been the head principal of Carrington Cove Elementary, and now she's essentially my new boss.

"Okay, well I'll let you get settled before the teachers start arriving. I'll introduce you officially at the staff meeting this Wednesday, but I'm sending out an email to the staff shortly."

"Sounds great."

Alaina leaves my office and I turn back to the box that holds my degrees and credentials, pieces of paper that I may never have earned if I hadn't had Chase. As if he knew I was thinking about him, my phone chimes in my purse with the sound of a text message. When I see my son's name on the screen, I can't help but brace myself for what he's going to say.

Chase: *This school is so small, but my science teacher is cool.*

Smiling, I type out a response.

Me: *It is small, but that means you'll become close with your classmates.*

Chase: *I already met a few of the guys on the baseball team.*

Me: *I'm excited for you, honey.*

Chase: *Gotta go, Mom. Next class is about to start.*

Me: *Love you. Have a good day.*

Chase: *Love you too.*

I hold my phone to my chest and breathe out a sigh of relief. Everything is going to be okay, especially if I can avoid seeing Grady until Chase graduates from high school.

The second his face pops into my head, I groan, tossing my phone back into my purse and trying to focus on arranging things in my new office. But, like every other time I've thought of Grady these past weeks, our night together plays back through my mind like a montage of black and white snapshots.

Me seeing him in the bar.

Me flirting with him, even though I knew I shouldn't.

But God, he looked so rugged, so manly, so much hotter than he did as a teenager—even though he was attractive back then as well.

Me wondering what his lips tasted like as I watched him sip from his whiskey.

His eyes staring up at me while his head was between my legs.

The way his face tightened as he sank into me.

The sounds he made as he came, and the sounds he drew from me each time he gave me an orgasm, each one stronger than the last one.

It was just supposed to be one night—a few hours to give in to my curiosity, let myself live a little and be with someone who I knew was safe.

Grady was always a safe place for me.

Then why didn't you say goodbye to him before you left, Scottie? Why leave him like that?

"Ugh," I groan out loud, fighting with myself for the umpteenth time. It's not that I didn't want to say goodbye, but I couldn't. I couldn't bring myself to say those words to him before—not when

I found out I was pregnant and changed my number at Andrew's request, and I sure as hell couldn't say them that night.

Fifteen years ago was one of the hardest times of my life. Reporters were calling me non-stop, wondering why I wasn't playing in the upcoming season as planned. I was on track to make the national team, but I couldn't tell them—not until it was too late to hide the reason. And by then, I was old news.

I was also in a relationship with a man whose child I was carrying, desperately trying to convince myself that marrying him and building a family was the right thing to do—that we owed it to Chase. Even if it meant I would be tied to him for the rest of my life.

I should have listened to my gut. Andrew turned out to be one of my greatest mistakes, and severing my friendship with Grady was another.

Pushing Grady away was one of the hardest things I've ever had to do. Watching him succeed, seeing him achieve his dreams just reminded me that I wouldn't be chasing my own. And seeing him again only solidified what I already knew—he is the type of man you keep forever, the type who deserves everything he could ever dream of. And here I am, a mess—a single mom with an ex I wish would jump off a cliff, and a son who needs me now more than ever.

So I let myself be selfish for just that one night, to take what I wanted, what I needed, and live in a fantasy of what it would be like to be with Grady Reynolds.

But that's all I got. That's all I deserved. That's all I would allow myself to have.

So I left without telling him and headed back to my life, the one I had chosen all those years ago.

My mom told me he stopped by her house looking for me just like I knew he would. That's why I left before Christmas, days before I planned to—because I couldn't stand the thought of seeing the look in his eyes when I told him that he and I were just a one-night thing.

But that was before I got the call from my mom about the job offer and the house.

"It would be good for Chase," she said, and as a mother herself, I knew her heart was in the right place.

So I sat down and made a list of pros and cons. And ultimately, I knew this move was what my son needed. If I had it my way, I would have stayed far away from Grady and his magic dick.

The boy I once knew grew into a man who still made heads turn everywhere he went. Now I know it's only a matter of time before we cross paths and have the inevitable awkward conversation about why I'm here.

But I'm not going to worry about that until it happens. I can't. I have too many other things to focus on right now, like getting my office together.

So that's what I do, ignoring the calls from Andrew that I know will eventually come and organizing the contents of my desk and hanging my degrees up on the wall.

Once I'm done, I sit back and take a deep breath, reminding myself that everything is going to work out for the best. Until another wave of nausea hits me, just like it did on the road a few days ago, and I throw up my breakfast in the trashcan under my desk.

Chapter Five

Grady

"Are you trying to use telepathy to fix that transmission, or are you having a stroke?" Chet asks me, breaking me from the staring match I'm having with the piece of the engine sitting on the bench in front of me.

"What?" Blinking, I turn to him, his brows furrowed with curiosity.

"You were zoned out, man. I was watching you for several minutes before I finally decided to say something."

I heave out a sigh. "I got distracted."

"Seems to be a pattern with you lately."

"What do you mean?"

Chet moves around me, grabbing a wrench from the toolbox. "I don't know. For the past couple of months, you've been grumpier than normal. I swear, the crease between your eyebrows is permanent now." He reaches up and pushes his thumb against the spot in question, and I shove his arm away.

"Don't touch me."

Laughing, he backs away. "Then unclench, man. I mean, if you're that wound up, download Tinder and try to find someone to help alleviate the tension. You know what I mean?"

Scowling at him, I turn back to the transmission and reach for the rag on the table. "That's the last fucking thing I need."

"I disagree. You need to get laid or buy a punching bag. One or the other, but you need something to pound into, if you catch my drift."

"You can take your drift and shove it up your ass."

Chet chuckles and then heads back to the car he's working on. "I'm telling you...Tinder. You'll feel better."

Growling, I grab the driveshaft and prepare to replace the worn bushings as I ruminate over Chet's advice.

Getting laid is what put me in this piss-poor mood in the first place. That head of curly hair, green eyes that continue to haunt me at night, and a smile with perfect pink lips that I can't stop envisioning sucking my cock.

Scottie fucked me up for the second time in my life, and this time is even worse than the first because now I know what she feels like wrapped around me.

But it wasn't just the sex. It was hearing her voice again, laughing with her, anticipating the next words that were going to come out of her mouth. She transported me back in time, to a point in my life where I was optimistic, still working toward something, still wondering what the next few years were going to bring.

Now, every day just feels dreary, annoying, and anything but optimistic, especially since Scottie walked out on me after our night together.

Her mom basically told me not to chase after her. How do you catch someone who doesn't want to be caught? And better yet, why should I try? By leaving the way she did, she made it clear that she wanted nothing more from me than sex. Any other man would be ecstatic that a woman he slept with wasn't expecting more.

But I'm not like other guys.

And Scottie isn't like any other woman I've been with.

"Fuck, I'm pathetic," I mumble to myself as my hands move on their own. Normally, I would use a project like this to drown out the noise in my head, to slip away from reality and give myself something else to focus on. But now, the only thing my brain seems to want to fixate on is a woman who exited my life again just as abruptly as she did the last time.

I glance back at the Nova, seeing Scottie splayed out on the hood again, my head buried between her legs as I lapped at her pussy, and my dick grows hard against my jeans. That night she told me I should rebuild that car, and fuck if I didn't listen. In fact, I have a few parts coming next week and the seats are being reupholstered at the end of the month. The new headlights are installed, along with new gauges for the dash, and then it's just a few tweaks to the motor—new spark plugs, pistons and piston rings, bearings, and gaskets—before registering her for the road so she's legal for me to drive around anytime I want.

As I lay there that night, holding Scottie in my arms, I imagined the two of us cruising up and down the coast in that car, her wild curls flowing around her as the ocean breeze drifted in through the windows. Stopping on the side of the road so I could fuck her on the bench seat, then waiting until it got dark so I could bend her over the hood and fuck her again.

Now when I stare at the car, anger fills my chest, my jaw grows tight, and I curse myself for letting myself get wrapped up in a woman—an issue I've never had before.

"Grady, there's a customer here that wants to ask you about a custom exhaust for their car." Lindy, my receptionist and bookkeeper, pops her head into the garage, pulling me from my thoughts.

"I'll be right there."

She slides back behind the door that separates the reception area from the garage as I stand from the stool I was sitting on and head to the sink to wash the grease from my hands. Back when I was playing baseball, it was grass and dirt under my fingernails mixed with grease. Now it's only grease that seeps its way into my skin, marking me with this new life, no matter how hard I scrub to get rid of it.

Although, come Monday, it'll be both grease and dirt again. Much to my dismay, I agreed to try coaching the high school baseball team, yet another decision influenced by that night with Scottie. And even though I regret it now, I'm not going to back out. I made a commitment, and I'm going to see it through because that's who I am—or at least, that's who I'm trying to be, despite questioning my life choices daily. From what I've heard, that's normal. But all I know is, normal sucks.

***

Sipping my beer as I lie back in my recliner, I watch the highlights on ESPN, much like I do every night. Thank God it's Friday, which means I have tomorrow off. Chet manages the garage on Saturdays, and we're only open until two in the afternoon, so he gets a few extra hours off as well.

My eyelids struggle to stay open as the words and images on the TV become blurry. I set my beer on the coffee table, fold my hands over my chest, and promise myself I'm only going to shut my eyes for a few minutes. Hours pass before the sound of breaking glass jolts me from a deep sleep.

My pulse instantly spikes. I jerk my head toward the window that overlooks my property, seeing flashes of light move around in the distance near the garage.

"What the fuck?" Launching myself from my recliner, I head for the window, peering through the blinds as a few figures move around the building, their flashlights casting shadows against the ground and walls. "Oh, hell no." I stalk toward my room and head straight for my gun safe, entering the code and grabbing my shotgun. I shove a few shells in my pocket before slipping on my shoes and ripping my front door open.

I don't plan on shooting anyone, but I know that the sound of a shotgun being cocked is enough to make anyone think twice about what they've done.

Carrington Cove might be a small town, but that doesn't mean there aren't bad seeds here like anywhere else. It's moments like this that I'm glad I installed an alarm system in the garage when I bought the place from Mr. Rogers. He never saw the need for it, but I wanted to protect my investment. There's a lot of money sitting in that shop, and as my phone vibrates in my pocket, alerting me that the sensors have been tripped and the police notified, I'm grateful the alarm is silent. It gives me a chance to surprise the intruders myself.

Noise and voices echo from inside the garage as I get closer. I think I saw three shadows, but there could be more men than that.

"Come on!" one of the voices whisper-shouts. "You're running out of time."

"I don't know if this is a good idea," another voice whispers back. I draw closer to the building, slipping inside the front door and tiptoeing through the office they just went through.

"Don't be a pussy. You want to be on the team, right? Then prove it."

The more I listen, the more aware I become that these voices don't belong to men. Hell, one of the kids sounds like he just went through puberty.

Holding my gun, I debate what to do. I don't want them to piss their pants, so I set the gun by the door and reach for my phone, ready to turn on the flashlight. I wait for the right moment to make my move. Sirens wail in the distance, so I know the police are almost here, but I'll be damned if these kids get away before I get a chance to let them know whose business they fucked with.

"Hurry up!"

A loud crash of metal on metal assaults my ears, followed by laughter. When the sound of breaking glass follows in a matter of seconds, I rip open the door. "Hey!"

Three teenage boys twist to face me, eyes wide and terrified. The one holding the baseball bat drops it to the floor and freezes while one of the others screams, "Run!"

I barely have a second to realize the kid with the bat crushed the hood in on the Nova before they all take off in different directions. Since bat boy thought vandalizing my car was his idea of a fun Friday night, I run after him.

I lose track of where the other two boys went as I close in on bat boy, who is sprinting toward the back exit. With a quick lunge, I grab the hood of his jacket and yank him back.

"No!" he shouts as he falls to the concrete floor, still trying to wriggle free. But I pounce on him, pinning him to the ground beneath me, holding his hands at his sides.

"Gotcha, you little shit!"

"Get off of me!"

"Yeah, like that's going to happen."

The sound of a boot hitting a door pulls my attention to the reception area, and three police officers come barreling into the garage, their guns poised.

"Hands in the air!" Frank, one of the officers I know fairly well, yells when he sees me pinning the kid to the floor.

"It's me, Frank. I caught one of the kids who broke in, but the other two got away."

The kid beneath me struggles to throw me off, but I've got a hundred pounds on him, easily. I've put on a shit ton of muscle because working out became one of the only things I could focus on after my career ended. But I give him points for at least continuing to put up a fight. He's gonna need that gumption to get out of this.

Frank lowers his gun, signaling to the other two officers to do the same. "Where did the other two go?"

"Outside, I think. They probably slipped through the back."

"Go check outside," Frank tells his companions before walking over to us. "What's your name, kid?" he asks the boy, who's finally stopped moving.

He scowls up at Frank, his jaw clenched. "I'm not telling you."

"Well, we can do this the hard way, then." He reaches for the radio attached to his chest. "I've got a suspect in custody. Attempted burglary, trespassing, breaking and entering, and he's not willing to talk. I'll be bringing him in to stay the night in a cell. Get it ready for him, will ya?"

"You're taking me to jail?" the kid cries out in disbelief.

"If you don't want to talk, a night in a cell should help change your mind really quickly."

"Fine. My name is Chase. Chase Warner," he grates out and then looks up at me. "Can you get off of me now?"

I glance up at Frank who nods. "I'll put him in cuffs. He's not going anywhere."

Once I stand up and Frank secures the kid with his hands cuffed in front of him, sulking against the wall, I walk over to the Nova to assess the damage. Frank tries to get ahold of the kid's parents.

"Fuck." Staring at my car, I clench my jaw so hard my teeth threaten to crack. The hood is wrecked, dented so deep in the middle that I know there's no salvaging it. One of the brand-new headlights I just replaced is shattered too.

Glaring back at the kid, I debate going over there and asking what the fuck his problem is, but Frank strides up to me before I can move. "His mom is on her way."

"Good. Any luck catching the other two?"

Frank shakes his head. "Unfortunately, no. The best bet we have is getting the kid to squeal on his friends."

"Snitches get stitches, Frank. The kid isn't going to talk."

"Maybe, maybe not. Once I tell the mom he's facing charges of trespassing, vandalism, and breaking and entering, she might force him to talk."

I snort. "Anything else we can charge him with?"

Frank leans closer to me, lowering his voice. "You're certain you want to press charges?"

I gesture to my car. "Are you looking at the same classic car with the dented in hood and busted headlight that I am?"

Nodding, he takes a step back. "I get it, but he's a kid."

"Who broke into my garage, destroyed my car, and..."

Before I can finish, the door from the reception area swings open violently and the last person I expected to see races in. "Chase! Chase?"

"Scottie?" My feet move toward her on instinct.

"Grady," she breathes out, her hair as wild as her eyes. "Where's Chase?"

I spin my head around, wondering if I'm being punked. "Wait..."

"Oh my God." She pushes past me, heading right for the kid, her robe open and flowing behind her.

Fuck.

The kid's name is Chase.

Scottie's son's name is Chase.

This is Scottie's son.

And my night just got a lot more fucking interesting.

Chapter Six

Scottie

"What the hell is going on?" I stare down at my handcuffed son, trying to wrap my head around this. My lungs are barely taking in air, but I'm certainly wide awake now.

When Chase asked if he could hang out at his new friend Jared's house, I was so damn excited that he was making friends that I didn't think twice before agreeing. I never imagined something could go wrong—so terribly wrong.

I was also ecstatic thinking about the fact that I could go to sleep before eight o'clock without feeling guilty for not spending time with my son. The exhaustion and persistent nausea have been wearing on me all week. It was all I could do to make it to Friday.

And now, as I stand in the same space as Grady, the other issue I've been avoiding looms over me, reminding me that I have to tell him my news eventually. But tonight is definitely not the time, given our current circumstances.

"Ma'am, your son was caught trespassing, breaking and entering, and vandalizing Mr. Reynolds' business tonight." The officer explains what transpired since he didn't get a chance to on the phone. As soon as I heard that my son was being arrested, I cut him off and asked for the address, shaking with nerves as I raced toward Grady's Garage.

I already knew that avoiding Grady was no longer possible, but this is not how I envisioned our reunion going.

"Chase Allen Warner! Have you lost your damn mind?"

"It wasn't my idea!" he yells, as if that excuse is going to get him anywhere.

I pull my robe tighter around my body and peer around at the destruction in the garage. "That's funny—because you're the only one in handcuffs right now, so how the hell are you supposed to convince me that someone else is responsible for destroying Grady's car?"

Chase's eyes dart to Grady and then back to me. "You know this guy?"

Grady grunts, crossing his arms and narrowing his eyes. "Ha. Yeah, we know each other."

"Shit," my son mutters, hanging his head.

"Watch your language and start talking," I demand.

With his eyes still focused on the ground, Chase begins to mumble. "Jared said he wanted to take me and the other kid somewhere, have us prove that we wanted to be on the team."

"What team?" Grady interjects.

"The baseball team," I answer for my son as Grady huffs out a breath.

"Of fucking course," he grates, running his hand through his hair as he starts to pace the floor. But I can only track his movement from the corner of my eye because my main focus is my kid and how badly I want to strangle him right now.

"So they convinced you to break into the garage and vandalize a car?" I shriek, my voice echoing off the walls of the garage. "And you just listened to them?"

"What's the other kid's name?" The officer chimes in.

Chase's eyes dart to the side, but I bend down, grab his chin, and force him to meet my gaze. "Tell the officer right now before this gets even worse for you, kid."

"Trent. Trent McDonald," he mutters.

"And Jared? What's his last name?" The officer scribbles on a notepad.

"Brown," Chase says as I release his chin and stand up straight again. But as I do, a wave of dizziness hits me, and I feel myself starting to sway.

"Whoa, Scottie." Grady grabs me before I fall, holding me in his arms.

And God, he smells good. Like soap and sweat. His scent—it's one of the few things that hasn't instantly triggered my nausea.

Absolutely not, little one. I refuse to be one of those pregnant women who eats soap or craves dirt. Get it together.

Rubbing my stomach, I let Grady guide me over to a chair. "Are you all right?" he asks, concern etched on his face.

I peer up at him, wondering how on earth I'm going to get through this.

One thing at a time, Scottie.

"Yeah, I just got up too fast."

"Mom?" Chase calls out to me, pleading with his eyes. My son doesn't do this shit. Sure, he's a teenager and makes stupid choices more often than not, but this is beyond stupid. This is illegal.

I look up at Grady. "I'm so sorry about this."

"Which part?" He folds his arms across his chest and glares down at me.

"Not here," I say soft enough that he can hear me, but quiet enough that Chase can't.

Grady glances over to my son but returns his gaze to mine quickly, giving me a curt nod. His eyes, they're full of anger. I'm sure he's pissed about his car, but I'm also not so naïve to think that some of that anger isn't reserved for me.

The officer clears his throat, breaking through our moment. "Sorry to interrupt, but I need to know what you want to do, Grady. Do you want to press charges?"

I stand from the chair, placing a hand on his chest. "Grady, please. I know you're pissed, but this is my kid. I promise, we'll pay for the damages, but—"

"I don't know." His jaw clenches as I wait for him to continue. "I think we all need to cool off and maybe we can sit down and talk tomorrow," he says, cutting me off.

My shoulders fall as I sigh with relief. "I'd appreciate that."

The officer nods, scribbles another note on his pad, then proceeds toward my son, unlocking the cuffs from around his wrists. "You're free to go home with your mother tonight, son, but this isn't over. You've just had your first brush with the law, and if I were you, I'd be hell-bent on making it your last. Otherwise, you and I will get to know each other very well, and I'm not someone you want to be friends with."

Chase stares at the ground and nods.

"Thank you, officer."

"Frank Davidson, ma'am." He reaches out to shake my hand.

"Scottie Warner. And again, thank you for calling me."

"Of course." He tips his chin toward Grady and then leaves the three of us alone.

"Grady…" I start, but he shakes his head at me and starts heading for the door.

"Warner," he mumbles, shaking his head. "Definitely not Scottie Daniels anymore."

"Warner is my married name."

He glares at me. "I'm putting the pieces together, Scottie."

"Look, I know it's late, but..."

"I meant what I said, Scottie. I need..." He winces as he looks back at me. "I need some time to wrap my head around this."

Knowing better than to push any further, I swallow down my rebuttal and gesture for my son to follow me out to the car. Chase launches from the floor and stands behind me. "Can I come by tomorrow then?" I ask.

Grady doesn't meet my eyes, but I can see the strain in his muscles as he clenches his fists. "Yeah, that should be fine. What time?"

"Probably the afternoon."

"You know where I live," he says, and in that moment, I feel like it's a dig, a reminder that I've been in his home, in his bed, and I left without saying goodbye.

But there will never be a goodbye between me and Grady because, no matter how much I wish I could let him be, that's virtually impossible now that I'm carrying his baby.

***

"Give me your phone." The second we walk through our front door, I face my son head-on.

Chase hands over the device willingly. "I'm sorry, Mom."

"Sorry isn't going to fix this mess, Chase." *And you're not the only one who has things to fix here.* "I'm so disappointed in you." He nods, not daring to argue. "You broke the law tonight, and you're not even fifteen! Do you realize that if Grady decides to press charges, this could follow you around for years? This could affect your entire future!"

"But you said that you know him, so can't you talk to him? Get him to cut me some slack?"

"Slack?" I shriek. "Just what do you think he should do, Chase? What if I *didn't* know the man whose business you broke into? Huh? What would you propose I do then?" He shrugs, avoiding my eyes. Pinching the bridge of my nose, I say, "Look, it's late. I need sleep and a level head to even begin to think of how I want to handle this. But just know, you are grounded until you're eighteen."

His head pops up. "Eighteen?"

"If you're lucky. Now go to your room." I point down the hallway, and he wisely obeys, walking to his room and shutting the door behind him.

As the door clicks shut, I let out a long, shaky breath, the reality of the night sinking in. Heading back to my room, I shut myself inside and enter the bathroom, studying myself in the mirror.

I'm twenty all over again, holding my stomach as I take in a few deep breaths, wondering how on earth I'm going to handle this. Nothing prepares you for being a parent, and I sure as hell have never had to deal with anything like this with Chase. Sure, he has problems putting his laundry in the basket instead of on the floor right next to it, his room smells like rotten feet no matter how much Febreze I spray, and his idea of communicating most of the time is rolling his eyes or grunting. But he's a good kid.

This was supposed to be a fresh start for us. Instead, I feel like we came in full throttle, only to run headfirst into a brick wall. And to top it all off, now I'll have another child to raise and wonder what kind of trouble they'll get into. How am I supposed to navigate all of this on my own?

I should have guessed I was pregnant weeks ago, but with the move, my mind was focused on other things. I didn't even realize I missed my period, and the nausea didn't start right away, same as when I was pregnant with Chase. With him, all of my symptoms started later in the first trimester and lasted well into my fifth month. Here's hoping this pregnancy is easier, but given my age, I'm even more nervous about what to expect.

I have one child with a man I can't stand, a child who thought breaking the law to fit in with his new friends was a good idea, and another on the way with a man that can barely stand to look at me right now. And if Andrew finds out about this? I don't even want to think about how he'll react and what he might do.

History is repeating itself, and I'm the fool who thought I'd learned from my past.

Tomorrow I will talk to Grady, ask for forgiveness for me and my son, and let him know that he's going to be a father. I will stand my ground, assure him that nothing between us has to change, and then we can just both move on with our lives.

I've done this before, and I can do it again. Only this time, I'm not going to let my heart get involved. That's how I got in trouble in the first place, and the last thing I need is heartache on top of everything else.

***

Just after three in the afternoon, I pull into the driveway of Grady's house and shut my car off. Chase is under the supervision of my mom and Gigi while I'm gone so I don't have to worry about him getting himself in trouble again. I haven't told them what happened last night yet, but they know something's up since Chase looked like a puppy dog with his tail tucked between his legs when I dropped him off, *and* he's without a cell phone.

Grady steps out the front door just as I stand from the car, and god, he looks *good*.

Wearing a simple gray t-shirt and jeans, his light brown hair freshly cut, and his feet bare, he stares at me as I make my way to his wraparound porch and climb the five steps that lead to the front door. His arms are straining against the sleeves of his shirt, those biceps that I remember biting into as he made me come so hard I nearly passed out.

"Hi," I say, trying to gauge his mood and forget about our hot night that led to me being pregnant.

"Hey." He holds the door open so I can enter the house and follows me inside.

In daylight, I can finally take in his home. The night I spent here was fully in the dark, so I couldn't appreciate the home he's built for himself.

The walls are a light gray and the décor features shades of blue, ranging from sky blue to navy. A plus gray couch and matching recliner stand out in the living room, facing a massive television that takes up nearly an entire wall. Framed articles from his baseball career hang proudly on the walls around the space. Through an opening in the wall, I glimpse the kitchen through that separates the two rooms, and a hallway to my left leads to his bedroom—a place I remember all too well.

"Scottie?" he says, pulling me from my thoughts.

"Yeah?"

"I asked you if you'd like something to drink."

"Oh, sorry." I push my curls from my face. "Sure. Water would be great, thanks."

He nods and heads for the kitchen, bringing me back a glass of ice water, gesturing for me to sit on the couch as he takes a seat in his recliner to my right.

I take a sip, set the glass on the coffee table in front of me, and then meet his eyes. "Grady, I'm so sorry. Again."

"For which part?" His words are curt, and I know he's referring to my leaving without a word, but I have to handle the matter with Chase first.

"About last night. Believe me, my son will be suffering the utmost punishment from me, and we will pay for all the damages, but I'm begging you, please don't press charges."

Leaning forward, bracing his forearms on his thighs, he stares at me. "I'm not going to press charges, Scottie."

A sigh of relief leaves my lips. "Thank you."

"I remember what it was like to be fourteen and wanting to fit in. But this situation is more complicated than that."

"What do you mean?" *Does he know about the baby? How could he know? I haven't told anyone yet, not even my mom.*

"Your son said that these boys are on the baseball team?" he asks.

"Yes..."

"Well, I'm one of the new coaches."

My stomach drops. "Oh."

"Yeah." Leaning back in the recliner now, he begins to rock. "The new coach reached out to me back in December, right before..."

Our night together. I nod, but don't say anything.

"I wasn't even entertaining the idea, but then you suggested it, and I..."

"I'm glad you decided to coach, Grady," I tell him, offering a small smile. "It'll be good for you. And the boys. They'll learn so much from you."

Silence stretches between us and then he finally asks, "Why didn't you tell me you were moving back, Scottie?"

I sigh and lean back into the couch. "Because I didn't know I was until about three weeks ago." His brow furrows, but he doesn't say anything. "Carrington Cove Elementary was looking for a new assistant principal and my mom called me about the job. It's not uncommon for administrators to change schools mid-year, and life down in Georgia has been taxing lately, so…" I rub my palms on my jeans. "My son and I needed a fresh start. Then, not even a few days in…"

"He went and got himself in trouble," he finishes for me.

"Yeah." Sitting up again, I stare right into his eyes. "Can Chase work off the damages, Grady? Please? I don't want to just write you a check. I want my son to learn something from this. He needs to think long and hard about the consequences of his actions so he never thinks about doing something like this ever again."

Grady clears his throat. "Yeah, I think that could work. The yard needs some help. He can pull weeds, organize scraps, stuff like that. Maybe I can make him scrub engine parts, get some grease under his fingernails."

I glance at his hands, remembering how they felt on me, callused from hard work. I'd never been touched possessively like that. He ran his hands over my curves like he was tracing the lines of a classic car—and I felt every ounce of appreciation of my body in his touch.

"Perfect." Relief rushes through me. "And he'll be working off his debt at my house as well."

"But at practice…"

"Don't take it easy on him there, either. Make him run, do push-ups. I don't care if he throws up."

The corner of his mouth tips up. "You'd like that, wouldn't you?"

I shrug. "Like I said, I want him to regret every second of his choice."

His smile falls. "This means we're going to be seeing a lot more of each other," he says, as if the words pain him.

Staring down at my lap, I nod. "Yeah, we will." Lifting my gaze, I see him staring at me. "But, there's something else I need to talk to you about."

"Now you want to talk? You usually just disappear without a thought," he spits out, and the anger he's been reining in finally comes out. I could see it in the tick of his jaw, but Grady has always been good at keeping his composure.

"That's not fair, Grady," I whisper.

He stands from his chair, placing his hands on his hips. "Really? You're going to talk to me about fair?"

I launch myself from the couch so I'm standing now too, facing him. "What do you want from me?"

"I want to know why you left without saying goodbye, damn it!" His voice booms through the room.

It startles me, but I hold my ground. "Because it was just supposed to be one night."

"You really only wanted one night with me, Scottie?"

Shaking my head, I look off to the side. "I didn't expect to see you again, Grady. And when I did, I just…"

"You just thought, 'Hey, I haven't seen that guy in seventeen years, and he looks like a good lay.'"

"No. That wasn't it."

"Then what? Was the sex not satisfactory?"

My hands start shaking from the adrenaline running through me, but I give him a steely gaze. "You're being an ass."

He points a finger at me. "And *you're* lying to me. There's a reason why you ran that night, and I'm pretty damn sure I know what it is, but I'm wondering if you have the guts to tell me."

Throwing my hands up in the air, I reply, "What do you want me to say?"

"I want you to admit that it meant something to you, and you ran because you were fucking scared!"

His words feel like a slap, the impact of reality hitting me all at once.

Because he's right. That night did mean something, but it doesn't matter now. Everything changed when those two pink lines appeared.

"Grady…"

He closes the distance between us, holding me by the upper arms and lowering his voice. "One night, Scottie? You honestly thought that one night was enough?"

"We shouldn't have even had that, Grady," I manage to squeak out.

"Why?" He drags his nose up the side of my face, his breath hot on my skin. And my entire body comes alive.

God, how can this man have this effect on me? He's my friend, *was* my friend for years. And one night together completely changed how my body responds to him?

It was just sex, two consenting adults in it for a good time.

It wasn't supposed to mean anything.

You're so stupid for even thinking that it wouldn't, Scottie.

"Because I'm pregnant, Grady," I whisper, letting my admission float out in the space between us.

He freezes, his chest rising and falling so slowly in front of my eyes that I'd think he stopped breathing if I didn't see the evidence for myself.

Taking a step back, he releases my arms and I gaze up at him, his expression unreadable. "You're what?"

I clear my throat and declare with more assertion this time, "I'm pregnant."

Grady barely blinks for a few beats. "Um...how?"

Blowing out a breath, I turn away from him and begin to pace the room. "Believe me, I've been asking myself the same question, but you know, condoms don't always work."

He runs a hand through his hair. "Jesus. I, uh..."

"I know this is a lot."

"You think?" He turns to me, his brows halfway up his forehead. "When did you find out?"

"Just this week. Something was off with me. I threw up a few times, and then finally realized I missed my period." I shake my head, palming my face. "I should have known sooner, but life was crazy with the move and new job, and..."

"Okay." He blows out a breath, nodding slowly, absorbing this new information. "So what now?"

"I called Dr. Rivera. I have an appointment next week." Given my age and the fact that I'm already eleven weeks along, they wanted to see me as soon as possible. "Look, I know this is a lot to take in, and I'm sorry that the timing of all of this isn't better, but I wanted you to know. You deserve to know."

Grady takes a seat in his recliner again, staring off into space. "Scottie..."

"Don't worry, Grady. I'm not asking for anything from you." His head snaps to meet my eyes. "My focus is on Chase right now, and we can figure the other stuff out later." The longer he looks at me like I'm a stranger, the more eager I am to leave.

Reaching for my purse, I toss it over my shoulder and head for the door. "Look, I need to go."

"Scottie!" he calls after me.

I turn back to face him for a moment. "Take some time, Grady. We can talk again soon." And then I open the door and race out to my car, needing some space so I can break down in private. I tear out of his yard as the first few tears begin to fall, and my hands continue to shake as I grip the wheel.

"Why are you crying, Scottie?" I say to myself, signaling to turn onto the main road so I can get back to my son and deal with my family.

Why *am* I crying?

Because telling Grady he was going to be a father and seeing his reaction was a lot harder than I thought. Not only did I turn his life upside down, but he looked at me like I was just a figment of his imagination.

What did you expect, Scottie? And besides, you don't want anything more from him, right?

I guess I just figured the next time I had a child, things would be different. I would be in love. The child would be planned and prayed for.

I never imagined going through the same experience twice. And honestly, after Chase turned ten, I sort of assumed that I was only meant to have one kid.

I love my son and having him forced me to grow up and view life very differently. But nothing could have prepared me for this—for encountering a man from my past who awakened the old me, the girl who was good at having fun, disregarding consequences, and living in the moment.

Looks like I channeled her a little too well—because now I'm in a predicament that I'm unequipped to handle. I'm not sure what I want, and nothing prepared me for how Grady makes me feel.

All I know is that I refuse to let my heart get involved this time.

I can handle this on my own, and that's the way it has to be—because Grady has the ability to destroy me, and I can't crumble again. There's no way I'd survive it twice.

Chapter Seven

Grady

Laughter and screams filter out from the living room as Lilly holds up her latest present and tissue paper goes flying everywhere. Today is my niece's birthday party and I'm here, like the supportive uncle that I am. But seeing kids running around, screaming and crying, is just another reminder of how my life is about to completely change. Dealing with this as an innocent bystander who can come and go as they please has been my favorite part of my uncle status since Bentley was born eleven years ago.

But now? I'm going to be the newest member of the parent club, and I'm still having trouble wrapping my head around it.

I close the front door behind me, taking a deep breath before moving deeper into the house. Clusters of adults fill the living room, but then I hear my sister's voice in the kitchen, so I head in that direction.

"Penn, could you..."

"I'm on it, babe." He kisses her on the cheek, heads to the pantry to grab a trash bag, and then moves into the living room to start picking up the mess that Lilly is making with wrapping paper and bags.

"Look at you. You speak and he moves." Willow, Dallas's girlfriend, says. She and Astrid are close friends now, and I'm grateful my sister has someone she clicks with. Willow fit into our little group seamlessly after she moved here.

Astrid rolls her eyes at Willow. "No, we're a team. He helps. I help." She sighs wistfully. "It's amazing."

"And how's it been living together? You still think all his weird quirks are cute?"

Laughing, Astrid replies, "There's been a few bumps here and there, a little tiff or two. But the makeup sex is worth it."

Willow grins. "Can't argue with you there. When Dallas and I fight, it actually makes me horny."

"Uh, did I walk in on a conversation that I shouldn't be a part of?"

Astrid whips her head in my direction. "Dear lord, did you poke your finger in a light socket?"

"What?" Bringing a hand to my head, I realize my hair is sticking up on all ends. I try to pat it down, but it's no use. Sighing, I say, "No. It's just been a long weekend."

"What happened?" my sister asks, moving to serve slices of cake onto plates.

No sense in beating around the bush. Carrington Cove is a small town, so I'm surprised she doesn't already know. Though, my sister is busy managing her own business and raising two kids. "The garage got broken into Friday night."

"Oh my God, Grady! Is it bad?" My sister's reaction is louder than necessary, but I appreciate her concern.

Penn comes rushing over, concerned by her outburst. "What? Is everything okay?"

"Yes. No." Astrid turns between me and her boyfriend. "The garage was broken into? Seriously?"

Dallas steps up next to Willow. "Dude, I fucking heard someone talking about that at the hardware store this morning. Did you catch the guy?"

Groaning, I rub the back of my neck. "Uh, yeah. I caught one of them. It was some kids. Three teenagers. Two of them escaped, but we got their names from the other kid."

Astrid shakes her head, continuing to serve cake. "Damn. I swear, if Bentley ever did something like that, I'd make sure he didn't see daylight again for a very long time."

"Yeah, well I think his mom had the same idea." I've seen Scottie pissed before, but Scottie as a pissed off mom? That was a new experience.

And it was kind of fucking hot.

"You met the kid's mom?" Penn asks.

"They called her to come pick him up since he's a minor and I hadn't decided if I was going to press charges or not."

"Why wouldn't you? He smashed in the hood of the Nova," Dallas says. "At least that's what I heard."

Penn winces. "Shit. The Nova?"

"I don't give a fuck about the car," I grumble, hanging my head. The break-in is only part of the shitstorm I'm facing now. But I have to tell someone. Keeping the news of my impending fatherhood is eating me up inside. I have so many questions, but mostly, I'm wondering how the fuck I'm going to manage everything that's been thrown at me recently.

Looks like your life isn't boring anymore, is it, Grady?

Astrid puts a hand on my back, rubbing in circles. "Grady, what's going on? I feel like you're upset about more than the break-in."

When I lift my head and meet my sister's eyes, I know instantly that everything is going to be okay because I have her to lean on. She's the best mom that I know, and she can help me make sense of all of this—my feelings, both about being a dad and about Scottie.

"The kid's mom is a woman I slept with a few months ago, right around Christmas. And when she came to talk to me yesterday about how to make this right, she also dropped a bomb on me that I wasn't expecting." I look around at Penn, Dallas, and Willow, realizing they're all listening too. So I drop the news. "It looks like I'm about to be a dad."

Astrid's eyes bug out as she stutters, "I—I'm sorry?" She shakes her head. "Did...did you just say that you're going to be a dad?"

Willow leans in closer to my sister. "Astrid, that's exactly what he just said."

She swats her friend away and bends her knees so our eyes are at the same level as I continue to brace myself on the counter in front of me. "Grady...how are you...what can I..." She blows out a breath. "Holy shit."

"Say that a few more times and you might be where I'm at." I barely slept last night and I'm definitely feeling the effects of it today.

Penn and Dallas share a look, and then Dallas steps forward. "Well, let me be the first to say it since everyone else's brains have short-circuited." Reaching out his hand to shake mine, he says, "Congratulations, man."

Penn repeats the gesture, saying, "Welcome to the club."

I huff out a laugh. "Yeah, thanks, I think."

Penn isn't my niece and nephew's biological dad, but he's been a part of their lives since they were born. And since Brandon died, he has stepped in and filled that role, even though he never intends on replacing their father. But he's a dad to those kids, no doubt about it. Maybe I need to pick his brain about this too.

Astrid reaches for my hand, covering it with her own. "Let me serve the cake and then we can talk, okay?"

"Yeah. Sounds good."

Dallas comes up beside me and hands me a beer. "You look like you could use one of these."

"Definitely." I pop the top and drain half of it before looking out over the house full of people once more. This is going to be my life from now on—birthday parties, screaming kids, diapers, and late-night feedings.

But I guess the first question that needs answering is, is Scottie going to let me be there for that? How involved does she want me to be in this kid's life?

She left in such a rush yesterday, and I still don't have her fucking phone number, so I haven't had a chance to ask her about what this is going to look like.

Is she going to move in with me? Where is she even living right now? When is she due? How is this going to work with our jobs? Will we need daycare? What about Chase? Does he know he's going to be a big brother yet?

Regardless of the lack of answers I have right now, at least I know this—I'll be damned if I'm not there for every moment I can be. Astrid and I grew up without our dad in the picture. He left just after Astrid turned two. I was five and barely remember him, but what I do remember is that he wasn't there—not for birthdays, Christmases, or baseball games. He wasn't in pictures, and I always had to explain that my dad wasn't around.

That will *not* be my child's life. Scottie and I have a lot of shit to figure out, but I know for certain that I will be there for everything, and she can't deny me that opportunity. I am going to be in this child's life, even if Scottie doesn't want me in hers.

But can I be the father I didn't have? Is that a part of a man that's instinctual, or will I feel like I'm trying to fill a role I was never meant to play?

"Fuck." I drag a hand through my hair, making it look worse, I'm sure, then drain the other half of my beer, toss the can in the recycling, and head to the bathroom. When I come out, my sister is standing there, waiting for me. She pulls me back to her room, shuts the door behind us, and takes a seat next to me on the bed.

"Grady." She rubs my back again. "Talk to me."

"It's Scottie, Astrid."

"Scottie.... Scottie..." Her eyes widen in recognition. "Wait. Scottland Daniels?"

"Yup." I throw myself back on the bed, staring blankly up at the ceiling.

"I saw her in town a few months ago, around Christmas. She stopped by the bakery with her mom and grandma."

"Well, that was when I ran into her, so..."

"And you two..."

"Slept together," I finish for her. "I'm sure I don't need to explain how babies are conceived."

She slaps my stomach, making me wince. "Don't get snarky with me. I'm just trying to process this out loud, okay?"

"Sorry."

"Walk me through it. I thought you guys were just friends, at least back in high school you were, right? What happened? But spare me all the dirty details, okay?" she wrinkles her nose. "You are my brother, after all."

Sighing, I sit up and replay that night—seeing her at the bar, talking and flirting even though we were just friends before, how she made me feel, taking her back to my place, and how she left without saying goodbye.

Astrid's eyebrows pinch together as she listens, and when I get to yesterday, when Scottie told me about the baby and then took off, she smacks me in the back of the head. "What the fuck was that for?"

"You let her leave, Grady."

"What was I supposed to do?" I rub the spot her hand connected with.

"Not let her leave while she was clearly upset."

"Well, we both were."

"But she's carrying your baby, so you can't be mad..."

"Why not?"

"Because she's pregnant! That's the reason!" She throws her hands up in the air. "You can't be mad at a pregnant woman. It's a rule. Her mind is not her own, and neither is her body. Hormones make you do crazy shit."

"But..."

She holds up her palm to stop me. "No. I get it. She left and didn't say anything, but I'm sure she had a reason. Hell, she lived in another state at the time. Adults can have sex and it mean nothing more."

"But it meant something to me, Astrid," I admit, my voice low. I think the part that's getting to me the most is that there are feelings involved, at least on my end. I felt it that night and every day after she left me without a backward glance.

Her face instantly softens, and for a second, I think she's back on my team. "I can tell, but that doesn't sound like that's what she wants."

"I don't know what the hell she wants," I say, growing more irritated. I want to talk to her, but at the same time, I'm still pissed at her. "She ran off and... fuck." I stand from the bed and start pacing. "I have so many fucking questions. My life is about to completely change."

My sister smiles. "I know."

"Why are you smiling? Are you enjoying watching me spin out of control here?"

She joins me on the other side of the room, gripping my arms so I stop moving. "I'm smiling because my brother is about to be a dad, which means I'm going to be an aunt. And you're going to be an amazing dad, Grady." She cups my jaw. "You're the best uncle, you're great with kids, and when it's your own child, I promise it's even better."

"How do you know that? I haven't even had a fucking long-term relationship, Astrid, and I'm almost thirty-six." Sweat beads at my temples as my stomach churns. "I have no idea how this is supposed to work, and I…"

"You need to talk to Scottie."

"I don't even have her fucking phone number. She left before I could ask her for it, for the second time."

"Then get it." She taps the side of my head. "You're not stupid. You should have some idea of how to find her."

Blowing out a breath, I admit what I'm really feeling. "I never imagined this would be how I had a kid, Astrid. I always envisioned that if I had a shot at being married and having a family, it would be mornings waking up next to my wife, waiting with her as she took a pregnancy test, being excited and knowing that starting a family was what we both wanted. And at this point, I was starting to accept that a life like that wasn't in the cards for me."

She raises her eyebrows and walks away from me. "Yeah, well, life doesn't always work out the way we think it will, Grady."

My sister sure as hell knows what it's like to have your world flipped upside down, but this? This is new territory for me. The last time my world spun out of control was when I could no longer play baseball for a living. But back then, the only person I had to worry about was myself.

Now, it's not just me that's affected by this. It's Scottie *and* Chase. It's both of our families.

And this woman—seeing her again made me realize how fucking lonely I've been. My sister has been pushing me to date for months, but I knew it was a lost cause. Single women in town hit on me all the time, but they all want me for the wrong reasons.

Scottie, though, she really knows me. She knew me before baseball became my job, before I became this grumpy mechanic who doesn't know what the fuck he's doing with his life.

She's different. She always has been, and now she's having my baby. But I want more. I want *her*.

"I want a family, Astrid," I say, breaking the silence.

Spinning around to face me, she clarifies, "What?"

"I want more than just weekend visits. I want what you and Penn have." I gesture to the other side of the house where Penn is holding the party together while we talk.

Smirking, she crosses her arms over her chest. "Weren't you just telling me a few months ago when I suggested you start dating that you were better off alone? That you didn't think that life was meant for you?"

"Yeah, but..."

"So now because Scottie is pregnant, you want that? Are you sure, Grady?" Her face grows serious. "Because as a single mom, I'm going to tell you that the last thing that woman needs is some man who *thinks* he knows what he wants but is going to change his mind down the line."

Shit. She's right. I need to make sure I can be the man she needs, the father and partner that she deserves before I commit to this one hundred percent—because when I commit to something, I go all in, and Scottie can't have any doubts about how I feel.

"Be really freaking sure that you are ready for everything having a family entails, Grady, because if not, at least you can both go in knowing where you stand." And then she narrows her eyes at me. "If it was any other woman, would you feel the same way?"

"Like what?"

"Wanting a family, trying to be in a relationship with the mother of your child?"

I shake my head instantly. "No." And I can say that with certainty.

"You care about her," Astrid declares, and I nod. "I can see it in your eyes, hear it in your voice."

"There was always something there, even back in high school, but I never let myself go there. I had baseball to focus on and Scottie was the same way about softball. But I liked her. I always did."

"And now?"

"Now we're having a baby, and that night wasn't just a fluke. I wanted more, but she left before I could talk to her about it." I brush a hand through my hair. "She fucking flipped my world upside down…"

Astrid folds her lips in as she smiles. "Oh my God, my brother is in love *and* he's having a baby!"

Rolling my eyes, I watch as she jumps up and down with excitement. "Relax. I have to talk to her first, remember. But fuck, Astrid…" Shaking my head, I continue, "If I don't try to at least make this work, if I don't take this as a sign that life has a way of pointing you in the right direction if you pay attention, then I'll regret it. I know there's a ton of shit to work out, but I owe it to myself, and to this child, to try."

My sister pulls me into a hug. "You do. My big brother is all grown up," she teases as we squeeze each other.

"I'm going to need you to get through this." It's at this moment that I realize my hands are shaking as Astrid holds me closer.

"I'll always be here, Grady. I love you and I promise, you will get through this."

"Love you too, sis."

She pats me on the back and releases me before saying, "Now go figure out what your future looks like before this baby gets here. You might think you have all the time in the world, but believe me, it goes by faster than you think."

Chapter Eight

Scottie

"I'm pregnant."

Silence falls in the room as I wait for a reaction from the two most important women in my life, the reasons I moved back to Carrington Cove in the first place—because I knew I'd have their support. I just didn't think it would be for this.

"Goodness gracious, Scottie." My mother stares at me from across the couch in her living room. Gigi is sitting in a chair in the other corner, and I'm stationed on the loveseat across from them with my legs tucked underneath me.

I left Grady's yesterday feeling uneasy about everything, especially leaving him with little explanation, once again. But I figured he needed time to process and so did I, so I went home and made dinner for Chase and me, then slept for ten hours before waking this morning knowing I couldn't keep this from my mom and grandma any longer.

I've only been back in Carrington Cove for two weeks, and my life has already taken another turn.

Hey, universe? Yeah, it's me, Scottland! I'd like to get off of this ride now, please!

"Yeah."

"How are you feeling?" my mother asks, after a few minutes of processing.

"Nauseous and tired. It was the throwing up that finally made me question it. I mean, before Grady, I hadn't had sex in almost two years. Andrew hadn't touched me in forever, and the idea of sleeping with some stranger just didn't appeal to me, you know?"

Gigi snickers. "Well, that Grady is walking sex on a stick, so it's no wonder that he knocked you up on the first try."

We actually had sex three times that night, but that detail isn't necessarily relevant at this point. I roll my eyes and look back at my mom. "I'm about eleven weeks by my calculations, which puts me due in the middle of September. My appointment is this week, so I'll know more then."

Blinking, my mother stares across the room at me before snapping herself out of it. "First of all, you're not alone in this, Scottland. Okay? Carrington Cove is home now, and Mom and I will be here in whatever way we can." Gigi nods. "And second, have you talked to Grady yet?"

"I did yesterday."

"And what did he say?"

I stare at my lap, picking at the hem of my sweater. "He was surprised." I mean, we both were. We used a condom, and I know I'm not on the pill, but all I keep thinking is I should have kept taking my birth control after the divorce. It would have at least been another layer of protection.

"And what does he want? I mean, are you two…"

"No," I cut her off. "I can't go there, Mom."

She glances at me sympathetically. "Scottie…"

"No. I tried to make things work with Andrew and look how that turned out."

"Andrew Warner is a piece of shit who cares about no one but himself," Gigi interjects, pounding her fist on the arm of the chair she's sitting in. "You did what you could and what you thought was best at the time, Scottland, but he was never going to be the man you deserved. He's a liar and a cheater. If it weren't for the fact that he gave you Chase, I'd hunt him down and light his pants on fire myself."

Letting laughter escape my lips, I stare at my grandmother. "Thank you, Gigi."

"But Grady..." my mother chimes in.

"Is my friend," I finish for her. "We are *friends*."

"Who bumped uglies," Gigi says as my mother snorts. "Doesn't sound like just friends to me."

Sighing, I adjust myself in my spot. "Look, I blame it on the alcohol, okay?"

It wasn't just his brown eyes, which felt like portals to the past, or his smile that made my vagina clench, or the way his arms bulged against the sleeves of his shirt, or how being in his presence again reminded me of how he used to make me feel when I was younger—seen and understood.

Nope. I couldn't blame it on any of those things, either. Just the alcohol. That's the story I'm sticking to.

"So how is this going to work?" My mom leans against the arm of the couch, resting her chin in her hand.

"We'll co-parent. It's not like I need a partner. Hell, I did this practically on my own the first time."

"Is that what he wants?"

"I don't know yet, since we haven't talked about it, but I can't see why not. I mean, he has his own life, his business to run, and a life here that *I'm* changing. I don't need to upend it any more than I already have."

My mother narrows her eyes at me. "Is that what he said?"

"We didn't talk much. I told him the news, he was in shock, so I left him to process."

My mom and Gigi share a look, then Gigi focuses back on me. "Scottie, I know this isn't what you were looking for when you moved back, baby, but maybe this is all happening for a reason."

I huff out a laugh. "Yeah, that I didn't listen well enough in sex ed and I never should have gone off the pill when Andrew and I divorced."

She shakes her head. "Children are a blessing, and regardless of how this works out with Grady, you know your mother and I are here. Please don't forget that."

Tears fill my eyes. "I know. I'm sorry, though…"

My mother stands from the couch and comes to sit next to me. "Why on earth are you apologizing?"

"Because history is repeating itself and I have no idea how I'm supposed to do this again. God, I just wanted a fresh start—for me and my son." I wipe my nose on the sleeve of my sweater, curling into my mother's arms, allowing myself to finally fall apart, although I could also blame that on the hormones.

I hate that I feel stuck between the past and present, like all my past choices are cycling through again. I've already visited this rodeo and it was chaos—a long road of figuring out that you can go into something with the best of intentions, but ultimately, life is going to work out the way it's supposed to, and people will disappoint you no matter what.

That's why I think it's just better if Grady and I stay friends. If we tried for more and it didn't work, I wouldn't bounce back from that destruction. Our lifelong friendship has already shifted because we slept together, and now that we're having a child, I think it's safe to say nothing will ever be the same. But that doesn't mean we can't freeze where we are and just try to make the best of it.

It's the only solution that doesn't leave me vulnerable again. I barely feel like I'm back on solid ground after my divorce. I don't need to step in quicksand once more.

My mom sways us back and forth, comforting me the only way she can. "You are not alone." She takes a deep breath. "Grady doesn't seem like a man that walks away from his responsibilities. You need to talk to him. Even if you don't want to be involved with him romantically, he is your friend. You know him. Do you honestly think he would let you do this on your own?"

"That's the thing, I *don't* know him."

My mother releases me and arches a brow. "Scottie, am I really supposed to believe that? All I can remember hearing from you back in high school was Grady this, and Grady that..."

"But it's been seventeen years. We aren't the same people we were back then."

She brushes my curls from my face and wipes a tear from my cheek. "Then get to know each other now. You obviously felt comfortable enough to sleep with the man, so lean into that and see where it takes you. That man is *not* Andrew. I saw it in his eyes when he came here looking for you back in December, Scottie." I look straight into her eyes, trying to grasp the truth of her words.

"What did he look like?" I ask, not sure I want the answer, but my grandmother interjects before my mom can answer.

Gigi clears her throat. "Was the sex good at least?"

"Mom!" my mother exclaims, glancing over her shoulder at my grandma as I sniffle through a laugh.

"What? If you're gonna get knocked up, it's gotta be worth it. I mean, I remember the night your father and I conceived you and my God, he rocked my world that time…"

My mother shakes her head as we share a laugh. "Gigi, it was…" I let out a sigh because there aren't words eloquent enough to describe how Grady touched my body, how safe he made me feel, how sex with him was so intense that it scared the shit out of me.

She claps slowly. "Then the man did his job. And if he can do that right, there's probably a lot more he's capable of too."

***

"Come to momma." As soon as I open the door to Smells Like Sugar, which used to be the Sunshine Bakery when I was a kid, cinnamon and sugar assault my senses and intensify my craving, which is why I'm here before I head into work this morning.

Last night, as I went to bed, I got the strangest craving for something with cinnamon and apples, and when I woke up, the craving was amplified. So here I am, preparing to eat my weight in baked goods since it's the only thing that sounds delicious at the moment.

"Oh. Hi, there."

I glance up from the display case to find Astrid, Grady's sister, standing on the other side of the counter. Seeing her just reminds me that I'm having a child with her brother, and she's going to be my kid's aunt.

Jesus, this is getting more complicated by the second.

"Hi, Astrid."

Her friendly smile seems genuine, but I have no idea if Grady has shared our news with her yet, so I feel uneasy standing in front of her right now. But if I don't get an apple fritter in the next five minutes, I might chew someone's head off."

"I know about the baby."

Okay then. No beating around the bush. I guess I have to appreciate her directness. "Um..."

She rounds the counter and comes out to the side I'm standing on. "Look, this doesn't have to be awkward. In fact..." Her smile grows. "I'm really freaking excited because I get to be an aunt. I swear, I never thought Grady would ever have kids, especially after these past few years." She rolls her eyes and pulls me by the hand, closer to the case. "But everything happens for a reason, right?"

My eyes must be bugging out of my head. "Yeah, that's how the saying goes, isn't it?"

She waves me off. "Anyway, just know that I'm here if you need anything, including sweet treats." Pointing to the display case, she bounces her eyebrows. "I've got a little bit of everything. What is the baby in the mood for this morning?"

I'm trying to regain speech after her reaction, but I don't get a chance to respond before the chime above the door rings out. A striking blonde woman waltzes in, looking like she just stepped off the cover of a magazine in her business attire and heels.

"Willow! This is Scottie," Astrid announces to the woman, whose eyes immediately widen.

Willow's expression mimics Astrid's, and suddenly I'm very aware that far more people know about me and my situation than I anticipated. Turning to me, she plasters a smile on her face and then reaches out to shake my hand. "Oh my gosh! It's so nice to meet you."

I reciprocate her gesture as I stare between the two of them. "Likewise, although I'm sure you already knew who I was based on your reaction."

Astrid bumps her shoulder against Willow's. "I told her I knew about the baby."

Willow sighs, rolling her eyes. "You have to forgive my friend here, Scottie. Astrid is one of my best friends, but she is insanely excited about becoming an aunt. I haven't heard her talk about anything else since she found out on Sunday."

"My brother came to my daughter's birthday party looking like he hadn't slept and told us what happened with your son and…" She drops her eyes to my stomach.

My hand moves there instinctively. "Oh."

"We're not judging you," Willow interjects. "Believe me. I swear, just looking at Dallas could get me pregnant, so I can imagine how hard it was to resist Grady."

Astrid smacks Willow's arm. "Ew, that's my brother!"

Willow shrugs, still looking at me. "Sorry, girl, but the men in this town…" she tsks. "There must be something in the water in Carrington Cove." I fold in my lips to hide my smile. I can't speak for their men, but I know the second I saw Grady that night, all grown up and far more muscular than he was in high school, my ovaries started dry humping the air.

Astrid pushes Willow aside and glances back at the bakery case. "Anyway, what can I get for you this morning? Any cravings?"

"Actually, yeah. That's why I stopped in. Those apple fritters look delicious. I'll take two please." Each one is nearly as big as my head, but I don't want to risk not having enough.

Astrid nods, moves back to the other side of the counter and grabs a bag, reaching for the fritters and sliding them inside while Willow pulls my attention to her again. "So, you just moved back here, Scottie?"

"Yeah. I've lived in Georgia for the past fifteen years, but I got a job opportunity I couldn't pass up, so my son and I moved here."

"Your mom and grandma come in here all the time," Astrid adds as she moves to the register. "In fact, weren't you here with them back in December?"

"Yes, I was."

"I thought so." I hand her my card, but she waves it away. "Nope. Your money is no good here. These are for my future niece or nephew, so it's on me."

"Astrid, that's not necessary."

Willow places her hand on my arm. "Just let her. Trust me, you don't want to argue with her. You won't win."

Astrid plasters an award-winning smile on her face and hands me the bag with my goodies. "She's right."

Sighing, I take the bag from her. "Well, thank you. You didn't have to do that."

"I know, but it's my business so I can do whatever I want." Her eyes soften. "And I want you to know that I'm here if you need anything. I know that we don't really know each other, but I remember how close you and my brother were, and I know he's taking this seriously, Scottie. Grady isn't the type of man to walk away from his responsibilities, okay?"

"I know that."

"And you can trust him. Hell, I'd trust him with my life."

I want to trust Grady. I want to believe that this will all work out easily, but my past has proven otherwise. "I appreciate that. In fact, could I get his phone number from you by chance? We haven't exchanged that information yet. Our last two conversations were a little strained."

She pulls her phone from her back pocket and sends me Grady's number via text after I give her mine. "And now I have yours too."

"Thank you." I make a mental note to text him later and then check the time. "I need to get going. Work calls, you know?"

Willow and Astrid nod. "It was really nice to meet you, Scottie," Willow says.

"Likewise."

"And I'm serious. Reach out if you need anything. We take care of each other around here and you're practically family now," Astrid says.

"If you don't reach out, she will probably hunt you down and insert herself in your life anyway," Willow adds. "That's what she did to me when I moved to town."

"Hey! Don't act like you didn't appreciate my offer of friendship," Astrid admonishes, making me laugh. "And I'm pretty sure you were the one with the addiction to blueberry muffins, so you hunted me down first."

Willow walks over to her and pulls her in for a hug. "I'm just kidding. Of course I did, Astrid. It's because of you, and Dallas too of course, that Carrington Cove started to feel like home."

This town hasn't been my home in years, but being back here again, seeing how people interact, and being surrounded by family has reminded me of what home should feel like. Georgia never felt like that. Sure, we had friends and coworkers we hung out with, but Andrew's family was never truly welcoming, and as our marriage dissolved, I felt more and more alone.

"Thank you. Both of you. I'm sure I'll be seeing you around." With a nod of my head, I exit the bakery feeling overwhelmed by my reality. Astrid seems genuine and she and Willow obviously have a strong friendship, but my focus right now needs to be on how to navigate my relationship with Grady. Oh, and telling my boss that the employee she just hired will be going on maternity leave in roughly six months.

On the drive to work, I inhale one of the apple fritters, moaning with every bite. My stomach is finally happy, but my nerves are still going haywire. Let's just hope today goes by quickly and smoothly without any other surprises for me. I don't think I could take any more at this point.

***

"Okay, well..."

"I'm sorry, Alaina."

My new boss shakes her head at me, tapping the desk in front of her. "Don't you dare apologize. You're having a child and should be celebrating that. Hell, at least you're dating. I can't remember the last time I spent a few hours alone with a man." Her eyes bug out. "Oh god, I can't believe I just said that. That was unprofessional, wasn't it?"

"Not at all. I get it. That's how I ended up in this situation, unfortunately. The father and I...we're not romantically involved. It was just...unexpected, obviously."

"I see." She brushes her bangs from her eyes. "Well, it's okay. We can work around this. You're not due until September, so we'll just start the new year in August with someone to fill in for you temporarily, and then you can return later in the fall." She brushes her hands in the air. "See? No big deal."

Hearing her talk about the future that's only a matter of months away just reminds me of all the decisions I need to make and haven't even begun to think about yet.

"That sounds agreeable."

"Of course. In the meantime, business will operate as usual. Just let me know if you're not feeling well or need a break, and we can work around that too."

Standing from the chair opposite her desk, I reach out to shake her hand. "Thank you for being understanding about this. The last thing I wanted to tell you after you just hired me is that I'll be leaving again in a few months." Shrugging, I say, "I guess I won't be employee of the year any time soon."

Alain ignores my outstretched hand as she laughs, rounds her desk, and pulls me in for a hug. "Scottie, you're having a baby. It's a beautiful thing and all that matters right now is that you take care of yourself."

Inhaling deeply, I say, "I'm trying."

She releases me and nods. "Good. Okay, we have that parent meeting in an hour, and then I have a few observations to complete today, so I'm going to get back at it."

"See you soon," I tell her before exiting her office and heading back to my own. When I close the door behind me and pick up my phone from my desk, I notice a text from an unknown number.

Unknown: *Hey. It's Grady. We need to talk.*

Jesus, I haven't even texted him yet, so this is a surprise.

Me: *How did you get my number?*

Unknown: *My sister.*

Astrid. Duh. I knew this was coming, but something about his message just makes my anxiety spike for the tenth time this morning.

Me: *Okay, I agree we need to talk, but I'm at work right now.*

While waiting for his reply, I program his number into my phone, instantly being teleported back in time when I did this the first time. Seems we've both secured new cell phone numbers since then.

Grady: *Can we talk tonight then? I have a bunch of questions and my head is spinning. I need to know how this is going to work, Scottie.*

Me: *Tonight is fine. Can you come over to my house though so I don't have to leave Chase?*

I know my son can fend for himself, but since his breaking and entering incident, he does not have any privacy or trust from me.

Grady: *Absolutely. Send me your address. I'll bring dinner.*

Me: *You don't need to do that. My address is really easy. I'm renting the house right next to my mom's. Apparently, you remember where she lives.*

Grady: *Yeah, I do. What time works best for you?*

Me: *Six?*

Grady: *See ya then.*

I stare at my phone, rereading our texts and trying to gauge how he's feeling, but texts are so difficult at conveying tone and emotion. No matter how he feels though, I have to stand my ground. It's like I told my mom and grandma, I can't go down the same road twice. By ending up pregnant, I've already made the turn, but I'm not racing down the hill toward a delusional happily ever after again. That hill leads to nothing but a twisted up stomach, and the possibility of losing all control.

I set my phone to the side, wake up my computer, and get to work answering emails. I make a list of everything I want to accomplish today and start flipping through files for students I am scheduled to meet with to go over academic and behavior concerns. But before the first bell rings, signaling the start of school, my phone vibrates with a call.

I nearly drop my phone when I see who is calling.

Clenching my teeth, I toss the phone back on my desk and don't even bother responding because I know damn well that engaging in that conversation will only make my blood pressure spike.

And I don't have to answer to him anymore. I'm not his wife, and thanks to him, I may never want that title ever again.

***

"How many people do you think live here?"

Grady stands on the front porch of my house, his arms laden with bags. "This isn't all food, but a lot of it is. We had a busy day at the shop and I'm starving. I remember how I ate as a teenage boy, so I know Chase can put away some food."

I gesture for him to come into the house. "Well, thank you for bringing dinner, even though I told you not to. Guess you're not as good at listening as you were back in high school."

"You're welcome," he grumbles, casting me a glance over his shoulder from the kitchen as he sets the bags on the counter and heaves out a sigh. "Before I forget to ask, does Chase know…" His eyes dip down to my stomach and I cover the baby growing inside of me on instinct.

"No. I figured we should talk first before I let him know, especially given the fact he'll be essentially working for you in the coming weeks."

Grady nods, the scowl still on his face. "I think that's smart."

"He's in his room. Should I call him out here?" Standing in front of Grady now, especially after our last two interactions, has made me nervous. But god, he looks so handsome, even though his grumpy disposition is off-putting. He's freshly showered and wearing dark jeans and a plain black t-shirt, looking just as delectable, if not more so, than he did that night that changed the trajectory of our lives.

"Maybe we should talk first. I mean, what is your schedule like? I'd like to be accommodating to you both if I can, especially since I know he'll have baseball practice starting next week."

"His tryout is tomorrow, right?" I ask as I lean against the other side of the counter. Since we moved here after the initial team tryouts, the coaching staff made an exception to give him a chance to play, especially because he's a pitcher—like Grady was.

"Yeah." Grady blows out a breath. "I'm supposed to meet with the coaching staff around noon, and then I guess I'm officially a coach as of tomorrow."

"You're going to be an amazing coach, Grady," I say, trying to decide if his lack of confidence is because of what's happening between us and Chase, or because he honestly doesn't think he'll be good at it. But how could he think otherwise? The man was unstoppable on the mound. I'm sure the boys on the team will be stoked to learn from him and see the game from his perspective.

"We'll see, won't we?" Shaking his head, he gestures toward the bags. "I hope you're in the mood for a burger. Dallas's restaurant, Catch & Release, has some of the best in town, and their onion rings are freaking amazing, so I figured it was a safe bet." He begins pulling containers out, popping the lids on them just as Chase comes out from his room and into the kitchen.

"Oh. I didn't realize we had company." My son and Grady lock eyes with one another as the energy shifts in the room.

"You remember Grady, right, Chase?" I ask awkwardly, as if the two of them could ever forget the night Grady pinned him to the ground and Chase ended up in handcuffs.

Chase's eyes narrow suspiciously. "What's he doing here?"

Grady clears his throat. "I'm here to discuss your schedule for working at my garage. I agreed to let you work off your debt instead of pressing charges."

"My mom mentioned that." Chase stares down at the ground, avoiding Grady's gaze when he says, "Thanks."

"I remember being a teenage boy, so I know that your brain doesn't work right most of the time. But I promise you, if there's a next time, the next person won't be as forgiving." Chase nods, still staring at the ground. "And we're going to be spending a lot more time together at baseball practice, so it's best that we put all of this behind us."

That last detail grabs my son's attention. I hadn't told him that Grady is one of the baseball coaches yet.

"What are you talking about? You're a coach?"

"Yup." Grady tips his chin, twisting to face my son head-on now as he crosses his arms over his chest. "And your mom tells me you're a pitcher, so guess who you'll probably be working with the most?"

Chase's jaw tenses. "Just perfect."

"This is why you shouldn't do stupid shit, Chase," I chime in. "Sometimes life can throw you a curveball and your past mistakes can come back to bite you in the ass."

Are you speaking to your son, or yourself, Scottie?

"It's going to be a learning curve for all of us," Grady grates out, sliding a Styrofoam container across the counter toward my son. "I brought plenty."

Chase's eyes dart over to me, silently asking for permission.

"Go ahead, Chase. Grady brought us dinner, which you can thank him for as well."

Chase reaches for the container, grabs a few sides of ketchup from the bags, then says, "Thanks," before turning to me. "I'm going to eat in my room."

Knowing it's probably for the best so Grady and I can speak candidly about everything we need to, I nod as Chase scurries down the hall, shutting his door softly, leaving Grady and me alone again.

"I hope you're ready to deal with teenage attitudes. I swear, sometimes I feel like I'm walking on eggshells in my own damn house."

Grady grunts. "Teenagers don't scare me."

I take a step closer to the counter and lower my voice. "Chase really is a good kid, Grady. I'm sorry that your first encounter with him was what it was." Our eyes lock. "But now that you and I..." I gesture to my stomach. "It's important to me that you two get along."

His Adam's apple bobs as he swallows roughly. "I'm in uncharted territory, Scottie, on all fronts." I watch his eyes dip down to my stomach. "But I promise, I will do everything in my power to make sure I'm in my kid's life."

I've heard those words before...But talk is cheap.

Do you honestly think Grady isn't a man of his word though, Scottie?

"Are you hungry?" He pushes a container toward me as the smell of charbroiled meat and salty french fries hits my nose, pulling me from my thoughts.

"Yes, which is weird since I've been extremely nauseous all week."

We grab our food and head to the dining room table, choosing two chairs right next to each other. Grady's body is almost too big for the chair, his knee hitting mine once he scoots in closer. We dive into our food, taking a few bites before he finally breaks the silence. "Practices should be done by five, so I was thinking he could come work at the garage one night a week for an hour or so, and then Saturdays. There's plenty of grunt jobs that he can do that my technicians would be glad to have taken off their plates."

"He doesn't usually have a ton of homework, so that should be good," I reply as I pop a fry in my mouth. "Oh my God, the batter on these is heavenly."

Grady juts his chin toward the bags on the counter that he didn't open. "I also brought a few apple fritters for you."

My head spins toward the kitchen and then back to him. "How did you..."

"Astrid told me," he says, his eyes locked on mine. "When she told me you asked for my number and shared yours with me, she also shared your latest craving." Shaking his head, there's a hint of a smile on his lips. "My sister is a little excited about the baby, just an FYI."

"Oh, I'm aware. I got a dose of it today when I stopped in the bakery."

Grady pinches the bridge of his nose. "I'm sorry. I can only imagine."

"It's okay." I pick up another fry. "Babies are supposed to be celebrated. A new life is coming into the world." As I stare down at my food, I can feel Grady's eyes on me. "I just…"

Grady's hand envelops mine, drawing my eyes to his. "I want this, Scottie," he says, the deep rasp of his voice coating me in warmth. "Please don't think otherwise, I just…it's a lot to wrap my head around and I have so many questions."

Taking in a deep breath, I put the fry down and turn to him. "Okay. Well, let's talk about it."

"You sure you're not going to run away again?" The corner of his lips lift, but I don't blame him for asking. My track record isn't the best.

"You're in my house, so there's not really anywhere for me to go."

His eyes bounce back and forth between mine. "Then tell me how this is supposed to work. What do you want from me?"

As I stare into his eyes, I ask myself that same question. I know what I can *handle* from him, but what I *want*? That's a question I'm not willing to answer—because if there's one thing I've learned in my life, it's that what I want isn't a factor in what I get.

"I want you to be as involved as you want. This is your child too, so…"

"I'm going to be a father, Scottie," he says with conviction. "The last thing I want is for my kid to grow up not knowing who I am or not being able to count on me."

Tears threaten to fall, but I manage to say, "Okay."

"But that means that we're going to be spending a lot of time together and I need you to talk to me and stop running away. I want to be involved in everything." He points a finger at the table, emphasizing his point. "I'm going to be at doctor's appointments, and I want us to make decisions together. I want us to be a team."

Oh my god. My hormones can't handle this.

Before I burst into tears, he stands from the table and goes over to the bags. "I have no idea what I'm doing, and I'm not above admitting that, all right?" He reaches in one bag and pulls out three books, one of which I recognize instantly because I own the same one—only mine is probably a few versions outdated.

"You bought *What to Expect When You're Expecting*?"

He holds up the book. "Yeah, but this one is for dads." I squint and see the subtitle on the cover. "And then there's another two that looked informative, so I'll read those once I get done with this one."

"Grady..."

"I also brought you some of these." He holds up a small plastic bag of ginger candies. "The lady at the store swore these helped with nausea, and I remember you saying that you weren't feeling great, so I figured it couldn't hurt to try them."

One tear slips down my cheek. "Wow."

He drops the bag on the counter and walks back over to where I'm sitting. "What's wrong?"

"Nothing."

"Are you sure? You're crying..."

"It's the damn hormones, Grady," I snap a little too harshly, but my body feels possessed. I forgot how quickly my mood can change. Poor Grady is in for a treat as this pregnancy progresses.

Wincing, he walks back over to the counter and pulls out the familiar pink box that I know is from Astrid's bakery. Bringing it over to the table, he pops open the lid and rips off a chunk of an apple fritter, offering it to me. "Do you need some sugar?"

Laughing through my tears, I grab it from him and take a bite, chewing through the emotions that are overwhelming me.

Andrew never cared this much when I got pregnant with Chase. He was more focused on finishing college so he could get a job and support us before our son was born. And back then, I admired that, but that was before I realized that it was his selfish side shining through, definitely not selflessness. He worked so he didn't have to accept that a child was going to change his life. He never once asked me how I was feeling, worried about doctor's appointments, or cared about decisions that I made about our son. He said he would. He said a lot of things in the beginning I should have questioned more.

But when Chase was born, he smiled proudly and smoked a cigar with his dad outside of the hospital like we were living in the 1950s. I should have known then that nothing was going to change.

"Thank you," I manage to say as I finish chewing.

Grady takes his seat again. "I want to be here for you." He reaches for my hand, intertwining our fingers like he did that night at Ricky's—the night I realized that, while time and distance can change circumstances, they do nothing to diminish unresolved feelings. "I just need you to let me."

"I'm used to doing things on my own, Grady," I squeak out. "I have for a long time."

"Well, get used to me being around because I'm not going anywhere."

Can I believe him?

I guess only time will tell.

"And Chase will be okay. He still has time to pull his head out of his ass."

God, he has no idea how much my son needs a male role model to look up to, how coming here was the best way to distance him from disappointment.

"Don't go easy on him, Grady. I know having someone like you to look up to could change his life."

Grady shakes his head as his eyes meet the floor. "Not sure he should aspire to be me, but I can at least teach him the value of hard work."

"You're the type of man I can only hope my son turns out to be," I whisper as our eyes meet.

Grady swallows and then clears his throat. "I have another question for you."

"Okay..."

"What about us?"

My heart skips a beat. This is exactly the conversation I was dreading, but the determination in Grady's eyes tells me that he's not brushing past it. "Uh..."

He scoots his chair closer to me as he reaches up to brush my curls from my face. The smooth trail of his finger down my jaw has me clenching my thighs together. "Us, Scottie. That night..." He trails off, shaking his head. "You can't tell me you didn't feel that."

I did. I felt everything, which is why I ran.

"Grady, we're...friends."

"Yeah, and even you said we unlocked a new level of friendship." The corner of his mouth tips up, but his eyes drop to my mouth as he licks his lips.

"That was before…"

"And what about now?"

Is he saying what I think he is? That he wants more with me?

I know I've dreamt of it, wondered and longed for another night with this man, especially after the last. But it's just like I told my mom and Gigi—I can't go down this path again. My heart has to stay out of this.

"Now we're friends who are having a baby together," I reply, watching the expression on his face morph from playfulness to confusion and then acceptance. "Friends who support each other, friends who have agreed to give my son a chance to right his wrongs and learn from his mistakes."

He clears his throat, drops my hand, and leans back in his chair. His stoic demeanor is unnerving, but there's too much at stake to cross that line again. My son needs to be my focus right now, and this baby growing inside of me.

Grady clears his throat before a knowing smile crosses his lips, and it makes me even more uneasy. "Okay then. Friends it is."

Not wanting to watch his jaw tick from the boundary I just erected between us, I stand from my chair and head into the kitchen, grabbing a ginger ale from the fridge and popping the top, sipping on it to ease the churning in my stomach. When I was pregnant with Chase, ginger ale was always in my house because it helped with the nausea, but I also just really love the taste of it. And I can't drink wine right now, which is what I would normally reach for given the tension-filled atmosphere.

The screech of a chair across the tile floor has me spinning around. Grady pushes in his seat, taking his take-out box to the trash and moving back to the counter to collect his books. "I guess I'll leave you to the rest of your night, then."

"Okay."

"Text me the details of your doctor's appointment, please, so I know when to be there."

"Sounds good."

"And maybe next week we can talk about living arrangements."

My stomach drops. Oh God, I didn't even think about that. I lived with Andrew after Chase was born. We were married. Does this mean that Grady wants us to live together?

"Uh..."

When his eyes finally meet mine again, he flashes me a smile that is almost placating. "Don't worry. We'll figure that out too." He kisses me on the temple and then moves for the door. "Have a good night, Scottie. Get some rest and keep growing our baby."

And then he leaves without saying goodbye, acting like he didn't just scramble my brain with unanswered questions.

This is going to be way more complicated than I thought.

Chapter Nine

Grady

"All right, boys. Line it up," commands Ryan Carter, the new head coach of the baseball team, as a group of teenage boys all make their way over to us. Once the chatter dies down, he continues. "We're gonna set up the 1-2-3 drill, but pitchers, you're going to be working with Coach Reynolds today."

My eyes meet Chase's with laser focus.

I'm not going to let our unorthodox meeting deter me from teaching the kid something about the game. That won't even be the last of our challenging interactions. Eventually, we'll have to discuss how I'm going to be in his life beyond this season and long after he's worked off his punishment with me. But I can't focus on that right now. I'm eager to see what he can do on the field.

To his side, Trent and Jared snicker, so I shift my focus in their direction, instantly extinguishing their cockiness. Ryan and I already discussed the incident at the garage, and those two boys are doing their own community service through the sheriff's department and running extra drills after practice. Their punishment starts today, so I'm sure their amusement with the situation will diminish considerably by tomorrow.

"You ready for this?" Ryan asks as the boys disperse and Chase and two other pitchers head to the mound with a bucket of balls. The team's catcher, Franklin, takes his place at home plate, doing a few stretches before he crouches low.

"As ready as I'm going to be." I've pitched in front of millions of people, but the pressure I feel right now is nothing compared to that. This is why I've been avoiding coaching.

What if I'm horrible? What if I don't live up to everyone's expectations? What if these kids only see a washed-up old man who had his shot at playing professionally and ruined it out of stubbornness?

"You've got this. Don't stress about being a teacher. Just do what feels natural, and they will learn. You know the game, so let that speak for itself." Patting me on the shoulder, Ryan heads to the other side of the field where the boys are grabbing equipment for their drill. I take a deep breath before striding to the mound where Chase, Nathan, and Max are waiting.

"All right. Since we haven't worked together yet, I want to see what you guys have got." Technically, this week is Chase's tryout for the team as well, so I definitely need to assess whether he has the talent to play with varsity or JV. He's only a freshman, but we spoke to his former coaches down in Georgia and they praised his talents. If he can take a starting spot from one of our juniors, it's going to make his chances of fitting in on the team even harder.

I know from personal experience.

But once they see him play, the boys will shut up quickly if he helps them win.

I know that from personal experience as well.

"Nathan, you're up first." Crossing my arms over my chest, I settle into my spot so I can study his movements. He's not bad, but he's not very controlled. He's tightening too much in his shoulders, which is costing him speed. After Nathan throws about a dozen pitches of varying accuracy, I let Max have a go. Max has more control, but he's inconsistent. One pitch is right on target, and the next is nowhere near the plate.

"Let's see what you've got, Chase," I say as Scottie's son shoots me a nervous glance before taking the mound. He takes his time agreeing with the catcher's call, but when he winds up and lets the ball loose, I swear, I see myself twenty years ago.

I clear my throat, not wanting to get too excited. "Again."

I keep him up there for longer than the other two boys, which they pick up on sooner quickly. After a good fifteen minutes pass, the boys get antsy.

Max chimes in first. "I think you should let us pitch again, Coach. I mean, everyone needs time to warm up, right?"

Chase looks between me and Max, and since I don't want to ruffle feathers just yet, I agree to let Max have another shot to prove himself. But he stands on the mound and tries way too hard the second time around, only building up his frustration. Nathan also takes another turn, but at the end, I think all four of us can agree that Chase has more talent in his pinky finger than the two juniors who probably walked onto this team.

I hear Ryan call his whistle from the other side of the field, requesting the entire team to gather around, so I gesture for the boys to jog over as I start to clean up the balls from the pitching practice. I shoot a text off to Ryan to let him know he has a new starting pitcher.

Once everyone is gathered around, Ryan makes an announcement. "One thing you all need to remember is that your behavior and choices are not just a reflection on yourselves, but on this team as well. They're also a reflection on us as coaches." He gestures between me, himself, and the other assistant coach, Brad. "But I want everyone to understand that your spot on this team isn't guaranteed. Moving forward, there will be a no-strike policy."

"What's that?" one of the players asks as I take my place next to Ryan, inserting myself into the conversation now.

"It means you get no more chances. You screw up? You're off the team." He shoots his glare at Chase's accomplices to the break-in at my shop. Their eyes find the ground as the other members of the team murmur amongst themselves. I remember what it was like to be in high school—rumors spread like wildfire. And with cell phones now? I can only imagine how many people in town and beyond know about the mess these boys got into.

"With that being said, I would like to announce that the newest member of our team, Chase Warner, will also be the starting pitcher in next week's game."

Nathan and Max instantly tense up, but Chase stands tall next to them. It's good to know he's aware of the talent he possesses. His mom would be proud, especially since she always advised me to own mine.

"Now, Chase, Jared, and Trent, you boys are staying after, but the rest of you, take three laps around the field and then we're done for the day."

The boys take off to rush through their run, while Ryan and I stare down at the three delinquents in front of us.

Ryan rubs his palms together with a pleased smile on his face. "Now, there's nothing I love more than serving punishment, especially when it's due. You three have no idea who you were messing with."

"Oh, we knew," Jared mutters under his breath.

"Say it so we can hear you, son," I bark, reminding myself that he's a minor and I can't touch him. But cocky boys like him—I remember them well. His insecurities are lurking right underneath the surface and that's why he convinced Chase to do what they did. He felt threatened, and with good reason, it seems. But it doesn't excuse his behavior.

"It was nothing," Jared replies, avoiding my eyes.

I take a step closer to him, his eyes widen, and then I lower my voice when I say, "It's not too late for me to press charges. I hope you realize that. I'm trying to do you a favor, so if I were you, I'd shut your mouth and do what you're told for the next hour and remind yourself never to do something like that again."

He visibly swallows. "The next hour?"

Ryan chuckles. "Oh yeah. We're not stopping until each one of you pukes."

Huh. Maybe this coaching gig might be a little fun after all.

***

"Scotland Warner?" The nurse calls out from the door that separates the waiting room from the office and exam rooms. My knees haven't stopped bouncing since I sat down, but part of that is because I'm at my kid's first doctor's appointment, and the mother of my child still isn't here.

"Scotland Warner!" She's louder this time, peering around the room.

I raise my hand like a kindergartener. "Um, hi."

The nurse looks me up and down. "No offense, Grady, but I don't think you're the pregnant woman I'm looking for."

I chuckle as I stand from my seat and move closer to her. Lowering my voice, I say, "I'm the father. Scottie isn't here yet and she's not answering her phone."

"I see." She peers down at her chart. "Well..."

The door chimes as the woman in question rushes into the office, swiveling her head around chaotically before her eyes land on me. "Oh my God! Sorry I'm late." Blowing her curls out of her face, she strides up to the nurse and me in a business-style dress that hugs all of her curves, stealing the breath from my lungs and making my dick harden in seconds.

I've seen Scottie in a uniform on the pitching mound and dressed casually in jeans and a t-shirt, but I've never seen her like this. Just the sight of her dressed like she's in charge makes me want to get sent to the principal's office so I can see what kind of punishment *she* can dish out. Or better yet, let's reverse the roles and I can punish her for denying what's between us all these years later.

Focus, Grady. You can revisit that little fantasy later.

"Well, let's get you back here then." The nurse gestures for us to follow her, but I hold the door open so Scottie can go ahead of me.

"Thank you."

"Of course." As she walks ahead of me, giving me the perfect view of her ass in that tight dress, I remember what that ass looked like bent over in front of me all those months ago.

I wonder if *that* instance was the time that did it, the one that knocked her up—because my memory likes to venture back to that night frequently, and how *that* orgasm felt like my soul was leaving my fucking body.

Perhaps that was the moment when our souls were creating a new one.

The nurse stops us in the hall to take Scottie's vitals. I watch her cringe as she steps on the scale and takes in her weight, rolling her eyes when she steps off and slides her heels back on to continue down the hallway.

"Here we are." The nurse opens a door to an exam room and motions for Scottie to take a seat on the bed. "We need you to undress from the waist down and cover yourself with the sheet."

"I know. This isn't my first rodeo." Scottie places her purse on an empty chair against the wall, irritation lacing her words.

The nurse doesn't even react. "The doctor will be in to see you shortly."

As soon as the door clicks shut, Scottie looks at me. "Do you mind turning around, please?"

"What?"

"I need to take off my underwear and get on the table, and I don't need you staring at me while I do it."

I close the distance between us, loving how she has to crane her neck back to meet my gaze. "Scottie, you do realize I've seen your pussy and your ass, right? In fact, I know them intimately."

I swear I see flashes of our night together shine through her eyes before she visibly swallows and takes a step back. "This is different. I'm…I'm in a vulnerable state."

Lowering my voice, I reply, "Having my face nose deep in your pussy wasn't vulnerable enough for you?"

Her eyes widen. "Grady…"

But before I say something else, I remind myself that pushing Scottie isn't going to get me anywhere, even though all I want to do in this moment is bend her over the exam table and remind her of how perfectly her pussy grips my cock, how insane our connection was and still is, and how her coming back to Carrington Cove couldn't have been a coincidence.

It's the resolution I came to when we spoke the other night at her house, when I asked her about us, and she blew it off like our night together meant nothing.

Well, I call bullshit. I could read her like a fucking playbook. She was pushing me away because she's fucking scared. But the thing is—I'm scared too, of a lot of things.

The one thing I *do* know, though, is that wanting her is not something I should be scared of. In fact, it's the only piece of our puzzle I'm sure of.

Before that night, I had no romantic interest in women, but that's because none of them were her. She's always been the one that broke the mold for me, something that is so blatantly clear now that we're back in each other's lives. Now, I need to play this right to prove to her that we belong together—not just because we're having a child together, but because our child could *never* be a mistake.

I take a step back and hold my hands up in surrender. "You're right. I'm sorry. I'll turn around."

She watches me cautiously as I slowly face the wall, shoving my hands in my pockets as the sound of her movements filters behind me.

"I can't believe I've already gained seven pounds," she mumbles as I hear the rustle of her clothes and the crinkle of the paper sheet.

"You look perfect, Scottie."

She scoffs. "Easy for you to say. You're the father. You aren't growing a human being, and your body looks like it was carved from granite."

I clench my jaw, waiting for her to finish covering herself so I can refute her statement, even though her comment about my body was slightly revealing. But I can't focus on that right now.

With a peek over my shoulder, I see her smooth the paper over her legs, so I take that as my cue to close the distance between us again. Peering down at her as she lies back on the exam chair, I make sure she's looking at me before I speak again. "You're right. I'm not growing a human. But you are, and that's such an incredible fucking thing. Hell, reading about everything your body goes through while pregnant makes my mind spin." I stroke her cheek with my finger, and for a second, I swear she leans into my touch before she catches herself and looks away. "I can't imagine what you must be feeling, but just know that no matter how your body changes, it will never change how sexy I find you."

Her eyes whip back to mine, widening just as the doctor knocks on the door. "Is everyone decent?" she asks through the door before Scottie answers her with a squeaky reply.

"Yes. Come in."

A woman who looks about the same age as my mom shuffles through the door, pushing her glasses up her nose before glancing at both of us. "Good afternoon, you two. How are we doing today?"

"Great," I reply as Scottie says, "A little nauseous."

The doctor laughs. "Well, that's to be expected momma-to-be." She casts her gaze to me, dropping her eyes down my entire body before looking away and clearing her throat. *Yeah, I get that reaction from women a lot.* "I'm Dr. Rivera, and I'm honored to be caring for you during your pregnancy." She smiles at Scottie and then glances down at her chart, flipping the page over. "Now, it seems you're about twelve weeks along?"

"Yes, based on my calculations," Scottie answers.

Dr. Rivera's eyes dart to me once more. "And I take it this is Dad?"

"No, I'm her brother," I deadpan.

The doctor glares at me slightly just as Scottie smacks my arm. "Grady!"

Dr. Rivera chuckles and then sets the chart down on the counter before wheeling over a machine that has a small screen and attached keyboard sitting right underneath it with far too many buttons to make sense. "It's okay. I appreciate sarcasm, but for the sake of Scottland and your unborn child, answering questions with honesty will allow me to give her the best care."

"Noted. My apologies."

Dr. Rivera does a few routine examinations, looking under the flimsy paper sheet covering Scottie's legs, and for a moment, I'm jealous that she's got a front-row seat to Scottie's pussy right now.

Fuck, something is really wrong with me.

Once the doctor is finished examining her cervix, Scottie lifts her dress above the sheet to expose her stomach. Dr. Rivera squeezes clear gel onto Scottie's skin and then takes a handheld device, moving along her abdomen as an image begins to form on the screen.

"Since you're further along, we should be able to see something on an abdominal ultrasound." She rubs the device around, clicking a few buttons until a white, kidney bean shape appears in the middle of the screen, followed by a rhythmic whooshing sound that fills the room and a flicker in the center of the figure.

"Is that…" I start to ask, but the words die on my tongue as the image of my child comes into view. I move closer to Scottie on the reclining bed, reaching for her hand instinctively as the sound of our child's heartbeat echoes around us. "Holy shit." I swear my heartbeat thrashes faster than the one on the monitor. I know how this all works but seeing and hearing it just makes this all more fucking real.

There's a human—a tiny, fragile human growing inside the woman beside me. Suddenly, the world as I know it feels like it's shifted, with Scottie and this little baby becoming the center of mine.

"Definitely twelve weeks," Dr. Rivera says, taking snapshots as the image moves on the screen, pulling me back to reality. Our baby puts on a show, kicking and wiggling, making Scottie laugh.

"Already full of energy," she murmurs, garnering my attention. When my eyes find her face, her eyes are full of moisture. I squeeze her hand, forcing her to look at me.

"That's our baby, Scottie."

Her smile is small, but it's there. "I know." Our eyes lock, and I'm held captive and speechless, forgetting we aren't alone until the doctor speaks, breaking the trance.

"Everything looks great, Scottland. Measurements are right on track. Your due date appears to be around September thirteenth." The sound of a printer fills the room as the doctor extracts a few pictures from the bottom of the machine and hands them to Scottie. "Here's a keepsake. You're doing a fantastic job growing that baby. Just keep up with your bloodwork, try to get in movement and plenty of water, and rest when you can. You are older now than during your last pregnancy, and while I wouldn't classify you as high risk, your body is going to react differently with age, so just be prepared for that."

"What about gestational diabetes?" I chime in before Scottie can say anything. "I know the risk increases with age."

Dr. Rivera's eyes flick over to mine as she takes her gloves off. "As long as Scottie eats a balanced diet, she should be fine. Routine blood work will let us know if there's cause for concern."

Scottie glares at me, but I don't give a shit. I have a right to ask questions too. "Thank you."

The doctor grabs the chart and makes a few notes before moving to the door. "You're welcome. I'll see you back in about four weeks. Take care, you two."

She leaves the room and Scottie turns to me once more. "I take it you've been reading?"

"I'm on book number two, Scottie," I reply, holding up two fingers. "I told you, I'm in this."

She gestures for me to turn around so she can get dressed again, and I oblige, even though I think it's bullshit. But one obstacle at a time. "I appreciate the concern, Grady, but..."

"But nothing, Scottie. You and this baby are my responsibility now," I grate out, trying to keep my composure, though my pulse is thundering in my ears. Seeing my baby just now caused something in me to snap.

"Yeah, I've heard that before," she murmurs so softly that I almost miss it.

"What do you mean?" I turn around to face her, but she shakes her head, stepping over to the chair where she left her purse earlier.

"Nothing, Grady. Let's just go."

Not wanting to fight with her or increase the tension between us any further, I hold the door open for her and follow her out of the doctor's office.

I walk her to her car, opening the door for her as she sets her purse inside. "So..." she starts as she spins to face me.

"That was fucking wild, Scottie," I breathe out, the image of my child imprinted on my brain. I shove my hands in my pockets so I don't reach out and smash my lips to hers.

God, I just want to fucking kiss her, hold her, and put her in a giant bubble so nothing happens to either of them. If this is how I'm going to feel until this baby is born, I might just have a fucking heart attack before I turn thirty-six.

She chuckles. "I know. I forgot how intense that feels. It's been so long since I had Chase. It's all coming back to me with each milestone."

"Shouldn't we find out the sex at the next appointment?" I ask. "You'll be sixteen weeks then."

"We can, if the baby cooperates." She licks her lips and tilts her head up at me. "Do you want to know?"

"I mean, I think it would make it easier to plan. What do you want?"

She rubs her stomach, the small bump now more noticeable to me after seeing it during the ultrasound. And fuck, it just makes her sexier. "I don't know. Part of me thinks it would be fun to wait, but the control freak in me doesn't think I could."

We share a laugh. "Okay, we'll find out then. I think it would ease some of the stress of the unknown."

"Okay."

"What about circumcision?"

"Um..."

"Well, if it's a boy, I don't want him battling with a turtleneck for the rest of his life, you know?" I say jokingly, but I'm actually serious. "You know that I'm circumcised, but..."

She holds a hand up. "No need to go any further. I agree, okay?"

I nod. "Good, but I don't think I could be in the room for that. I just might be the one to throw up if that's the case."

She covers her mouth, laughing. "Am I going to have to worry about *you* getting sick throughout this whole pregnancy?"

"No, just with that." I visibly shudder and resist the urge to reach down and cover my dick.

"Normally, the father should be concerned about the mother throwing up."

"I am." I reach out and stroke her arm, catching her off guard. But I retract my touch just as quickly.

Small steps, Grady.

Clearing my throat, I take my keys out of my pocket. "Okay then. Well…"

"Yeah." She brushes her curls back from her face. "I need to get back to work."

"I'll see you later though, right?" I ask.

"Yeah. I'll have Chase there by six."

Nodding, I start walking to my truck backwards, keeping my eyes on Scottie. "Keep growing our baby, Scottie," I say as primitive pleasure races through me.

She rolls her eyes at me. "Like I have a choice."

Yeah, you do, Scottie. You have the choice to let me in, I say to myself.

And as I drive back to the garage, I think about how I need to make her see that. But I know that I can't figure this out on my own.

Operation Get My Baby's Momma to Give Me a Chance is underway, and it's time to call in reinforcements.

***

"We can talk more about it on Friday," my sister says through the phone as I sit in the office of the garage, waiting for Scottie and Chase to show up. Astrid insisted that I call her today after the doctor's appointment and let her know how it went, but I barely got two free seconds after returning to the garage before I had to help a few of the technicians with their jobs.

"Okay. I'm gonna hold you to that, though."

She chuckles. "I promise. I just have to get this order done before I leave here, and the phone is still ringing with last minute orders."

Easter is this week, so the bakery is swamped. "Okay, see you at Lilly's dance class."

"Thanks again for taking her."

"Not a problem."

We end the call and I toss my phone on the counter in front of me, letting out a long sigh. My niece takes dance classes two nights a week, and occasionally, my sister asks me to take her until she can get there to pick her up. I don't mind. Hell, I actually love watching my favorite little girl in the world twirl around in a tutu. But now I realize that being a dance *dad* might just be in my future.

If we have a little girl, will she be interested in dance? Or will she be a tomboy I can teach how to throw and hit a baseball better than any boy her age? If we have a son, will he love the game like I did, or will he prefer football or video games?

Will my child be shy or outgoing? Quiet or loud?

Visions swirl through my mind at an alarming rate, accompanied by the memory of what my baby looked like on the screen just hours ago.

The sound of a car door slamming shut outside interrupts my thoughts, and I stand from the chair to peek through the blinds.

Scottie is saying something to Chase as they walk up to the garage, and Chase looks less than pleased to be here. By the time I'm done with him, he won't be any happier.

The chime above the door rings out. "Grady?"

"Right here," I reply instantly, startling her as Chase remains close to the door.

Her hand flies to cover her chest. "Jesus."

"Sorry." I move to the other side of the counter. "Chase." I tip my chin at him, but he doesn't acknowledge me. Funny how now that we're not at a baseball field or his house, his demeanor has changed.

I hate that my first encounter with this kid went down the way it did, especially given circumstances between Scottie and me now. I know things would be easier if he liked me, if we could see eye to eye. But I think about how I'd feel if he were my kid and did what he did. I think about how I'm now this kid's coach. I think about the kind of role I play in his life beyond the next few weeks or months.

We have to find a middle ground, and I hope we find it soon.

"Chase, don't be rude."

"Coach," he says with no emotion.

"I'm Grady here, Chase. I'm your mom's friend and the man who you owe work to, all right? At practice, I'm your coach, but not here."

His shoulders relax a bit, which makes me wonder if he thinks his debt will translate to the baseball field as well. I know Ryan worked these boys hard the other night, but I told him afterward that Chase will get the bulk of his punishment working with me.

Chase simply nods before I turn my eyes back to Scottie.

And fuck, does she look beautiful. Each time I see her, the desire to make her mine intensifies. "When should I pick him up?"

I glance at the clock on the wall. "Two hours should be good. I'm gonna have him work outside until it gets dark, then move into the garage to scrub some parts."

She nods. "Sounds good." Turning back to her son, she says sternly, "Listen to Grady and do whatever he tells you to do, got it?"

"Yeah." His eyes never leave the ground.

Sighing, she looks back at me. "Thank you. See you in a bit." But then she gets as close as she can before whispering, "Remember, he doesn't know about..." Her eyes flick down to her stomach and back up, pleading with me.

"I know."

"I'll tell him, I promise. I just..."

I grab her hand and squeeze it. "It's okay. One thing at a time."

She flashes me a tight-lipped smile, one I wish would reach her eyes. But this day has been a roller coaster of emotions, so I can't blame her for being apprehensive, especially since she's leaving her son with me.

Once Scottie leaves, the silence between Chase and me grows louder by the second. I clear my throat and move to open the door leading to the garage. "Follow me."

The lights are still on inside, but I head toward the back where I store some garden tools and other items I use regularly. Metal hooks on the wall hold rakes, shovels, and clippers for yard work. For the next few weeks, that's what Chase will be responsible for.

"I told your mom the yard needs some TLC, so that's where you're going to start."

He grumbles, "Whatever."

I fight the urge to roll my eyes at his attitude, one he didn't dare give me on the baseball field earlier this week, and instead hand him a rake and a hula hoe, motioning for him to follow me outside.

"Weeds. They never stop growing here, especially in the spring. You need to clean them out." I gesture to the field in front of us, a good thousand square feet covered in weeds that are almost to my knees.

"All of these?"

"Yup." I pat him on the shoulder. "You won't get it done today, so you can finish over your next few shifts here."

"This sucks," he grumbles, stalking away from me, dragging the hula hoe behind him.

"Yeah, well so does the dent in the hood of my car." He glares at me over his shoulder but doesn't say anything in return. "I'll be in the garage doing some paperwork. You can stop at dark."

Chase gets to work, pushing the hula hoe through the dirt, anger fueling his movements. And as I watch him, I see it—all of the irritation lurking beneath the surface, an anger that I recognize and have lived with for several years, mostly since I lost baseball.

I was irritable as a teenager too. Especially during games, when I saw other dads cheering on their sons, knowing mine would never do the same. And I wonder if that's true for Chase as well?

Scottie told me she's divorced, and it wouldn't take a rocket scientist to figure that out since her last name changed. But if she moved her son to Carrington Cove, where the hell is this kid's dad? I know if Scottie took my kid and left the state, I'd be scouring every square inch of land looking for them both.

Shaking my head, I walk back toward the garage, wondering if I should dig deeper into her marriage to understand why it ended. The last thing I want to do is repeat history, for her or myself. I don't want to become a man Scottie can't count on. I don't want my son or daughter to grow up in a divided family.

I glance over my shoulder at the angry boy pulling weeds from the dirt. I don't want him to feel like another man is entering his life only to leave it eventually.

I wait as long as I can until there's barely a sliver of daylight left in the sky before I head out to where Chase is working. I expect to see his energy level sated, for him to be covered in sweat, but much to my surprise, he's not working on the weeds.

He's practicing his pitching stance, winding up before throwing an imaginary baseball at the corner of the yard.

"You're leaning too far forward," I say, startling him.

"No I'm not."

"You sure about that?"

He reaches down, picks up the hula hoe, and starts working again as if we weren't in the middle of a conversation.

"You know I could teach you a few things…"

"I don't need your help."

"Everyone has room to improve."

Chase sighs. "Look, you may be friends with my mom, but we don't have to be friends, okay? I'm sorry I broke into your garage and smashed your car, but beyond working to repay you for that, we don't need to talk."

I cross my arms over my chest as the sky around us grows completely dark. "Don't forget I'm your coach too."

"Yeah, I'm aware," he mutters, running the tool through one more weed before standing up tall. "Am I done out here?"

I groan, realizing that the person I may need to work on my relationship with the most is the boy standing right in front of me. He's not my kid, but he's Scottie's son, and the older brother of our child. I refuse to fight with him. There has to be a way we can figure this out.

"Yeah. Come on. I have another job for you."

"Joy."

Chase follows me into the garage and over to the steel sink where we scrub engine parts. I found a bucket of odd parts and ends, stuff that I'm sure I don't even need anymore, but the point is to get this kid's hands dirty. Mr. Rogers used to save this job for me when I worked here after school. I didn't understand the point of it back then, but now I do, and maybe Chase will figure it out too.

"Steel pads are in the bucket," I say, pointing to a small container beside him. "Soap is above you, and I highly recommend wearing an apron."

"You want me to clean these?" His eyes survey the grease-covered pieces of steel. "Is it even possible for these to get clean?"

"Yup. It's possible." I pat him on the shoulder and start to walk away, but before I can stop myself, more words spill out. "You know, I used to do the same thing."

"What are you talking about?" Chase replies, still staring down into the sink full of engine parts.

"Practice my pitching without the ball." Our eyes meet, and though he's acting like he doesn't care about what I have to say, his eyes show curiosity. "How often do you do that?"

He swallows visibly. "More than I should probably admit."

I nod once. "I can tell. That's what sets you apart, Chase. That's why I told Coach Carter you should be the starting pitcher, not Max or Nathan."

"I don't need you doing me any favors," he snaps.

"Believe me, the last place I would do you a favor is on the baseball field." I walk back over to him and point in the sink. "This favor is for your mom, just so you know. But on the field? There's no room for error, no place for players who don't earn their spot."

"Well, now the whole team hates me, so thanks for that."

I lower my voice and continue, "It's easy for people to be jealous of *what* you've got, but not *how* you got it." His eyes bore into mine. "It comes down to hard work, Chase. If they put in the same effort, they could have your talent. Believe me, I know what you're going through."

For a moment, I see a flicker of understanding in his eyes, a realization that we have more in common than not. His face softens, and his scowl begins to fade. But then he clears his throat, grabs an apron from the sink, and reaches for a steel pad, running it under the water. "No, you don't."

A small part of me wants to argue with him, but the adult part of my brain tells me tonight isn't the time. We have a long road ahead, and there will be moments to bridge the gaps that separate us.

At least, I hope so.

"I'll be in the office if you need me," I say as I walk away. As I settle behind the counter, waiting for Scottie to return to pick him up, there's a dull ache in my chest that won't subside. It's half for the woman I want, and the other half for her son who has his own challenges to face, some I'm now responsible for as well.

***

"How'd it go?" Scottie asks as soon as she walks through the front door nearly an hour later. She's changed from her dress into casual pants and a plain white t-shirt, but she still looks strikingly beautiful.

I rise from my chair, pulling up my jeans. "Well, do you want the truth?"

Her face falls. "What did he do?"

"Nothing horrible," I say, brushing a hand through my hair. My shirt rides up a little, flashing a sliver of my abs, and Scottie's eyes focus on the sight. I wait for her gaze to return to mine, smirking in her direction.

Her glare is icy, probably because I caught her staring. "Continue, please."

"He's just pissed, Scottie."

"Well, he has no one to be pissed at but himself." She crosses her arms over her chest, pushing her breasts together. And maybe I'm just imagining things, but her boobs look bigger than they were earlier today.

She catches me staring this time, clearing her throat to regain my attention.

Is this how it's going to be for the next six months? Stolen glances, catching each other staring, and denying what's really between us?

I refocus on the matter at hand. "I don't think it was just anger about the work." I hold my hands up in frustration. "I might be way off base, but my gut is telling me there's something else bothering him."

Scottie blows out a breath, dropping her arms to her sides. "What did he say?"

I tell her about catching him practicing his pitching and how the boys on the team are giving him a hard time because he's starting at the game tomorrow. And when I tried to explain how I can relate, he brushed me off.

"Yeah, sounds about right," she says, shaking her head.

"So it's not just me? I mean, I'm not here to be friends with the kid, but…"

"You're a man, Grady. That's all you had to do to piss him off. Having a penis is why Chase is giving you that attitude."

My brows furrow. "Uh, can you explain further, please?"

Scottie leans on the counter that separates us. "He doesn't trust you because you're a man. The one man in his life he should have been able to count on never kept his word, so…"

Recognition races through me. God, I remember that feeling well—wondering why my father never stuck around. Wondering if all men were like that—leaving their kids behind without a second thought.

Knowing that Chase has experienced that just fuels the anger coursing through me. "Fuck, Scottie."

She shrugs, but brushes a tear from her cheek. "It's part of why we moved here," she whispers. "I was tired of watching my son suffer, tired of seeing him disappointed when his father wouldn't keep his word."

I shift my gaze back to Chase, who's still standing at the sink, scrubbing engine parts. That ache in my chest intensifies because now I not only have to ensure my own child never feels that disappointment, but I also want to show Chase that there are men who do keep their word.

"You did the right thing, Scottie."

"I know, but it doesn't make it any easier. And now he's got a target on his back because of baseball. I was hoping that might go away too, but…"

"He's really fucking talented," I say, cutting in. "I swear, watching him yesterday was like…"

"Watching you," she finishes for me, her eyes locked on mine.

"Yeah."

Silence stretches between us. I stare at her, feeling like I'm a teenager all over again, getting lost in her eyes. But now, as adults? The connection is even more powerful.

We're connected not just by friendship now, but by the life growing inside of her.

Scottie is the only person who really knew who I was before baseball. And her son has that same passion for the game—a passion only someone cut from the same cloth can recognize in another.

"I won't let him down, Scottie," I declare, breaking the silence. "Or you."

"You—you can't promise that, Grady." Her voice is shaky and her lips are trembling, but it's the fear in her eyes that tells me how fucking vital it is that I prove I'm serious.

Standing tall, I assert, "Yes, I can."

She swallows and then pushes herself off the counter. "I need to get my son home." Walking around me, she heads into the garage. "Chase?"

He looks over his shoulder at her. "Yeah?"

"You're done for the day," I tell him .

"Finally," he mutters, tossing the steel pad into the sink.

"Say thank you to Grady," Scottie warns as Chase pulls the apron from his body.

"For what?"

Scottie glares at her son. "For not putting you in jail!"

He rolls his eyes before walking past me. "Thanks."

Scottie sighs as Chase leaves the garage, not bothering to wait for her. "Same time on Saturday?"

"Yeah. Have you, uh…decided when to tell Chase about the baby?" I hate the sound of desperation in my voice, but keeping this from him is only going to make matter worse.

"Um, not really."

"Well, there's a game tomorrow, so maybe you can tell Chase about the baby on Friday. That way he knows before he comes back on Saturday. Fridays won't work in the future, just an FYI. I have to take my niece to her dance class sometimes on Friday nights for my sister, so Saturdays will work best."

"You're a dance uncle?" Scottie teases.

"And damn proud of it."

Something briefly sparks in her eyes, a glimmer of appreciation maybe, or reverence, but I can't be quite sure because she darts her gaze from mine in a flash and heads back for the office to follow Chase to her car. "Have a good night, Grady."

"Keep growing our kid, Scottie," I call after her.

The smirk she gives me over her shoulder is one I won't soon forget. I've seen it before, and now my mission in life is to make sure that I never have to live without it again.

Chapter Ten

Grady

"Tighten it up!" I call out to Chase on the mound. Our eyes meet and he nods—thank God—taking my coaching seriously. The kid might have a fucking attitude at the garage, but on the field, he's actually fucking listening.

I'll take what I can get.

Chase waits for the call from the catcher. They agree on the pitch, and then he hurls the ball toward home plate, striking out the kid at bat.

"Hell yeah!" Scottie cheers from behind me, and I can't help but laugh at her outburst.

It's our first home game with Chase pitching and me as a coach, and that rush? The thrill of the game, the strategy, and the laser focus it takes to win at baseball? God, I didn't realize how much I fucking missed this.

My gut was right on the money about putting Chase on the mound. The other boys are starting to come around too, as we end the top of the sixth inning, up by seven runs.

"Nice job, kid," Ryan tells Chase as he runs past him into the dugout.

"Thanks, Coach." Chase takes a seat on the bench, chugging from his water bottle as a few of the other players congratulate him.

Ryan turns to me after sending our first player up to bat. "The arm on that kid."

"I fucking know it." Chewing my gum, I watch Ryan call out to the players up to bat. Then murmurs behind me catch my ears.

"Looks like Reynolds found his new protégé," one of the boys mutters from the bench.

"Maybe he'll be able to prove that he's not washed up after all," the kid beside him replies.

I spin on my heels and close the distance between me and the kids, narrowing my eyes at Trent and Jared. Of course it's these two running their mouths.

"You have something to say to me?" I grate out, attempting to rein in my rage because fighting with punk-ass teenagers wasn't on my agenda for the day, let alone my life as a thirty-five-year-old man.

"Nope," Jared snickers, covering his mouth with his hand.

Ryan rushes over to me as the rest of the team crowds around. "What's going on?"

I glare down at the boys. "Nothing."

Chase peers up at me from the bench, his brow furrowed because he must have heard what they said. And I'm sure he's wondering why I didn't say anything back.

Why didn't I tell Ryan how disrespectful and out of touch those boys are with reality?

Because the opinion of a sixteen-year-old boy isn't relevant.

Spinning around, I go back to the edge of the dugout, hanging my hands over the railing while I will my heart to stop racing. I clench my fists together, taking in deep breaths and blowing them out as one of our players gets a double, putting us on base.

"You sure you don't want to tell me what's going on?" Ryan asks, taking his spot beside me again.

"It's not important."

He drops his voice and says, "Jared is a fucking douche."

I twist my head to meet his gaze. "Are you allowed to say that about a kid?"

"I can if it's the truth. His dad is always on him about being the best at the game, and thinks his kid walks on fucking water, but the truth is, he's mediocre. If he practiced as much as he ran his mouth, he'd be a much better ballplayer."

I huff out a laugh and direct my eyes back to the field. "I never thought the hardest criticism I'd face in this position would be from the kids."

"Take it as a compliment. They're in the presence of baseball royalty." He places his hand on my shoulder.

"Ha."

"You're right where you're supposed to be, Grady. And even if the only kid you get through to this year is Chase, your expertise could change that kid's life." I turn to face Ryan again. "All it takes is one person's influence to change the entire path we travel."

Ryan walks away from me to hustle the boys together as we prepare to go back on the field. The pitcher on the other team struck out our next three kids at bat, but we're still ahead with three more innings to play.

As I watch Chase take the mound again, I glance back at Scottie. She's snapping pictures of her son on her phone, smiling. Then she places her phone in her pocket, beaming as she watches him do his thing.

But the pride on her face? It's so mesmerizing that I can barely look away.

I should be watching the game. I should be coaching, which is what I'm here to do.

But all I want to do is watch *her*.

Is that how I'll feel one day watching our kid do something they love? Will the nerves of watching them succeed, intertwined with the fear of seeing them fail, ever go away? What advice will I give my child when they encounter haters like I just did?

The responsibility of my impending fatherhood slams into me for the hundredth time, feeding my own insecurities about my capabilities as a parent. I'm terrified to let my child down, to not say or do the right thing, but I know that Scottie can teach me how to navigate that. Hell, she's a remarkable mother. The love she has for Chase practically oozes from her pores. Her entire life changed when she had him and she instantly fell into that role without a backward glance.

But can I do that too?

I had to walk away from baseball completely because losing it was the worst heartbreak I've ever suffered. Being around it again, though, reminds me of the joy it brought.

And that's what being around Scottie again feels like too.

My eyes find her belly, concealed by her blouse, but I know there's a bump there.

My kid will be here in less than six months. My life will look completely different.

But I'm the one in control of how it looks, right?

For once, that truth radiates from my mind.

I have the choice of where to go from here. For the past five years, I felt the complete opposite. But now, my future is so clear—and it includes Scottie and Chase.

I just hope I don't strike out with no one to blame but myself...again.

***

"Sorry I'm late." My sister comes up next to me as I watch my niece dance through the small glass window in the waiting room for parents. It's Friday night which means I'm on dance duty like Astrid asked me to be, and the truth is, watching Lilly smile and twirl around is exactly the distraction I need right now.

"You're not late. There's still fifteen minutes of class left," I say, pulling my sister into my side and kissing the top of her head.

"For a moment there, I thought I might be. We have so many orders for tomorrow that I felt guilty leaving early, but Tanya assured me she had it under control."

"I could have taken her home if you needed me to."

"I know, but you and I needed to talk anyway, right?" Our eyes meet and she winks up at me.

"Yeah." I blow out a breath. "Outside?"

Astrid's eyes move around the small room filled with people. Other parents are corralling their kids as they play with some toys on the rug in the center of the room, and several other parents are engaged in their own conversations. I don't usually converse with people while I'm here because I'm much more interested in watching Lilly dance. "Probably best."

We exit the room and round the corner of the building, out of sight and earshot. "So, how are things going with Scottie?"

"Well, not much has developed since our appointment on Wednesday, but some things are happening with Chase."

Astrid crosses her arms and draws her brows together. "Like what?" I spend the next few minutes recounting my interactions with him at practice and when he was working at the shop, as well as his performance during the game yesterday. By the time I'm done, emotion is written all over Astrid's face. "God, Grady. My heart hurts for the kid."

"I know."

"I mean, we know what it was like to not have a father around, but we never really remembered what it was like when he was there. His absence was normal. There was no whiplash of wondering if he'd actually show up when he said he would because he was never there to begin with, you know?"

"Yeah."

"And as far as baseball, I think you're right listening to your gut. Hell, you know the game inside and out. If Chase is as good as you say he is, foster that. He will come around, eventually."

"How do you know that?"

She smiles up at me. "Because everyone needs someone to look up to."

"I don't know if I'm the person he should be looking up to…"

She cuts me off. "That's funny. Because I *know* that you are. You're strong, loyal, confident, determined, and hardworking." She pauses, emotion clogging her voice. "That's why *I* look up to you, Grady. And Chase can learn those things from you too."

"Fuck, Astrid." I pull her into my chest, squeezing the shit out of her because I needed to hear that. "Why do you gotta say shit that makes me want to cry?"

She laughs. "I love you. You're the best freaking brother and you're going to be an amazing dad. But I'm pretty sure you're not just worried about this stuff with Chase," she says as we part.

I run my hand through my hair. "I need to wear down Scottie, Astrid," I admit, shaking my head. "She's so fucking stubborn. I can tell she wants me, and the more time we spend together, I know she is what I want, but..."

Astrid puts her hand up to cut me off. "Think about her history, Grady. I mean, look at how Brandon scarred me, how hard it was for me to let Penn in—this man I knew practically my entire life but *still* didn't want to hand over my heart to." Astrid sighs. "It's going to take time. You can't expect for her to change her mind overnight, but if you think she feels the same way, at least you know the battle is worth fighting."

"I'm not a patient man, Astrid."

"You're patient when it matters," she counters with an arched brow. "Is Scottie worth taking things slow?"

"Yes," I reply without hesitation.

"Then show her you're serious. Give her time and let her see that you're not going anywhere."

I nod, taking in her advice. "I can do that."

"Good. Because you're building something real here, Grady. That's worth the wait."

Chapter Eleven

Scottie

"So, how was school?" I push my spaghetti around on my plate, my appetite dissipating the longer I avoid telling my son what I need to. I have no idea how Chase is going to react to the fact that I'm having another child, let alone that the father of his future sibling is Grady.

"It was fine." Chase takes a bite of his garlic bread, keeping his eyes on his plate.

"It's been a few weeks now since we moved. Any classes that you like the most?"

When he finishes chewing, he replies, "I actually really like my math teacher. I mean, math sucks, but she's funny and explains things really well."

"That's great."

"Yeah." Another bout of silence stretches between us as I take one last bite of my pasta and push it to the side. Chase notices that I haven't eaten much and furrows his brow. "You okay, Mom?"

Sighing, I lean back in my chair and clasp my hands together. "Well, yes and no, honey. I—I need to tell you something."

He sets his fork down and wipes his mouth with his napkin. "Okay..."

"I..." *Just say it, Scottie. Rip off the Band-Aid. You're not going to be able to hide it much longer anyway.* "I'm pregnant."

Chase's mouth falls open slightly, but he doesn't say anything. He just stares at me from his seat across the table.

My heart is hammering against my rib cage and my stomach threatens to expel the small amount of dinner I just ate, but then my son practically yells, "When the hell did you have sex?"

"Chase Matthew!" I scold, shocked by his outburst. I definitely wasn't expecting *that* to be his response.

He visibly shudders and then stands from the table, putting distance between us. "You're...you're not..." He groans. "You're my mom!"

Standing from my seat, I cross my arms over my chest. "Yes, I am. But I'm also a woman, and..."

He holds his hands up in the air. "Please, for the love of God, don't say anything else." He closes his eyes and takes a few deep breaths.

"Jesus, I never imagined this being your reaction!"

My son and I had the sex talk about three years ago because I wanted him to hear things from me, not his friends or something online. I was honest with him, letting him know sex isn't just for procreation, but for pleasure too.

And now I feel like that conversation is coming back to bite me in the ass.

"I'm sorry, Mom," he finally says on a sigh. "But..."

"Look, I know it's hard for you right now to look past *how* this happened, but the fact of the matter is, you're going to have a little brother or sister in September, Chase."

That information sinks in quickly, and he rushes back over to me, pulling me in for a hug. My son is two inches taller than me, and I know he's not done growing. It feels so odd feeling dwarfed by him in this moment, but I'm grateful that he's able to comfort me because I've been in knots keeping this from him, and this baby isn't just changing my life. It's going to change his too.

"I always wanted a sibling," he mutters as he squeezes me.

"Sorry it's happening so late," I counter sarcastically, which makes him laugh. But then I remember that I have one more detail he needs to know. I separate myself from him and then look up into his eyes. "There's something else, though, Chase."

"What is it?"

"The father…" I start, inhaling deeply before his eyes bug out as if he didn't think about that piece of information. "It's Grady."

Chase's face falls and then his spine straightens. "Are you serious?"

"Yes, which made your break-in at his garage all the more complicated."

Chase takes a step back from me. "Does he know?"

"Uh-huh." I watch the wheels spin in my son's head as he walks from side to side, wearing a line in the carpet. "I didn't find out until that day that you broke in to his garage, but I told him the day after."

"And you've been keeping this from me all this time?" he says, his voice rising.

"Don't yell at *me*, Chase! You shouldn't have been anywhere near that garage in the first place!"

"It wasn't my idea!"

"It doesn't matter," I counter, lowering my voice once more. "You were the one that did the damage and went along with the idea, so you are guilty, a lesson that I hope you freaking learned from. You don't have to be in charge to still reap the consequences of a choice."

"And what about the consequences of having sex? Shouldn't you have used protection when you and Grady..." he trails off, shaking his head and visibly shuttering.

"We did! We did and it still failed!" I shout back, even though I never imagined sharing this much detail about how his sibling was conceived. "But let this be a lesson to you too that things don't always work, even when you prepare for them. And maybe in the future, you should use two condoms anytime you choose to have sex!"

Uh, not sure this is the time to give your son advice, Scottie.

Chase plants his hands on his hips, as if *he's* the parent that's disappointed in *me* right now. "So what does this mean? Are you two getting married?"

"No," I reply instantly. "No. We're just friends. We knew each other a long time ago in high school and now we're having this baby together, but we are not romantically involved."

"You don't want that?"

Well, there's another thing I didn't think we'd be talking about.

"I..." As I try to find the right words, Chase's eyebrows draw together. "I'm trying to keep things as uncomplicated as I can. I don't want another situation like with your dad."

My son's jaw flexes tight. "So what happens now?"

I close the distance between us and take his hand. "We keep doing what we're doing, and in a little less than six months, there will be a new baby to love on."

"And what about Grady?"

"He and I are figuring out how things are going to work between us. He wants to be involved in his kid's life and I'm not going to deny him that opportunity."

Chase rolls his eyes. "Yeah, we'll see how long that lasts."

My heart breaks in that moment for my son, for his tumultuous relationship with his own father, the one that has jaded him so deeply that he doesn't feel that he can trust men.

"Grady isn't like your father, Chase."

"Not now, maybe. But…"

"No. He won't ever be," I say, more resolutely than I feel because I can't have Chase discounting the man Grady is already. I know he has his own feelings toward him given their complicated relationship, but as his sibling's father, he can't think that way or say those things out loud. I don't want this child to hurt like Chase has, and I'm going to try to do everything I can to make sure that doesn't happen, including keeping my feelings for Grady locked up tight.

"What I need from you is to just keep working off your punishment, do what Grady says on and off the baseball field, and focus on yourself. Don't worry about what's going on between him and me. Anything we decide, we will let you know, okay?"

"I don't get a say in anything?"

I swallow hard. "If it affects you, then yes, of course you'll have a voice in the matter."

He scoffs but nods. "Fine."

"I'm sorry this happened. I'm sorry our fresh start is more complicated than I hoped it would be."

Chase pulls me in for another hug. "It's okay, Mom. This is a surprise, for sure, but…it might be kind of cool to have a little baby around."

The warmth in his voice eases some of the tension in my chest just slightly. "I love you. Having you come into my life was the most incredible thing I've ever experienced. I know this baby is only going to amplify the love in our lives." I look up at him. "You are the most important person in my life, Chase, and that won't ever change. Now

I get to make another child the center of my world, and I'm scared but excited too."

"I can't believe you had sex," he mutters, making us both laugh.

"One day you'll understand. There will be someone you're drawn to in a way you can't quite explain."

We part and, suddenly, memories of Grady and me from high school come flooding back.

It was always there—this connection I feel to him. But we're all grown up now, and the stakes are so much higher.

"I have some homework to finish," Chase says, pulling me from my inner turmoil.

"You're doing homework on a Friday night?" I ask as he carries his plate to the sink.

"Yeah, that way I don't have to worry about it on Sunday. I'm pretty sure that after working at Grady's tomorrow, I'm going to be beat."

I stop him before he retreats down the hallway. "I'm proud of you, you know."

He scoffs. "Why? I did something really freaking stupid, Mom. I still can't believe that I listened to them." His gaze drifts off to the side of the room as he shakes his head. "I just wanted to fit in. I didn't want to feel like an outsider again."

God how I wish I could take away his pain and convince him that things get so much better after high school. He has so much talent, which has always caused problems on any team he's played on. But I hoped it would be different here.

I lift his chin and direct his gaze back to mine. "I'm proud of you because, even though you made a poor choice, you're taking the right steps to learn from it. That's all I can hope for as you grow into a young man. Own your mistakes and strive not to repeat them."

He nods and heads to his room, leaving me alone to consider my own words. I keep telling myself this is the same reason to keep my distance from Grady.

I just wish that my heart would get the message too.

***

"I'm sorry Jaxon is struggling with the divorce." Mr. and Mrs. Harrison sit on the opposite side of my desk, trying to hold a united front in this meeting despite the animosity I can sense between them. "But throwing a chair across the room is unacceptable behavior."

"My son is upset. I don't know what else to do," Mrs. Harrison says, glaring at her husband. "I mean, if my husband hadn't slept with his secretary, we wouldn't be in this mess in the first place!"

"Jesus, Tiffany," Mr. Harrison grates out. "This isn't the time or the place to bring that up."

"Why not? Your indiscretions are why our family is being torn apart!" Her voice carries in my small office, and suddenly, I fear that the point of this meeting is being lost.

I sympathize with the woman, I do. But mediating divorces is not part of my job description. My job is to hold the students at Carrington Cove Elementary accountable for their behavior and celebrate their wins with them.

"Look, I know things are tough right now, but what Jaxon needs is stability. Here at school, there is only so much we can do for him, especially if his behavior is endangering the safety of students and staff." I slide a paper across the desk toward them. "This is the behavior contract we will be implementing, and here is a copy of the suspension paperwork," I add, handing them another paper from the folder.

"Our seven-year-old is getting suspended! Are you happy with yourself?" Mrs. Harrison shouts at her soon-to-be ex-husband, launching from her chair, slinging her purse over her shoulder, and storming out of my office.

Mr. Harrison releases a long breath. "I'm sorry you had to hear all of that."

"It's okay." *But I secretly wish I could tell you what I really feel about you. Jackass.* "But my biggest concern is your son. We care about Jaxon and want to give him the best shot at being successful, but his behavior cannot continue like this."

Mr. Harrison nods as he stands. "I understand. Thank you for your time."

As I watch him leave, I slump back in my chair and let out the breath I'd been holding. Just being around that energy dredges up memories of my own divorce—how Andrew tried to shift the blame, how Chase acted out at first when he realized his dad wasn't coming home anymore—though, those last few years, Andrew was hardly around anyway.

I close my eyes and rub my stomach, feeling a bubble-like sensation move across my belly. My memory of feeling Chase move for the first time while pregnant with him is fuzzy, but my body remembers it well.

"Hey there, little one," I whisper, peering down at my growing bump that is becoming more difficult to hide. I know they say you show faster with your second pregnancy, but I was hoping I'd get at least a few more weeks before needing a new wardrobe. My old maternity clothes are long gone, and even if they weren't, they wouldn't be in fashion now, given that my last pregnancy was fifteen years ago.

The moment of nostalgia is interrupted by the buzz of my phone vibrating across the desk, flashing Andrew's name. I hit ignore, not caring if he knows I sent him to voicemail, and then wake up my computer, anxious to catch up on emails. His calls are becoming more frequent, which can only mean one thing.

But a knock on the door stops me before my thoughts can wander too far.

"Come in."

The man who walks in is the last person I expected to see—and definitely not someone I should be this pleased to see.

"What—what are you doing here?"

"Are you busy?" Grady asks as he enters my office, making it feel way smaller than it is. He's dressed in blue jeans and a plain olive-green shirt, his light brown hair freshly cut. My ovaries jump for joy at his appearance, but my brain whips them back into submission, reminding my entire nervous system that we aren't allowed to react to him like that.

"Uh, well..." I start, but he doesn't wait for me to finish, taking a seat on the other side of my desk. "I'm—I'm working, Grady."

"I know. I just..." He lifts the bag he's carrying and places it on my desk. "I brought you some stuff I thought you could use."

I arch a brow at him. "I didn't ask you to do that."

He glares at me. "I know you didn't, Scottie. I'm taking care of you, like I said I would."

My brain wants to protest further, but my heart lurches at his gesture. And at that exact moment, I feel that flutter of bubbles move across my belly, as if our baby is aware of its daddy's presence.

I reach for the bag and peer inside, puzzled by the assortment of items it contains.

"I finished my second book," he says as I start extracting items and placing them on the desk.

"What the hell was this book about?"

"How to care for your pregnant wife."

My eyes snap up to meet his. "But I'm not…"

"My wife. I know, Scottie," he says a little too harshly, but I let it slide. "But you are carrying my child, which means I'm still responsible for you. So, I brought you a few things to make work easier as you get bigger."

Rolling my eyes at the reminder that my waistline is expanding by the minute, I pull an apple fritter from the bag and inhale the aroma of sugar and cinnamon. "Nice touch."

"I thought that might make you happy. You're still craving them?"

I don't want to admit that I've eaten five of them this week, but I'm sure Astrid already told him. "Yeah, that hasn't changed, thankfully."

"Good. The other things should help with aches and pains."

I stare at the heat patches, eucalyptus oil, cushions for my shoes, and pregnancy herbal tea. "This is…"

"There's also a book for *you* to read," he adds as I pull out the book and fight the urge to roll my eyes again.

"The big book of baby names?"

"Yup. I already have some ideas, but I figured I'd let you do some research of your own before we have that discussion."

A wave of emotion comes over me. "You—you have names picked out?" How does this man manage to surprise me at every turn?

"A few, but I'm open to compromising."

Suddenly, I'm reminded of how many discussions we've yet to have about our child and everything that comes next. This man went out of his way to *bring* me things, *say* the right things, and make me *feel* things—and that's a big fucking problem.

The reality of it all hits me, and I quickly shove everything back into the bag, eager to get space from him. "Well, thank you for this, but I really wish you would have waited until I wasn't at work."

His brow furrows. "Is it a problem that I'm here?"

"I just..." I scoff, gesturing around the office. "I'm working, Grady! I've had a shitty day and it's only halfway over. I just had to suspend a second grader for throwing a chair in the classroom, and I have another parent meeting later about a bullying situation with our sixth graders." I place the bag in the corner of my office by my bookshelf. "This isn't the place for pregnancy talk, or..."

He clears his throat as he stands. "Fine. I get it. It won't happen again."

I can see the hurt lurking under the surface of his deep blue eyes, but he has to understand that there are boundaries. We're not together. This is something that a boyfriend or husband would do, and he is neither of those things.

But God, what would it be like if he were?

"Thank you."

"But you need to understand something, Scottie," he says, moving closer to me instead of the door. When he's only a few inches from me, he tips my chin up with two of his fingers and places his other hand on my bump, drawing a gasp from me.

It's the first time he's touched me—while pregnant, that is—and my body is eager for more instantly. A wave of security wafts through me, like I can let my guard down just because he's near.

But the truth is, he's the person I need it for the most.

"You can pretend like you are mad at me for being here, but I think you're just scared to accept my help and care," he says, making me feel like he can see right through me. "All I keep wondering is if I'm doing enough for you, if there's something you need that I can give you because I feel helpless in this situation, and I *hate* that fucking feeling. I can't grow our kid, Scottie." He shakes his head with a pinch in his brow. "I can't fucking help you with that, but I *can* take care of you, so that's what I'm going to do. And you. Can't. Stop. Me." He punctuates the last four words, making his point clear. "You need ice cream at midnight? Text me. You want your feet rubbed after a long day? I'll be at your house in fifteen minutes. And if you need anything else to help you relax," he says with a suggestive smirk, "I can help with that too." Licking his lips, he drops his eyes to my mouth and then back up to my gaze before saying, "Eagerly."

My knees threaten to buckle and my mouth gets dry before I swallow hard to coat my throat. I dart out my tongue to lick my lips, hating how his eyes dip right to the sight again, making me wish he'd just kiss me, toss me onto my desk, and fuck me into next week.

The hormones are increasing in my body at an alarming rate. I knew it earlier this week when I whipped out my vibrator and got myself off twice before I passed out the other night.

"Thank you," I say instead, knowing he at least deserves that from me.

The corner of his mouth lifts and then he takes a step back, satisfied with himself and the law he just laid down. "You're welcome. I'll see you tomorrow?"

"Yeah, at six. Chase will be there." Tomorrow is Wednesday, so my son is scheduled to work at the garage again. It seems to be working out well around his baseball practices and games, the last of which they won last night.

"Okay. See you then."

Grady leaves my office finally, giving me a moment to breathe before Alaina comes sauntering in. "Uh, was that Grady Reynolds?"

"Yeah." I sigh, moving back to my seat as I plop down in my chair, rubbing my stomach again.

"What was he doing here?" she asks, looking borderline starstruck. And I guess when a former MLB player moves back to the small town he grew up in, he is a little like a celebrity.

"Grady is my baby's father," I reply, gesturing to my bump.

Alaina's eyes go wide. "Damn, girl."

"Yeah. We, uh, were good friends in high school, and now…"

Alaina smirks. "So I take it he's taking his role in all of this seriously?"

"Ha. Yeah, a little too seriously." I point to the bag on the floor. "He dropped off a care package."

"Jesus. Marry him, Scottie," she declares, catching me off guard before snapping her fingers. "Marry him right now."

"What?"

"You'd be crazy not to. I mean, do you know how many single women in this town throw themselves at him every day?"

Just the mention of other women going after Grady has my pulse spiking. "Are you serious?"

"Oh yeah. It's embarrassing, really. I once saw him in the grocery store, and some woman ran her cart into a display of soda, knocking the entire thing over because I swear, she was trying to do the bend and snap from Legally Blonde to catch his attention."

I snort, and not in a classy way. Once I get ahold of myself, I reply, "I'm not going to marry the man just because I'm pregnant, Alaina." *Been there, done that.*

She fakes a pout. "But you'd be living out the dream."

"What dream?"

"The one where you marry the guy who was always just your friend, who also happens to be a famous former athlete, and is smoking hot, and then knocked you up one hot, steamy night together, tying you to one another for all eternity when you were really meant to be together all along."

I laugh at her. "That's the dream?"

"I mean, it's a mix of a few, for sure." She shrugs with a smile on her lips.

"My goal is to keep things as simple as I can, and that means no feelings and no marrying Grady."

Her lips curl up into a knowing grin. "Fine. But I'll tell you this—any man that stops by your work to bring you a care package so you're comfortable while you're carrying his child...is *not* a man that just wants to be your *friend*." With an arch of her brow, she exits my office and leaves my mind spinning even more than it already was.

I try to get back to work, try to focus on my job, but it's useless, especially as I inhale the apple fritter for lunch, and glance back at pictures on my phone from Chase's game yesterday.

Most of them are of my son, but I'm ashamed to say I snapped a few of Grady too—his baseball cap covering his eyes, his arms bulging against the sleeves of his jersey, his strong hands clapping as the boys made plays and smoked the other team.

A bolt of lust travels down my spine and straight between my legs as I scroll back through those pictures, but then a warmth spreads through my chest when I realize how extraordinary his gesture was, just like Alaina said.

I do *want* Grady. I'm fully aware of that.

But I don't *need* him to take care of me—because if he does, I'll start wanting more. And wanting something I can't have will only complicate this already tricky situation.

Chapter Twelve

Grady

"So, what do you guys think?" Dallas asks from the other side of the bar as Penn, Parker, and I all try the new burger he's thinking about putting on the menu. It's a classic beef patty with a potato cake on top that's a cross between a jalapeño popper and a hash brown. The outside is fried in a flaky batter, and the inside has mashed potatoes mixed with diced jalapeños and gooey, cheddar cheese. It's making me wish I was alone so I could properly appreciate it without judgment.

The moan of approval I let out is borderline embarrassing. "Fucking delicious," I say around a mouthful of food.

"You've got a winner here, brother." Penn echoes my sentiment.

"I would give up sex if I could eat this every day," Parker adds, drawing all our attention his way.

Penn wipes his mouth with his napkin. "Uh, I don't know about that."

Dallas stares at his youngest brother with confusion as well. "Yeah. There's no food I would choose over sex with Willow."

Parker glares at both of his brothers while I keep my mouth shut. I'm not having regular sex, that's for sure. But if I had the opportunity to fuck Scottie anytime she wanted, I would give up all food for the rest of my life.

"Thanks for rubbing in the fact that you both are getting laid regularly." Parker takes another bite, grumbling around his food.

"In a bit of a dry spell?" I ask, knowing how rough that can be. At one point, even your hand will start to think that you're pathetic.

"You could say that."

"You have that conference in New York coming up though, don't you?" Penn interjects. "Maybe you'll get lucky on your trip, turn that frown of yours upside down." He pokes his brother in the cheek as Parker swats him away.

Dallas and I share a laugh before he clears his throat. "Uh, not to shift away from Parker's lackluster love life, but I wanted to make sure you're all going to be at Willow's birthday party next Saturday. I'm trying to get a head count for the food."

Penn and Parker nod in unison. "You know Astrid and I will be there," Penn says. Astrid and Willow are best friends, so there's no way they'd miss it.

"I'm leaving the office early that day so I can make it on time," Parker adds.

Dallas turns his attention to me. "You coming?"

I take a sip of my Coke before replying. "Yup. I've had it on my calendar for months."

"What about Scottie?" Dallas asks as he wipes down the bar. "Are you gonna bring her?"

"I mean, I hadn't thought about it."

Penn shoves my shoulder, grinning. "This is your opportunity to introduce her to everyone!" he teases.

"I don't know if she can go, but I'll ask her." Hell, if I had it my way, she'd be going as my significant other, but I'm still working on changing our relationship status. One day at a time.

"How are things going with you two?" Dallas asks.

"They're...going." I blow out a sigh of frustration.

Penn winces. "That good, huh?"

I wipe my hands on my napkin and toss it onto my empty plate, the burger completely gone. "I don't know, guys. If I had it my way, Scottie would have a ring on her finger and would already be moved into my house."

Parker's eyes bug out. "Fuck. Really? Marriage already?"

Penn gives his brother a pointed look. "Not everyone is against marriage, little brother."

Dallas chuckles, but Parker glares back at Penn. "Well, get fucked over by your fiancée, and you'd be against it too."

"Anyway," I interject, steering the conversation back on track. "Like I said, I want that, but Scottie doesn't."

"That's what she said?"

"More or less, but I know she has feelings for me too."

Parker groans. "Oh god, are we gonna have to watch you two tiptoe around each other for years like Penn and Astrid did before they finally admitted their fucking feelings?"

Penn shoves his brother off his stool as Dallas shrugs. "Parker does have a point, Penn."

"We fucking figured out our shit, okay? But our situation was much more complicated." Penn turns to me now. "Did she give you a reason why she won't give you a chance?"

"I mean, she doesn't want to ruin our friendship, for one. But I feel like after we slept together, nothing was going to be the same again anyway."

"Valid point," Dallas says.

"But I have a feeling a lot of it has to do with her ex-husband."

Dallas winces. "Ex-husband drama can be complicated."

"Is he in the picture still?" Penn asks.

"I honestly don't know. I know he was a shitty father who let his son down a lot." But there's something else that she's not telling me, and I haven't been able to figure it out yet.

"How are things going with the kid?" Dallas asks.

"The kid has a chip on his shoulder, that's for damn sure," I reply. "But I don't blame him. When he's on the baseball field, though, he and I get along just fine. He's fucking talented as hell." The corner of my mouth lifts. "Reminds me a lot of myself at that age."

"Nice," Penn says.

"But at the garage, it's a different story. He doesn't want to listen and is clearly pissed about being there. I get it, but I was thinking maybe if I get him to help me fix up the car, he might not see it as a complete waste of time, and it could give us a chance to get to know each other better."

Penn nods. "That's a good idea, Grady. Especially because you're still going to be in his life once your kid is born."

"Exactly."

"I remember trying to bond with Bentley after Brandon died. Granted, Bentley was a lot younger than Chase and already knew me, but it was still tough. One day when I corrected something he did, he got mad and told me that I wasn't his dad." Penn shakes his head. "It fucking killed me because I know how badly he wishes Brandon were still here, but since he isn't, all I could do was explain that it's okay to have other role models in your life."

Penn's words force me to swallow down the lump in my throat because I know that feeling well. Mr. Rogers was the man I looked up to in so many ways, and he taught me everything I know about cars. If it weren't for him, I probably would have gotten in a lot more trouble as a kid and I wouldn't have had something to keep me sane after losing baseball.

"So, you think the car thing could help?"

Penn nods firmly. "Yes. He's going to push back, of course, but for every push he gives, you just push back harder. He'll come around."

Dallas chimes in. "We see it a lot with the boys we coach, Grady." Dallas and Penn coach a soccer team each year in the fall. Most of the boys on the team have fathers in the service, so they aren't around for large stretches of time. I can't imagine having a dad who comes in and out of your life like that. It makes me grateful that at least mine left and never returned because suffering that whiplash could be even harder to fucking deal with.

"Okay. I'll give it a shot."

Parker, who'd been silent during this discussion, clears his throat dramatically. "Well, now that you three have a plan for how you're going to save the world, one broken boy at a time, I gotta get back to work." He starts to stand from his chair, but Penn grabs his shirt by the collar and yanks him to his chest. "What the—"

Seething, Penn grates out, "Just because you've written off having a family doesn't mean you get to mock ours."

Dallas and I stand, ready to break them up if need be.

Parker glares up at his brother. "Jesus, calm down."

Penn shakes Parker slightly. "No, you need to watch your fucking mouth, Parker. Raising another man's kid is fucking hard. Putting their needs before your own is a noble fucking thing. And maybe you should consider that you're also one of those broken boys inside, too scared to let anyone in because you were hurt once."

Parker clenches his jaw. "Fuck you, Penn."

"Right back at you, brother."

"Okay." Dallas rounds the bar and steps between the two of them, pulling Penn's hands from Parker's shirt. "That's enough."

Penn steps back, but his anger remains palpable. "He needs to watch his fucking mouth. Just because he's unhappy with his life, doesn't mean he gets to talk down to us about ours."

After a few tension-filled moments, Parker pulls his wallet from his pocket, tosses down some cash, and glares at all three of us. "I don't need this shit," he says, turning and walking out of the restaurant.

"You know he isn't going to be able to move past his shit until he's ready to," Dallas says to his brother.

"I don't care. I said what I needed to say to him." Penn throws a twenty-dollar bill on the bar and then drains the rest of his drink. "I need to get back to work." Penn exits the restaurant just as quickly as his younger brother did.

"Well, that turned sour quickly."

Dallas looks at me. "Parker has been in a fucking mood for months. Penn and I think it has a lot to do with how we've changed our lives for the women we love. He had that once, and…"

"Yeah, I know."

Dallas runs a hand through his short, black hair. "I hate seeing him so jaded. He wasn't like this before Sasha fucking betrayed him."

"Something like that would change any person, Dallas."

He looks me dead in the eye. "I know, and I'm afraid it will prevent him from ever trusting another woman."

His words strike me right in the chest. "Fuck, that's it."

"What?"

I reach for my wallet, throw a few bills on the counter, and shove it back in my pocket. "Nothing. You just made me realize something I wasn't seeing before."

"Okay..."

"I've got to go," I say as my mind starts spinning.

"Glad everyone was in a hurry to leave today," he murmurs behind me as I exit the restaurant and head back to the garage, realizing that what Scottie needs is a reason to trust me, proof that she can count on me, and so does Chase. At least now I have a better idea of how to make them both see that I'm not here to hurt them.

In fact, it's quite the opposite.

I want to give them each what they need and deserve—someone to trust if they fall, because falling in life is inevitable, and I refuse to let them feel like they're alone anymore.

***

Sitting in my recliner, flipping through the pages of my third book about pregnancy and becoming a father, I listen to this week's MLB highlights in the background, stifling a yawn. It's crazy to think there was a time when I was on that television, my face plastered on the screen during these same highlights. Now, I'm coaching kids who have no idea how much work and determination it takes to get to that point and preparing to be a father, while the woman carrying my baby is pretending she doesn't have feelings for me.

My, how things have changed.

The conversation at Catch & Release between me and the Sheppard boys keeps playing on repeat in my head. When Dallas said he feared his brother wouldn't trust another woman again, it made me realize that I had been walking around feeling the same way—that is until Scottie walked back into my life. That's how I know that fighting for her is worth it. She's the only woman I've ever wanted to fight for, so

I've spent the entire day thinking about how I can help her see that she doesn't need to fear the future we could share. She just has to give us a shot.

My phone vibrates on the coffee table, and when I see who the text message is from, a lightning bolt of adrenaline races through me. I close the book, set it on the table, and pick up my phone to read the message.

Scottie: *Does that offer to fulfill my cravings still stand?*

I sit up in my chair eagerly, holding my phone between my knees as I type out my response.

Me: *Absolutely. What do you need?*

Scottie: *An orange popsicle.*

Me: *That's very specific.*

Scottie: *No commentary needed. Can you bring me a box or not?*

Me: *Your wish is my command, babe. Be there soon.*

I launch from my chair, change into a pair of clean jeans, slap a ball cap on my head, grab my keys, and head for the grocery store. Scottie's request tells me she's letting me in, albeit in a small way, but still. I'll take it.

I race through the store to the freezer section and grab the first box of orange popsicles I see—the classic Big Stick variety, a favorite I remember from the days of chasing down the ice cream truck in my neighborhood. I pay for the treats and then try not to speed as I cross town and pull into Scottie's driveway.

The curtains on her mother's front window move, drawing my attention over there as I get out of my truck. I'm sure her mom knows about our situation, but I'm curious what her thoughts are and wonder if maybe she can talk some sense into her daughter.

One obstacle at a time, Grady.

As I knock on Scottie's door, the bag rustles in my hand, stirred by the breeze sweeping across the front porch. The door swings open, and there's Scottie, stealing the breath from my lungs and making my dick ache, longing to show her just what she does to him.

She's fresh from the shower, wearing an oversized gray t-shirt and navy sleep shorts, with her hair wrapped in a towel. Her skin is glowing, her feet are bare, her toenails painted a soft yellow, and I can see her small bump just underneath her shirt.

Mine.

"Special delivery for Scottie Daniels," I announce, holding up the bag. She motions for me to come in while I simultaneously will my dick to calm down.

A heavy sigh of relief escapes her as she smiles. "Thank you, Grady. I can't explain why these sounded so good, but when my brain locked onto these, I couldn't think of anything else." I follow her into the kitchen, and she takes the bag from me, setting it on the counter. "When I was pregnant with Chase I had the same craving. Maybe it means I'm having another boy."

"That might be true, but all the books say every pregnancy is different." She takes the box of popsicles out of the bag and her face falls. "What's wrong?" I ask.

Her eyes stay locked on the box of Big Sticks for so long that I'm afraid she's fallen asleep with her eyes open. But when they finally meet mine, they're full of tears. I react immediately, closing the distance between us. "Shit, Scottie. Are you okay?"

She brushes a tear away. "Um, yeah. I just..."

"What?"

"These aren't the ones I wanted," she cries, sobbing into her hands, falling apart right in front of me.

I have no idea what to do in this moment except pull her into my chest. "Fuck. I'm—I'm sorry."

Her words are muffled as she buries her head in my chest. "I wanted the ones with the two sticks, you know?" She pushes back from me, gesturing with her hands as if holding a popsicle with two sticks. Tears flow down her cheeks and snot drips from her nose.

"Why didn't you say that?" I ask, bewildered by the intensity of her reaction.

"You should have just known!" she yells back at me, shocking me. "You're supposed to know!"

I hold my hands up in surrender, not sure what else I'm supposed to do. Here I was thinking I was saving the day, being of use like I told her I wanted to be, but I wasn't prepared for this reaction. "Scottie..."

She stands there, shaking her head. "I'm sorry, I just..."

I pull her gently back into my arms. "Everything's going to be okay," I murmur. Before she can say anything else, I decide that maybe a distraction is what she needs. So that's what I give her. I tip her chin up so I can look into her tear-filled eyes, and then I slant my mouth over hers, swallowing her gasp.

But then, without a moment's hesitation, she wraps her arms around my neck and meets my tongue thrust for thrust, moaning and burying her hands in my hair, knocking my hat off my head in the process.

I back her up into the fridge, knocking something off the top of it, but it doesn't faze us. My cock presses against my jeans, begging to be let free just as I reach down and pick up her leg, wrapping it around my waist. She pushes her pussy against my cock, rubbing herself along every inch of me she can reach as we grasp for one another, with so much tension and need in the kiss that it feels like we couldn't have stopped this if we tried.

It's magnetic, this pull between us. We're two polar opposites that have no choice but to be drawn toward one another. But as soon as I run my hand up the inside of her thigh, wanting to feel her and make her come more than my next breath, she shoves me away, both of our chests heaving.

"Scottie..."

Her hand comes up to her mouth, covering it as her wide eyes stare up at me. "What the hell, Grady?" Her next words come out as a whisper, while my heart hammers so wildly that I can hear it in my ears. "Why did you do that?"

"I didn't know how else to calm you down," I admit, even though kissing her felt instinctual, just like taking care of her does.

Her voice is shaky. "You—you shouldn't have done that."

"It didn't seem to bother you while you were kissing me back," I counter, which was a very bad idea.

Her eyes narrow into slits, but before she can fire something back at me, Chase rounds the corner. His eyes dart between us, picking up on the intensity as we stand just a few feet apart.

"I heard a noise and came out here to see what was going on," he says. "Is everything okay?"

I turn away from him, grabbing my hat from the floor while trying to hide the erection still pressing against my pants. Scottie rips the towel from her head, tossing it onto the counter before wiping under her eyes where tear streaks still glisten in the florescent lights.

"I'm fine," she says, plastering a fake-as-shit smile on her face.

"Why are you crying, Mom?"

"I brought the wrong damn popsicles," I grumble, looking over my shoulder at Chase, who is growing more concerned by the minute.

"Popsicles?"

"Yeah," Scottie manages to say, finding her voice again. "But it's okay. The baby just wanted a specific kind..."

Chase rolls his eyes. "Another man making her cry. Doesn't surprise me."

"Hey!" Scottie snaps, chastising her son.

"You're pregnant with his kid and he's making you cry!" Chase points accusingly at me. "Not a good sign, Mom."

"Chase Matthew!"

If I wasn't so thrown off right now, I'd say something to defend myself. But ultimately, there's only one way to fix this. I turn back around now that my dick has calmed down and grab my keys from my pocket. "I'll be right back."

"Grady!" Scottie calls out to me, but I'm already heading out the door, needing some space to clear my head.

"I'll be back with the right popsicles, Scottie," I say, closing the door behind me. I fix my ball cap as I walk back to my truck, wondering how the fuck one simple errand turned into attacking this woman with my mouth and wishing I could do it again.

By the time I return with the correct popsicles, it's after nine. Scottie opens the door, her expression guarded as I step inside. She doesn't even bother opening the bag I hand her.

We just stare at each other across the island, waiting for the other person to speak first. Luckily, she breaks first. "I'm sorry, Grady."

"No, I am." I blow out a breath, tossing my hat onto the counter beside the bag. "When the cashier noticed I was back again for more popsicles, she said next time I should send you a picture to make sure it's exactly what you want. Apparently, it's a very common first-time-dad mistake."

A small smile graces her lips. "I'm sure. But my reaction was a little..."

I raise my hand to stop her. "You're fine, Scottie. I told you that I'd never let you down, and I did, so all I was trying to do was fix it."

She bites her bottom lip, uncertainty in her eyes. "I don't usually cry over popsicles, Grady. It's just the hormones, and my heart was set on the ones with the two sticks." She holds up two fingers like a peace sign. "It really wasn't a big deal, but in the moment, it felt like it was."

I slide the bag closer to her. "Then eat one, Scottie, so we'll both feel better, and then I think we need to talk."

She nods, pulling a popsicle out, discarding the plastic wrapper in the trash, and then sucking on the frozen treat, closing her eyes and moaning as she does.

My dick instantly gets excited again over the sound, but the last thing I should do is mark this woman with my mouth again.

"So good," she moans as her lips stretch over the orange ice, and suddenly I'm transported back to the night when her lips were stretched around my dick.

Fuck. "I'm glad it's what you wanted."

"You're really sweet for going back out and getting these, especially after how I reacted."

"Anything to make you stop crying."

Glaring at me, she takes a seat in a big, cushioned chair in her living room. I plop myself onto the couch. "I want you to know that I yelled at Chase after you left."

"He's not my biggest fan, and I'm sure now that he knows about the baby, it's only going to take more time for him to come around."

"He never should have said those things to you." Her eyes drift toward the hallway. "I don't know what's gotten into him."

"He doesn't trust me yet. Neither of you do," I say, echoing my thoughts from earlier today.

Scottie's tongue freezes as she eats her popsicle. "What do you mean?"

Knowing that I have to push her, have to get her to open up to me, I ask the question that's been on my mind. "What happened with your ex, Scottie?"

She swallows hard and lowers the popsicle, a trickle of juice sliding down her wrist. "I..."

"I need to know what I'm up against. I want to know about your past to avoid making the same mistakes—for you *and* Chase."

Tears well in her eyes. "Why are you so concerned about that?"

Leaning forward, I reach for her hand, stroking the top of it with my thumb. "Because I'm not going anywhere, and the last thing I want is resentment in our family."

She can deny it all she wants, but she and Chase are my family now—by blood, and hopefully one day, by choice. I know she's not there yet, but hopefully she will be soon, especially if our kiss was any indication of the sexual tension lurking beneath the surface.

Her eyes fall to the melting popsicle in her hand before she stands from the couch and races to the sink, dropping the popsicle and washing her hands. I can see the tremble in her limbs as she returns, sitting back in her chair and nervously figuring out what to say.

"I told you Chase hasn't had the best example of a man to look up to. His dad preferred strip clubs and other women over spending time with his own family. The straw that broke the camel's back for me was when he took my son to the Gl-Ass Company, his favorite strip club, and left him in the car for two hours before he remembered he brought him."

"Jesus Christ." I run a hand through my hair.

"Yeah, he's a piece of work, and the last person I want my son to be around. Chase saw me cry too many times, saw us yell at each other a lot, especially toward the end when I finally stood my ground." She stares off to the side of the room. "I should have left sooner, and I hate myself for not."

"You can't blame yourself for someone else's actions, Scottie. You did leave, which took courage, and that's what matters."

She brushes a tear from her cheek. "Yeah, but now my son..." She shakes her head. "He needs you, Grady." Her admission shocks me.

So, I'm good enough to be a role model to her son, but not good enough to be her partner?

Remember what your sister said, Grady. She's been hurt and is obviously placing a lot of blame on herself. Cut her some slack and keep pushing for what you want.

"I'm not a saint, Scottie."

"No, and I never said you were. But you're loyal, honest, and hardworking. That's all I want Chase to aspire to be."

"He has to get used to me being around. We're going to be a family, whether you and I are together or not. I was thinking...what if he helped me fix up the Nova?"

The corner of her mouth lifts. "I think he'd like that."

"I think so too, if he could dial back his attitude long enough to actually listen to me." I shake my head, leaning back into the cushion. "I don't know how you deal with that every day."

"Being a parent is tough. There are days when I feel like I'm nailing it, and many more when I feel like I'm failing. Before I had Chase, my mistakes were my own, but as a mother, I constantly wonder how my choices are going to affect my son. It's exhausting."

"I don't want to fail my kid," I admit on a whisper, hoping she understands that she's not the only one struggling. And fuck, I just want us to struggle together.

Does that make me a sap?

No, that makes me a man who knows what he wants—to actually be vulnerable with a woman for the first time in my life.

"You won't—*because* you care about that. The only thing you can do is keep trying, Grady."

"Keep trying?" I ask, and then continue before I can think twice. "With Chase, or with you, Scottie?"

Her eyes widen and she slinks back, clearing her throat when she realizes my meaning. "You—you can't kiss me again, Grady."

I scoff. "If you think I'm done kissing you, you've got another thing coming, babe."

"I'm serious."

I lean forward so she can see straight into my eyes when I say, "So am I." Her breathing grows shallow again, and all I can think about is our kiss from earlier. But when she remains silent, I hit her with another thought. "I think our moms should meet."

"What?"

"I mean, I'm sure they know each other to some extent, but since this baby will join us all together, it would be nice for us all to sit down and share a meal, you know? Practice for the holidays and stuff."

She closes her eyes and sighs. "Yeah, I guess that will be something to talk about moving forward, huh?"

I smirk in her direction before I stand. "Yeah, we have a lot of things to talk about, Scottie."

She peers up at me, licking her lips. "Anything I should be prepared for?"

"Nothing you don't already know but are too afraid to address."

***

Chase wipes the sweat from his forehead as I lead him into the garage Saturday afternoon. He's just finished pulling weeds, which I could have very easily hired someone to do, but hopefully the blisters he has on his hands will make him think twice before letting some knuckleheads talk him into doing any more stupid shit. And now? It's time to give this kid something that he can take from this lesson and use throughout his life.

"Are you gonna make me scrub engine parts again?"

I stop in front of the Nova and turn to face him. "Yes, but not just for the hell of it." I gesture to the car behind me. "You broke this, so now you're going to learn how to fix it."

He eyes me wearily. "I don't know anything about cars."

"That's why I'm going to teach you. You didn't know how to pitch the first time you picked up a baseball, did you?"

"No."

"Exactly. You have to learn. Plus, having someone help me repair this car means it will be on the road sooner." I'm not gonna lie, the idea lights a fire of anticipation in me. This car has been sitting here neglected for years, and apparently all it took was a kid smashing in the hood and headlights for me to finally do something with it.

I meant what I said to Scottie the other night—I need to get this kid to let his guard down around me and I really think this is the key to making that happen.

"I'd rather just scrub engine parts," he mutters, looking anywhere but at me.

"No, you wouldn't. Trust me. Once you start taking this thing apart, you're going to want to learn how to put it back together."

"I don't get how you went from pitching in the MLB to turning a wrench," he says, his eyes still narrowed into slits.

"Actually, it was the same type of offer I'm giving you." Gesturing to the garage around us, I say, "I used to work here during high school, keeping the yard clean and doing grunt jobs. But then one day, the owner, Mr. Rogers, offered to teach me about cars, and I'm glad he did. I loved baseball, Chase. Still do. But the game can be taken away from you in an instant." I snap my fingers for emphasis.

"You seem to be speaking from experience," he replies sarcastically.

"You think?" It comes out like a joke, and thankfully I see a small crack of a smile on his lips before it vanishes just as quickly.

He takes a step closer to the car, surveying the damage he did with the bat that night. "How do we fix the hood?"

"I found a guy in Kentucky that has a scrap yard. I'm going to pick up a new one in a few weeks."

He clears his throat before darting his eyes to me. "I'm sorry."

Two words. That's all it takes for me to lower the last little bit of wall between us. I'm ready to move forward. I just hope he is too. "I appreciate that."

A small nod is all I get in return, but I'll take it. Popping the hood, I say, "You're going to help me take the engine out today and then we'll start tearing it apart while I wait for other parts to get here."

Sighing, he follows me to the engine hoist and helps me roll it over to the car. It takes us a while to get the engine out of the body, but once we do, Chase stares at it like it's an alien that just landed. "I have no idea what any of this is."

"I didn't either, but you'll catch on. Pulling an engine apart and putting it back together is actually a bit like mastering baseball."

His brows draw together. "How the hell do you figure that?"

Chuckling, I say, "Each component in an engine is critical to making it work, just like each player on the field. Everyone has their role, and they all need to work together to perform their best. Same with an engine. Once you understand all the parts and how they work together, you can make it run smoothly."

Chase rolls his eyes. "You sound like some old man trying to impart wisdom."

"I'm not that old," I counter, but Chase doesn't say anything else for a while. He watches me work as I begin draining the fluids from the engine, then take off the exhaust manifold. But when he finally speaks again, his question startles me and makes my pulse spike.

"Why didn't you say anything to Jared and Trent when they were talking crap about you at the game last week?"

Spinning to face him, I notice a clench in his jaw. I'm not sure why he's bringing this up now, but I oblige him. "Sometimes saying nothing is the best response."

"But they made you look stupid."

"No, they made themselves look stupid."

He licks his lips. "They made you sound washed up, like you're trying to turn me into you."

"I don't care what they think about me, Chase. I know who I am and reacting would only give them what they want. I'd rather just make them eat their words through *my* actions. Their shit-talking says more about their own insecurities than it does about me or you. And trust me, the sooner you realize that, the better you'll be at shutting out the noise."

"I don't need your advice, Grady."

I drop the wrench on the table and take a step toward him, hoping that closer proximity will help him really hear me. "Have you ever thought that maybe you do? That I might understand what you're dealing with?"

"No, you don't!" His voice rises and the disdain is back, but if he wants a fight, I'm going to give him one. I haven't tried that technique yet, so let's see what happens.

"Yeah, I do, Chase! Shit, watching you play ball is like seeing myself at your age." I pound a fist into my chest. "I can't tell you how fucking proud I am of you each time I watch you take the mound, when you actually fucking listen to my coaching instead of arguing with me like you are now!"

"You're not my dad!" His voice echoes in the garage, drawing the attention of the last two technicians who are preparing to leave for the day. "Stop trying to be!"

I close the gap between us and look right into his eyes. "I know that...because if I were your dad, I never would have let you move seven hours away from me!"

Tears form in his eyes as we stare each other down, both of our chests heaving. Sadness, hurt, and anger reflect in his eyes—emotions I'm all too familiar with myself.

When I speak again, I lower my voice, hoping to decrease the tension. "But. My kid is going to be your sibling, so I *am* going to be in your life, Chase—because I sure as hell won't abandon them. We can figure out how to get along, or these next four years are going to be hell for both of us. Once you turn eighteen, you can make your own path, but until then, we need to make this work."

His eyes drift to the side of the garage, but he doesn't move as a tear trails down his cheek. When he speaks again, I can barely hear him, but the words are still powerful. "I didn't want to come here, but my mom thought it would be best."

"I know." Reaching out, I place my hand on his shoulder, but he still doesn't look at me. "And I know that me being in your life wasn't in that plan, but I'm a firm believer that everything happens for a reason."

As soon as I say that, his eyes return to mine. "Even you losing baseball?"

I inhale deeply before replying. "At first, I was so angry about it, and it's taken me a long time to accept. But you know what's helped?"

"What?"

"Having your mom back in my life. And coaching."

He blinks. "My mom?"

"Yeah." I sigh before reaching for a rag to wipe off my hands, grateful the tension from us yelling is dwindling. "She was a huge part of my life before I made it to the MLB, and seeing her again reminded me that there is a life beyond the game. And now that we're having a kid, it's like a new chapter of my life is about to begin, and for the first time in five fucking years, I'm excited about it, Chase." The clench of his jaw softens. "And you're a part of that new chapter."

"Why aren't you marrying my mom?" he asks, shocking me, quite frankly.

"Maybe you should ask her that question." Probably not the most mature answer to give him, but if I had it my way, she and I would already be planning our future together.

I turn back to the engine, picking up where I left off. A few seconds later, I feel Chase come up beside me, leaning over my shoulder to see what I'm doing. "What do you need me to do?"

And just like that, instead of fighting our circumstances, we start working together on our project.

Now if only I could get his mom to come around.

***

"You didn't have to bring him home," Scottie says as I set bags of food on her kitchen counter. "But selfishly, I'm glad you did since you brought dinner too."

The smell of the burgers and onion rings I picked up from Catch and Release wafts through the air as Chase and I pull the boxes of food out of the bags. When I texted Scottie my offer, she said the craving for today was the same burger I brought before, so I couldn't help but oblige her request.

"I'm starving," Chase grumbles as he shoves three fries into his mouth from his container.

"Grady worked you hard today, huh?" Scottie asks.

He nods. "Yeah, but taking the engine for the Nova apart was actually kind of cool."

Scottie shoots me a curious look. "Cool, huh?"

Chase shrugs as he grabs a cup of ranch, a handful of napkins, and his drink. "Yeah, Mom. Cool." He heads down the hallway and calls out, "I'm gonna eat in my room and then shower."

I wait for his door to close and then lean over the counter to whisper, "He looked like I was asking him to play Operation and every time he touched the engine, it was going to electrocute him."

Scottie snorts. "Well, at least he was invested and not out to mess anything else up."

I reach for my burger and bring it to my mouth, but before I take a bite, I say, "We had a good day, Scottie."

Her smile is soft and there's a hint of emotion in her eyes. "I'm happy to hear that."

"Your son is actually pretty funny when he's not being surly and acting like nothing I say matters."

She smirks before popping an onion ring into her mouth. "I'd like to think he got that from me."

"Hopefully our kid will too."

She clears her throat and grabs her box of food, walking over to the table. When she sits down, she rubs her belly. "This baby is super excited for this meal."

I follow her over, taking my food and drink with me as well. "Are you feeling movement yet?"

"Yeah, but not from the outside."

"Just the flutters, right?"

She stares at me while she chews. "It's frightening how much you now know about pregnancy, Grady."

"I don't like not knowing things." I shrug. "But I'm looking forward to being able to feel our kid kick."

She rubs over her stomach again. "I already feel bigger than I should, but maybe that's because I didn't find out right away."

I drop my eyes down her body before lifting back to her gaze. "You look fucking perfect to me, Scottie." A tinge of pink graces her cheeks, but she doesn't say anything. And before she can flip a switch on me and lecture me about us remaining friends, I move the conversation to another topic. "So, do you have plans next weekend?"

Scottie wipes her mouth with a napkin. "I don't think so. Why?"

"Well, I was thinking we could have dinner with our families Friday night. Your mom and grandma can come over to my place, and I'll invite my mom, Penn, Astrid, and the kids so everyone can meet, like we discussed the other night."

Her eyes go wide for a second before she nods. "Jesus. No easing me into this, huh?"

I dip my eyes to her stomach. "We're kind of on a time crunch, remember?"

She nods slowly. "Um. Okay. That should work."

"Good. And then on Saturday, Dallas is throwing a birthday party for his girlfriend, Willow, at their house on Bayshore Drive. It's right on the beach and our whole friend and family group will be there."

"I only met Willow once at Astrid's bakery, Grady. I don't really know her."

"Doesn't matter. Dallas insisted that you come, and I want you to meet my friends." She winces, but I press on. "Your life is here now, Scottie, and I want to bring you into mine, to establish that you and I will be a package deal, especially once the baby comes." I look her straight in the eyes, cover her hand with mine, and say, "Come with me."

Her eyes dart down to our hands. "Just as friends, right?"

I swallow down the urge to argue. "Sure." But little does this woman know that I plan on making it very clear to everyone that she's carrying my baby.

She nods timidly, but then finds her confidence again. "Yeah, okay. No sense in hiding, I guess. Everyone's going to know about us sooner or later."

I wink at her. "I agree, although I'm sure most people around town have already heard rumors." I take my hand back and pop an onion ring into my mouth. "Now, what about the weekend after that? Do you have plans then?"

She swings her head around the room before her gaze lands back on me, looking perplexed. "What the hell is going on right now?"

I stifle a laugh. "What do you mean?"

"I mean, I'm sitting here talking with a man who actually wants to make plans." She places a hand over the center of her chest, feigning shock. "My heart can't handle this right now. I thought men like you were just a legend that some women talked about, but never truly existed."

Rolling my eyes, I lean forward and lower my voice so she has to lean in to hear what I'm about to say. "When are you going to learn that I want to spend as much time with you as possible, Scottie?"

Her tongue darts out as she licks her lips and speaks softly. "I'm just not used to this. I guess—I guess I'm still trying to wrap my head around it."

"Well, get used to it faster. Because the sooner you understand that I really want you in my life, the easier things will be for us down the road."

"What happens down the road?" she whispers, and her eyes drop to my lips for just a second. But as soon as she realizes she's unintentionally inching closer to me, she jolts back in her chair and looks away from me, breaking the moment.

"Scottie..."

"What did you have in mind for the following weekend, Grady?" Her response is curt as she picks up her burger and takes a huge bite of it, her cheeks bulging out as she chews, avoiding my gaze while I study her for a minute.

The woman is so damn stubborn that she can't admit what's right in front of her. And even though it's only making the frustration in me build, it's also a welcome reminder that it's only a matter of time before she breaks—and I'll be right there to catch her when she falls.

"There's a man with a scrap yard in Kentucky who has a hood for the Nova."

Her eyes meet mine almost instantly. "Oh! That's great."

"Yeah, I got lucky, but I have to drive to go pick it up."

"Okay..."

"I want you to come with me." When the idea sparked to life in my mind the other day, I knew it was the perfect way for us to spend time together, away from everyone else—to remind Scottie of the connection we share, to let her see what it would be like to be mine, to build the trust that I know she needs before she'll let me in completely.

She nearly chokes on her burger. When she's finished coughing, her eyes bounce back and forth between mine. "You mean like a…"

"Road trip," I finish for her. "Yeah."

"The last road trip I was on, I threw up on the side of the road." I try to stifle my laughter, but it comes out. "It's not funny, Grady!"

"I'm sorry. I know it's not, I just…"

"It's your fault I threw up that time, all right!" She points a finger at me. "You and your stupid, superhuman sperm."

My laughter dies almost instantly and she stares at me, shocked. "Kinda makes you wonder if this was all meant to be, doesn't it, Scottie?"

She freezes as we lock eyes. My heart is racing, waiting to see if she'll make the first move, or if I should launch myself at her to kiss the shit out of her again.

Before either of us can move, Chase comes back into the kitchen freshly showered, burping obnoxiously loudly to signal his arrival. And I have to admit, I'm impressed. "Damn, that was good."

Scottie blinks and the spell cast between us is broken. "Chase!" she admonishes.

"What?"

She stands from her chair, taking her food with her. "I taught you better manners than that."

He rolls his eyes but listens to his mother. "Excuse me."

"Thank you."

After Chase washes his hands, he looks over at me. "Thanks for dinner, Grady."

"You're welcome." The tightness in my chest dissipates a bit knowing that today was a huge turning point for us. When he heads back down the hall, Scottie yawns loudly. "Did you have a tiring day too?"

"I just cleaned while Chase was gone. The floors were disgusting, but now I'm kind of regretting doing all that work. My feet are killing me."

I stand from my chair, tossing my container in the trash. "I can help you with that."

"How?"

I wiggle my fingers in the air. "Remember, I offered foot rubs anytime."

She bites her bottom lip in contemplation. "I don't think that's a good idea, Grady."

"Your feet hurt, and I have healing hands. Don't overthink it, Scottie," I say, gesturing for her to follow me into the living room. I sit on one side of the couch and she sits on the opposite end. I yank her feet into my lap, rubbing under her arch.

The moan she lets out is music to my dick. "Oh God, that feels good."

"See? And you didn't want this."

She leans her head back on the arm of the couch and closes her eyes. I watch her eyelashes flutter and study the curves of her changing body as my hands move over the tops of her feet. She lets out little mewls of pleasure as I work over her arches, kneading and rubbing the muscles that she's using to keep herself standing all day. And all of those sounds just remind me of our night together—her head thrown back in pleasure, the curse words leaving her lips as my cock hit her perfectly deep in her pussy, the way her nails dug into my back as she climaxed over and over.

God, I want this woman more than I've wanted anything in my life—even the chance to play baseball again.

"Grady?"

"Huh?" I say, oblivious to the fact that she was talking since my mind was otherwise occupied.

"I said thank you for today—for dinner and for this."

"I told you, I'm here if you need anything." I trail my fingers up her calf, moving closer to the inside of her knee and then just barely grazing her thigh.

I've read the books, I know that her hormones are running rampant, that her libido is about to spike and she's going to need a release, or twenty. And if this woman won't let me in emotionally, perhaps relating to her physically again will remind her of the connection between us, the connection that has always been there and she can continue to deny, but it won't change anything.

We've already shared another kiss. There's so much more that I can do to drive her wild before our inevitable reconnection.

Her pupils dilate, her breathing starts to get heavier, and then I put the final nail in the board as I dart my eyes to the space between her legs and say, "And I mean anything, Scottie. Fucking anything."

Chapter Thirteen

Grady

"You sure you don't want some help?" Astrid says, hovering over me like I'm about to do something wrong.

"I'm grilling chicken and hot dogs. How can I fuck that up?"

"I don't know." She shrugs as Penn wraps his arm around her waist, pulling her into his chest. "I just don't like standing around not helping."

"If I asked you to stir the pasta salad, would that help ease your anxiety?"

She wriggles free of Penn and darts to the fridge. "Absolutely."

Penn and I laugh at my sister. "I swear, you're more nervous than I am."

Astrid brings the bowl of pasta salad over to the counter. "I just want everything to be perfect for you," my sister says affectionately. "I know you want this and—"

"I'm working on it, Astrid," I cut in, glancing nervously toward the door. I don't want to risk my mother overhearing the reason for this dinner before I can tell her myself. That is, if she hasn't already found out from the rumor mill. The past few weeks have been insane and the last thing I wanted was to tell her this news over the phone.

I know Scottie's mom and grandma know, but I wanted to have more answers for the questions my mother will inevitably have. Astrid's already reprimanded me for keeping this from Mom, but between trying to get Scottie to open up to me and Chase to stop fighting me at every turn, my head has been a mess.

"Have things gotten any better?" Astrid asks, stirring the pasta as Penn nurses a beer from his perch on a stool at the island. Bentley and Lilly are watching some show called Bluey that they're currently obsessed with in the living room.

"Yes, with Chase at least."

Astrid's face lights up. "Well, that sounds promising."

"It's definitely a step in the right direction."

Penn clears his throat. "Melissa just pulled up."

Astrid and I turn to look out the front window just as our mother shuts her car door, walking carefully up to the front porch with a casserole dish in hand.

I quickly rinse my hands in the sink and nod toward Astrid. "I'm gonna go talk to her before Scottie and her family get here."

"Good luck!" my sister calls out as I make my way to the front door.

I open it just as my mom approaches and steps onto the porch. "Hey, Mom."

She beams, perching up on her toes to kiss my cheek. "I have to say, this invitation was a pleasant surprise. It's usually your sister who's coordinating our family dinners."

"Well, I might have had an ulterior motive," I admit, leading her inside.

Her brows arch. "Is that so?"

"Yeah. Follow me." I lead her down the hallway, dropping off her casserole dish in the kitchen as we make our way to the den, a state-of-the-art game and movie room I insisted on when I built this place. "You might want to sit for what I'm about to tell you."

My mother lowers herself into one of the recliners, eyeing me cautiously. "You're scaring me, Grady."

Running a hand through my hair, I say, "No need to be scared, but I do have some news that's going to surprise you."

"Okay..."

"I'm going to be a dad," I blurt out, watching as the shock ripples across her face, her jaw dropping.

"What?"

"I'm having a kid in September...with Scottie Daniels."

That has her eyes widening even further. "Your friend Scottie from high school?"

"Yeah, Mom. We, uh, reconnected back in December, and then she moved back to Carrington Cove last month. She found out she was pregnant just after she moved back, and now..."

"You've known this long and you didn't tell me?" she says, placing her purse on the floor beside her chair and giving me that motherly scowl of disappointment.

"Well, I've only known a couple weeks, but...yes."

"Why?"

"Because I knew you'd have questions, and I didn't have any answers to give you."

"And now?"

I blow out a breath, suddenly feeling like a kid who just got in trouble. But I'm not. I'm a full-fledged adult who's about to have a kid of his own. So, I lay it all out there. "Now, I'm still figuring things out. I'm nervous about all of this change. I'm excited to be a dad but also scared I'll fuck up. And I'm frustrated because I want a relationship with Scottie, but she's made it clear she doesn't even want to try. I don't know if we're going to be living together, if she's going to keep working and we'll need daycare, or anything about what our life is going to look like—because the only life I see is the one where she's my wife."

My mother's hand flies to her chest as I continue. "Her son is on the baseball team too, which makes our situation even more complicated, but he's finally starting to come around. And I just…"

She stands from her chair and walks over to me. "Breathe, Grady," she says gently, and I do, since I'm nearly out of breath after my word vomit. "Now, do you think she feels the same about you?"

"I do, Mom. I can fucking feel it."

Smiling, she pats me on the shoulder. "Then do what you've always done and keep working for what you want. Put in the effort, even when it's difficult." She shakes her head as she crosses her arms over her chest. "I have to say, I always thought you had a thing for her back in high school."

I rub the back of my neck. "I did, but…"

"Baseball was your focus." She nods. "I know. And now?"

"She's my focus, Mom. Her, her son, and our kid. I want a family, and today she's coming over with hers so we can all get to know each other better. I'm trying to be patient, but it's hard. I don't want her to choose me because I've pressured her to. And her ex did a number on her. But this girl…" I look across the room and it all becomes so clear. "She's always seen me for me, not my skills on a pitching mound or how much money I have. We've had a connection since we were kids, and seeing her again just made me realize that my feelings were real—*are* real." I take in a deep breath. "She's the one, Mom." Lowering my voice, I admit, "I think she always has been."

"If there's one person in the world who deserves this, it's you, Grady. It's time for you to live your life for yourself and your happiness—not just for baseball." She smiles up at me with tears in her eyes. "I was always afraid that you would end up resenting the game when you realized what it could cost you."

"Like a family?"

"Yes." She nods softly. "Part of me always wondered if you'd ever have this, and now... Well, I can selfishly say I'm grateful to be welcoming another grandchild into our lives, but mostly..." She cups my face, making me feel like a boy again who needed her comfort in times when I doubted myself. "I'm so happy for you, Grady. You're going to be an amazing father."

"Even though mine wasn't around?" I whisper, voicing one of my biggest doubts.

"Especially because of that. You know what it felt like not to have that type of presence in your life, so be the man you wish you had to look up to." I nod, choking down the lump forming in my throat, knowing that she's right. "And since you've told me your news, I guess it's time to tell you mine."

"You have news?"

Fighting to contain her smile, she says, "Yes. I met someone. His name is John. We've been talking online, and he lives in Castle, about an hour away. We've discussed him moving here. He works remotely, and I don't want to leave Astrid without my help, and now you might need my babysitting services as well, so…"

"I want you here for more than just watching my kid, Mom."

She chuckles. "Good to know."

"Does he treat you well?"

"Yes, he does." The blush that graces her cheeks tells me that I probably don't want to know all of the reasons for that answer.

"Then I can't wait to meet him."

"And I can't wait to see Scottie again and welcome her into the family."

I pull her in for a hug, inhaling deeply, grateful that even though I only had one parent growing up, she was the one I had. "I love you, Mom."

"I love you too, Grady. And I can't wait to watch you be the dad you never had."

I follow my mom back to the main part of the house, and I see Astrid chewing on her thumbnail as we enter the kitchen.

"I take it you knew about my newest grandchild?" Mom asks her.

"I did, but only because he told me at Lilly's birthday party."

My mom turns to me. "I was there!"

"I know, Mom, but..." Before I can finish, the doorbell rings, which means Scottie is here. I point a finger around the room to all of my family members. "You'd all better be on your best behavior. Remember, I'm trying to win this woman over."

Penn shakes his head, Astrid smirks, and my mother pats me on the shoulder as she moves for the front door. "Don't worry, Grady. We're not the most obnoxious bunch of knuckleheads you could have for a family. It could always be worse."

***

"You need to join the gardening club," Scottie's mom, Lisa, tells my mom as we all sit around the table, gorging ourselves.

When I asked Scottie what she was craving, she told me barbecue chicken wings, and as I watch her devour them across the table, licking her fingers, I'm happy that I was able to make *her* happy.

The sight of her licking her fingers might also prevent me from standing up from my chair anytime soon, but it was all fucking worth it. Both of our families are getting along well, the food turned out great, and the woman carrying my child looks even more beautiful than the last time I saw her.

Things are all headed in the right direction.

"Katherine Sheppard has been trying to get me to join her club for years, but I have a black thumb, ladies. Not a green one."

Lisa groans. "Darn."

Gigi, Scottie's grandmother, chimes in. "And don't bother asking Scottie either. The only time she ever touched grass was when she was kicking it up while running around on a softball field."

Scottie stops eating for two seconds long enough to realize her name was mentioned. "What?"

"Nothing, dear. Get back to feeding my next grandchild." Gigi waves her off.

Scottie glares at her grandmother but goes back to eating. She said that her nausea has finally started to subside, and since then, she's called me three times to bring her something she was craving. Luckily, no orange popsicles again, but I haven't fucked up since that night, so I'd say I'm getting better at this.

"Oh!" My mother exclaims, turning to Scottie. "You're due in September, right?"

"Yes..."

"Does that mean you'll still be playing in the Carrington Cove games, Grady?" my mom asks.

Scottie mumbles around a mouthful of food. "They still do that?"

"Some kids at school were talking about that," Chase interjects. "What is it?"

"Every fall, the town hosts a weekend-long competition where teams fight for bragging rights and the Cove Cup. Each team is sponsored by a local business, and the winning team's sponsor gets to display the cup proudly for the next year," I say as Penn snickers beside me. "Dallas won last year, and I had every intention of trying to strip him of his title, but if Scottie has the baby before then, well…"

"You could still compete," Scottie says to me.

"I could, but I'm sure I'd rather be with you and the baby."

We stare at each other while our family looks on, but this woman is crazy if she thinks I would leave her alone with a newborn to go run around town fighting for a piece of plastic that doesn't mean nearly as much to me as she does.

Penn clears his throat, breaking the moment. "You know, you could always be on my team this year instead of being captain of your own. That way if you can't make it, it'll be easier to fill in for you."

Astrid pats Penn's cheek. "I'm going to be on Penn's team this year too. We talked about having one for the bakery and one for Penn's business, but it doesn't make sense to manage two teams."

I nod in agreement. "I think that sounds like a good option for me too."

Penn leans over the table now, smirking. "Plus, then all three of us could gang up on Dallas and knock him off his throne. He'd be livid."

The gleam in his eyes speaks to the competition between brothers. "That'd just be the cherry on the cake, wouldn't it?" I ask.

"Can I be on the team?" Bentley asks around his corn on the cob.

Astrid pats him on the back. "Not yet, baby. You're not old enough."

He swats her away. "I'm not a baby, mom. I'm eleven."

"Chase is old enough though, isn't he?" Scottie asks.

I clear my throat and look over at Chase. "He is. I'm sure Penn could use the manpower if you're interested."

Chase shrugs. "Yeah, I'm in."

"The best part of the games for me is the shirtless men," Gigi chimes in as Scottie and her mom both roll their eyes. "Do you play the games with your shirt off, Grady?"

"Jesus, Gigi. Can you not?" Scottie shakes her head.

Gigi just waves her off. "If you're not going to appreciate the fine specimen of a man that knocked you up, then this old broad will." She pushes a bowl of chips toward her granddaughter. "Just keep growing that baby, Scottie."

Scottie's mouth drops open as I stifle my laughter. Astrid giggles, and Lisa and my mom share a look.

"Hey, I'm more than just a baby factory, you know."

"Mom, please don't refer to yourself as a baby factory." Chase grimaces as he takes another bite of his hot dog.

Lilly decides to chime in at this moment. "Where do babies come from?"

The whole table goes silent as Astrid's eyes bug out and then lock onto mine.

"Uh..."

Chase nearly chokes on his hot dog, Penn stifles his laughter behind his fist, and all three of the matriarchal women sitting at the table share a look before Gigi pipes up. "Well, Lilly, you see... First, you need a handsome looking fella who has a package that intrigues you..."

"Mom!" "Gigi!" Lisa and Scottie shout at the exact same time as the rest of us old enough to know what sex is lose our composure.

Fuck. I can't remember the last time I laughed this hard.

"Lilly, you and I can have this conversation later," Astrid finally says, deflecting my niece's curiosity for the time being.

Lilly simply shrugs. "Okay. I'm done now, so can I get up from the table?"

"Yeah, me too," Bentley says.

Astrid nods. "Yes, but please clear your plates," she says as the kids get up from the table.

"Chase? Do you wanna see my uncle's backyard? He's got a soccer goal back there for me to practice on when I come over."

Chase stands from the table, shoving the last bite of his hot dog in his mouth as he mumbles, "Sure."

Scottie glances at me. "You put up a soccer goal for him?"

"Yeah. He doesn't have space for one at Astrid's, so I put one here."

"He has a backstop back there too," Astrid adds, a pleased grin on her face. "You haven't shown that to Chase yet, have you?" She directs her question to me.

Staring at my sister, I say, "No. Haven't gotten that far yet."

Scottie eyes me from her seat. "I might never get my son to leave this place now."

Everyone chuckles before standing from the table, leaving the two of us alone.

I shift in my chair, turning to face her. "How was the food?"

Leaning back, she rubs her stomach. "So good. Thank you for this. And I'm sorry about my grandma. She lacks a filter and I forget that other people don't know how to react to her sometimes."

"She's a hoot, Scottie. I can see where you get your sense of humor from." Scooting closer, I continue, "I'm happy to have everyone here." I reach forward and place my hand on her stomach just as our eyes meet. "And I should be thanking you."

"For what?" Her reply comes out as a whisper.

"All of this," I say, gesturing around my house full of people I love, full of family.

"I haven't done anything, Grady."

I stand from my chair, towering over her as I tip her chin up so she can look me in the eyes. "You're giving me a life I've always wanted, Scottie." Leaning down, I press a soft kiss to her lips, taking her by surprise. I don't push for more, just lips on lips, reverence and gratitude expressed physically. "I never thought I'd have this."

When I stand back up to full height, her eyes are still closed, lifting open slowly before bouncing back and forth between mine. "Grady..."

I take her hand and help her stand. "Come on. Let's go out back and watch the kids play."

For the next hour, the ladies sit on the back porch and talk among themselves as Penn and I play with the kids. Chase pitches to Lilly and Bentley, and Penn shags balls from the grass as the kids hit them.

"Anybody want a refill?" I ask before going into the house, eager for another beer myself. Once I get everyone's requests, I enter the kitchen through the French doors from the patio. I open the fridge to grab the drinks, and when I close the door, I find Lisa, Gigi, and my mom all standing on the opposite side of the kitchen island, staring at me.

"Uh, do y'all need something?"

Gigi doesn't beat around the bush. "I wanna know how long it's going to take for you to wear down my granddaughter," she says.

"Okay..." I draw out the word, momentarily stunned.

"If I have to watch her eye fuck you one more time, I'm going to throw her on top of you myself."

Setting the drinks on the island, I brace myself for this conversation. "I don't think that will be necessary, and honestly? It will probably just piss Scottie off even more, so let's not."

My mother nods. "I'm seeing it too, which is why we all decided to come in here and say something." She looks at Lisa and Gigi.

"Are y'all trying to meddle in our lives right now?"

Scottie's mom nods, smiling. "Of course. That's what mothers do. I once read a book series where the mom meddled in all her sons' love lives, and I don't think I've ever read something more relatable than that. In fact, she then taught her daughters-in-law how to meddle. It's our duty to teach the future generations, so if you have a girl, just know she will learn this talent as well."

I rub the back of my neck. "I don't know whether I should feel supported or scared."

"I know my daughter, Grady, and *she's* scared," Lisa says. "She never was until she had Chase, but being a mother changes you in so many ways that a man will never understand. I don't think I have to tell you that my daughter became jaded and scarred by the man she had a child with before. But you're not him, and she just needs to see that."

I blow out a breath and shove my hands in my pockets. "I'm trying."

"Well, try harder," Gigi says sharply.

"Look, I know you're all invested in this, which I'm not sure is a blessing or a curse at this point," I say, narrowing my eyes at all three of them. "But Scottie and I have to do what's best for us and I don't want to push her before she's ready."

Lisa rounds the counter, standing right in front of me. "Just don't let her push you away, Grady. Please." There's a hint of desperation in her voice and pleading in her eyes. "I know I sent you away that morning you showed up looking for her, but she asked me to. Now, after seeing you two together..." She shakes her head. "You're the kind of man who can show her what real love is."

"I won't give up on her," I say, even though I have no control over the woman. All I can do at this point is keep proving she can trust me, keep getting her to give in to my touch, and try to be involved as much as she'll let me.

"You both deserve a second chance at happiness," my mother says. "And this baby deserves you two together—not because that's what's expected, but because you two were meant for each other."

Fuck, I feel that too.

"What's going on?" All four of us spin our heads in the direction of the French doors where Scottie stands, assessing us with her gaze.

Lisa reaches for the drinks I placed on the counter. "Just helping Grady take the drinks out. He only has two hands, you know?" Holding four cans in her arms, she moves around her daughter and heads back outside.

"Subtle, Mom," Scottie mutters.

"I was just headed to the bathroom!" my mother exclaims before scurrying down the hall.

Scottie turns to Gigi, placing her hands on her hips. "And you? What's your excuse?"

Gigi smirks at me, wiggling her eyebrows. "I was just telling Grady that if you don't want to go on that road trip with him, I will." She takes a chip from the bowl on the counter, pops it in her mouth, and heads back outside.

"Jesus," Scottie says under her breath, pinching her nose as she moves further into the kitchen.

"You told your grandma about the road trip?"

Her head lifts and her eyes connect with mine. "Yeah. I wanted to make sure her or my mom would be home so Chase had supervision if I decided to go."

Moving closer to her, I pull her into me, loving the fact that our child rests between us when I do. "And what did you decide?"

She worries her bottom lip between her teeth. "I guess it would be kind of fun."

I want to fist pump the air, but refrain. "Kind of fun? *What* kind of fun?"

Rolling her eyes, she pushes against my chest, creating space between us. "Don't get any ideas, Grady."

Before she gets too far from me, I pull her back into my chest. "I promise to make it fun, Scottie. For both of us."

Her throat bobs as she swallows. "And how do you propose to do that?"

Lick your pussy until you scream. Suck on your nipples until you can't take it anymore. Bury myself inside of you and stay there for as long as you'll let me. Lay next to you and laugh until we can't keep our eyes open anymore.

"By asking you questions about parenthood."

Her lip quirks up. "That's your idea of fun?"

"I need the truth about what to expect, Scottie," I say, not wanting to scare her with my honest thoughts. "I feel like these books are fucking sugarcoating things and I don't like to be unprepared, remember?"

"Yeah, I guess there are things about babies that you just have to learn through experience."

"That's how I feel, but you have that experience, and I don't."

Sighing, she steps away from me. "Fine, I'll answer your questions as long as you let me pick the playlist."

"You can't play NSYNC the entire time, though," I plead, making her laugh.

She rubs her stomach and then grins at me. "Oh, Grady. You have no idea what you just agreed to."

Yeah, I do—because I just got this woman to agree to stay with me for forty-eight hours straight—so I'm pretty sure she's the one who has no idea what's about to happen when we're alone, and I can't fucking wait to show her.

Chapter Fourteen

Scottie

"Holy crap. I forgot how incredible the coast is here." As my eyes scan the expanse of ocean stretching out in front of me, I try to think back to the last time I actually stepped foot on the sand in Carrington Cove. It was so cold when I came back here in December that the idea of going near the water didn't even enter my mind. And since I moved back, well, I've been a little preoccupied.

Grady's hand rests gently on the small of my back as he leads me toward the front of the house. "It is. Willow inherited this house last year. That's what initially brought her here from D.C."

"What an amazing gift."

He chuckles softly. "Dallas didn't think so. He's always wanted this house, so he and Willow had it out a bit at first. But as they sorted things out, they fell for each other, and now it's their home together."

I glance up at him. "Sounds like it all worked out for them."

His eyes find mine as we come to the steps that lead to the wraparound front porch. "Sometimes the unexpected *can* work out, Scottie." Before I can say anything in response, he presses a soft kiss to my lips—something he keeps doing, even though I told him not to—and then leads me up the steps and to the front door where people are walking in and out of the house, moving between the tables and chairs set up on the sand under a white tent and the living room of the magnificent beach-front property Willow now owns.

"You're here!" Astrid shrieks as she emerges from the kitchen, glass of wine in hand, and quickly closes the distance to where Grady and I stand.

"You act like you didn't just see us last night," Grady tells his sister as she pulls me in for a hug.

She swats at his chest. "Don't be an ass, Grady."

"How many glasses have you had already?"

She glares at her brother. "This is my first one, thank you very much." She sticks her tongue out at him, drawing a burst of laughter from me. Turning her attention back to me, she says, "I'd offer you a glass, but..."

I rub my belly just as Grady does the same. God, he's so eager to touch our growing child and to show me affection that it's messing with my head.

I wish he would just fucking listen like I asked him to. *No touching. Just friends.*

But I can't seem to find the words to tell him to stop either.

Because you don't want him to, Scottie. Duh!

"It's okay. I mean, I certainly miss alcohol, especially in social situations like this, but it's just one of those sacrifices I know is temporary."

She nods. "Right. Once you hold that little baby, every ache, pain, and missed glass of wine is all worth it."

I reach down to stroke my bump again, feeling those bubbles grow stronger with each passing day.

Last night, I had a dream about the baby. We were in the hospital and I was holding our child, who had light brown hair and blue eyes just like Grady. I couldn't tell if we had a daughter or a son, but the way this man looked at me—like I had given him everything he'd ever wanted in this life—made me cry in my sleep. I glanced down at our child for one second to admire the human we created, but when I looked back up, he was gone—vanished into thin air. And then he never returned.

It woke me up from a dead sleep, the torture of my worst fears slashing through one of the most incredible moments of my life.

It's part of the reason I wish I could have that glass of wine to take the edge off the anxiety I feel racing through my body—because the closer Grady and I get, the more I feel like he's going to change his mind. It's what Andrew eventually did, and I didn't want to accept it. I kept blaming myself, believing that *I* must be the problem.

I know now that he was a selfish narcissist, and I didn't do anything wrong. But I swore to myself I'd never trust another man again.

I just didn't think Grady would be the one I'd want to let in. Add on my mother and grandmother meddling last night, and well? My entire body is antsy for more than one reason right now.

"Come on," Astrid urges, pulling me by the hand over to the kitchen where a group of women are standing. The house has a mostly open concept except for one wall that separates the kitchen from the living area. There's a wide cutout in the wall that allows you to peer between rooms. The cabinets are dark navy with white marble countertops, the hardwood floors are classic and stained in a light oak shade, and all of the décor is in shades of blue and white, with pops of teal scattered throughout. The nautical vibes make me wish I had a home this close to the ocean to enjoy serenity like this.

"You're just going to steal my date from me?" Grady calls after her, but the title he gave me is catching me off guard more than Astrid is right now.

"I've got her. Go grab a beer. The boys are outside playing cornhole." She waves him off as we reach the kitchen and she places her wine glass on the island. "Do you want something to drink?"

I admire the display of food spread across the counter and island, including a tiered stand of cupcakes that I know Astrid had to have made. "Um, water would be great, thanks."

"We have water with cucumber and lemon in it if you want that?"

I scrunch up my nose. "No thanks."

Giggling, she grabs a bottle of water from the fridge and hands it to me. "That didn't sound good, I take it?"

Twisting the cap off, I take a sip of water. "No, unfortunately. I'm usually all about stuff like that, but this baby wants nothing to do with fruits and vegetables, which is really frustrating when you're supposed to be eating healthy foods, you know?"

A woman standing beside me inserts herself into our conversation. "God, when I was pregnant with my son, all I wanted was chocolate ice cream, so I definitely understand that struggle."

"Apple fritters have been my obsession lately, especially the ones from Astrid's bakery."

Astrid beams proudly as the woman to my left extends her hand. "I'm Shauna, by the way."

"Scottie."

"It's nice to meet you."

"Likewise."

"How do you know Astrid and Willow?"

My hand finds my bump. No time like the present to let the truth fly, right? "Well, I'm having a baby with Astrid's brother."

Astrid squeals. "I'm going to be an aunt!"

Willow comes around the corner now. "Astrid, that squeal is going to attract the geese outside."

Shauna and I laugh as Astrid shrugs. "Not sorry."

"Scottie! You're here!" Willow closes the distance between us and pulls me in for a hug.

"Happy birthday!" I tell her.

"Thank you." She inhales deeply with a smile on her lips. "Thirty-five and finally feeling like I'm right where I'm supposed to be."

Shauna clears her throat. "And who do you have to thank for that?"

Willow rolls her eyes. "You, I guess." Willow glances back at me. "Scottie, Shauna is my best friend from college. She lives in Texas now with her real-life bonified cowboy husband, and she's the one who convinced me to come down here when I inherited this house."

"Grady was telling me a little bit about it as we were walking in. What an adventure."

"It was, murderous geese aside." I glance at Astrid, who chuckles behind her wine glass. "But it led me to the love of my life." She stares out the window at Dallas and the other guys where they stand together, nursing their beers. "Carrington Cove became my home and I'm so grateful for that."

"I, for one, am happy to no longer be the only girl in the family," declares a shorter woman with long black hair as she joins our conversation. She reaches her hand out to me. "I'm Hazel, the youngest Sheppard sibling and only girl, until Willow balanced things out, that is."

Astrid chimes in. "Hey. I'm part of the family now too, you know?"

Hazel grins. "Yeah, but Willow was first, and she broke down Dallas. You've got to give her credit for that."

"Aw, I love you too, Hazel." Willow pulls Hazel in for a hug.

Shauna tsks. "Now, don't you start crying, birthday girl. We still have hours of this party left."

Willow laughs as she grows emotional. "I can't help it," she says as she fans her face, making all of us chuckle as well.

I can feel my own emotions starting to build, forming a lump in my throat because I know how it feels to not belong. I felt out of place for the past fifteen years, living a life I chose because I felt like I had to, not because that's what I wanted. And having genuine friendships is a lot more difficult than you'd think. I had female friends back in Georgia, but most of them were from my association with Andrew. As soon as we split up, it was clear where their loyalties lay.

But now, being back in Carrington Cove, there is a peace that's come over me—a sense of purpose and belonging, despite my pregnancy and the issues with Chase.

Maybe it's having my mom and Gigi in my life every day. Maybe it's working at a job with a boss I love.

Or maybe it's the man standing out in the sand, the one who's giving me another child and another chance to get this right, and these women who have welcomed me into their circle without a second thought.

God, I want him. I want to trust him. I'm just so fucking terrified.

"Hey, honey?" A deep voice behind us catches everyone's attention, and we collectively spin around to take in the giant man holding a baby striding toward Shauna.

Jesus Christ, this man looks like a tree—thick, hearty, and definitely rugged.

"I'm pretty sure Hudson is hungry," he says, stopping right next to Shauna. *So this must be her husband.*

Shauna intercepts their son. "Sounds about right. My boobs were burning so he must have sensed it." She plants kisses all over the baby's cheeks before moving toward the couch to nurse him.

"Oh God. Nursing. How did I forget about that?" I face-palm my forehead.

"Are you planning on nursing?" Astrid asks me as Willow fills a glass of wine for herself.

"I did with Chase, but not for long. I didn't have any idea what I was doing, so it didn't go well. But with this one," I say, rubbing my stomach again, "I think I might want to try again."

Astrid sighs. "I loved nursing, but when I was done, I was so glad."

"I'm looking forward to getting my body back, but I'm also trying to soak up each of these moments for as long as I can," Shauna says from the couch, peeking at her son under her nursing cover.

"How old is he?" I ask, moving closer to her.

"Almost nine months. He's definitely more interested in solid food now, but he still likes to nurse, especially when he's tired."

I take a seat on the cushioned chair beside her. "My first son is fourteen, so it's been a long time since I've done the baby stage."

Shauna nods in understanding. "Well, Hudson is our first, so I'm still learning. But if you ever need someone to talk to, I'm here. I can give you my phone number before I leave."

Gratitude rushes through me. "Thank you. I appreciate that."

"Of course. We moms have to stick together, you know? I didn't realize how much my identity would change just by having my son."

"Oh, I understand that more than you know."

Shauna lifts the cover up, staring down at Hudson nursing as his eyes drift close. "But having Forrest by my side has made it easier. I seriously don't know what I would do without him." She looks back up at me and says, "Is your husband excited about the baby?"

Her question makes my stomach drop because Grady isn't my husband. I don't have one of those this time around.

As I fumble for a response, a voice behind me says, "He is, although he's not her husband yet." I turn and lock eyes with Grady as he makes his way to my side.

I stare up at him from my seat on the chair, my pulse thrumming in my body as I process the words he just spoke. "Uh, you came out of nowhere."

He tucks one of my curls behind my ear. "I came in here to check on you. You okay?"

"Um, yeah. Just talking about babies with Shauna."

Grady nods, smiling at Shauna. "Forrest was showing this little guy off outside," he says, gesturing to the baby who is now fast asleep in a milk coma.

Shauna readjusts her nursing cover, clasps her bra back in place, and then situates Hudson over her shoulder to burp him.

Jesus, this is going to be me again before I know it.

"Do you mind if I hold him?" Grady asks, startling us both.

"Sure. He needs to burp still, but who knows if he will since he's passed out." She hands him a receiving blanket. "Just use this to cover your shirt in case he spits up.

"I've held babies before, so I know the risks. It's just been a while."

"When have you burped a baby?" I ask as Shauna passes Hudson to Grady, his big arms supporting the baby on his shoulder.

And my clit starts to throb.

Good lord, this man holding a baby should be my new screensaver.

Yup, this image is going in my diddle bank for later.

"I have a niece and a nephew, remember?" he says to me, patting Hudson's back as his hips start to sway. "I wasn't around much when they were babies because of baseball, so I need the practice, you know?"

Shauna smiles at me knowingly. "Well, he's a natural, so at least you won't have to worry about him freaking out on you. Forrest was very cautious at first."

Her husband walks over to the couch now, taking a seat beside her. "Forgive me, but I didn't want to be the one to drop him first, all right?"

I snort. "God, I'll never forget the time that Chase rolled off the bed right in front of me. I cried on and off for an hour, thinking I'd wrecked him for the rest of his life."

Grady furrows his brow. "How the hell did that happen?"

I look up at him. "Don't act like it couldn't happen to you, all right? I looked away for one second and...boom. He was on the ground."

Shauna nods in understanding. "That's how it works. Hudson rolled off the couch because I was watching television and trying to fold laundry at the same time."

"She called me at work, crying hysterically," Forrest says. "But babies are a lot tougher than you think. At least that's what my mom told me, and he's fine." He stares up at his son, smiling proudly.

I inhale deeply and blow it out. "Just remembering all of this is starting to make me feel overwhelmed."

Shauna leans forward in her seat. "Don't be. You're already a mom and you'll slip right back into a rhythm the second time around. At least, that's what I keep telling myself." She glances over at Forrest and then back to me. "We haven't really told many people, but I'm expecting again."

"Aw, congratulations," I say, reaching out for her hand.

"Thank you."

Forrest clears his throat as he stands from the couch, leaning down to kiss the top of Shauna's head. "I'm gonna take Grady back outside, but just holler if you need anything."

She peers up at him and nods. "Okay. I love you."

"Love you too, baby." He presses a soft kiss to her lips and then motions for Grady to follow him outside, still holding a sleeping Hudson.

"You gonna be okay?" Grady asks me before trailing after Forrest.

"Yes, I'm good."

"Okay." He takes a few steps away, but then turns back, stopping right next to my chair, holding the baby to his chest as he leans down and plants a kiss to the top of my head. "Just let me know if you need anything, all right?"

Shauna folds in her lips to hide her smile as I reply, "I'm a big girl. I'll be fine."

"Don't argue with me, Scottie. You'll lose every time. When are you going to accept that?" he says, flashing me a wink before finishing his trek outside, leaving Shauna and me alone again.

Willow, Hazel, and Astrid scurry over with their wine in their hands just as Shauna speaks. "Okay, so what the hell is going on with you two? Because he said he's not your husband yet, but you don't seem to want him to cater to you, which I'm telling you, is a lot better than it sounds." She places her hand on her chest. "And that's coming from a type A control freak who never thought I'd let a man take care of me like Forrest does, but God, it's so hot."

Willow laughs as Astrid raises her brows at me.

"Well, uh... we're just friends who are having a kid together," I say, shrugging. But I feel uneasy the second the words leave my lips. "You know, kind of like a Ross and Rachel type of situation?"

"Uh, that man wants to be more than just your friend," Shauna says. "He wants to be your baby daddy *and* your lover. Jesus, woman, I say just let him!"

Willow snorts. "I second that! My God, Scottie…I don't know how you resist that."

Sighing, I close my eyes and Astrid clears her throat. "I'm kind of in an awkward position right now because I know you're all lusting after my older brother, but putting that aside, I really want things to work out with you and Grady, Scottie. So, I'm going to join in on the peer pressure."

Hazel chimes in, and I peer up at her now. "I take pictures for a living, and the way that man looks at you? Totally camera-worthy, just saying." I roll my eyes, but inside, my pulse is hammering. "I can only hope to find a man that looks at me like that one day," she adds.

I look around the group of women. "Y'all just don't get it," I murmur.

"Then explain it to us," Astrid urges.

Before I get a chance to respond, the door flies open, and Dallas comes barreling inside. Scanning the room, his eyes quickly land on Willow.

"There's the birthday girl." His deep voice sounds like gravel as he walks over to her, pulls her into his chest, and covers her mouth with his, drawing whistles and cheers from everyone in the house.

"Here I am. Are you okay?" Willow asks, brushing his hair from his eyes.

He swallows roughly and then says, "I'm more than okay, Goose. In fact, it's time for me to give you your gift, but I need everyone to come outside for that." He motions for us to follow him. "Come on. The sun is about to set anyway, and you don't want to miss it."

Shauna and I both stand from the couch and follow everyone down the porch and across the sand to the white tent that covers a wide square of space, chairs and tables stationed underneath, covered in white linen tablecloths and vases full of yellow flowers. The sun is inching toward the horizon in the distance, lighting up the sky in oranges and yellows that are breathtaking.

God, I missed this place. Carrington Cove was once home and it's starting to feel that way again.

Clutching my water bottle to my chest, I watch intently, eager to see what Dallas has planned for the woman he so clearly adores. Suddenly, two strong arms wrap around me from behind, pulling me into an unexpected embrace.

"Jesus, Grady."

"I'm sorry. I didn't want to scare you, but..."

"You have to stop touching me like this," I whisper as Dallas leads Willow to the front of the tent, a group of people gathering around them.

"I can't," he whispers in my ear, pressing a kiss to the skin just under my earlobe, sending a shiver down my spine as his hands move over my bump. "And I don't want to."

I tell myself it's just from the breeze wafting off the ocean, but he and I both know the truth. "Grady..."

"Shhhh...Dallas has something big planned—I just know it."

I don't bother arguing with him because Dallas calls everyone's attention to where he and Willow are standing, his hand holding hers.

"I want to take a moment to thank everyone for gathering here today to celebrate the life of this amazing woman standing next to me." Cheers and applause ring out. "Many of you know how Willow and I got our start, and it wasn't an easy one." Laughter fills the space, leading me to believe there is much more to their story than I know.

"But I didn't realize what I was missing in my life until she waltzed into it." He turns to her and murmurs echo through the crowd.

"Oh my God. He's going to propose, isn't he?" I whisper.

Grady squeezes me tighter. "He's in love."

My heart lurches at his words, hammering wildly as if I'm the one who's about to be asked one of the most important questions of my life, and all I can envision is Grady being the one to ask me.

I didn't get a proposal from Andrew. It was more of a declaration.

"We're getting married, Scottie. Our kid deserves that."

What our child really deserved was a father who cared.

A tear streams down my cheek. *Ugh, stupid hormones.*

Dallas drops to one knee, Willow gasps, and the crowd pulls out their phones to start recording and taking pictures.

"You are the love of my life, Goose." She laughs at the nickname. "Fate is more powerful than we'll ever truly know, but I think you and I can both attest to that given how we ended up in each other's lives." She nods. "I don't want to live another day without knowing that you'll be my wife. I love you more than I ever thought I could love someone. You are my future, my best friend, and the woman I was made for." He reaches into his back pocket and pulls out a ring without a box. "Willow Marshall, will you marry me?"

"HONK! HONK!"

Everyone's attention shifts to the right as a gaggle of geese interrupt one of the most important moments in Dallas and Willow's lives.

"Oh my God!" Astrid shrieks and Willow shakes her head, laughing.

"I told you that you'd attract the geese!" Willow shouts at her best friend before dropping Dallas's hand and marching toward the birds. "Listen up, you heathens..." But she doesn't get very far before Dallas pulls her back to him, laughing along with everyone else.

"Come on, Goose. It's only fitting that the geese want to be part of this moment."

Willow rolls her eyes before Dallas drops to his knee again, just as Grady presses another kiss to my temple and pulls me in closer.

"Do you want to fight off geese with me for the rest of our lives, baby?"

She covers her mouth, giggling as tears flow down her cheeks before finally shouting, "Yes!"

Dallas launches himself from the ground and everyone goes crazy, clapping wildly and shouting cheers of congratulations as the geese continue to honk in the background. They seal their engagement with a kiss, and then Dallas slides the ring onto her finger, admiring how the diamond looks on her hand.

I wipe under my eyes and nose, so emotional over someone else's happily ever after, but hating that I can't just let myself have my own.

"I need to use the bathroom," I say as I shift out of Grady's arms and head back to the house.

"Scottie?" he asks, concern etched on his face.

"I just need some tissue," I tell him, not bothering to turn around. But honestly, I need to be alone. I need to let this wave of emotion flow through me so I don't look like a crazy person crying over a proposal between two people I barely know.

Locking myself in the bathroom, I take a seat on the toilet and grab tissue, letting the tears flow. I cover my mouth to hide my sobs, and then take a few deep breaths as I fight to gather myself.

I wish I wasn't so conflicted about where my life is headed. I wish I didn't feel so hesitant to let Grady in when he is making it clear that he wants me. And I wish that I could feel more joy this time around instead of feeling anxious about all the decisions I still need to make before this baby gets here.

Grateful that I grabbed my purse before I came in here, I take a look at myself in the mirror and then get to work fixing my makeup. I carry an emergency kit with me for these moments when my emotions get the best of me, which is happening more often the further along I get in my pregnancy. I just didn't expect it to happen here.

When I finally feel composed enough to return to the party, I open the door to find Astrid waiting for me, biting her fingernail.

"Sorry, I took so long," I say, but she just smiles back at me.

"I just wanted to make sure you're okay. Grady said you ran away from him."

Covering my heart with my hand, I reply, "My emotions just got the best of me. I have these breakdowns and once they start, it takes me a minute to calm down."

She nods. "I understand. That happened to me a lot when I was pregnant with my daughter." Then she tilts her head, eyeing me. "But I'm wondering if something else got to you too." We stare at each other for a few seconds before Astrid straightens her head again and takes a deep breath. "Look, I know things are awkward between you and my brother right now, but I really just want to support you in any way I can, Scottie—as a friend, a fellow mom, and a future aunt to your kid."

"I—I appreciate that."

"Would you like to have lunch or dinner with me sometime this week?" Her suggestion catches me off guard, but honestly, I think it would be nice to have another woman to talk to. I really like Shauna, but she does live halfway across the country. And Astrid's right, she is going to be family soon.

"Oh, uh… Yeah, I think we could make that happen."

"Good. I'll text you tomorrow. Is that okay?"

"Sure."

She reaches out for my hand. "I'm serious. I have no ulterior motives here, but I think you and I have something in common, and I want you to know that you're not alone."

***

I'm sitting at the table in Catch & Release, waiting for Astrid to show up on Wednesday night just after I dropped Chase off at Grady's Garage. When Astrid texted me to meet up, this seemed like the most logical time to make it happen, but I'm not going to lie, I'm nervous about what she meant when she said we have something in common.

"You play darts?" An old man wearing a veteran's hat comes waddling up to the booth.

"I'm sorry?"

"Do you play darts?"

Not sure if I should take him seriously, I reply, "I have, but it's been a long time."

He hikes up his pants that are being held up by suspenders anyway. "No worries. I can teach you the game again."

"Oh, Harold. Leave her alone." Astrid waltzes up to the table, wrapping her arm around his shoulders. "She isn't here to play darts with you."

"But we need a fourth," he whines, making me smile.

"You boys are just going to have to find someone else to join your game tonight."

He grunts. "Fine."

The two of us watch him walk up to the next unsuspecting woman as Astrid slides into her seat, shaking her head. "Sorry I'm late."

"Don't apologize. I haven't been here very long."

"Okay, good. And sorry about Harold."

"He seems harmless."

"He is, but he and his friends are always scouting for women to play darts with them. The next time you see Willow, ask how her game with them went." Astrid smirks as a server approaches, greeting her like she's a long-lost friend. We place our orders, and I opt for the burger and onion rings, the only thing I've had from here that I know will satisfy my growing hunger.

"You seem like a little bit of a celebrity around here," I say once our server takes off.

Astrid smiles and leans back in the booth, surveying the restaurant. "I used to work here before I owned the bakery."

"Oh. I didn't know that."

"Yeah. After my husband died, I was working here and at the bakery just to make ends meet. Brandon's death benefit paid off the house, but I was a stay-at-home mom before he passed, and overnight I became a single mom who needed to start earning an income to survive."

The mention of her husband has my heart racing. "I'm so sorry about your husband."

"Thank you, but that's part of the reason why I wanted to talk to you, Scottie." She adjusts herself in her seat. "I get the feeling that you and your husband didn't have the best marriage."

I scoff, but nod. "What makes you say that?"

She winces. "Details that my brother has shared with me, but mostly, I see something in your eyes that I recognized in myself."

"And what's that?"

"Fear," she says bluntly, making my heart rate climb even more.

Swirling my water glass, I take a sip and then say, "Well, you're not wrong."

She nods curtly. "And if I'm on the right track, I'm guessing that's the reason you're hell-bent on keeping my brother at a distance."

"God, Astrid." I bury my head in my hands as tears threaten to spill from my eyes. "I'm such a fucking mess."

She reaches across the table to pull my hands from my face. "No, you're not. You're human and have been through some shit that very few can understand. No one can blame you for how you feel, but I want you to know that I felt that way too, and it took me four years before I was finally willing to risk my heart again."

"How did you do it?" I groan, frustrated but feeling relieved to be able to talk to someone about this.

Astrid huffs out a laugh. "Girl, it wasn't easy. You have to consider that Penn was my husband's best friend growing up, and also *my* friend. So, not only were we risking our friendship, his bond with my kids, and our lives that were so intertwined, but also the trust that he shared with my late husband."

"That sounds complicated."

"It was, especially because Penn thought my marriage was perfect, but the truth was...it was far from it."

I swallow hard. "I know that feeling well."

"Well, I wanted to share my story with you because I want you to know that if there is anyone who understands what you're going through, it's me." She smiles softly. "I hate that we have this in common, but I also think it's important for you to know that I've been there too. I totally get how hard it is to let someone else in again after you've been hurt, after your belief in love and partnership has been destroyed. Especially when they're also a friend, which makes the risks even greater."

Tears start to well in my eyes again. "I feel like I'm right back where I was when I found out I was pregnant with Chase, and I just don't want to make the same mistakes."

"I hear you."

Sighing, I close my eyes and lean my head against the back of the booth. "I can't go through that again."

"Yes. All valid."

"Your brother was my friend, *is* my friend, and the thought of potentially hating him one day like I hate my ex just kills me."

"Keep letting it out, Scottie." I pop my eyes open and look at her. "I'm not going anywhere. I'm not here to judge. I just want you to be able to talk about it because honestly, keeping it inside is what almost broke me and Penn. Telling him the truth allowed us to move forward, and I know you're not there yet, but you need to give those fears life so you can start to let go of them."

A tear streams down my cheek, but I brush it away and start to tell Astrid my story. She sits there and listens, nods and asks questions when they're warranted. But most of all, she doesn't tell me to move past it, to give her brother a shot, or that life is too short to hold a grudge.

She allows me to feel my feelings—be angry, terrified, and guilty for where all of my life choices have led me.

She becomes my friend, the first genuine one I've made in a long time.

"How do you feel?" she asks after our food is long gone, she's told me more about her life, and I've finally run out of things to say.

"Lighter somehow."

"Good." She picks one last fry up from her plate, pops it in her mouth, and then pushes her plate away.

"Thank you for that—for listening."

She reaches across the table and grabs my hand. "You're welcome. I hope it helped."

"It did. But I still don't know what to do about your brother, Astrid."

She shrugs. "It's okay because you'll figure it out. Sometimes we just need to take that first step, you know? That's what I had to do with Penn. Lots of baby steps to get where we are now."

My hands instinctively move to my stomach where my baby is growing. "Baby steps."

"Yup. They may be small, but you'll still get where you need to be eventually." She clears her throat. "Before I forget, I wanted to talk to you about your baby shower."

My eyes bug out. "Oh, Jesus. I haven't even thought about that."

"It's okay, but if you're willing, I'd love to throw it for you."

"Oh my God, Astrid. You don't have to do that."

"Nonsense. You know how damn excited I am about this baby, Scottie. Please, let me do this for you. Willow wants to help too."

Biting my bottom lip, I ask, "Are you sure?"

Astrid rolls her eyes. "Yes, that's why I'm offering."

"Okay," I relent. "Thank you. I appreciate it so much. I had a small one for Chase, but obviously I didn't keep anything and there are so many new things out there now that it feels like an entirely different world."

"I'm so excited!" She bounces in her chair, making me laugh. "You two are finding out the sex, right?"

"Yeah, in a few weeks."

"Good, makes it easier to plan and pick a theme. And don't forget to register. There's an adorable boutique on the boardwalk that has pretty much everything you could need, but you should also do some online registries so people can send gifts directly to you."

"God, things have changed since I had Chase."

She nods. "Yeah, but the way a baby changes your life will always be the same—for the better."

"Ain't that the truth," I reply.

She winks at me and says, "So can the right man in your life." She takes a sip of her water. "Just wanted to remind you of that too."

***

"Come on, Chase! You've got this!" I stand on the bleachers, cupping hands around my mouth, shouting loud enough so my son can hear me out on the pitching mound.

It's the top of the ninth inning and the score is tied. All Chase has to do is strike out this kid, and then our team will be up at bat, getting a chance to score at least one more run before the game is over to secure the win. Thank God for the home team advantage.

"Relax!" Grady yells, pulling Chase's eyes across the field to the dugout. Chase nods and shakes out his jitters again, knowing he only has one more pitch to deliver and then his job is done for the night.

My focus has been split all evening between watching my son and the man whose baby I'm carrying. After my dinner with Astrid last night, I slept better than I have in months. I can attest that it was just exhaustion after a busy weekend and crazy work week, especially since it's spring and the end of the school year is winding down. But honestly, I think it was just getting a lot of tension I'd been carrying out in the open.

I'm so grateful to Astrid for offering up her friendship and support. Before we left, she assured me she would keep our conversation to herself, which I appreciate. I want to tell Grady in my own time. With each passing day and each tender kiss, I feel myself more willing to let my guard down.

Grady is *not* Andrew, and I know deep in my gut, he never will be. Taking a huge leap of faith is still hard, though, and I'm fighting with myself over how I work past that.

But I want to. At least I'm getting firmer in that choice. And the physical attraction I feel toward the man is definitely not dwindling either.

"God, he's so sexy." A woman's voice to my left pulls me from my thoughts.

"I agree. But since he came home, he hasn't even looked at a woman."

"Girl, do you know how many make-believe noises I've had to think of just for an excuse to take my car to his garage?"

The other woman giggles. "Yup. I've been there too."

The first woman sighs. "Maybe he's gay."

A snort escapes from me because I'm certain I know who they're talking about. Grady? Gay? Um, pretty sure after the filthy things he whispered to me and did to my body, no one would ever believe that claim.

"No, I've heard he actually went home with some woman from Ricky's a few months ago, so that can't be it."

My pulse hammers as I continue to listen. "Obviously it was just a one-night stand, then, because I've heard he's still single."

My hackles rise. I understand the allure of this man. Hell, I've admired him longer than I care to admit, and on and off for years before that. And now, I'm carrying his baby and still fighting my attraction to him. But hearing these women drool over him and speculate about his life is making me irritated, and dare I say, jealous.

He's mine, I want to say with a glare that tells them to back off.

But I can't say that—*because I won't let myself be his*.

Chase strikes out the final batter, launching a celebration among the crowd here to cheer on the home team. Smiling, my son races into the dugout, high-fiving Grady, who quickly looks back to find me, grinning from ear to ear. He gives me a wink and then turns his attention back to the team, getting his players ready to go up to bat.

Carrington Cove High School scores two runs in the bottom of the ninth, making the final score 5-2. The boys erupt in celebration of their win, jostling Chase around, congratulating him on his performance on the mound.

When the celebration has died down, I make my way down the bleachers and onto the field. When I spot Chase, I walk over and tap him on his shoulder. He spins around and his face lights up as he pulls me into his arms and lifts me off the ground. "Mom! We won!" He spins me around a few times before planting me back down on the ground.

"You did so good! I'm so proud of you!"

"He did amazing," Grady says, striding up to both of us. He holds a fist out to bump with Chase, who returns it enthusiastically, and then turns his attention to me. "Did you enjoy the game?"

"Of course," I say as he wraps his arm around my waist, pulling me to his side.

Chase studies us with curiosity before one of the other players calls him over to where they're standing. "I'll be right back, Mom."

"Okay, I'll be here."

Grady tips my chin up so I meet his eyes. "He did so fucking good, Scottie. Kept his cool, used the strategies we've been practicing all week. Hell, I thought the pressure was going to get to him there at the end, but he took his time and made the right call with the pitch. He's a fucking natural."

Smiling while fighting tears of pride, I say, "I love watching him play. He's so in his element out there."

Grady nods and then reaches down to place his palm on my growing belly. "Did this little one enjoy the game too?"

Those flutters I'm getting used to feeling now move across my belly, right under Grady's hand, but he doesn't notice, so I don't say anything. He probably can't feel it yet. "They did."

"Good. This kid needs to accept right now that baseball is just going to be a part of his or her life, in one way or another."

"So coaching wasn't such a bad idea after all?" I tease.

He cups the side of my face. "I'm glad I listened to you, Scottie. I fucking needed this."

The crack in his voice makes me want to comfort him because I know how hard this decision was for him. We only talked about it briefly that night back in December, but I could see the conflict in his eyes. I know what it was like to lose the game, but when you dedicate your life to something like that, it never fully leaves you. It just isn't the center of your world anymore.

Grady's eyes bounce back and forth between mine and then I hear the women from earlier snickering behind us.

"Who is that? Are they together?" one of the women says to the other.

"I don't know. She looks familiar, though."

Unwilling to listen to any more, I just react. Pressing up on my toes, I plant my lips on Grady's, marking him as mine as I pull his head down and block out the women's chatter.

Grady doesn't even hesitate, melting into the kiss as he pulls me in tighter, cups my jaw again, and dances his tongue against mine while the sounds around us fade away.

What are you doing, Scottie? You aren't supposed to be kissing this man, remember?

Yeah, but I'll be damned if I let these women even think they could have a shot with my baby's daddy.

I swat away those worries and drown in the kiss instead, wrapping my arms around his neck, twisting my tongue against his, groaning when his hand buries in my hair and gives it a gentle tug.

I'm so enraptured in the moment, feeling my entire body heat up, that I forget we're at a high school baseball game until my son comes over and metaphorically throws cold water on us.

"Jesus, Mom." I break away from Grady instantly, just in time to see my son cover his eyes. "So this is how my future sibling was conceived?"

Grady smirks down at me. I resist the urge to meet his gaze, fully aware of what he's thinking, and I refuse to give him that satisfaction. "Chase, I..."

He holds a hand up. "Let's just pretend that didn't happen. Although the entire team saw you, which isn't great."

"I'll handle the team," Grady says.

"I thought you two were just friends?" Chase asks, but the truth is, I don't have an explanation for him right now because I'm the one that crossed the line this time, not Grady.

"We are," I say as Grady huffs beside me. "But look, we need to get going, okay?"

Chase rolls his eyes. "Fine. Let me go get my stuff." He races toward the dugout, leaving Grady and me alone.

I slowly lift my eyes to meet his and am taken aback by the look he's giving me. "Yes?"

Crossing his arms over his chest, he says, "Nothing."

I narrow my eyes, mimicking his stance. "Nothing? That's what you're going to say to me?"

"Yup." He nods once and then leans down to kiss my temple. "See you tomorrow morning?"

Tomorrow we're leaving for our road trip to Kentucky, which means I had to take the day off, but I honestly don't mind. I could use the break. But now, after I just kissed the man I told to stop kissing me, I'm thinking the timing of this all couldn't be worse.

Stupid hormones and jealousy.

"Um, yeah. I'll be ready."

"Good. We have a long drive and lots to talk about." He intensifies the glare he's giving me, making his eyes appear even smaller. "*A lot* to talk about, Scottie. And I just hope you're ready for it." I swallow roughly. "Sleep well, keep growing our baby, and I'll see you soon."

Jesus Christ. What have I gotten myself into?

Chapter Fifteen

Grady

"She did what?" Astrid asks through the phone as I shove my last pair of shorts into my duffle bag.

"She fucking kissed me in front of everyone at the game." I can't fight the smile spreading across my face, thinking back to how brazen Scottie was in that moment. I heard the women behind us talking, and hell, it's not like I don't hear that shit practically everywhere I go in this small town. But the way Scottie reacted to their words is a really clear indication that she feels what I feel—*possessiveness*—which means we are definitely on the right path to getting her to admit that she has feelings for me.

"So what did you say to her?"

"Nothing."

My sister grows quiet. "Um, why not?"

"Because I could tell she was freaked out by it, and honestly, I didn't *need* to say anything. She fucking kissed me, Astrid. That means she wants me, and that's all I need to know."

She wants me, and I'm tired of us both pretending she doesn't.

"Don't push too hard, Grady," my sister cautions. "Just because she kissed you, doesn't mean she's ready for more yet."

"I know, but it means she can't deny our connection, Astrid. And fuck, I'm tired of denying it too. This trip is the make-or-break point. I need her to open up to me, to give me a shot. We can go slow, but if I don't at least try to get her to see that she doesn't need to be scared of me, then I'm going to regret it."

"God, this is so romantic," my sister says through the phone. "I feel so invested and really want everything to work out. For both of your sakes, I hope she doesn't make you wait as long as I did with Penn."

"Your situation was a little different though too, sis."

"Yeah, but still, the fear is the same. Make her feel safe, and then she'll let her guard down."

"Protecting her and our baby is the only thing I can think about most days."

"Please promise to call me after your trip and let me know how it goes, okay?"

"I promise. Give Bentley and Lilly a kiss for me."

"I will. Good luck and be safe, Grady."

We say our goodbyes and then I end the call, shoving my phone in my pocket before zipping up my bag and slinging it over my shoulder, eager to get to Scottie's house to pick her up. When I pull into her driveway, I see her outside on the lawn in front of her mother's house, talking to Lisa and Gigi.

"Good morning, ladies!" I call as I step out of my truck.

Gigi grins at me and Lisa sends a wink my way, but Scottie is standing with her arms wrapped around her body, almost as if she's trying to comfort herself. But her eyes? They're dancing appreciatively up and down my body. The weather is supposed to be warm this weekend, so I'm wearing khaki shorts, a navy shirt, and, of course, a baseball cap.

The way Scottie is looking at me right now tells me she likes what she sees, and the feeling is mutual. She has on a light pink sundress that fits snugly at the top but is loose enough around the waist to conceal her growing stomach. For a second, I'm disappointed, but then she uncrosses her arms and the fabric stretches across her bump, revealing the evidence of our growing child.

Mine.

These two are mine and it's only a matter of time before Scottie accepts it.

"I appreciate you two looking after Chase while I'm gone," she says to her mom and grandma, turning away from me as I join their circle.

"Of course. Don't worry about him. We'll make sure he stays out of trouble."

"I already threatened him if he tries to pull any type of shit," Gigi says with an arch of her brow.

"He'd be a fool to double cross you, Gigi," I say.

"Any man would. Maybe I should share with him what happened to the last man that pissed me off…"

Scottie sighs and pinches the bridge of her nose. "As much as we'd love to sit around and let you regale us with tales of your insanity, we have a long drive ahead of us and really should be going."

Gigi rolls her eyes. "Fine, but you two had better be careful. I can't handle raising another teenager. I barely survived getting this one through high school," she says, jutting her thumb at Lisa.

"Oh, I wasn't that bad," Lisa protests.

"Do we need to share your crazy antics with the group?" Gigi teases, popping her hip and hand out at the same time.

With a laugh, I say, "I'd love to hear these stories, but another time." Reaching for Scottie's hand, I pull her toward her house.

Gigi calls out to us before we get too far, "I'd tell you two to use protection, but it seems kind of redundant now!"

Scottie groans and I stifle my laughter, leading her to her front door. "I can't even apologize for her anymore."

"It's fine," I say, not wanting to dwell on her family because she and I are the only thing I plan to focus on this weekend. "Are you all packed?"

"Yes. My bags are inside. I just need to use the bathroom and then we can go," she says, opening the front door and leading the way inside.

"I'll grab your stuff."

"And I'm just warning you, Grady," she says, pulling my attention to her as she rubs her stomach. "This kid likes to eat and put pressure on my bladder, so there might be a few more stops on our journey than you planned."

"Scottie, I'll stop a thousand times if you need it, okay?"

Her smile is soft and directed right at me. "Okay."

I watch her walk down the hallway and then I grab her small suitcase and bag. I head out to my truck to deposit them in the back seat. A few minutes later, Scottie emerges, locking the door behind her. She traipses down the steps over to the passenger side of the truck, where I'm waiting to help her inside.

"I guess chivalry isn't dead," she says as I open the door, take her hand in mine, and help her up into the truck.

"Definitely not. But it's also about the risk of you falling while trying to get in my truck."

"I'm not a klutz, Grady."

Brushing her curls from her face, I cup her jaw and direct her gaze to mine. "Didn't say you were. I'm just taking extra precautions since the last thing I want is for one slip to jeopardize you or our baby, Scottie."

She blinks a few times but doesn't say anything, so I press a quick kiss to her forehead, shut her door, and then round the hood to hop into my seat. "Seat belts on."

"Yes, Dad."

"The daddy kink isn't one I'm interested in, unless it really does it for you. Then I might reconsider."

She smacks my shoulder as I back out of the driveway and head for the highway, drawing a laugh from me. And as soon as we get on the open road, my pulse returns to normal, even though the clock just started ticking and I still have a lot of work to do.

***

"Bye, bye, bye!" Scottie sings while doing the famous hand movements that accompany the NSYNC song she's currently torturing me with. "God, I still know all the words all these years later."

"I can see that," I grumble before signaling and switching lanes on the highway.

She cackles beside me as she scrolls through her phone for her next choice of punishment. "Okay, I can take a hint. I honestly haven't listened to boy bands in years, but I had to torture you a bit just for old times' sake."

"Hey, if it makes you and the baby happy, then I can handle it."

Scottie adjusts herself in her seat, selecting a country station that I appreciate wholeheartedly, and then turning toward me. We're only an hour into our drive, but already I feel like having her in my passenger seat is the only way I ever want to drive anywhere again. "You know, it doesn't have to always be about me and the baby, Grady."

"Yes, it does."

"What about you? What do *you* want?"

I shoot her a glance over my shoulder, a look that says she knows what I want, and that shuts her up instantly. "Exactly."

She turns back to face forward and then silence stretches through the cab as we cruise along the highway. After about fifteen minutes, she says, "Are we driving all the way to Coal City today?"

"No. We're gonna stop in St. Paul, Virginia tonight. I have a hotel room booked and we'll finish the drive in the morning. I'm sure you'll want to move instead of sitting for the entire eight-hour drive. I figured we'd want to stretch our legs, get some dinner, and relax a bit."

"I could have made it the entire trip, Grady. I wish you would have asked."

Yeah, but if I did, then I wouldn't have had the excuse to take you to dinner tonight and stay in a hotel room with you.

"It's okay. I don't mind. I'm just grateful you agreed to come with me. It gives us time to talk, you know?" I'm also drowning in the scent of her perfume that's embedding itself in the interior of my truck, which means it's going to smell like her for weeks. And I'm definitely not complaining.

She clears her throat. "Ah, yes. The parenting advice that you wanted. Well, no time like the present. Ask away, Grady."

I nod, checking the navigation on my dash, making sure I'm not going to miss a turn for a while and then start the first place my mind goes. "Do you want an epidural when you deliver?"

"That's not about parenting."

"No, but I still want to know these things. I want to be on the same page going into delivery so we're not arguing about shit in the hospital and in case something happens, I need to be able to speak for you."

She lets out a sigh. "I had an epidural with Chase, but I think I might want to try having this one naturally. I guess I'll know once I get in there and if the pain gets to be too much. It's been a long time, but I know I'm strong enough to do it without the drugs."

"I won't judge you either way. I just want you to be comfortable and safe. You and the baby." I reach over and place my hand on her stomach, rubbing small circles over our child.

"I felt a kick from the outside the other day," she says. "That means you might be able to soon."

"I'm ready for that." Clearing my throat, I take my hand back and continue asking her questions. "Do you plan on nursing?"

"Yes. I didn't do it for very long with Chase, but I would like to try this time. If we use formula, I'm okay with that too."

"Selfishly, I want to be able to feed the baby as well, so whatever you decide I'll go along with."

"This is your kid too, Grady."

"I want my kid to be fed, Scottie. I don't care what that looks like, honestly."

"Okay. What else?"

"How do you feel about co-sleeping?"

"Jesus, you really did read all of those books, didn't you?"

"Yes, Scottie. Now answer the question."

"How about you tell me what *you* think about it?" she counters, putting the pressure on me.

"Honestly, I'm a little afraid of rolling over and squishing my kid. I know it can make things easier in the beginning, especially for nursing in the middle of the night, but a bassinet on the side of the bed might be easier and safer."

"You make it sound like we'll be sleeping in the same bed, Grady."

"Do you think I'm going to leave you alone in the beginning, Scottie?" I say, refraining from just telling her that this *will* happen, she just doesn't realize it yet. Sadly, I think this woman has forgotten how dedicated I can be to something that's important to me—and now that's her.

"I mean..."

"We need to figure out our living situation still," I say, not letting her finish. "I don't want to miss out on stuff, and if we were in the same house, it would be much easier for me to be involved."

"That's a big decision, Grady," she replies, her voice shaky.

"I know, but it's important to me. If there is one thing I want, Scottie, it's that."

There. Now I can use her insistence that I have a say to my advantage.

"We don't have to decide anything now, but I obviously have more room at my place—for you, Chase, and the baby."

"I'm not sure that's a good idea," she whispers.

Casting a glance at her briefly, I say, "Why? Afraid it would be too hard to resist me then?"

She blinks and then hits me with a reply that tells me tonight could change everything. "Yeah, I think it would."

***

"Twelve diapers in a day?" I pop a piece of pizza crust in my mouth, trying to rein in my shock.

"Yup." Scottie points her own crust at me from across the table. "Especially in the beginning. And don't be surprised if you're peed and pooped on by your kid. It's going to happen."

"How many times can I expect to be woken up in the middle of the night?"

Scottie grins. "You sure you want me to answer that question?"

I wince. "How bad can it get?"

"Well, there was a three-night stretch where Chase screamed from eleven at night to four in the morning for no reason. I swear, I tried everything to get him to calm down, but nothing worked. I felt like the worst mother on the planet because I couldn't calm my baby, but it's very normal for babies in the beginning to cry like that."

"Where was your ex?"

Scottie scoffs. "Andrew was in our room complaining about how loud the baby was, but never once offered to help soothe him."

Fury races through my chest. "Don't take this wrong, but every time you talk about your ex, it makes me want to throat punch him."

She grins, so at least I know she still doesn't harbor feelings for the guy. "Believe me, I want to too."

I feel like the moment to push is here, but at the same time, I don't want to ruin our night. We pulled in to St. Paul less than an hour ago, and the only options for food around our hotel were barbecue and pizza. Scottie chose pizza, so here we are, sitting in a booth in a mom-and-pop restaurant, talking about parenthood like it's the most natural thing in the world.

But I want to know more. I need to know why this woman is so hell-bent on keeping me at arm's length. So, risking turning this evening sour, I decide that now is the opportunity to get her to open up.

"Why did you marry him, Scottie?"

My question catches her off guard. "Excuse me?"

Leaning forward in my seat, I clasp my hands in front of me and look her square in the eye. "From what you've told me, the guy was a piece of shit. He didn't care about you or Chase, so I want to know. Why did you marry him?"

Her eyes bounce back and forth between mine for so long, I think she might run out of the restaurant to avoid answering the question. But then she takes a deep breath, blows it out, and starts talking.

"Andrew and I got married a few months before Chase was born. I did what I thought I was supposed to do—marry the man I was having a kid with and give us a shot at being a family. We were in love, or so I thought, and the last thing I wanted to believe was that my life would amount to nothing because it didn't go according to my plan. Softball wasn't an option anymore, so I decided to give all my time and energy to my family. I always wanted kids, I just didn't think it would happen that soon." I nod, urging her to continue. "But very soon after our wedding, I realized the man I thought I knew wasn't him at all. Andrew never was a doting father. He didn't help or spend a ton of time with Chase. As Chase got older and could play sports, I thought maybe that would change. And it did for a while, but then Andrew started missing practices and games. He would come home late, and many nights I would soothe my crying child to sleep because he missed his dad, wanted his dad there, but he never was."

She stares down at her lap for a beat until she pops her head up, straightens her spine, and the fierceness I've always known her to possess comes back into her eyes. "I was feeling sorry for myself, accepted my fate, until one day, I thought about the example I was setting for my son. I was showing him it was okay to accept less than what he and I both deserved, and that's when I knew we had to get out. I was teaching but knew I could make more money as an administrator so I pursued that, and while I did, I made plans to leave him."

My throat grows tighter as I wait for her to continue.

"Andrew controlled our finances, but he didn't share anything with me, so I started putting my own money aside, and waited until I knew that he wouldn't be able to hold financial security over my head. He works for a very wealthy law firm down in Georgia and was working on being named the next District Attorney in our county. A divorce would look bad for him, but I didn't care, especially after the strip club incident. We divorced two years ago, but he continued to hurt Chase. So, we left."

"How did he react?"

Her gaze drops to the table. "I don't know."

My pulse spikes at her response. "What do you mean you don't know?"

As if on cue, her phone starts vibrating across the table, Andrew's name flashing on the screen. She lets it go until the call ends and looks back up at me. "Andrew doesn't know that Chase and I left. At least, he didn't at first… But I've been getting more phone calls from him lately, so I think he may have figured it out."

"Fuck, Scottie." I grind my teeth together, feeling as if things make much more sense now, but also that there is even more to figure out. "You took his kid to another state without telling him?"

She tilts her head, and her voice is firm as she says, "The last time Chase saw his father was almost a year ago, Grady. The last time they even spoke was two months before we moved. My son doesn't deserve that. He deserves someone who values him and is invested in his life." Sighing, she continues, "If Andrew's been by the old house, he knows we're gone, but I refuse to live in fear of what he might do. I've spent too long basing my decisions on that man, and I owe Chase a better life than that."

"Legally though, he still has rights."

She stiffens, narrowing her eyes. "I'm aware of that, but if he knows what's good for him, he'll relinquish them. Chase is old enough to have a say in court, and I have proof of Andrew's extracurricular activities at the strip clubs that can always come out if need be."

"Why didn't you bring that up when you two divorced? Terminating his rights?"

"Because I wanted to believe he would value what little time he'd get with his son, but I should have known better than to think that even a divorce would change him."

I take a long sip from my beer, processing all this new information. "Do you think that's enough to keep him away? Or make him agree to give up his rights?"

"I don't know, but I was willing to take the risk when we left."

"Do you think he could be looking for you in Carrington Cove?"

"Maybe, but that would mean leaving his life down in Georgia, and that man cares about no one but himself."

I brush a hand through my hair, eyes fixed on the woman across from me. "God, Scottie." My mind is racing with so many thoughts, but the one that prevails is the one I choose to voice. "You're so fucking strong—do you know that?"

Her brows draw together. "Not sure *strong* is the word I'd use, Grady. I put up with too much shit for too many years…"

I reach across the table for her hands, clasping them in mine and intertwining our fingers. "But you left. You planned, made sacrifices, and took risks for your son." Shaking my head, I continue, "You're exactly the mother Chase needs, and I couldn't ask for a better mother of my child. You're fucking amazing."

Tears form in her eyes. "I don't feel amazing."

"How do you feel?" I say, lowering my voice so only she can hear it.

"Scared, Grady. So scared of repeating my mistakes."

"The only way that happens is if you trust the wrong people." I take her hand and place it over my heart. "Do you feel like you can trust me?"

She swallows hard, her voice a whisper. "I want to."

"I can work with that, Scottie. That means we're already halfway where we need to be."

***

"Um, why is there only one bed?" Scottie glances around the room as I bring in the last of our bags. The hotel room is a mix of rustic and modern with finished wood details and iron accents.

And yes, there's only one bed.

"This was all they had left. Don't worry, I don't bite."

Scottie huffs out a laugh. "Ha. Um, you're a liar because I've been a victim of your biting."

I glance at her over my shoulder as I hoist her suitcase onto the stand in the corner. "Eager victim, or enthusiastic participant?" Her cheeks flush, confirming what we both already know. "We're adults, Scottie. We can handle this, right?"

Grumbling, she walks to the bathroom, shutting herself inside as I fight the pleased grin on my face. I take a moment to unpack a few things while Scottie uses the restroom and when she emerges, she stares back at the bed like it's a volcano preparing to erupt. "I'm gonna take a shower."

"Okay." Gesturing to the bed, I say, "I'm gonna see if there's a movie or show on that we can watch before we call it a night."

She nods, grabbing a change of clothes from her suitcase and her toiletry bag before heading back to the bathroom. I hear the water turn on and instantly, all I can think about is her naked, covered in soap suds as water cascades down her changing body, wishing I was in there to appreciate it—a body I can't stop fucking thinking about worshiping and owning again.

"Jesus, Grady," I mutter to myself, contemplating how the rest of the night is going to play out. After Scottie's confession in the restaurant, I feel like I'm on high alert. I know her ex has no idea where we're at right now, but the idea that the man could show up at any time and cause more strife in her life makes me want to take matters into my own hands—not only for Scottie but also for Chase.

That kid has become as much a part of my life as Scottie has in the past month, and when we get back home, I have to do something to make sure I don't lose them too.

Any man that would let either of them go is a fucking idiot as far as I'm concerned.

They're mine now though, and that's all that matters.

I turn on the television, flipping through the channels, hoping there's something for us to watch that could help Scottie feel more at ease. A rerun of *Friends* catches my eye, so I stop there, loving that no matter how many times I watch this show, it never gets old. Ironically, the episode on the TV is the one with Rachel's baby shower, which just seems fitting given our circumstances.

"Just so you know, I know what a Diaper Genie is," Scottie says, coming out of the bathroom, drying her hair in her towel. "This episode always makes me laugh."

Fuck, she looks so sexy—no makeup, oversized t-shirt and small shorts that barely peek out from the hem of her shirt. And her nipples—they're standing at fucking attention, enticing me.

"I'm glad one of us does," I say, trying to conceal my growing erection as I adjust myself on the bed. But hell, I'm always fucking hard around this woman, so it's not like I can hide it completely.

"Did I tell you that Astrid offered to throw me a baby shower?"

"No, but that doesn't surprise me."

Scottie removes the towel from her head, hanging it on the hook on the bathroom door, and then moves closer to the bed, reaching for a bottle of lotion she set on the nightstand earlier. She pumps the bottle a few times, places her foot on the edge of the mattress, and then begins rubbing lotion into her smooth skin, all the way up and down those silky legs of hers I just want wrapped around my fucking hips again.

Jesus Christ, this is torture. And it was all my idea. What the fuck was I thinking?

"It almost made me cry, but then again, most things do right now."

I close my eyes and take a deep breath. I decide I should probably shower so I can jack off before I have to sleep next to this woman all night. If I had it my way, I'd be buried inside of her when I come, and even though I hoped we'd get to that point again eventually, I am not expecting our night to end that way.

"I'm gonna get in the shower," I announce, standing from the bed and walking over to my suitcase, trying to conceal the bulge in my shorts.

"Okay."

Taking my change of clothes into the bathroom with me, I turn on the water and wait for it to warm up. I reach for my dick the second I'm under the warm spray.

It's easy to forget what you're missing when you haven't had sex for a long time. And even though Scottie and I slept together almost five months ago now, I still remember every detail of that night. I know what she sounds like, feels like, smells like, and tastes like. And knowing all of those things makes being a gentleman that much fucking harder.

As I pull on my length, I think back to the image of her on my Nova, legs spread, pussy wet, moans leaving her plump lips. That familiar tingle races down my spine as I tighten my grip and move faster over my cock.

"Fuck," I groan on a whisper as the first spurt of cum hits the shower wall, leaving my body in ribbons that I wish I could see painted on Scottie's skin instead. When I'm spent, I finish washing my body and then get dressed, feeling a little more at ease before reentering the room.

But as soon as I see Scottie sitting up against the headboard with her shirt rolled up, staring down at her bare stomach, rubbing her bump in soft circles, my dick grows hard again instantly.

Fucking hell.

"Whatcha doing?" I say as I run the towel through my hair, hanging it on top of Scottie's on the back of the door.

She darts her eyes over to me and they immediately darken when she realizes that I don't have a shirt on.

Yeah, I might have made that choice on purpose.

"The baby is moving." She pats the bed, indicating I should join her. When I settle in next to her, she grabs my hand and places it on her stomach where our kid is doing somersaults. "Can you feel it?" A tiny push hits my hand, and I swear, I feel my heart crack open in my chest. "Did you feel that?"

I chuckle as my lips spread into a grin so big it hurts my fucking cheeks. "A little."

She moves my hand to another spot, and the movement I feel there is more pronounced. "That was a big one," Scottie says through a laugh.

"Yeah, I felt that one more, for sure."

Scottie and I sit there for a few minutes, soaking up the miracle growing in her stomach before she says, "You know, I haven't said thank you to you."

"Yeah, you have."

She shakes her head. "No. Not just for bringing me food I'm craving or rubbing my feet when they hurt…but for this." She presses my hand into her stomach. "For this child, Grady."

Fuck. This woman is killing me. "I know it wasn't planned, Scottie, but I wouldn't want to have a child with anyone else."

Our eyes lock on one another as my pulse hammers in my neck. For one second, I contemplate moving closer to her, seeing what she would do if I tried to kiss her, but then she yawns, breaking the moment. "Sorry."

Clearing my throat, I move my hand from her skin and stand from my spot. "No problem. It's definitely getting late. We should probably head to bed so we can get on the road early in the morning, right?"

She nods, moving from her spot in the bed, swinging her legs over the side, preparing to stand. "Yeah. I'm tired."

I give her privacy to do her nighttime routine, and then I enter the bathroom to do the same. The entire room smells like her, imprinting her scent on my brain, making me long to have this smell around for the rest of my life.

When I go back to the main room, Scottie is turned on her side in the bed, facing away from me. I take my spot closest to the door, the side I insisted on having. Scottie didn't understand my reasoning until I explained that I want to be the first person an intruder encounters, rather than putting her or the baby at risk. She rolled her eyes but went along with it and, honestly, I would have slept on the floor next to her if she hadn't.

I settle into the bed, lying on my back and staring up at the ceiling as the noises from outside filter through the room, along with Scottie's light breathing. "Good night, Scottie."

"Good night, Grady."

Silence stretches between us for so long, I think she's fallen asleep. But then she surprises me when she whispers, "Grady?"

My voice cracks when I answer. "Yeah?"

"Do you mind massaging my lower back, please?" She groans. "I'm in a lot of pain from sitting all day, I think."

"Fuck, Scottie. I'm sorry." Rolling over, I scoot closer to her and grip her hips, pulling her toward me.

"It's not your fault. It's part of growing a human. My hips always hurt because they're opening up for the baby."

Pressing my thumb into her lower back, I start to work out the tightness in her muscles, all the while feeling my dick grow harder in my shorts. But instead of trying to keep Scottie from feeling what she does to me, I move closer, pushing myself into her ass.

"Grady..."

"I'm not going to apologize for what you do to me, Scottie."

She lets out a long sigh. "Keep touching me."

"I didn't plan on stopping."

Her groans of relief fill the room as I rub and push into her hips and back, relieving the pressure. But when she speaks next, I nearly choke on my saliva.

"Did that offer to help with anything I need still stand?"

My hands freeze. "Anything."

She rolls onto her back as I pull my hand away from her, staring up at me from the bed. I can barely remember to take in a breath as she bites her bottom lip and says, "I'm so horny, Grady."

Jesus fucking Christ.

"Don't ask for something you're not one-hundred percent positive that you want, Scottie."

She reaches up and places her hand on my shoulder, moving her palm down my bicep and to my forearm before grabbing my hand and placing it between her legs, where I instantly feel the heat of her pussy. "I want it. I—I need it."

"Fuck, baby." I rest my forehead on hers as all of the blood in my body rushes to my cock.

"I'm so on edge, and you said..."

She doesn't get a chance to finish her sentence because I cover her mouth with mine, my restraint snapping. My pulse fires rapidly as my tongue dances against hers with so much force and passion that I'm afraid I'm going to overwhelm her.

But my hesitation is gone, my need for her is raging, and as soon as she pulls me down to her, I take what she's offering—for both of us.

"I'm dying here, woman," I say, grabbing her hand and placing it over my cock that feels like fucking steel at this moment.

"Me too. God, touch me, Grady. Please."

I kiss her deeper, rubbing her pussy through her shorts as she pushes her pelvis against my hand. "I want to do everything to you, Scottie. You have no idea how hard it's been not touching you like this again."

"Yes. I want it all. Fuck me. Own me." Her breaths are erratic. "Touch me everywhere. Make me come until I lose count."

Breaking our kiss, I push up from the bed and sit against the headboard, much like she was earlier. "Come here." I gesture for her to sit between my legs as my cock tries to climb out of my shorts, but he'll get his turn. First, I'm going to make this woman come all over my hand. Then my mouth. And then my cock. And then we're going to do it all over again.

"Take your shorts and underwear off." With her lip between her teeth, she stares at me while I watch her undress, ripping her shirt over her head as well, and then she crawls over to me, twisting around too soon because the sight of her tits and her swollen belly with my child is enough to make me come already.

"God, you're so sexy like this. Carrying my baby," I whisper in her ear as I reach around her, encasing her in my arms before cupping her breasts. The moan that leaves her lips is like a symphony only made for me. I twist and pinch her nipples softly at first, getting a feel for what she can handle. "Like that?"

"Harder."

Increasing the pressure, I tweak and turn her nipples in my fingers, feeling my cock twitch between us. Her breasts have definitely grown since the last time we were together, and I can't wait to show her how much I appreciate that change, how much I appreciate her body and how it's transformed as she grows my child.

"Yes," she mewls as her head falls back to my shoulder and her legs widen.

"How wet are you, Scottie?"

"Soaked, Grady. God, I need your fingers. Please touch me. Make me come until I can't breathe."

I dip my hand down over her stomach, stopping to appreciate that curve, and then travel down to her slit, dragging my index finger through her wetness. And she's right—she's fucking drenched.

"So greedy." I circle her clit softly with the tip of my finger. "You need this, don't you?"

"You have no idea how badly." Her nails dig into my forearm as I work her up slowly, but by the way she's already struggling to breathe, I'd say she's primed and ready to come.

"Tell me you're tired of fighting this," I say, stopping all of my movements as she tenses in my arms.

"What?"

I turn her head to face me with my hand that was just on her breast as my hand between her legs stays poised right at her clit. Looking into her eyes, I say, "Tell me that you're tired of fighting our connection, Scottie, and I'll make you come all fucking night."

Her eyes widen just slightly, but then she reaches up, drags her nails through the scruff on my jaw, and says, "I'm tired, Grady. I want you and I—I need you. I'm just…"

I place my finger over her lips to stop her. "That's all I needed to hear. The rest we can figure out later." Without missing a beat, I capture her lips with mine, kissing her hard as my finger goes back to working her over. I bring both of my hands between her legs now, pulling hers over my knees so she's completely exposed to me. The fingers of one hand slide right into her tight heat as my other hand puts more pressure on her clit.

"Oh God. Yes, right there…"

"Are you gonna come for me, Scottie?"

"Yes!"

I rub deeply inside of her, finding her G-spot and putting pressure there as wetness floods my hand. "Fucking squirt for me, Scottie. Let me see it and feel it."

With a few more strokes, she detonates, drenching the bed beneath her, covering my hand in her orgasm and convulsing in my arms as she struggles to breathe, but I don't let up.

"Grady…Grady, I can't," she breathes out as I keep playing with her, knowing that she's sensitive, but I don't stop.

"Yes, you can, baby. I'm not even close to being done yet." My hands keep moving, stroking her deeply, circling her clit until she comes once more, breathless and panting but satisfied, just the way she deserves to be.

With a press of my lips to her temple, I help her off me, spinning her so she's flat on the bed. I stand up, push my shorts and underwear down, stroking myself as Scottie watches me, licking her lips as her eyes drop down to my cock.

"He's all yours, baby. But first, you're going to get my tongue because tasting you the first time made me realize that I have a new drug of choice...and that's your pussy, Scottie."

Her lips curl in a delighted grin as I climb on the bed again, situating myself between her legs, dipping my head to her pussy and lapping up her releases that I worked for. "So fucking good."

Her hands bury in my hair. "God, Grady...yes!" She fucks my mouth as I eat her out, grinding herself on my face. "More. Please, more!"

I push two fingers inside her as my tongue explores her cunt, licking her clit, spearing her opening in tandem with my fingers, and building her up again like a man fucking starved.

For the past five months, I've been fasting, waiting for the perfect time to fuel my body with what it needs—and that's Scottie.

I reach up and play with her nipple with my free hand as my tongue continues to tease and torture her between her legs. Her pussy tightens around my fingers, and that's when I know she's about to explode again.

"That's it, baby. Give it to me," I mumble against her, and a few moments later, she's screaming, letting everyone know how good I'm making her feel, soaking my hand and making me hard as stone.

And I don't give a shit who hears.

"Fuck," she groans as I crawl up her body, pressing a kiss to her stomach, nervous about how rough I can be with her in her state, but trying not to focus on anything but what makes her feel good.

I lap at her nipples on my ascent, kissing and groping her breasts, giving them the attention they deserve—because in a few months, these won't belong to me anymore. And I want my fill before that happens.

"Grady…"

"Yeah, Scottie?"

"I need your cock."

Chuckling, I reply around her nipple. "I'm going to give it to you, dirty girl." She groans, turning her head to the side as I hold myself above her face. "Look at me, Scottie." I wait for her to turn back to face me, and when she does, I reach for my dick and drag it up and down her slit. "I want to memorize the way you look as I stuff you full of me." Gently, I press into her, letting her adjust to my thickness. Her back arches off the bed as she lets out a sigh of contentment, but our eyes are still connected as I work myself inside her, trying to keep my composure because feeling her bare, knowing that we don't have to worry about protection this time, is blowing my fucking mind.

"Fucking hell, Scottie."

"I'm not going to break, Grady. Fuck me, please."

I lean back on my heels, holding her legs open wide as I watch my cock disappear inside her, my length coated in her wetness, her pink flesh pulling and sucking me in as I pick up my pace. Her breasts jiggle and bounce with each of my thrusts, but when our eyes meet, I know that this woman has made my life complete, and fucking her for the rest of my days is the only thing that I want.

"You're dripping, Scottie." My dick glistens in the dark as I keep sliding in and out of her.

"It's so good…"

Keeping myself propped up on my hands, I hover over her face, lowering my lips to hers, kissing her and connecting with her, taking in every moment, every thrust, every moan that leaves her lips. My cock grows harder, that tingle in my spine warning me that I'm not going to last much longer if we keep this up, so I slow down and wait for Scottie's eyes to pop open before I say, "I want you to ride me, baby."

She nods in agreement, and after we shift around on the bed, I watch her slide down my cock again, getting a front row seat to this woman in all of her exquisite glory.

I never knew the sight of a pregnant woman could make me go fucking insane, but I think it's because it's Scottie, and she's carrying *my* baby that I feel like I can't get enough.

She lifts her hands and buries them in her hair as she swirls her hips over me, rubbing her clit against my pelvis while hitting that spot inside of her that I know will set her off.

"That's it, Scottie. Fuck that cock until you come. Break for me."

Her breathing picks up speed. "I'm almost there."

Pushing myself up, I hold her to my chest and latch onto her nipple with my mouth, sucking and nibbling while I tweak the other one, giving her every sensation that I know she loves, that I know she needs, so that when she finds her climax, I can let go with her.

Her hips move up and down, her stomach rubs against my chest, I pull her mouth to mine, and seconds later she screams against my lips, taking me over the edge with her. White hot pleasure sears my limbs, makes me dizzy, and leaves me breathless as we both come down from the high of being with each other again.

Slowly, still encasing her in my arms, I lower us to the bed so we're both lying on our sides. After we gain control of our breathing, I open my eyes to find Scottie staring at me, the wheels in her mind clearly spinning.

"Don't freak out, Scottie," I say, cupping the side of her face that's slick with sweat.

"I'm not."

"Are you sure?" Stroking her back, I wait for her to respond.

"Yeah. It's just…"

"What, Scottie? What are you thinking?"

She pauses but then says, "I'm just wondering how soon until we can do that again."

It takes a second for her words to register, but when they do, I tip my head back and let out a laugh that runs through my entire body. "Jesus, woman. Can I get a minute to recover, please? I'm not that young anymore."

Giggling, she pushes my hair from my face. "Don't take too long, Grady. My body is wound up tight and it seems your cock is the only thing that can cure that."

Rolling over her once more, careful not to crush her beneath me, I stare down into her eyes and say, "Good thing you're finally admitting that. Now buckle up because it looks like sleep isn't in your future tonight. We have lost time to make up for, and I'm taking advantage of every second."

***

"That's it. Squeeze my cock, Scottie." I'm sitting on the corner of the bed, and Scottie is riding me, facing away from me so her back is to my chest. With my hand between her legs, I find her clit and make slow circles around the nub as she moves up and down. "Go slow, Scottie. Feel every inch."

"You're so thick," she moans, wrapping an arm around the back of my neck as her hips roll and glide in a rhythm that is making my legs shake. "God, I needed this."

"Fuck yes. Jesus, I want to bend you over and fuck you so hard."

"Please…"

Knowing she wants that too, I lift her off me and spin us around, pushing her down so her torso is on the bed now. She props herself up on her forearms, glancing back at me as I drag my crown through her slit.

"Don't tease me."

I give her ass a little slap. "Patience."

"I need to come," she whines, dropping her head to the comforter.

Sliding back inside of her slowly, she lets out an erotic moan when I push all the way in, bottoming out and circling my hips before drawing back out and repeating the process.

"Yes…oh, fuck!"

I must have hit the magic spot because she's coming quickly, shaking and screaming into the mattress as I stroke her deep and hard, waiting for her to reach the end of her orgasm before I let myself take my own.

When the last drop leaves my body, I collapse onto the bed next to her, my hand covering my chest as I regain my composure. This is the third time we've had sex tonight, and as much as I want to keep going, I know we need to rest too.

I roll over and pull her into my chest, kissing her shoulder and running my hand over her stomach while she faces away from me. "You okay?"

"Uh-huh."

"You sure I didn't hurt you?"

She glances over her shoulder to look at me. "No, Grady. You took care of me and gave me exactly what I needed."

I rest my forehead on her shoulder now. "Fuck, I needed it too." The yawn that leaves her lips makes me laugh. "I think it's time we sleep though, Scottie."

"Fine."

After we both use the bathroom and put our clothes back on, Scottie turns on her side again, but this time I pull her closer to me, breathing her in as we drift off.

"What happens now, Grady?" she whispers as sleep overtakes us both.

"Now we sleep, Scottie. The rest can wait."

Chapter Sixteen

Scottie

"Grady..." My eyes peek open and see the sun cutting through the curtains on the window in our hotel room, but that's not what woke me up. The man between my legs doing wicked things with his tongue is.

"Your pussy is so fucking addictive, baby."

Burying my hand in his hair, I let him work his magic, exploding on his tongue in record time, which is astounding to me since I lost count of how many orgasms he gave me last night.

As soon as we went to bed last night, my body couldn't relax.

My chest is wound tight, my hormones are running wild, and Grady said he would help me with whatever I needed—and what I need more than anything right now is sex.

All I could think about was the man lying beside me, the one who told me how strong and brave I was, the one who has been nothing but a constant in my life since he reentered it, and even back before we reconnected. This man that has told me numerous times how much I mean to him, and even though I'm terrified, I can't keep denying how I feel.

I wish I could tell the future, that I could see that the risk of letting him in would be worth it, but it's just not possible. What is worth it, though, is trusting him—something that I feel is the biggest obstacle we face, but one I'm ready to conquer if it means getting this right with him. I just know I have to take things slowly so I can get there.

Sure. Grady making you come until you can't walk is taking things slowly, Scottie.

He's just scratching an itch for me that he created when he impregnated me with his super sperm, okay?

As soon as I come down from my release, Grady crawls up my body, kissing my stomach where our child is growing on his way up, hovering over my face as he reaches my head.

"Well, that's one way to wake up."

"That's the only way I want to wake up from here on out, Scottie. With my mouth on your pussy."

I can feel my cheeks start to heat from his words. "Not sure that's possible."

"It would be if you were in my bed every night." He rolls to the side, propping his head up on his arm, facing me. I realize he stripped my shorts and underwear off while I was still asleep.

"Grady..."

He reaches for my hand, threading our fingers together. "Don't overthink it. We had sex, Scottie. I was doing what you needed, what you asked for..."

"I was horny," I explain, even though it was more than just that. "The hormones..."

He thrusts his rock-hard erection into my pelvis. "Tell the truth. You remembered how good we were together and needed to make sure it wasn't all in your imagination. That's why you told me you wanted me to massage your back last night."

With a shaky breath, I admit, "Fine. I did want you. I *do* want you. You're right, okay?"

His grin is lethal. "Damn. You admitting that is music to my ears."

I roll my eyes and then pull his lips to mine, savoring our kiss, making sure this is real. It feels real, so strong and overwhelming that it's terrifying. But God, this man. I didn't know there were men like him.

And he wants *me*.

Grady lowers his forehead to mine. "The first step to accepting you have a problem is admitting it," he teases as I push against his chest, but he just holds my hand against his skin as he holds my gaze with his eyes.

On a shaky breath, I ask, "But...what happens now?"

His eyes bounce back and forth between mine before he says with confidence, "Now Chase and I work on putting the car back together, I keep coaching, you keep growing our baby, and we keep fucking because it seems like you need that and I'm more than willing to take care of that for you."

I can't help but laugh.

God, how am I supposed to resist this man?

I think the answer to that question is—I don't. I just let him in, one step at a time.

***

"Pleasure doing business with you." Grady reaches forward to shake hands with Carl, the man we drove all this way to meet.

"I hope this helps you get your girl on the road sooner rather than later."

"It will, believe me. Finding a hood to replace is like finding a needle in a haystack. I appreciate you answering my call."

"Don't mention it. The pleasure was all mine." Carl directs his eyes to me. "And congrats on the baby. Not sure a Nova would be considered a family car, but…"

Grady laughs. "It's more of a passion project, but our family will definitely enjoy it when it's done."

I stand back and let Grady finish tying down the hood in the bed of his truck while letting his declaration swirl around in my brain. After our conversation this morning in bed, he made love to me one more time and then we got dressed, stopping by a small café near our hotel for breakfast before finishing the drive to Coal City, knowing that this trip has changed so much between us.

I know he wants more than just sex, but for now that's what I can offer him. He didn't say anything else to me about our future, so I'm not sure where his head is, but I can't worry about that when my own mind is spinning with questions and what-ifs. After fighting something for so long, it's hard to change your outlook overnight. But after last night, all I know is that I can't deny my feelings any longer or what my body needs—and apparently, that's Grady's cock.

"You ready?" Grady wipes the dust off his hands as he hops down from the bed of the truck, looking so delicious with a smudge of dirt on his cheek and his arms bulging against the sleeves of his simple gray shirt.

"You're a mess." I walk over to him, lick my thumb, and then reach up to wipe the dirt from his face. But he catches my hand before I can touch him, pulls my thumb into his mouth, and sucks it—*hard*.

Dear Lord. My vagina just clenched.

"That…that wasn't what I was after," I say when he releases my thumb with a pop.

"I know, but you didn't hate it, did you?"

Trying to hide the whimper that wants to escape my lips, I swallow and say, "Are you just going to torture me now that you know how addicted I am to sex?"

He smirks at me before pulling me into his chest. "Maybe."

"That's not very nice."

"On the contrary, I think the things that I do to you are *very* nice—and a little naughty too." The gravel of his voice sends a shock wave to my clit, and if he doesn't stop, I'm going to end up fucking him on the side of the road multiple times on the drive back home.

I've never been this horny in my life.

"Come on, Scottie. Let's get on the road. We're already behind schedule, and I'd like to get you home at a reasonable hour so you can ride my cock again later if that's what you want."

Chuckling, I let him help me into the truck, and then we make the long drive home, getting home late, but not late enough to prevent Grady from giving me two more orgasms before we both pass out.

Chapter Seventeen

Grady

"I'm nervous." Scottie squeezes my hand again as we wait in the exam room, eager for the doctor to come in and do her ultrasound. She's right between four and five months along, which means we could determine the sex on an ultrasound if the baby cooperates, but if not, we'll have to wait longer.

I never considered myself an impatient man, but between Scottie initiating sex between us and wondering if this appointment is going to go the way we want, I'm feeling more and more on edge.

Our road trip ended the way I hoped it would, with Scottie giving in to our connection. But as soon as I saw the look on her face in the light of day, my own fear surfaced—the fear she'll regret us sleeping together again. So instead of asking her to explain what her expectations are between us now, I didn't push for anything. And now, I'm in yet another limbo status of my relationship with my baby's mother.

"Why are you nervous?"

"Because I don't want you to be disappointed," she says, startling me.

"Why would I be disappointed?"

She rubs circles over her stomach. "I don't know. What if you have your hopes up for one gender, and it's the opposite?"

"Scottie, I don't care if it's a monkey, as long as it's healthy, okay?"

She stares up at me with a pinch in her brow. "If it's a monkey, we have a whole other set of problems to deal with, Grady."

Laughing, I press a kiss to her forehead just as Dr. Rivera comes into the room. "Well, hello there."

"Hey, Doc." I keep Scottie's hand in mine but stand up tall now as Dr. Rivera crosses the room to her chair.

"How are you feeling, Scottie?"

"Pretty good. The nausea is finally gone, and there's a lot of movement from the baby."

"Good," Dr. Rivera replies, flipping through Scottie's chart.

"And she's definitely aroused more," I add, which has both the doctor and Scottie snapping their heads in my direction.

"Grady!" Scottie hisses.

Hiding my grin, I say, "What? It's true." Scottie has no reason to be ashamed of her need for my cock, but making her blush is quickly becoming a favorite activity of mine.

Dr. Rivera clears her throat. "Well, increased libido is normal in the second trimester. As long as it's comfortable for you, Scottie, sex is perfectly safe."

Scottie glares at me. "Good luck getting laid now."

Squeezing her hand again, I turn my attention back to Dr. Rivera, who is also fighting a grin. "All of your labs look good though, so what do you say we have a look on the ultrasound. Are you two interested in finding out the sex?"

"Yes," Scottie and I say at the same time.

Dr. Rivera chuckles. "All right then. Just don't be disappointed if the baby gets shy on us. It happens fairly often, especially with the girls."

As she lifts Scottie's shirt and squeezes clear gel on her skin, I bring Scottie's hand to my lips and gently kiss her knuckles. The doctor maneuvers the ultrasound wand, trying to get the right angle of the baby. "Everything looks great. Baby is measuring on track." Dr. Rivera clicks around on the screen, taking measurements and then moves the wand around, trying to get a clear view of the baby's anatomy.

"Oh my gosh." Scottie leans forward in her seat, trying to get a closer look at the screen. But I don't see a damn thing. In fact, there is nothing between this kid's legs.

And that's when it hits me.

"Looks like you two are having a girl!" Dr. Rivera exclaims. Just then, the baby moves and presses her legs together just long enough to confirm her lack of a penis.

"Holy shit." I look down at Scottie just as she stares up at me. "We're having a girl."

"I don't know how to raise a girl," Scottie says with a pout of her lips, but there's an excitement in her eyes as well.

Dr. Rivera chuckles as she takes a few pictures of our daughter's profile, and then prints out a strip of pictures for us to take with us. "Each sex has its own set of challenges, but the teenage years are what you really can't prepare for either way."

Scottie sighs, leaning back on the bed, but my mind is still swimming.

I'm going to have a daughter.

Dr. Rivera hands Scottie the strip of pictures. "Keep doing what you're doing, Mom. We'll see you both in a month."

After Scottie gets situated and we schedule our next appointment, I lead her back out to my truck and help her inside. I insisted on picking her up from work to drive her to the appointment together, and now that I know I have a daughter on the way, the world just completely shifted beneath me.

"So, she's not allowed to date until she's thirty, and I may need to buy more guns—I already have a few at home."

Scottie slaps my arm as I continue to drive back to Carrington Cove Elementary. "Oh, stop it."

With a grin, I glance over at the mother of my child, picking up her hand and kissing the top of it. "We're having a girl, Scottie."

"Yes, Grady. That's the third time you've said that now."

"I'm gonna get to be a dance dad."

She laughs at me. "Well, at least you already have practice with that."

"There's going to be pink and purple everywhere."

"How do you feel about that?"

I take a deep breath. "Honestly, I'm overwhelmed all over again, but this time it's an exciting overwhelm. Now I can prepare for more things that were up in the air—like the nursery."

Scottie's eyes dip down to her stomach. "Yeah. It just became very real."

"Did you doubt that it was before?" I tease.

Smiling, she shakes her head. "No, but I raised a boy, Grady. Raising a girl is something I don't have any experience with."

"We'll learn together," I reply. "Plus, Astrid will go through everything with Lilly first, so we'll get to watch her as sort of an experiment."

Scottie nods. "Good point."

"So when do you want to start getting her room ready?"

Scottie's head whips over to me so fast, I swear, I hear it crack. "What?"

I quickly glance over at her. "What do you mean, 'what'?"

"Grady, I...we don't need to worry about that yet."

Irritation builds in my chest, but I keep myself in check while breathing to relieve the pressure. "Scottie, we're having a baby in four months. There's a timeline, sweetheart."

"I know that, and I don't appreciate you insulting my intelligence."

My head rears back on my neck. "I'm not insulting you, I just..."

"Well, that's what it feels like." She crosses her arms over her chest and stares out the passenger window.

"Scottie..."

"You can't just make decisions without me, Grady."

I push my hand through my hair. "I'm not bringing anything up that you're not also aware of, but you've got to meet me halfway here."

Her head whips back in my direction. "And you need to understand how difficult it was for me to take a step forward with you. I mean, my God, we *just* found out we're having a daughter, *just* left the doctor's office, and you're already talking about me moving in. We've been sleeping together for a week! We're not together..."

I shake my head, clenching my teeth and the steering wheel beneath my hands. "Thanks for reminding me of that fact you've made abundantly clear, no matter how much I try to get you to see..." I let my words trail off because the things I want to say aren't going to make this situation better.

"You know what? Let's just not talk about it anymore, okay?"

I want to push. I want to tell her that shutting down on me isn't how we're going to be able to work through shit, but I also know that she's emotional, hormonal, and scared. And I need to take a minute to pause as well because if I don't, I might end up saying something that I can't take back.

As I pull into the parking lot, I turn into the bus circle that leads right to the front office. When I shift the truck into park, I turn in my seat to face Scottie as she gathers her purse from the floorboard, avoiding my gaze.

"Scottie..."

"I need to get back to work, Grady." She reaches for the door handle, but I grab her other arm before she can, pulling her across the seat to me and smashing my lips to hers.

She refuses to open to me at first, but with the second pass of my tongue over her lips, she moans and lets me fuck her mouth with my own as I bury my hands in her hair, those curls that I can't get enough of. I claim her for as long as she'll let me, remind her of our connection, and help her relax all while working us both up for later.

When I pull back, her eyes are still closed. She slowly opens them and when our gazes meet, her bottom lip starts to tremble.

"I'm sorry," I say before she can speak, cupping her jaw with my hand. "But if you shut down on me, we're never going to get through this. I need you to be able to talk to me, Scottie. Tell me how you're feeling instead of ending a conversation before it starts."

"It's just a lot. I need some time, Grady. Moving fast is the last thing I want to do because I don't feel like I'm in control that way." She pauses then says, "Hell, I don't feel in control when I'm around you at all."

I nuzzle my nose against hers. "The feeling is mutual, baby. You make me feel like a piece of my heart exists outside my body, and I want to do anything and everything I can to protect it." I cup the side of her face. "But if you don't meet me halfway, this isn't going to work."

With a pleading look in her eyes, she asks, "Can we table the discussion about the nursery then, please?"

"Okay. But just know that it's happening, Scottie. You and our daughter will be living under my roof where I can look after both of you. And Chase will be there too."

She leans forward and presses a kiss to my lips but doesn't reply to the declaration I just laid out there. "I'll see you later."

"Keep growing our baby girl, Scottie."

When she turns back to the door, I watch her step down from the truck and walk toward the office, taking my resolve with her.

Baby steps. That's what I keep reminding myself. But my baby is stepping into this world sooner rather than later, and her mother and I need to get on the same page soon. Otherwise, I'm not sure what world she's going to be coming into, and I don't like that feeling at all.

When I get back to the garage, reality shifts on its axis as I consider what's most important regarding raising a daughter, and the first thing that comes to mind is safety. In a flash, one threat I've failed to forget surges through me with urgency, so before I can push it off any longer, I make the phone call I've been meaning to since I got back from Kentucky.

"Law Offices of Timothy McDonald. How can I help you?"

"Hi, Mabel. It's Grady Reynolds. Is Tim available to chat by any chance?"

I hear some muttering in the background. "Actually, he is free. Hold on one moment while I transfer you to his line."

"I appreciate it."

The line goes silent for a moment before the boisterous voice of Timothy McDonald fills my ears. "Grady Reynolds! Gotta say, I wasn't expecting a phone call from you today, or ever, really."

"Usually I'm not in need of your services, Tim. But it seems things have changed."

I hear paper rustle around through the phone. "Well then, what can I do for you? You got into some legal trouble, I take it?"

"Not exactly. It's actually a friend of mine that needs your help."

"I see. What seems to be the issue?"

And so I tell him, preparing for the worst obstacle that Scottie and I will have to face before we can truly move forward.

But I have to make sure that my family is taken care of—all three of them now.

Chapter Eighteen

Scottie

"How was your trip?" Astrid asks as we walk through the baby boutique on the boardwalk that frames Carrington Cove. The reflection of the sunset off the water is breathtaking as I admire the view from inside the store. It's Wednesday night and Chase is at Grady's working on the Nova, so I figured it was the best time to meet up with Astrid and knock an item off my to-do list—registering for my baby shower.

Plus, I feel like I need someone to talk to about how I'm feeling, and Astrid is the first person that came to mind.

"Hello? Earth to Scottie." She waves her hand in front of my face, breaking through my stare.

"Sorry."

Her grin is assuming. "That good, huh?"

"If you're implying what I think you are, that makes this conversation even more awkward."

Astrid laughs. "Look. I know my brother has sex, all right? I mean, you *are* pregnant with his child." She nudges my shoulder jokingly. "Grady has only told me that things went well, and I'm dying to know if that means you took anything that we talked about to heart."

Sighing, I pick up a beautiful gray and teal blanket from the shelf, smoothing over the soft fabric with my hand while avoiding her eyes. "I did, and I'm..." I turn to look at her now. "I asked him to do something for me that only he can, and he delivered...multiple times."

Astrid folds her lips in, trying to stifle her squeals. "Oh. My. God..."

I set the blanket back down and begin to walk away from her. "It's not that big of a deal."

She scurries after me to keep up. "Um, yes it is. This is huge. And, selfishly, I'm so happy that you're trying to move forward, Scottie."

Spinning to face her now, I say, "I'm terrified, but I can't deny what's there, Astrid. Your brother is the type of man you don't let go of, and..." I glance around the shop, making sure there's no one to overhear us. "I'm so horny."

She chuckles. "Oh, yeah. I remember those days during the second trimester. Brandon was on deployment during my second pregnancy, so my vibrator became my best friend."

"Well, I think mine is about to break." We share a laugh. "But of course, it's more than just about sex," I say, sighing wistfully, thinking back to how this man has cared for me since he found out he was going to be a father, and how dedicated he has been to building a relationship with my son as well. Tears form in my eyes before I know it, and then Astrid's smile falls.

"Oh no. What's wrong?"

I wave my hands in front of my face. "I can't even tell you what's wrong. I have no control over my emotions right now, and I hate it." Pulling a tissue from my purse, I dab under my eyes. "My feelings are all over the place, my body hurts every day as this little girl grows, and I'm feeling overwhelmed just being in this store right now." My eyes move all over the shelves full of baby products, many of which I'm completely unfamiliar with because it's been so long since I've needed any of this stuff.

Astrid rubs my shoulders and pulls me into her side. "Everything is going to work out, Scottie. There's no reason to stress. You have a support system this time. Your family is here, Grady is fully committed, and *I'm* here for anything you need."

I hand her the scanner for the baby registry, which is the whole point of this visit anyway. "Can you just start scanning things, please?"

Keeping her arm around me, she guides me down the aisles as I gather myself. "Of course. You gonna be okay?"

Stuttering through a shaky breath, I reply, "Yeah."

The beep of the scanner is the only sound for a few minutes until Astrid breaks our silence, releasing me from her embrace. "I don't want to upset you again, but I have to ask you one more thing."

"All right."

"Did you tell my brother about Andrew? Like...all of it?"

I nod. "Yes. He knows everything now."

"And how did he react?"

I think about that night at the pizza parlor, how Grady actively listened as I told him my story, and the words he said to me once I revealed the whole reason and circumstances surrounding my return to Carrington Cove.

"You're exactly the mother Chase needs, and I couldn't ask for a better mother of my child. You're fucking amazing."

"He told me I am strong and brave. That I am a good mom...."

Astrid beams with pride for her brother. "Sounds like he's a smarter man than I thought."

I take a few steps before something I've been thinking about comes out. "How come as women and mothers we constantly feel inadequate? Like our life choices have stronger consequences because we have others that rely on us so much? That one wrong move can scar our kids, our partners, or ourselves for life?"

Astrid hums. "I often wonder that myself. But I also know what a blessing it is to be given the responsibility of being a mother." She scans the store before turning to face me. "The fact that you care so much is a testament not just to the woman and mother you are, Scottie, but to the one you're continually growing into. No one is perfect, but part of life is learning and growing from our imperfections. It took me a long time to accept that."

"I feel like I should have things figured out by now. Like, I'm old enough to know better, and do better. You know?"

She reaches forward and places her hand on my shoulder. "If there's one thing I've learned in the last year, it's that everybody grows differently, and I think our environment has a lot to do with that. Carrington Cove might just be the climate you needed to break through the ground you've been buried under, the shield you've been using to protect yourself. This baby girl is already so loved, so wanted. And Grady clearly wants you too. I'd say, that's already a promising start to a new journey this time around."

Smiling, I blink away my tears. "Thank you."

"Anytime. Take this one day at a time, okay? Let the people here love you, protect you, and help you through this new, exciting phase of your life. And remember, sometimes you have to fall to learn how to pick yourself back up and do things differently. You just might find it's even better the second time around."

***

"God, right there." The water cascades down my back as Grady keeps fucking me from behind in the shower.

Chase spent the night at Jeremy's house, one of the boys on the team, so naturally, Grady and I decided to take advantage of not having him here. Although, before my son left, I told him that if I got a call from the cops tonight, I'd take him to juvenile hall myself.

"I wish you could see yourself right now, Scottie," Grady growls in my ear, thrusting harder as he wraps his arm around my shoulders, pulling me closer to his chest. "So fucking beautiful, so perfect, taking my cock like it was made for you, sucking me in and milking me."

My moans echo off the shower walls as Grady's other hand travels over my stomach and down to my clit, rubbing soft circles around the bundle of nerves, helping me get to the finish line faster.

"You have no idea what you do to me, how hard you fucking make me," he says, lining his lips up to my ear before biting down on the skin of my neck as my heart twists in my chest at those words.

"Grady…"

"Come on my cock, Scottie. Shatter for me." And that's all he needs to say before I splinter, shaking as I fight to keep standing. Grady keeps thrusting, letting me fall forward as I brace myself on the shower wall and he fucks me hard and deep, chasing his own release.

"Jesus fuck," he groans before he stills and lets out a heavy sigh.

"So good," I mumble as he spins me around and pulls me close to his chest—well, as close as I can get due to the growing belly between us.

Our daughter kicks me hard in the ribs, making me wince.

"You okay?" he asks, brushing my wet hair from my face as the water continues to fall down against his back.

"Yeah. The baby just kicked me. I don't think she liked being rattled around."

Grady plants a chaste kiss on my lips. "Well, let's finish getting cleaned up then so you can relax. Lord knows it's been a long week, and this next week will be even busier."

"Are you ready for the season to end?" I ask him as he slathers my body with soap and runs his hands all over my skin. I just came, but the feel of his hands on me is making me want to fuck him again.

God, I'm a heathen. I think I'm starting to understand how people become sex addicts.

"Yes and no. It's definitely been exhausting since I'm not used to having that type of schedule. But I've really loved every fucking minute of it, Scottie. Our last game is this week and it feels bittersweet." He cups the side of my face. "Thank you for making me see what I didn't want to."

"I'm glad you found a piece of baseball to keep in your life. You seem happier."

With a stoic look on his face, he says, "It's not just baseball that's made me happier, Scottie."

I brush off his words as I twist around to face the wall and gather myself before my heart explodes. With each passing day, I'm falling for him and imagining our life together, but neither of us has initiated that conversation, and it sure as hell isn't going to come from me.

I barely feel like I'm finally starting to get the hang of this new normal where this man caters to me and fucks me anytime I ask, which is uncharacteristically often given my changing body and mood swings. But part of me can't help but wonder if sex is the only thing we have going for us right now. Grady hasn't brought up the baby's room again since I squashed that conversation a few weeks ago, and honestly, I don't know if he will after the way I acted.

I just wanted some time to let things sink in. I get him wanting to make decisions and expect answers from me, but the truth is, I'm coming up with the answers as I go right now. For once in my life, I'm trying not to think too hard about the future—even though our daughter will be here in less than four months, and I need to have some idea of what our life is going to look like before then.

Once we're all clean and dressed, we settle into my bed. Grady leans back against my headboard while I rest my head in his lap, facing the television. And this moment—it feels so normal, so natural, like this is what things between us should be like.

But how long until it goes sour? Can just being near someone always feel this soothing, or is it inevitable that feelings change over time?

I don't know anyone in my life who's had a relationship or marriage last, especially not happily. Grady and I aren't married, but I'm sure he'd want that one day, and the last thing I want is for us to end up resenting one another down the road.

I just don't see how that could happen, given how strongly I feel about this man and how different those feelings are from what I felt with Andrew.

But can I really trust and believe that this won't end in turmoil like it did for me the last time?

My heart says yes, but my head is still protesting the idea, trying to keep me safe, trying to make me cautious. And the only thing holding us together right now is sex. What happens when that's off the table? Will this man even still want me after he sees what childbirth is like and what it does to my body?

"Grady..."

"Yeah, babe?"

"What happens when our daughter gets here?"

He brushes my hair from my face. "What do you mean?"

"Well, in a few months I'm going to be as big as a house and probably won't want sex anymore. And after I deliver, I can't have sex for at least six weeks."

His brows furrow as he stares down at me. "Where is this coming from?"

"I don't know," I say, tracing circles on the comforter beneath me, hoping he can't see how unnerved I feel at the moment. God, being a woman sucks sometimes. There's never a quiet moment in our minds. "I just figure once sex is off the table, you won't…"

He presses a finger to my lips, stopping me mid-sentence. "Don't even say another word." I gulp down my reply, waiting for him to continue. "Do you honestly think that the only reason I'm here is for sex?"

"Well, no, but…"

He pulls me up and guides me to his lap, our daughter resting between us. "Scottie Daniels…"

"I'm not Daniels anymore."

He fixes me with a glare. "I'm sure as fuck not calling you by another man's name when you're carrying *my* baby." My clit twitches from that comment. "But you will always be Scottie Daniels to me, until you take my last name," he declares, making my heart race even harder. He sighs, taking in a deep breath before continuing. "Scottie Daniels, will you go on a date with me?"

I nearly laugh because that was the last thing I was expecting to come out of his mouth. "What?"

Our eyes lock. "I want to take you on a proper date, Scottie. We never did that, and if I hadn't been so wrapped up in baseball back in high school, I would have asked you then. But you know how that all worked out. And now, even though we're already having a kid together, it seems you need to be reminded that I want more with you. Maybe I should just show you—if you'll let me, that is."

My lips curl up into a smile that burns my cheeks, and suddenly a wave of relief and excitement washes over me. "You want to take me on a date?"

"That's what I said, baby."

"When?"

"How about next weekend?"

Gnawing on my bottom lip, I take a moment to contemplate his proposition. Yet, deep down, I know this is Grady's way of demonstrating what I need to see and hear. And if ever there was a sign that I should keep trusting this man, this is it. "Okay."

He buries his hands in my hair, bringing my mouth to his. "Good girl. See? You just need to follow your heart, Scottie. It's trying to speak to you. I just wish you would listen."

"My head keeps getting in the way."

"Well, tell it to knock it the fuck off."

I bark out a laugh. "It's not that easy. I've spent most of my adult life overthinking, Grady. It's going to take time to change that."

When his lips touch mine again, my entire body warms from head to toe. "At least you're trying, Scottie. That's all I ask. And soon, you'll realize you don't have to carry the mental load alone because I'm here, and I'm not letting you go again. No way in hell."

***

"Don't let them get in your head, Chase!" Grady yells from the dugout, trying to help calm my son who currently has a runner on each base. The Carrington Cove High School baseball team is down by three runs at the top of the seventh inning, but it's still anyone's game.

Chase hasn't been playing his best, though, and as a parent, there are few things worse than watching your kid deal with immense pressure and not being able to do much about it.

"You've got this, Chase!" I scream from my seat in the bleachers. I would stand, but this baby girl is putting a ton of pressure on my sciatic nerve lately, so sitting is just a better option so my legs don't give out on me.

"Timeout!" Grady calls to the umpire, who nods his head and echoes the call.

I blow out a breath, watching Grady walk toward my son, hoping he can give him the words of encouragement he needs right now. Biting my nails, I watch the two of them as my daughter does somersaults in my belly.

"I know, peanut. Big brother's got this, though." I rub a few circles around the spot where I feel her. "When you're old enough to understand how nerve-racking this is, I'll remind you of this moment."

Grady pats Chase on the shoulder and then heads back to the dugout, straightening his ball cap while popping a fresh stick of gum in his mouth.

God, he's so fucking hot. Tonight, I'm gonna make him keep that hat on him while I ride him.

I push away my dirty thoughts and focus back on my son as he stands on the mound again, looking more calm and in control. He goes to wind up the pitch, but the runner on third gets a little too far off base, so Chase hammers the ball to the third baseman, who tags the runner out.

"Yes, Chase! Great job!" I scream, clapping my hands wildly.Chase gets the ball back and goes back to waiting for the call from the catcher.

After two shakes, he gives a nod and then winds up and throws the pitch, striking the batter out at the plate.

I can see his grin from here, so whatever Grady said to him was exactly what he needed to hear.

Unfortunately, the boys still lose 7-6, but my son walks out of the dugout proud, and he should be. He pitched one hell of a game.

As soon as I waddle over to him, he pulls me in for a hug. "Hey, Mom."

"Hey, baby. You did great. I'm so proud of you."

"I hate losing."

"Can't win them all, but you did amazing. You kept your cool under pressure, which is a sign of maturity and strength, honey."

"Yeah, I guess."

I reach up and push his hat from his face so I can see it, so gratified with the young man he's becoming. Our move to Carrington Cove may have started off rocky, but he's changed so much and for the better, and I know it's because of the man who entered our lives, the same one striding over to us right now.

Grady stretches his hand out to shake my son's. "You did phenomenally, Chase," he says, before turning to me. "Wouldn't you say so?"

"I was just telling him that."

"Thanks," Chase says, his cheeks turning slightly pink.

Grady steps closer to him and lowers his voice. "You made me really fucking proud out there, kid. I'm honored to be your coach."

Emotion clogs my throat instantly, watching this man talk to my son the way his own father should have.

Chase nods, his face stoic, before he puts his hat back on and then leans down to kiss my cheek. "I'm going to grab my bag and say bye to the guys."

"Okay. Think about where you want to eat for dinner. Your choice," I call out to him as he nods and then jogs over to the dugout.

I turn back to Grady, trying to keep my emotions in check. "So, how do you feel, Coach?"

He takes a deep breath. "Really fucking proud, Scottie. Even though we lost, I couldn't have been prouder of how all of the boys played."

"You should be." Staring up at him, I continue, "Just out of curiosity, what did you say to Chase in the seventh inning when the bases were loaded?"

Grady grins. "That's between him and me, Scottie."

"That's how you're going to be? Really?"

"Yup." He wraps his arm around my waist and guides me toward the gate that leads out to the parking lot. "I can't tell you all of my winning moves."

"How come?"

"Because the game isn't over yet, and until it is, you keep some plays close to the vest."

Chapter Nineteen

Grady

"This is definitely not how I anticipated spending my Thursday afternoon," Dallas says as he follows me into the baby boutique. Parker, Penn, and I already ate our weekly lunch at Dallas's restaurant, but then I asked them if they'd be willing to help me out with something for Scottie, and shockingly, they all said yes, so here we are.

"What are we after?"

"A crib." I pull my phone from my pocket and open the website where our registry is. Scottie and my sister handled putting this list together, but sometimes when you want something done, you've got to do it yourself. Shoving the phone in their faces, the guys take note of the item we're looking for, and they nod.

"Got it." Parker scours the store, which is quite bigger than it appears from the boardwalk. "I've gotta say though, I'm in uncharted territory."

"You're a doctor. Surely you know something about caring for babies," I say.

"I'm a doctor for animals. Their babies are much lower maintenance."

Penn picks up a stuffed duck and inspects it. "Have you guys decided on a theme for the room?"

My eyes land on a onesie that has a pink ruffle around it like a tutu, so I pick it up, knowing there's no way I'm not getting that for my daughter. "Not yet, but I wanted to surprise her." Dallas and Penn both wince. "What?"

"Not a good idea, man," Penn says. "Trust me. When it comes to decorating, you want your woman's input."

Dallas nods in agreement. "Willow and I had our first fight after moving in together over the color of rugs we wanted to put in the house. It was brutal."

Parker rolls his eyes. "Don't listen to them. I think what you're doing is a top-notch boyfriend move." He clasps a hand on my shoulder, even though I'm about four inches taller than him. "Scottie will love it."

Penn juts his thumb at his brother. "Don't take advice from the only single guy here, Grady. Trust me."

Parker flips his brother the bird. "Fuck you." He takes off down one of the aisles, leaving me alone with Penn and Dallas.

"I can hold off on colors and stuff, I guess. But I want to start getting something together. I want her to see that having a place for our daughter could actually make her feel more at ease instead of overwhelming her. And I want that place to be in my house where eventually I want her and Chase as well."

"I take it things are a little rocky then?" Penn asks.

"Not rocky, just…bumpy."

"Hitting a few bumpy bumps?" Dallas suggests.

"What the fuck are bumpy bumps?"

He shrugs. "I don't know. I heard Willow talking about some book thing and she kept saying it over and over again, and I guess it just sort of stuck in my head."

"Well, I'd go over all the bumpy bumps for Scottie, but right now they feel like the kind of hills you go up and down on a fucking roller coaster."

Penn clasps me on the shoulder. "Just be patient. You guys have a lot going on right now and she's hormonal, which doesn't help."

"Don't talk about her hormones, okay?" I say a little too defensively.

"Not trying to offend, but you have to remember that her pregnancy is an additional dimension you're navigating on top of your relationship."

After we got home from Kentucky, I talked to the guys about the developments between us without going into too much detail, but Dallas and Penn both agreed that I did the right thing just letting things progress naturally. But after we found out we're having a daughter, my patience has failed to exist anymore. Hence why I'm shopping for baby shit before Scottie has the baby shower because I can't fucking wait anymore. Regardless of how things work between us, I'm going to need a room for my daughter in my house, so I want to be prepared.

As we round the corner at the end of a new aisle, the sight before us makes me, Dallas, and Penn all stop in our tracks.

Parker is staring at the display of breast pumps, taking each one and bringing it up to his own nipples, as if trying them on for size.

"What the fuck did we just walk in on?" Dallas grumbles.

Penn blows out a breath. "I swear, he must have been adopted."

Pinching the bridge of my nose, I speak loud enough for Parker to hear. "Watching you right now makes me question how people trust you to operate on animals."

Parker's head spins to face us as he drops the breast pump, the sound of it hitting the floor echoing around us. Scrambling to pick it up, he says, "Uh, I think the animals are starting to have an influence on me." Parker sets the breast pump down and stares at it with a look of concern on his face. "This place is having a weird effect on me too, so I think it's time for me to go."

"Yeah, I think trying to milk yourself is a surefire mark of insanity," Penn mutters as Parker flips him off and Dallas snickers beside him. Parker heads for the door and doesn't look back as he exits the shop, leaving the three of us alone again.

"Okay, we need to focus. I need to get enough stuff to start putting together this room." I look around the shop until I find the store associate restocking one of the shelves and head right over to her, assuming that Penn and Dallas are right behind me. But five minutes later, I hear the telltale sound of walkie talkies going off in one of the aisles.

"We need diaper cream and wipes, stat!"

"10-4. Roger that!"

A tube of diaper cream goes flying past my face, landing in Penn's arms as he catches it like a running back in the NFL, cheering as he races around the store.

I take my phone out of my pocket, send an S.O.S text to my sister, and wonder why the fuck I didn't just ask for her help with this in the first place.

Fifteen minutes later, I'm standing at the counter, prepared to drop almost a grand on furniture and necessities for my kid when my sister breezes through the entrance of the store, her long hair thrown up in a clip and her apron still tied around her waist. She must have come straight from the bakery.

"Is everything okay? Your text said it was an emergency."

"Yeah, I'm okay, but I need your opinion on this stuff," I say, gesturing to the mountain of boxes, bags, and containers stacked next to the counter. The attendant helping me is more than pleased with my purchase, seeing as how she probably works on commission.

Astrid gives me a confused look. "What are you doing?"

"I'm buying shit for my daughter's nursery," I say matter-of-factly. "I want to surprise Scottie, and asked the boys to come with me, but turns out that was a big fucking mistake."

Dallas comes around the corner, muttering into one of the baby monitors again. "Uh oh. Momma Bear number one is here. I repeat, Momma Bear number one is here."

Penn runs from the back of the store and stops dead in his tracks as he meets Astrid's icy glare. "Oh. Hi, babe."

"What the hell are you two doing?" With her arms crossed over her chest, she glares at both of them. "This is your idea of helping?"

Dallas and Penn both hang their heads in shame, and I'm not going to lie, the sight is making me fucking tickled pink.

But then she turns to face me. "And you thought that these two children would be better assistance than your sister, who is already a mother and happens to know the mother of your child pretty darn well?"

"Uh…"

"Idiots. All of you." Astrid takes the baby monitors from Dallas and Penn, and hands them over to the attendant. "I believe these belong to you."

"It's no trouble. Honestly, this happens more than you might think when men come into the store."

Astrid flashes her a placating smile. "I'm sure." Spinning to face us all again, she says, "Dallas and Penn, you two can leave. Your *help* isn't needed anymore."

Penn smacks Dallas on the back of the head. "See? You got us in trouble."

"It was your idea, dipshit."

They continue to argue as they make their way out the front door of the store before my sister locks eyes with me again.

"I'm sorry. You're right. I wasn't thinking, but shit, I'm out of my element here, Astrid."

"Which is exactly why you should have called me." She checks the time on her phone. "Now, I have fifteen minutes before I need to be back at the bakery. Tell me what's going on."

I blow out a breath as the attendant starts wrapping up a few of the items I purchased. "I want to surprise Scottie with something, but I need to know if I'm totally off base here."

"Well, you know I have no problem giving it to you straight, big brother. Now ask away."

"I told Scottie that we needed to start putting together a nursery, preferably at my house, but she freaked out."

"You *told* her this was happening?"

Rubbing the back of my neck, I say sheepishly, "Kind of?"

She smacks the back of my head now. "I was wrong. You're an idiot too."

"Ow!"

"You should know better than to tell a woman she's going to do anything, let alone insinuate that she's going to live with you without first asking how she feels about it."

"I know, but damn it, Astrid. I can't live apart from them."

"But you can't force Scottie to make that decision in the blink of an eye." She snaps her fingers in front of my face. "So what are you buying all of this stuff for, then? You know her shower is next month, right?"

"Well, I was thinking of setting up a nursery at my house so she could visualize a space for our daughter and maybe start to see herself there too." I shrug.

The smile she gives me allows a wave of relief to wash through me. "That's really sweet, Grady, but what if she still says no?"

"Then at least I'll have a room ready for my baby girl when she's with me." It's not what I want, but at least the time, effort, and money won't be for nothing.

She taps her finger to her chin. "Okay, then I support this. But, I have another idea that might win her over a bit too."

I pull her into my chest. "What would I do without you?"

She holds up her thumb and index finger with an inch of space between them. "You wouldn't be this close to getting your dream girl and dream life."

Let's just hope she's right about that.

Chapter Twenty

Scottie

"This is where you wanted to take me on our date?" I stare up at the house that I haven't been to since the summer after high school, wondering what the hell is going through this man's mind.

Grady took me to a steakhouse a few towns over for dinner, and then he drove us back to Carrington Cove, but wouldn't tell me where he was taking me. And now that we're sitting outside of Grady's high school buddy Derek's house, I'm beginning to question this man's sanity.

Grady laughs as he gets out of the truck and rounds the front to my side to help me out. "Just trust me."

"When I'm worried about a trespassing charge, that's hard to do. I mean, if I get the cops called on me, my son will never let me live it down. You do remember our recent run-in with the law, don't you, Grady?"

He takes my hand and guides me across the street to the front lawn. "We're not going to get arrested. I've already cleared it with Derek's parents. They know we're here, but they're in Florida visiting friends." He taps his temple. "If you haven't figured it out by now, I'm a planner, Scottie."

I can only shake my head as Grady lifts the latch on the house's side gate, leading me into the backyard. And suddenly, a wave of memories from the night I was last here comes rushing back to me.

Grady points to the side of the yard with a smirk on his lips. "You might not recall, but that's where you did a keg stand."

"Are you trying to remind me of how crazy I was back in the day? Because I'm aware."

He chuckles. "No, but that was the moment I realized you were unlike any other girl I'd ever met, and I knew I was really going to fucking miss you when you left."

My heart begins to pound. "Oh."

"Come on."

He leads me back out front and over to the tree where we sat that night, and as soon as my eyes see the tire swing still hanging from the thick branch, I turn to face him. "Are we here to remind me of when I puked all over the grass right here because of that keg stand?"

He throws his head back and laughs. "No, but I'll never forget that because you were always so concerned about me getting sick and you puked pretty violently that night."

"Karma has a way of catching up to you, Grady. Don't forget that."

He leads me over to the swing. "Wanna hop on?"

I stare down at my belly that feels like it's getting larger by the minute. "Not sure I can fit."

"Yeah, you can. I'll help you."

With Grady steadying me, I thread my legs through the tire, and he begins to push me gently, rocking me back and forth.

I wait a few moments before I ask, "Why are we here, Grady?"

"Nostalgia. Memories. Feelings," he says cryptically. "That night could have changed our lives if I had just acted on what I wanted back then, Scottie."

Silence stretches between us as I think back to the night we were here last. "Do you remember what we talked about that night?" I finally ask.

"Every word of it."

"What's the part that stands out the most?" I whisper as Grady pulls the tire to a stop and comes around to face me.

"You asked me if I was ready for what comes next," he says, his eyes locked on mine.

And suddenly it feels hard to breathe. "Okay..."

"Come here." He helps me out of the tire swing and then pulls me into his chest, or as close as we can get since my belly is making that harder to accomplish. Cupping my jaw, he says, "I think it's time that I tell you what I want—what I see coming next for us."

I swallow down the lump in my throat. "Oh..."

"Scottie," he starts, but my phone rings in my pocket, interrupting the moment.

Glancing down at it, I'm worried when I see my mom's name on the screen. "Uh..."

Grady nods. "It's okay. Answer it."

"I'm sorry. She knows I'm out with you, so it's weird that she's calling," I explain as I swipe across the screen.

"Hello?"

"Scottie," my mother says, urgency in her tone.

"What's wrong, Mom? Is Chase all right?"

"You need to come home."

"Mom, you're scaring me."

"It's Andrew, sweetie," she says as I feel my stomach drop. "He's here."

***

By the time Grady pulls into my driveway, the tension between us is so palpable that you could cut it with a knife. Part of me is eager to hear what he had to say and upset that we were interrupted, but the other part of me is terrified, dreading what brought Andrew all the way to Carrington Cove. Deep down, though, I think I know exactly why he's here.

Just when things started to feel like they were moving in the right direction, the past had to come back and remind me of my poor choices. Seems like this is a battle I'll never win.

When Grady helps me down from the truck and Andrew sees my stomach, he starts laughing. "Jesus Christ, Scottie. You moved this far just to be unmarried and pregnant again? Seems like some things don't ever fucking change, huh?"

"You'd better watch how you speak to her," Grady interjects, standing in front of me, shielding me from one of the biggest mistakes of my life.

"Who the fuck are you?"

"The man you'll have to answer to if you don't show Scottie some respect."

"Respect?" Andrew laughs. "Funny. You know, I could have shown up with the cops since Scottie chose to move out of state without fucking telling me, but I didn't. How's that for respect?"

I stand next to Grady now, finding my resolve to face the consequences of my actions and the man who doesn't deserve my fear or sympathy. "What I find funny is you deciding to show up now, after all this time."

"My job is demanding, Scottie. You fucking know that."

I roll my eyes. "Yes, it always was more important than anything else, Andrew, including your family."

"Which I think is reason enough for you to leave," Grady chimes in.

"I have every legal right to be here. My wife and kid live here, and…"

"Ex-wife," Grady corrects him sharply, "and a son you haven't seen in over a year."

Andrew takes a step closer to Grady, even though Grady towers over him by several inches.

God, I don't know what I ever saw in Andrew.

And as my blood boils in my veins, I wish for a way to get him to leave our lives for good. Sadly, when you have a child with someone, you're connected to them forever.

Andrew puffs out his chest. "I don't know who you think you are, but—"

Cutting him off, Grady lowers his voice, but it doesn't make him sound any less threatening. "I'm the man who's having a baby with your ex-wife, the man who gets to love and protect her now, and the man who gets to show your son what it means to actually be a man of his word."

Oh my God. "Grady…"

Andrew fires back. "Well, she broke the law by taking my son out of state without informing me."

Grady starts to laugh. "You know, that's rich coming from you, Andrew Warner." Andrew's eyes narrow but Grady doesn't miss a beat. "You see, I knew this time was coming. When Scottie told me why she decided to move back here, I knew you'd come back around at some point, trying to exercise your perceived power. Men like you always do." Grady moves to his truck, swings open the door, and retrieves a manila envelope. Slamming the door shut, he strides back over to us and thrusts the envelope to my ex. "I wanted to make sure you knew the stakes before you started making threats."

I watch anxiously, my pulse hammering in my ears, as Andrew takes the envelope. I can't deny that I am also a little curious about what's inside.

What the hell has Grady been up to?

"You think you can threaten me?" Andrew snarls as he pops the metal clasp and pulls a thick stack of papers from the envelope. His eyes dart back and forth over the words, and as he flips through the pages, his skin goes white.

"You sure you want to get the cops involved, or a judge, for that matter?" Grady asks, folding his arms over his chest, watching as my ex seemingly accepts his fate.

"Where did you get this?" Andrew is seething.

"I have friends, important ones, who know how to track down the right information when necessary," Grady replies coolly, nodding toward the stack of papers. "Now, if you'll take out that last packet, you'll find a petition for voluntary termination of parental rights."

My stomach drops and the ground seems to sway beneath me. I steady myself on Grady's arm before my knees buckle underneath me.

Grady had legal paperwork prepared so Andrew can't fight me.

If I was on the fence about how I feel about this man before, this settles it.

"I don't have to sign shit," Andrew snaps.

Grady takes a step toward him. "You don't *have* to, but if you want to push this, I'll take immense pride in airing your dirty laundry in court. I also have friends in the press, which would do wonders for your legal career, wouldn't it, Warner?"

Andrew's face contorts with anger. "You mother fucker!" He lunges forward, but Grady's quicker, stepping between Andrew and me. He extends his arm, closing his hand around Andrew's throat before he can get any closer.

"Don't think I won't snap just because Scottie is here. Technically, you're trespassing on her property, so we're within our rights to defend ourselves. But I don't think that's what either of us wants, is it?" I clasp my hands over my mouth as Andrew struggles to breathe. "Do you need a pen?"

Andrew bobs his head up and down as Grady releases him and pulls a pen from his pocket, shoving it into his chest. "Here."

Wheezing, my ex-husband scribbles his name across the pages that fell to the ground, and for the first time in months, I feel like I can breathe.

"Smart choice." Grady takes the papers from Andrew and puts them back in the envelope. "Now, I suggest you get the fuck out of town. Forget you ever knew this woman and her son, and remember that someone is always watching, Andrew. Always."

Andrew dips his eyes up and down my body before he grates out, "You know what? Keep her. Her and that kid are the greatest mistake I've ever made."

My heart cracks in my chest as I watch him walk down the sidewalk, back out to his car, and drive off. And then I start to sink down to the ground.

"Oh, no you don't," Grady says, kneeling and catching me before I hit the ground as a sob escapes my lips. "It's okay, baby. It's okay. He's gone."

My body is shaking uncontrollably. All the fear, all the regret—it's leaving my soul through my tears as Grady lifts me in his arms and starts to carry me to the front door.

"Grady! Grady!" My mother's voice breaks through my crying, but I keep my face buried in Grady's chest. "Is she okay?"

"I've got her, Lisa." He assures her, pressing a kiss to the top of my head. "Andrew's gone and he won't be coming back, I can promise you that."

"I was watching in case he got out of line, but I wanted to keep my distance too." Her voice is shaky. "What did he say?" my mother asks as she starts stroking my back. "Scottie, baby. Are you all right?"

Grady hoists me tighter in his arms. "She's going to be. I need to get her inside. That was a lot of stress on her and the baby and I need to make sure they're okay. I'll text you."

My mother presses a kiss to my cheek. "He's gone, baby. You're safe now."

Little does she know just how true that is, especially here in Grady's arms.

Grady opens the front door and takes me straight to the couch. Depositing me carefully on the cushions, he props my feet up on a pillow as I fight to take in breaths.

Is this what a panic attack feels like?

"Breathe, Scottie. Breathe." He pushes my hair back from my face, kissing my forehead. "I'm going to get you some water. Just keep taking deep breaths."

By the time he returns, I feel like my heart rate is getting back to normal, and when I finally open my eyes, he's on his knees by my side, holding my hand, and staring at me like he's afraid I might disappear.

"Grady..."

"I'm sure you have questions, but I need you to calm down a little bit more before we talk. Your pulse is through the roof, and that's not good for the baby, Scottie."

I nod, closing my eyes and resting my head back against the pillow as our daughter moves around in my stomach. On instinct, both Grady and I place our hands there, silently comforting one another and absorbing the fact that she's okay and the drama from earlier is over—hopefully for the rest of my life.

"What was in the envelope?" I ask when I finally feel more at ease.

Grady pushes a hand through his hair and then takes a seat on the couch, placing my legs back across his lap so they're still propped up. "After our road trip, when you told me about your situation with your ex, I knew it was only a matter of time before he came back. So, I called up Timothy McDonald, the lawyer in town, and had him draft up the form."

"Why didn't you tell me?"

He twists his head to face me, flashing that panty-melting smirk of his. "Because the game wasn't over yet, and until it is, you keep some plays close to the vest."

I crack a smile, remembering what he told me after his pep talk with my son during his last baseball game. "Smooth."

He chuckles. "I knew getting him to sign it wouldn't be easy, so I needed leverage. A buddy of mine I played with in San Francisco worked with a private investigator when he was going through his divorce because he was fairly certain his wife was cheating on him. I got his number and had Andrew followed for a few weeks. We discovered all kinds of extracurricular activities your ex likes to partake in, including fucking the wife of one of the judges in his district. So, I made sure to include those pictures in case he wanted to fight back."

"Is that what made him look like he was going to throw up?" I ask, thinking back to how white Andrew looked as he flipped through the stack of papers.

"Probably. Or it was the picture of him snorting cocaine off a stripper's bare chest."

I close my eyes and shake my head. "Jesus. I can't believe I ever married him." But then I remember his words from earlier and my eyes well again. "He was *my* greatest mistake, Grady." I look across the room so he can't see what hearing that actually did to me, how betrayed and hurt it made me feel—not because I still have feelings for the man, but because without him, I wouldn't have Chase, and I don't see how any parent can regret their own child.

Grady tugs gently on my hand, pulling my attention back to him. "Scottie, don't you dare fucking believe a word that piece of shit said, okay? He may consider you two his greatest mistake, but for me? Realizing that you and Chase belong in my life was my defining moment." Instantly, it gets hard to breathe again. "The second you reentered my world, I knew what had been missing. His loss is my gain. You've completed my life, Scottie. You, your son, and this baby girl." He places his hand back on my belly. "And I'll keep reminding you of that until the end of time if you'll let me."

So many emotions are moving through me right now, but the one I'm choosing to focus on is *love*.

I tried to fight it, tried to deny what's really between us, and I can sit here and make up more excuses about why letting him in scares the shit out of me.

But at the end of the day, this man could never hurt me. Hell, he went out of his way to help me, care for me, and protect me and my son from the man who never deserved us to begin with.

I love him.

"I want that, Grady." Nodding, I swing my legs off of his lap and move to straddle him, holding his face in my hands. "What you did for me tonight? That's love. What you do for me every day? That's love. How you listen, how you show up, how you make me feel like I don't have to live in fear anymore? That's the kind of love I didn't know existed."

Grady cups the side of my face and speaks the words my heart already knew. "I'm so fucking in love with you, Scottie." The gravel in his voice travels right down the center of my chest, coating my entire body in warmth. "You're my best friend, and the woman I'm meant to be with. No one else ever stood a chance. Do you realize that?"

"I do now. And I—I love you too. So much that I'm terrified and overwhelmingly happy at the same time."

He takes a deep breath. "Then stop fighting this, and let me love you forever."

"Kiss me," I breathe against his lips. And he does until we're both out of control with need for each other, but he stops before it gets too far.

He lets out a sigh of relief, planting his lips on mine again. "Fuck, Scottie. You have no idea the brick you just lifted from my chest."

"I might have a little idea...I feel like I've been carrying a similar brick myself."

He lowers his hand to our baby, rubbing my stomach softly. "I want this life with you, for us to be a family. I want that so fucking much..."

"Me too. There's still a lot to figure out, but I'm done fighting this. I love you and that's all that matters."

"You are the love of my life, Scottie Daniels."

"I'm not Daniels anymore."

He tilts my head to the side, stroking my cheek. "No. And soon you'll be Scottie Reynolds, so we won't have to argue about this anymore."

"You love arguing with me, Grady."

The corner of his mouth tips up. "I do, but I love loving you more. And I plan on doing that for the rest of our lives."

***

"That's it, Scottie. Open up for me."

Closing my eyes, I focus on the feeling of Grady sliding in and out of me, lying behind me while he keeps my legs open with his arm under my knee.

"I can't get enough of you," he whispers in my ear. "Your heart, your mind, your body."

"Grady..."

"I love you. I'm so fucking in love with you, woman. You own me. You're the reason I can fucking breathe again." His lips find my neck, kissing and licking the skin.

"I love you too." He flicks his hips a bit and hits a spot inside of me that's making my orgasm build quickly. "Oh yes, right there..."

"Come with me, Scottie."

"Keep going..."

We don't say anything else as Grady continues to work my body over, thrusting in the perfect tempo that helps me reach my release. And as the first screams leave my lips, I hear him groan behind me until we're both shivering with aftershocks.

Sex has never been like this for me.

It's because I wasn't having sex with Grady Reynolds.

After cleaning up, I leave the bathroom to find Grady leaning against the headboard. I try not to stare, but it's useless.

The man is fucking perfect.

"Ready for round two already?" he asks, a smirk on his lips.

My body says yes, but my mind remembers something I've been waiting to show him when the time is right. And after tonight, that time is definitely now.

"I have something for you," I say, walking to my closet. I slide the door open and reach up to the top shelf, taking down the shoe box that is barely holding together after all these years.

Grady sits up taller. "What is that?"

I settle beside him on the bed and pop the lid off the box as the scent of old newspapers fills the air. "I told you I'd be rooting for you, Grady," I say, pushing the box toward him.

With a pinch in his brow, he begins to pull out article after article from his career, spanning almost ten years of accolades and his World Series win.

He's silent for so long, I start to grow nervous as he keeps taking out paper after paper, magazine articles, and even an old jersey I bought when he was drafted to the San Francisco Giants.

But when he peers up at me with tears in his eyes, I know that the love we've had for each other has run deep for far longer than we both realized. "I can't believe you kept all this."

"I can't believe you thought I wouldn't."

"Come here," he says, motioning for me to come closer, his voice thick with emotion. As I nestle into his side, he cups my chin and guides my gaze to meet his. "If I didn't love you before, this would have sealed the deal for me."

"That's how I felt when you pulled those papers from your truck tonight." The corner of his mouth lifts, but I continue. "I was always watching, Grady—every game, every milestone, I was invested. We may have lost touch through no one's fault but my own, but you were still very much a part of my life."

He leans his forehead on mine. "I don't want to question what if, but…"

I press a finger to his lips. "Don't. We're right where we're supposed to be. You and me, and our baby." He moves his hand to my stomach. "But I was always proud of you, and now even more so because you are the man I've always known you were supposed to be. And I love you so fucking much."

Grady slides us down to the bed, and I rest my head on his chest. He strokes my back, drawing circles with his fingers. "So, are you ready to agree to move in with me now?"

I chuckle. "I guess I don't have a valid argument against that anymore, do I?"

"Not at all."

I twist my face so I can look at him. "Yes, we can live together."

"I already have a room ready for the baby."

Rolling my eyes, I say, "Doesn't surprise me."

"Did you think I wasn't going to at least have something in the works?" he says, a hint of sarcasm in his tone. "You might have been on the fence about that, but I was serious."

"Did you paint the walls pink?"

"All I have is furniture. I was hoping we could finish the rest together when you pulled your head out of your ass."

"Hey!" I reach up to twist his nipple, but he grasps my hand before I can, twisting his body so he's hovering over me now.

"You're the most stubborn woman I've ever met, Scottie. Knowing my luck, our daughter is going to get that from you too."

"You're going to be outnumbered, Grady."

"I have Chase on my side still, at least for the next few years."

"Then what happens after he's gone off to school or moves out?"

He cups the side of my face. "Then it will just be me and my girls, and Chase—the way it should be—the way it always was supposed to be, babe. And I couldn't ask for anything better."

***

"So what does this mean?"

I'm sitting across from my son in our living room. It's Sunday morning after the night that made me realize all my sacrifices to get to this moment were worth it. Before Chase came home from his friend's house, Grady left to grab donuts—and apple fritters, of course—to give me a chance to talk to Chase alone. I wanted him to be able to voice any concerns freely without Grady around.

"This means that Grady and I are going to be together, and before your sister comes, we're moving in with him." As Grady and I lay down to sleep last night, I realized my life was about to change quicker than I had anticipated. But it feels right. I just hope my son supports this development.

Chase scoffs, but I can hear the teasing tone in his reply. "Seems kind of backwards seeing as how you're already pregnant."

"Watch it," I chastise him, but can't deny that he's right. "I know it seems out of order, but the truth is, Grady and I have a past and our feelings from back when we were younger only seem to have grown. Yes, we're having a child and that wasn't planned, but what we do have the ability to choose is the chance at being a family, and we both really want that."

Chase studies me for a moment. "What about Dad?"

"Grady knows your father isn't involved in our lives anymore. He knows that we left and have no intention of going back. But there's something important you should know as well." I take a deep breath and prepare to tell my son the truth about his dad. "Your father relinquished his parental rights, Chase."

"What does that mean?"

"That means that legally, you no longer have to see him."

I see my son's jaw clench as he processes this information. "Mom…I really hate him."

His words slash right through my heart. I stand from my chair and move to my son where he sits on the couch. Placing my hand on his shoulder, I lean into him. "Don't hate him, Chase. He doesn't deserve that energy from you, and hating someone takes a lot of energy, believe me."

"He's the worst dad. Honestly, I feel relieved that he's not in our lives anymore."

I let out a sigh of relief. "Me too. But the best thing you can do is learn from him, Chase—learn what kind of man *not* to be. I hope that one day when you find the person you want to be with, you devote time and energy to your relationship, and you cherish that person and show them how much they mean to you every day. Because if your father taught us anything, it's exactly what not to do. And when you have kids of your own, be there for them. Stick to your word. Be like…"

"Grady," he finishes for me, glancing over at me now. A tear falls as I nod, so grateful that my son has that man as an example to look up to now—and that he chose us.

Chase nods, silent for a few moments. When he speaks again, though, his words tell me that I'm taking the right step forward. "I like Grady, Mom. He's a good man."

Speaking around the lump in my throat, I say, "He is."

"He's taught me a lot."

"Me too, Chase."

"This kid is lucky to have him as a dad," he continues, reaching down to touch my stomach.

"Yeah, she is." I look my son in the eyes. "But she's just as lucky to have you as her big brother, Chase."

***

Two Weeks Later

"Hold that right there." Grady bends over the fender of the Nova while Chase holds something in place. With a wrench in his hand, Grady reaches down into the engine compartment, flicks his wrist a few times, and then stands tall again. "Perfect."

"It's gonna run, right?" Chase asks, wiping sweat from his brow. I watch the two of them from the doorway separating the reception area of Grady's Garage from the garage itself.

It's Saturday evening and Chase has been here since eight. When my son practically launched himself out of bed this morning, I thought something had to be wrong. Turns out, this was the day they planned to put the motor back in the car, and he was desperate to see if his newfound knowledge was worthwhile.

My stomach growls as my body reminds me that dinnertime is upon us, but I just don't have the heart to interrupt the two of them yet.

This is how our life is supposed to be.

Taking a deep breath so I don't overwhelm myself with that train of thought, I lean against the doorjamb and continue to watch my son learn from the man that has taught him more in the past few months than his father did in his entire life.

Grady pats Chase on the shoulder before wiping his hands on the rag he pulled from the back pocket of his jeans. "It better. Otherwise, we have to take the whole engine apart again."

"Really?" Chase asks in disbelief.

Grady laughs. "Maybe. Let's just hope we put it back together correctly the first time around."

"I wonder what it's like to drive a car like this." My son steps around the front end, running his hand down the lines of the body, tracing the door handle and back fender. Grady hired someone to give the car a new coat of paint while they rebuilt the engine, so the body is now sparkling in a beautiful midnight blue, a tad lighter than it was the night I laid my body on this car.

"Wanna find out?"

Chase's eyes pop up and lock with Grady's. "Really?"

"Yeah. Once she's street legal, I can teach you how to drive it. Keep in mind, this classic doesn't have all the bells and whistles new cars have."

Chase shakes his head. "I don't care. I'm in." He takes a few steps closer to Grady as they both stare down at the engine compartment. "I can't believe we took that whole thing apart and put it back together."

Grady places his hand on my son's shoulder. "I couldn't have done it without you, Chase. Thanks for your help."

My son simply nods, and before I start bawling for the second time today—the first was when I dropped my apple fritter in the grocery store parking lot—I clear my throat, gaining their attention. "How's it going?"

They both spin to face me simultaneously. Chase flashes me a proud grin, but Grady's grin speaks of dirty promises as his eyes dip up and down my body, the kind of promises that I know he's good at fulfilling.

"We got the engine in," Chase says. "Now, we just hope it starts."

"Can you check now?"

Chase looks back to Grady as he pulls the keys from the pocket of his jeans. "No better time than the present." Dangling the keys in front of my son's face, he says, "You wanna do the honors?"

"Shit. Really?"

"Chase!" I exclaim.

"Sorry." He swipes the keys from Grady's hands and practically jumps into the driver's seat as Grady walks over to me, pulling me into his chest.

"Hey there." He leans down and presses a kiss to my lips.

"Hey, yourself."

"How was your day?" He reaches down and places his hand on my bump. "Both of you."

"We're doing okay. Getting hungry though."

"Me too. As soon as we know if all our work was for nothing, we'll go grab some food, okay?"

"Sounds good."

Leaning down to line his mouth up to my ear, he whispers, "And then I'll eat you for dessert."

"I missed you," I whisper back to him.

"Missed you too, Scottie." He presses a kiss on my neck. "I love you."

"Love you too, babe."

A shiver races down my spine, but part of that may be from the roar of the engine as the car comes to life, echoing throughout the garage and pulling our attention back to my son.

"It works!" Chase yells over the noise, pushing his hand up into the air through the driver's side window.

"Fuck yeah!" Grady beams with pride, pulling me into his side as Chase revs the gas and the engine continues to growl.

"Sounds good!" I shout loud enough so Chase can hear me.

"It does." Grady turns to me and says, "He did good, Scottie."

"He needed this," I tell him.

He tucks one of my curls behind my ear. "Yeah, I needed it too."

The baseball season is about to end, and as of today, my son has officially worked off his punishment for breaking into Grady's Garage all those months ago. Seems like "punishment" is too strong of a word to use now since that incident ended up being a blessing in disguise. And God, I'm so thankful for that—for this man and his patience, his heart, and the way he's shown up for me and my son in ways I never thought we'd have.

Chase kills the engine and steps out of the car. "God, it sounded good!"

Grady releases me and moves toward my son. "See? That sound right there was worth all the grease under your fingernails."

Chase laughs. "I don't know what feels better—striking out a batter at the plate, or hearing the engine I built come to life."

"I used to feel that way too." Grady shuts the driver's side door. "We still have a few things to finish up on the inside, but your mom is starving, so we'd better feed her."

"Yeah, this baby girl needs to eat," I say, rubbing my belly.

"I'm starving too." Chase moves to the sink to wash the grease off his hands.

"Better start upping your protein. We have three of our biggest games coming up," Grady says, eyeing me over his shoulder as he scrubs his hands beside my son.

"I don't see how we could lose. We've been on a winning streak pretty much all season."

Grady shakes his head. "Never go into a game cocky, Chase. Just because you won the last one doesn't mean shit. Each game is a new battle, and you should always play as if it's your last."

Something in his words strikes a chord with me.

My entire adult life has felt like a battle up until this point—fighting for my son, my freedom, and my worth.

But it turns out that the man that was made for me came into my life when I was fourteen. I just had to go through a lot of lessons and hurt to get back to him.

I don't regret our time apart, though. In fact, without those years, I wouldn't have Chase. But now, I have the promise of a future I never knew was possible, and it's all because of Grady—the boy who shared a passion for the same sport I loved, my friend that chased his dreams, even when mine shifted, and the man who loves me now, showing me that sometimes, when you fall, the right person will be there to pick you up and guide you to your next adventure—the one you were meant to take all along.

Chapter Twenty-One

Grady

One Month Later

"So, now that the season is over, how do you feel about your first coaching experience?" Parker asks me as he nurses his drink.

"It was harder than I expected in some ways, and exactly what I needed in others."

I know the season only ended two weeks ago, but I'm already excited for the next one. I signed a contract with the high school to return next spring, and since then, my mind has already been making notes of things we can improve on and tweak as the boys get older.

It feels so fucking good to have baseball in my life again.

Parker nods. "And this? How do you feel about this?" He gestures to the crowd of people around us.

I look around the white tent full of people we know and love, gathered here to celebrate our daughter's impending arrival. Astrid and Willow went all out throwing this baby shower, creating a beautiful theme of an apple orchard to pay tribute to Scottie's craving that hasn't dwindled at all, and Scottie looks absolutely breathtaking.

"I'm happier than I ever thought I could be, man," I tell him, searching the crowd for Scottie, only to find her just a few feet away, smoothing her pink dress over her bump, smiling and talking with Dolly, who runs the Carrington Cove Inn.

When Astrid and Willow told me they wanted to throw a coed baby shower, I was a little apprehensive about the idea. From what I've heard, baby showers are a sacred female-only event where discussions of childbirth and nipple creams take place.

However, now that the woman who owns me has finally let me in, I figured it would be more of an opportunity to celebrate Scottie and me moving in together officially this coming weekend, especially since any details of childbirth don't scare me anymore. I've read the books, and I've asked so many questions that I think Scottie has considered smothering me with her pillow multiple times by now. But in a few months, we're going to be parents, a family of four—and I can't fucking wait.

I just have one more thing I need to take care of before our daughter arrives, and hopefully that goes off without a hitch later.

"I can't believe I'm the only one still single now," Parker grumbles under his breath.

"I thought that's what you wanted?"

"I mean, it is," he says, a tad too defensively. "I came so close to getting married, but now that I dodged that bullet, I can't believe I ever considered it." He shakes his head before turning his gaze to mine. "Aren't you going to miss your freedom?"

I glance over at the woman who woke me up with her mouth around my cock this morning. "Nah. Freedom is overrated."

"Well, I won't be giving mine up ever again."

I hide my grin behind the rim of my glass. "Okay, Parker. Whatever you say."

"I'm serious. Casual hookups only."

"Sure."

"I met a smoking-hot woman in New York last month, actually. We met on the plane after I talked her down from a panic attack." He waggles his eyebrows. "And then we had a great night together."

"You didn't tell her the story of how you tried on breast pumps, did you?"

He glares at me before flipping me off and walking away. Part of me feels bad, but the other part knows that all it's going to take is the right woman to show up in his life and make him see the error in his thinking.

The right woman changes everything.

"You pissed him off already?" Penn asks, striding up to me.

"Of course. Doesn't take much these days."

"True story." He clasps his hand on my shoulder. "So, how are you feeling, dad-to-be?"

My lips curl up of their own accord. "Really fucking good, man."

"You look happy."

"Happy isn't strong enough of a word. The only thing missing is Scottie having my last name," I say, which surprises him.

"Are you two ready for that?"

"I am. But is Scottie?" I think out loud. "I want to believe she is."

"Then what's holding you back?"

"What are you two talking about?" Dallas comes up to us now, inserting himself into our conversation.

"Grady is thinking about proposing," Penn tells him.

Dallas turns his eyes back to me. "No shit. Well, I guess that makes sense. It's not like you guys aren't already having a baby together or anything."

"Exactly. And I want her to be my wife."

Dallas blows out a breath. "I know that feeling. If Willow didn't want to plan a wedding, I would have married her the minute after she said yes to my proposal."

Penn nods. "Astrid wanted to wait a year before we talked about it, but I bought a ring two months ago. The second that day comes, I'm sliding it on her finger."

I shake my head at my friend. "God, you sound the way I feel."

"And how's that?" Penn asks.

I look back over at Scottie, fighting the urge to growl as I look at her, swollen with my child. "Possessive."

Dallas and Penn nod in unison. "Yeah, welcome to the club," Dallas says, patting me on the back.

"All right, everyone. It's time to open presents!" My sister claps her hands, gathering everyone's attention. "If you could move into the tent, grab a cupcake as you sit down, and get ready to see just how spoiled this little girl is already, that would be great!" She says something to Willow, and then heads straight in my direction. "Hey, big brother."

I lean down and press a kiss to her cheek. "Thank you again for this."

"My pleasure." She lowers her voice and continues. "By the way, I have Chase and his friends on duty for later." She flashes me a wink and I feel a slight relief in my chest.

"Thank you."

"Yeah, I wasn't sure how we were going to coordinate all of that, but luckily, teenage boys can be pretty eager to help with the right bribe."

"What did you offer them?"

"A pool party at your house next weekend." She pats me on the shoulder and then begins to walk away. "You're welcome!"

Grumbling under my breath, even though I can't deny that my sister has been the biggest source of support for me throughout the past few months, I remind myself that all of this will be worth it once Scottie says the one word I need to hear from her later tonight.

As if my heart conjured her, Scottie waddles over to me, rubbing her stomach. "You ready to help me open gifts?"

I lower my head and press my lips to hers. "Of course, baby. How are you feeling?"

"Big as a house," she says, glancing down at our daughter.

I line my lips up to her ear. "You look so fucking gorgeous, Scottie. God, I want to defile you so badly."

She giggles. "You have issues."

"No, baby. You're carrying my child. There is nothing, and I mean nothing, that is sexier."

When she pulls her head back, she smiles up at me. "I love you."

"I love you too, Scottie." Taking her hand in mine, I lead her over to the chairs Astrid has positioned in front of the backdrop of an apple orchard. A sign that says *She's the Apple of Our Eye* hangs above the two chairs, and wooden buckets full of apples are scattered around the scene. As soon as Scottie takes a seat and I sit right next to her, we begin opening the gifts our family and friends have brought for us, only confirming for me how I'm right where I'm supposed to be in my life—with Scottie by my side, and hopefully soon, as my wife.

***

"What a day."

I lift Scottie's hand and press my lips to the top of it as I drive us back to my house. "You doing okay?"

She lets out a yawn, the fifth one that's left her lips since we left the baby shower. "Yeah, just tired. Who knew opening presents would be so exhausting?"

"Well, we were at it for almost three hours, so I agree…didn't know it could be that tiring."

The sun has set on the day, and even though the shower was over two hours ago, I had to keep Scottie at the house until night fell. According to Astrid, everything is in place, and as soon as we pull into the driveway, I'll be prepared to give Scottie one last gift for the day—which, in my opinion, is the most important one.

Scottie lets out another yawn. "I might even just skip a shower and go straight to bed."

"Aw, I was looking forward to scrubbing you clean."

She eyes me knowingly from her side of the truck. "Scrub me clean, or make me dirty first, Grady?"

I wink over at her. "Both, baby."

"Men. They only have one thing on their mind…always."

"Actually, I currently have two things on my mind, Scottie."

"Oh yeah? What's the other one?"

I don't have to reply because as soon as I pull into the driveway, the light from the electric candles in my front yard comes into view.

"Grady…what is that?" Scottie leans forward in her seat as I cruise toward my house, inching closer to our home and hopefully the beginning of our forever.

When I shift the truck in park, Scottie looks over at me with tears in her eyes. "What's going on?"

"Let me help you down," I say, exiting the truck and walking over to her side, taking in a few deep breaths to calm my nerves. I'm fairly certain this woman wants the same things I do, but it still doesn't diminish the nerves that I feel racing through me.

"Grady..." Scottie holds on to my hand intensely as I lead her over to the giant tree in my front yard, the one that currently has a tire swing and a baby swing hanging from two of the branches.

When we get to the baby swing, I spin her around to face me and prepare to deliver the most important speech of my life. "Scottie...the first time we sat together under a tree, all I wanted to do was kiss you. The second time I got you under a tree—this tree to be exact—I finally did. But now, I want to push our baby girl in this swing under this tree and watch her grow into the tire swing when she's old enough for that too." Scottie's eyes are filled with tears, but I keep going. "I want to marry you under this tree if you want that too, but all I care about is not wasting anymore time, baby. We found each other again on purpose, and our daughter is going to experience love and family better than you could ever imagine. That's what I want for my life, for *our* life, Scottie. So, I guess the question is, are you going to let me give it to you? Are you going to trust me enough to fall? Because I fell for you a long time ago and I don't ever want to stop falling in love with you. I want you in my life forever—as my wife."

"Oh my God."

I drop to one knee and pull the ring from my pocket that I've had in there all day. "Scottie Daniels..." She laughs at my use of her maiden name. "Will you marry me?"

With a trembling lip, she nods before whispering, "Yes."

That familiar intensity lifts from my chest as I slide the three-carat emerald cut solitaire diamond ring on her finger. Standing back up to my full height, I frame her face in my hands. "I love you."

"I love you more," she says, her voice thick with emotion. And there, under the tree, we seal our future with a kiss—a future we never imagined could be ours.

***

A Few Months Later

"All right. This is it. This is where we beat Dallas and bring the Carrington Cove Cup to Smells Like Sugar," Penn says as we huddle around in preparation for the last game.

Scottie is a few days past her due date, but she insisted I still play in the games and take Penn up on his offer to play on his team to try to dethrone Dallas. And we are so fucking close. One more competition and it's over.

Astrid jumps up and down. "Oh my God! I can't believe we're so close!" She looks past me and sticks her tongue out at Dallas and Willow, who are glaring in our direction.

"Isn't Willow your best friend?" I ask her before taking a sip of my water.

"Not today, she's not, Grady. Not today."

Chuckling, I glance over at my fiancée, making sure she's okay. Scottie is sitting in a chair under a big beach umbrella, trying to keep cool, even though it's hotter than Satan's asshole out here.

The past few months have been intense, and not just because of the heat wave rolling through the East Coast. As soon as Scottie hit her third trimester, she's been miserable. School is out for the summer, and she's officially on maternity leave now, thank God. But that means that she's been more than eager to give me a mile-long to-do list of things that need to be done before our daughter arrives.

Having her move in with me has been incredible because I get to go to sleep and wake up next to her, but when people warned me about the hormones and mood swings that were waiting for me as my fiancée approached her due date, I had no idea just how powerful they could get.

"Scottie is okay, Grady," Astrid says, catching me looking over at her for the hundredth time since the games started.

"I know, I'm just worried about her swelling. She's been complaining about it all morning and she said that her back has been killing her."

"All normal things at the end." My sister puts her hand on my shoulder. "She's in the shade, Chase is over there right now, and in a few minutes, we will be one step closer to winning this thing and then you can take her home, okay?"

I nod and glance down at my watch, noting that we have less than five minutes until they announce the next event. "You're right."

"Citizens of Carrington Cove!" Timothy shouts over the microphone as the crowd turns to face him and quiets down. "It is time for the final competition of the games!" Applause rings out among everyone.

"Grady!" Chase yells, racing over to us.

"The final competition will crown this year's winner from our final two teams: Catch & Release and Smells Like Sugar!"

"Grady!" Chase shouts again as he stumbles to a stop in front of me.

"What's up?"

"It's Mom. I think…I think the baby is coming!"

"Our final game is an egg and spoon race," Timothy continues, but my mind doesn't even process what he's saying anymore as Chase stands in front of me and his words sink in.

"Shit." I spin to my sister. "Astrid, I have to go."

"What? Now?" she whines. "But we only have one more game..."

"Scottie is in labor."

Her eyes bug out. "Oh my God! I'm going to be an aunt!"

"Yeah." I lean forward and kiss her on the cheek. "Good luck, sis! Beat Dallas's ass and I'll call you from the hospital!" I yell over my shoulder as I run after Chase, back over to my fiancée.

"Grady," Scottie says as she winces, pushing herself up from her chair. "I think this is it. This pain in my back...it won't let up."

Grabbing her hand, I help her stand and then lead her out to the parking lot behind the boardwalk, hoping the traffic isn't a nightmare to get through. People come into town from all over to watch the games, and normally, I'm all for it. But right now? I wish we lived somewhere else so I could get this woman to a hospital as quickly as possible.

"How far apart are the contractions?"

"A few minutes," she says, groaning as we keep walking, Chase trailing behind us. "Ow, shit. It hurts!"

"Fuck. Chase, go start the truck and get the AC going." I toss him my keys as he nods and races to my truck. "It's okay, baby. We're gonna get to the hospital as soon as we can."

"I'm sorry you had to leave the games," she cries as I hear my truck start in the distance.

"This is way more fucking important, baby. We're about to meet our daughter."

Scottie freezes in her steps. "Oh my God. Grady, I think she's coming right now."

"Fuck, really?"

"It hurts! Everything fucking burns down there." She squeezes my hand so hard that I'm afraid she might break my fingers.

"Okay, hold on!" I bend down and pick Scottie up, walking as fast as I can to the truck. "Chase! Call 9-1-1! The baby is coming now!"

"Holy shit! Really?"

"Don't cuss, Chase!" Scottie screams at her son as I open the back door to my truck and lay Scottie down on the back seat.

I have no towels, no gloves, nothing that would help with what's about to happen. So, I strip my shirt from my body, ask Chase to do the same, and lie one under Scottie's butt as I lift her dress and see blood already staining her underwear.

"Yes, we need an ambulance," Chase says as he stands on the other side of the door, talking in the phone and giving the operator as much information as he can.

"God, Grady! She's coming!"

I strip Scottie's underwear from her body and toss them to the floorboard of the truck, peeking between her legs to see my daughter's head beginning to crown. "Do you need to push, Scottie? I see her head."

"Yes!"

"Okay, push baby. Do what feels right."

Scottie screams as I watch her body do one of the most miraculous things I've ever witnessed.

I've pitched games in front of thousands of people, played a sport professionally for twelve years, and won a fucking World Series—but nothing will ever compare to the experience of watching my daughter come into the world.

With sirens wailing in the background, Scottie gives me one more push and I catch my daughter in my hands, bringing her up from the seat and right onto my chest as she cries and Scottie joins her.

"Oh my God," Scottie breathes out before pushing up on her elbows to see her.

"She's here, baby. She's here." I smooth my hand over our daughter's back and then reach for Chase's shirt to wrap around her as I hear the ambulance pull into the parking lot. "You did so fucking good, Scottie. Holy shit, she's perfect." Tears cloud my vision as I hold this little miracle in my arms.

"Let me hold her, Grady," she says through her own tears as I press a kiss to the top of my daughter's head and then hand her over to her.

Chase peeks his head around the corner, and when he sees the blood and details of childbirth, his face goes white. Luckily, I catch him before he faints and hits the ground. "Easy there, son."

"Is he okay?" Scottie shouts before looking down at our daughter. "Hello, baby girl. My goodness, you were in a hurry to get here, weren't you?"

"Excuse me, sir?" A paramedic gets my attention from behind me. "Is this where the mother is?"

"Yes! The baby is here. They are both doing good," I say, trying to keep my emotions in check.

I just delivered my daughter in the back of my truck, in a parking lot, with no preparation whatsoever.

And suddenly, I'm sliding to the ground to sit next to Chase so neither one of us passes out or throws up, because that would just make Scottie so fucking happy and put the cherry on top of this perfect yet crazy day.

Chapter Twenty-Two

Scottie

"There you go." I stare down at our daughter, Calliope Olive Reynolds, as she nurses and makes the cutest fucking noises. "I love you so much, little girl." Tears fill my eyes for the thousandth time in the past six hours, but I can't help it. Today was crazy, emotional, and overwhelming, but it all led to this moment and I'm so fucking happy that I can't help but let the tears fall freely.

"Hey, you're awake." Grady enters the room with a cup of coffee and a clean shirt.

"Yeah, she just woke up and was hungry, so…"

He comes over and sits on the edge of the bed, staring down at our daughter as she eats. Leaning over me, he presses a kiss to my head and brushes my curls back. "How are you feeling?"

"Sore. I guess I ended up doing this without drugs after all, huh?"

Grady chuckles. "Yeah, babe. But you did so fucking good."

I glance up at him, cupping his jaw with my free hand. "So did you. You brought our daughter into the world, Grady. How's that for a story?"

"Best start to this new chapter ever." He leans down and presses his lips to mine softly. "I love you so much. Thank you for the best gift I could ever ask for."

"Our lives are never going to be the same."

"I couldn't ask for anything better."

"Knock, knock!" I twist toward the door to find my mom, Gigi, and Chase walking in one right after the other.

My mom rushes over to the bed, leaning down to hug me. "Oh my goodness. Are you two okay?" she asks, peering down at the baby.

"We're good, Mom. Grady was amazing and the paramedics took good care of us until we got here and the nurses took over. The doctor has been by to check both of us out too, and everything is perfect."

My mother starts to cry. "I'm just so sad I missed it."

Gigi chimes in. "Me too, but I'm pretty sure Grady will knock her up again, so we'll just try to be here for the next one."

I roll my eyes as Grady laughs. "If I have it my way, there will definitely be another one, Gigi."

I glance up at my fiancé, eager to call him my husband soon, but we both agreed to wait until after the baby was born. "Um, we *just* had this one. Any chance we can wait at least a day before talking about baby number two?"

Chase inserts himself into the conversation. "Maybe you guys could not talk about making more babies in front of me, yeah? That would be great." He gives us a sarcastic thumbs-up.

Gigi puts her hand on his shoulder. "One day, you're going to find a woman you'll want to make babies with, and I'll be sure to remind you of this conversation if I'm still alive."

My mother pinches the bridge of her nose. "Jesus, Mom. Can we not talk about you dying today?"

Gigi holds her hands up. "No one lives forever. I'm just saying."

"Well, then maybe I should tell you that Calliope's middle name is going to be Olive, after you, Gigi."

My grandmother is speechless, and that never happens. "Oh shit. Are you trying to make me cry?"

"Cry or shut up. One of the two," I say, teasing her. She rushes over to the bed and stares down at her great-granddaughter. "I'm gonna teach this little girl everything I can about being a badass that doesn't take shit from anyone...until I die, that is."

"And we're back to talking about her dying," my mother grumbles just as there's another knock on the door.

Astrid and Penn stand there, my future sister-in-law beaming while fighting back tears. "Oh my God, she's here!" The two of them enter the room now, joining the crowd that's gathered.

"Did you tell her what happened?" I ask Grady, but Astrid answers for him.

"He called us as soon as you guys got to the hospital. I heard the second baby comes faster than the first, but damn!"

"Yeah, it was pretty crazy," I say before pulling Callie from my breast and covering myself back up. "Did you guys win the games?" I ask, hoisting Callie onto my shoulder and slowly starting to pat her back.

Astrid clenches her jaw. "No."

Penn rolls his eyes. "Astrid was too distracted by you guys running off that she kept dropping the egg and having to start all over, so we fell behind."

She slaps Penn in the chest. "Hey, you dropped the egg once too."

He shrugs. "I was worried too, I guess."

"Well, it's okay. You can always dethrone Dallas next year."

Astrid waves her hand through the air. "Enough about him. I want to meet my niece." She walks closer to the bed and glances down at the baby, instantly tearing up. "Oh my goodness, you guys. She's gorgeous."

"Looks like she has curly hair like her mom," Grady adds, pressing a kiss to the top of my head full of curls.

"I can't believe you delivered her," Astrid says to her brother.

"It was wild, but you know what? It was one of the best moments of my life."

And as I stare around the hospital room full of my family and the family I'm marrying into, I pause to let this blip in time soak in—because life can be tough and amazing, but it's those low moments that we go through when we fall that make the high ones that much more unforgettable and life-changing—and that's exactly what I feel in this moment.

Chapter Twenty-Three

Grady

Five Months Later

"Looking good, Daddy," Dallas says, chuckling as he wipes down the bar. It's Thursday, which means it's time for my weekly lunch with the boys.

I stare down at Callie in her carrier, strapped to my chest, sleeping as if the world around her doesn't exist. "Enough with the Daddy talk, all right? Just remember, payback is a bitch."

Penn snickers from his seat at the bar. "Yeah, it's a little disturbing. Just wait until your son calls you that, and then you'll think twice about using that nickname."

Dallas nods, clearing his throat. "Noted. But seriously, how's fatherhood treating you? That little girl looks so much bigger than she did last week."

"Well, she's five months now, so she's definitely hitting milestones left and right, but I think we're navigating our new normal pretty well." I kiss the top of my daughter's head. "Except the sleep deprivation. That still sucks, but she's getting better." Callie was waking up four times a night, but now we're down to two. Scottie takes one and I take the other so we can both get sleep, and she gets to also spend some time bonding with our girl. It's working well for us so far.

"It's crazy how fast they grow," Penn chimes in. "I remember watching Bentley and Lilly when they were babies, and it goes by so fucking fast. They continue to change now too, but in different ways." He shakes his head. "Having kids is wild, that's all I'm going to say."

"I can't fucking wait," Dallas interjects. "Only three more months and I'm going to join the daddy club."

Dallas and Willow got engaged last spring and married last summer, not wasting any time, and two short months later, they found out they were expecting their first child just after the Carrington Cove Games. Willow and Scottie have bonded a lot over pregnancy and motherhood, and selfishly, part of me is looking forward to having one of my closest friends be at the same place in life that I am.

Scottie and I got married on New Year's Eve at our house, surprising everyone when they thought they were just there for a party, but I didn't want to start the new year without her as my wife and her having *my* last name. I have a honeymoon planned for us over the summer after the school year is over. It will be our first trip away from Callie, but I think we both need it. Parenthood is rough, even if you approach it as a team.

But God, I love my fucking life. My girls and Chase—sometimes I still can't believe how things all worked out. It's a far cry from playing professional baseball, but it's exactly what my life was missing.

Being a stay-at-home dad has been an adjustment, but if there's one thing I've learned, it's that a schedule is key. It keeps everyone happy.

Before Callie was born, I asked Scottie what she wanted to do about her job. Needless to say, with the money I made in the MLB, there wasn't a need for her to work. And the garage does well, so it wasn't like we didn't have extra income. But Scottie was adamant about keeping her job because she loves working with the kids.

"So, has Willow entered her nesting phase yet?" I ask Dallas, taking a seat next to Penn. But Callie starts to stir as soon as I sit, so I stand right back up. It's her naptime, and if I don't let her rest, she'll be pissed off for the rest of the afternoon.

"Willow has taken the reins, and I've learned not to argue. She asks for my opinion here and there, but ultimately, I told her that as long as she's happy with the nursery and feels she has everything we need, I don't really care too much about the rest." Dallas shrugs, continuing to stock items behind the bar. "I just want to hold my son and hope to God the delivery goes smoothly."

Before either Penn or I can reply, Parker comes storming into Catch & Release with metaphorical smoke coming out of his ears.

"Uh, you okay?" I ask as he approaches the bar, tosses his glasses down, and blows out a breath.

"I don't even fucking know." He looks up at Dallas. "Can I get a beer, please?"

Dallas furrows his brow at his brother. "A beer? It's noon on a Thursday..."

"Just pour me a fucking beer, Dallas." Parker closes his eyes as he pinches the bridge of his nose and waits for his brother to slide a beer in his direction. As soon as the glass is within reaching distance, he picks it up and drains half of it before saying, "Fuck. My. Life."

Dallas comes out from behind the bar as Penn and I stand beside him, all three of us looking down at the youngest Sheppard, wondering what the hell is going on. But before any of us can say a word, a petite blonde comes smashing through the front door of the restaurant, her hair wild, her eyes scouring the room before they land on Parker leaning forward over the counter.

"Oh my God, Parker! There you are."

"Who the hell is this?" Dallas mumbles to me out of the corner of his mouth.

"No idea," I mutter in return as Parker spins around and meets the eyes of the woman who just crashed our lunch date.

"Cashlynn, what are you doing here?"

She brushes her hair from her face. "Well, you rushed out of the vet's office so fast that we didn't get a chance to talk."

Parker huffs out a laugh. "I think you did enough talking for the both of us."

"Should we say something?" I mutter as Dallas, Penn, and I continue to watch the conversation in front of us unfold.

Penn puts his hand on my shoulder. "Not yet."

"I'm sorry, I just..." The woman blows out a breath and then finally meets our eyes, covering her chest with her palm. "Oh God, I'm so sorry. I didn't mean to interrupt..."

"You're not, although I think we're all wondering how you know my brother here," Dallas says, gesturing to Parker.

Parker glares at his friend and then turns to me, Penn, and Dallas. "Guys, this is Cashlynn O'Neil."

"O'Neil?" I ask, wondering where the hell I've heard that name before. "Isn't that..."

"As in Dr. O'Neil, my boss?" Parker nods. "The one and only."

I turn back to the woman. "So you're..."

"Dr. O'Neil's daughter," Parker finishes for me. He shoots another irritated look at our surprise guest and then says something neither Penn, Dallas, nor I was expecting. "And as of today, my fiancée."

***

Not ready to say goodbye to Grady and Scottie? Download a special bonus epilogue here to get a glimpse at their future!

***

Curious about Parker's story? Don't worry. He's next. Someday You Learn is coming Spring of 2025 and you can pre-order here.

Also By Harlow James

Carrington Cove Series
Somewhere You Belong (Dallas and Willow)
Someone You Deserve (Penn and Astrid)
Sometimes You Fall (Grady and Scottie)
Someday You Learn (Parker and Cashlynn)
Somehow You Knew (Gage and Hazel)

***

The Ladies Who Brunch (rom-coms with a ton of spice)
Never Say Never (Charlotte and Damien)
No One Else (Amelia and Ethan)
Now's The Time (Penelope and Maddox)
Not As Planned (Noelle and Grant)
Nice Guys Still Finish (Jeffrey and Ariel)

***

The Newberry Springs (Gibson Brothers) Series
Everything to Lose (Wyatt & Kelsea)
Everything He Couldn't (Walker & Evelyn)
Everything But You (Forrest & Shauna)

***

The California Billionaires Series (rom coms with heart and heat)
My Unexpected Serenity (Wes and Shayla)
My Unexpected Vow (Hayes and Waverly)
My Unexpected Family (Silas and Chloe)

***

The Emerson Falls Series (smalltown romance with a found family friend group)
Tangled (Kane & Olivia)
Enticed (Cooper & Clara)
Captivated (Cash and Piper)
Revived (Luke and Rachel)
Devoted (Brooks and Jess)

***

Lost and Found in Copper Ridge
A holiday romance in which two people book a stay in a cabin for the same amount of time thanks to a serendipitous $5 bill.

Guilty as Charged
An intense opposites attract standalone that will melt your kindle. He's an ex-con construction worker. She's a lawyer looking for passion.

McKenzie's Turn to Fall
A holiday romance where a romance author falls for her neighborhood butcher.

Acknowledgements

Grady Reynolds.
This man STOLE my heart while I wrote his story, and to think, when I originally planned the series, he wasn't even included. But as soon as I started writing the first book, I knew he needed a story, and Scottie was the perfect heroine for him.

These two are one of those special couples that were hard to let go. In fact, their bonus epilogue could have been longer if I let myself keep writing.

BUT Parker is next and when I tell you I laughed my ass off while writing his book, I'm not exaggerating.

This series has been life changing—not only in my success as an author, but as a writer. I've pushed myself a lot in these stories and I hope my readers can feel the emotions I've poured into them. And hearing them in audio has been the icing on the cake!

We have two more books and then the series will be complete! But don't worry. I already have plans for what comes next

To my husband: Thank you for believing in me and cheering me on every step of the way. Thank you for traveling with me, investing in my success, and being my person, my best friend, the man that inspires all of my book boyfriends, and my official Book Bitch. I love you.

To my beta readers: Keely, Emily, Kelly, and Carolina: you four are the best voices I have in my corner. Each of you gives me the advice, feedback, and support that I need in your own way. I'm so grateful to have the four of you on my team still after all this time. I love you all and appreciate you more than you'll ever know.

To Kait, my P.A.: Hiring you has been one of the best decisions I've ever made. Your friendship and professional support have helped me so much this year. Thank you for being my newest cheerleader!

To Jess, my social media manager: You have single-handedly made my life better! I have so much more time to focus on writing and other aspects of my business thanks to you. Your time and creativity is appreciated SO much. Thank you from the bottom of my heart for doing what you do for me.

And to my readers: thank you for supporting me, whether you've been here since the beginning, or you're brand new. I LOVE this hobby turned business of mine. It's an amazing feeling to be able to create art for someone to enjoy and forming a relationship from that. I never take my readers for granted and know that there would be no Harlow James without you.

So thank you for supporting a wife and mom who found a hobby that she loves.

And a future career that I'm working toward with each passing day.

Connect with Harlow James

Follow me on Amazon

Follow me on Instagram

Follow me on Facebook

Join my Facebook Group: https://www.facebook.com/groups/494991441142710/

Follow me on Goodreads

Follow me on Book Bub

Subscribe to my Newsletter for Updates on New Releases and Giveaways

Website

Printed in Great Britain
by Amazon